The Torso

The Torso

Helene Tursten

Translated by
Katarina E. Tucker

First published in the English language in the United States in 2006
by Soho Press, Inc.
853 Broadway
New York, NY 10003

Library of Congress Cataloging in Publication Data
Tursten, Helene. 1954–
[Tatuerad torso. English]
The torso / Helene Tursten ; translated by Katarina Emilie Tucker
p. cm.
ISBN 1-56947-425-7
I. Tucker, Katarina Emilie. II. Title.
PT9876.3.U55T3813 2006
839.3'74—dc22   2005057749

10 9 8 7 6 5 4 3 2 1

The author would like to emphasize that the book cannot be used as a tourist guide, either in Copenhagen or in Göteborg. Streets, alleys, squares and other places are used with great freedom. In addition, none of the characters are deliberately based on real persons.

Sammie would also like to point out that he has never participated in the creation of mixed-breed puppies. He is the proud father of nine guaranteed pure bred ones.

The Torso

THE WIND GAVE NO warning of the ghastly discovery. Just the opposite. Even though it was early May, the wind blowing in from the sea was surprisingly mild and heavy with the smell of seaweed. The sunlight skipped and played upon the inner surfaces of the low waves in an attempt to pretend that summer had already come. It was one of those bonus days that can appear during the spring and then disappear just as quickly.

The woman and the black Labrador were alone down by the water. The dog was doing his best to get a laughing gull at the edge of the beach excited but it soared up a few meters* over the water's surface, flew a short distance, and lived up to its name.

The dog finally tired of the annoying seagull. At the water's edge he snatched up a large branch from among the driftwood left by the winter's storms. The branch was more than a meter long and difficult to balance in his mouth. Wobbling slightly, he set a course toward his mistress. With an appealing look he laid the branch, bleached gray by the sun and saltwater, at her feet. She bent and tried to break it into smaller pieces better suited to throwing but had to give up. Her toss was clumsy and relatively short, but the dog ran off eagerly. He proudly brought the branch back to his mistress, received praise and petting, let go of his pretty toy, and waited expectantly for her to hurl it again. The shiny black body shook with restrained power. When she threw the branch the dog instantly raced off.

This was a very pleasing game that the dog didn't seem to weary of. However, after a while, his owner's throwing power began to taper off. She finally walked over to a flat rock and sat down. She said loudly, "No, Allan. That's enough. I have to rest a bit."

The dog was absolutely crestfallen with disappointment. His tail,

---

* One meter equals 3.28 feet.

which had been wagging so proudly earlier, now pointed straight down at the sand. He nudged her hands with his nose a few times, but she quickly stuck them into her jacket pockets, turned her face toward the sun, and closed her eyes. She sat still for a long time.

When she opened her eyes again, she couldn't see him on the deserted beach. Alarmed, she got up and looked around in all directions. She laughed with relief when she spotted his tail sticking out from behind a large boulder, a little way into the water.

During the summer, children would play in an area between three high boulders that formed a small triangular pool one of whose angles pointed due west. The opening facing the ocean was narrow, barely half a meter in width. The kids screamed with joy when the gushing water surged through the boulders and poured down over them. The space was small but often ten kids succeeded in cramming themselves between the rocks.

The tide was unusually low so Allan had dared to venture out to the rock formation and had squeezed between the rocks that made up the base of the triangle. He had frozen there.

"Allan! Come here!" the woman called commandingly at the dog but he pretended not to hear. He suddenly disappeared behind the rocks. Grumbling, she headed down to the water's edge to summon him. She stopped uncertainly at the edge of the lapping waves. The water was ice cold.

"Allan. Come here! Come! Here!"

It didn't matter which commands or tone of voice she used. No sign of the dog could be seen. But she knew that he was out there between the rocks.

Angrily, she pulled off her shoes and socks. Swearing under her breath, she rolled up her pant legs and started wading out into the freezing water. Luckily, it was only ankle deep.

The rock formation was located about ten meters from the shore. When she was just a few meters from the opening between the boulders she detected a faint nauseating smell. Because she was angry it didn't really register until she had, with considerable effort, squeezed between the rocks.

Floating in the triangular pool was a black plastic bag with a hole where the gulls had been pecking at it. Allan stood still with his head inside the hole. The woman quickly waded over to the dog while yelling, "No! Allan! No!"

She gripped the scruff of his neck firmly. He growled and refused to let go of the contents of the sack. Summoning all her strength, she managed to lift his hindquarters and twist his body so that his back faced the water's surface and his legs stuck up toward the steel blue sky. Then he finally let go. Whimpering, he jumped into the water. Only his head remained above the surface. She quickly used one hand to push hard against his throat and with the other she got an iron grip on one of his front legs. She looked the dog straight in the eye the whole time, a low sound rising from her chest. He growled angrily again, and stared back, red-eyed. He finally quieted and looked to the side, to show that he was giving up. Slowly, she released him. It wasn't until then that she glanced through the hole in the sack.

At first she thought what she saw looked like the mark of a branding iron. She realized a second later that it was a tattoo.

Chapter 1

ONLY SUPERINTENDENT SVEN ANDERSSON, Detective
Inspector Irene Huss, and her colleague Jonny Blom were gathered in
the superintendent's office at the police station that evening. It was
almost seven thirty. The superintendent felt that it wasn't necessary to
call in th remaining inspectors from Violent Crimes as well. They would
have to make do with the two officers who had been at the crime scene.
The rest would be informed at "morning prayers" the next day.

They gathered around the desk with their steaming mugs of coffee.
Without any fancy introductory remarks Sven Andersson began.
"What do we have so far?"

"We got the call around lunchtime. An old lady had taken her dog
down to the ocean—"

Almost brusquely, the superintendent interrupted Jonny. "Where by
the ocean?"

"Near Stora Amundön. Or just south of it, just before Grundsö. A
small beautiful sandy beach called Killevik. There are some large
boulders shaped like a triangle. The lady's dog found a black plastic bag
in the triangle and—"

"Sorry to interrupt you, but the lady is two years older than I am and
three years younger than you, and her name is Karla Melander. She
lives on Klyfteråsvägen in Skintebo. Not far from Killevik," said Irene
Huss.

"Doesn't she have a job? How come she wasn't working in the middle of the week?" Andersson wondered aloud.

"She's a pediatric nurse and had worked over the weekend. Apparently she had yesterday and today off. Yesterday it was blowing quite
hard so they hadn't been down to the beach, but today the weather was
gorgeous. They've only been there once since Easter. The weather was
nice then, too, but ever since, it has just been wind and rain this miserable spring."

"Can we stop talking about the weather and get back to the essentials?" Jonny Blom said sharply.

Before the other two had time to answer, he picked up where he had been interrupted. "There was a large hole in the bag that was probably caused by birds. The dog evidently stuck his head in the sack and bit a body. It seems to be just the upper portion of a torso. The arms have been removed about ten centimeters from the shoulders. There is a distinct bite mark and the flesh is torn on the lower part of an arm stump. On the right shoulder, which was facing the hole, there is a large tattoo in different colors. That's what we could see. Forensics will have to come up with more information."

"So there's no lower half?"

"No. Based on size it appears as though the body was divided at the waist."

"You don't know if it's a man or a woman?"

Irene and Jonny looked at each other before Jonny responded with a trace of hesitation in his voice, "No. We don't know for sure but we discussed it. Both Irene and I believe that it looks like there is a large wound where the breasts should be. But it was difficult to see . . . the birds have been picking at it, and the body is quite decayed."

"Severed breasts. Sexual homicide! I'll be damned. That's about the worst there is. And then the other parts will have to be searched for," the superintendent said drearily.

He stood and went over to the map that was hanging on the wall. Göteborg and its surrounding areas, from Kungälv in the north to Kungsbacka in the south, were shown on the large detailed map. With his index finger, he followed the coastline from the entrance to the harbor down to Killevik. He used a short pin with a red plastic top to mark the precise place where the sack had been found.

He took a step back and examined the map for a while. Finally he turned toward the two detectives and said, "We need to find out how the currents run and how strong they are. There may also be a need to find out about the recent weather. We should know when there were storms."

"Storms? Why are we talking about the weather again?" Jonny whined.

"Because a body in the condition you have just described can't walk between the rocks and lie down in the calm water by itself."

Andersson gave Jonny a look as sharp as his tone of voice before he continued. "The body part could have gotten there a number of different ways. It could have been put there at the outset. Then you have to ask yourself why all of the body parts aren't in the same place. If they were placed in different locations along the coastline, more of them should have been found by now."

"There are a lot of small uninhabited islands west and southwest of Killevik," Irene said.

"Exactly. Tomorrow we'll have to search all of them. As well as the beaches south and north of the discovery site. Another possibility is that the sack floated quite a way since gases are produced when flesh starts rotting. . . ."

The superintendent stopped himself and Irene could see a look of nausea quickly pass over his face. He swallowed before he continued. "As I was saying, the sack might have floated and then been washed over the rocks during a storm. The waves crash over them when the wind is blowing hard. Maybe the sack tore when it was thrown against the rocks so that it couldn't wash out again as easily. That's why I'm interested in pinpointing recent storms. It may give us an idea of how long the sack has been there."

He fell silent, considering. The obvious follow-up question—after where were the other body parts—was, Who was the victim?

"When I talk to the reporters tonight I'm only going to say that we've found the upper part of the torso of a dead person. I'll say that we can't provide any more information until the medical examiner has conducted a more thorough examination."

Irene and Jonny nodded. At this initial stage of the investigation, there really wasn't much to go on. They didn't know the victim's sex. They didn't have a head, a lower body, arms, or legs, and they had no idea of the cause of death.

Chapter 2

"PART OF DISMEMBERED MURDER victim found at swimming place" was the caption in the *Göteborg Post*. Irene Huss read the article, eyes heavy with sleep. She had never been accused of being a morning person. Now she was trying to get her brain cells working with the morning's second cup of coffee.

Krister joined her at the breakfast table. Thudding on the stairs to the second floor warned of the twins' imminent arrival.

"Murder victim. Nobody knows yet if it's a murder victim," Irene muttered.

"It can hardly be a case of suicide," her husband countered, gently mocking her. More than anyone else, he was acquainted with his wife's bad morning moods, and he knew better than anyone how easy it was to tease her before she got a few cups of coffee in her system. But he had to be careful and not go too far. Then the whole day would be ruined for everyone involved.

"It very well could be," Irene hissed.

"Really? Good-bye, cruel world! Now I'm going to cut off my arms and legs and head in order to be absolutely certain that I'll die!"

Krister made a theatrical gesture and covered his eyes with one arm and with a closed fist raised the other to the ungracious powers above.

Irene said, "There are necrophiles. They steal dead bodies—"

She stopped herself when she saw her daughters standing in the doorway.

"Pleasant conversation you're having over breakfast," Katarina said dryly.

"What a horrible job you have, Mamma," was Jenny's comment.

That really hurt. Irene loved her job and had never wanted to become anything other than a police officer. More than anything else, she had always felt it was something meaningful. Certainly, there were aspects of the profession that were less than pleasant but someone had to do the job. It was hard to explain to two teenage daughters, one of whom wanted to become a singer in a band like the Cardigans and the other, a guide for survival courses in remote jungles and mountain ranges. (Katarina would definitely also consider traveling around to exotic and remote destinations for a travel program on TV.)

Irene took a large sip of extra-strong coffee in order to get herself ready for the day.

DURING MORNING prayers Superintendent Andersson informed his entire group about the little they knew with respect to the corpse discovered at Killevik. No new leads and no new body parts had been found so far. Andersson was waiting impatiently for what Forensics might come up with. Patience was not one of the superintendent's strong points.

In addition to Irene and Jonny, the group was made up of three more officers.

Birgitta Moberg was the other woman in the group. She was a slender blonde with bright brown eyes who looked significantly younger than her thirty years. Many men were deceived by her gentle appearance, but she was a woman with a mind of her own.

Hannu Rauhala was sitting beside her. His half-cropped hair was light blond, almost white. Usually he was quiet and reserved, but everyone knew that Hannu was extremely effective when it came to all types of inquiries and to investigating people.

The third inspector in the group was Fredrik Stridh. Despite the fact that he was twenty-eight years old and had worked at Violent Crimes for three years, he was still viewed as the "youngster." But his colleagues respected him for his never-failing good humor and his terrierlike stubbornness. He never let go if he caught the scent of a possible lead, no matter how faint it might be.

The only one missing was Tommy Persson, Irene's partner and best friend since the Police Academy in Ulriksdal. This morning he was lying on an operating table at the Eastern Hospital, being operated on for an inguinal hernia. He would be out for at least a week. Irene had called the night before and spoken with his wife, Agneta. In a conspiratorial tone she had confided to Irene, "Tommy isn't a bit nervous. But of course he's written out a will." Irene could hear loud protests from Tommy in the background, who was threatening his wife with unpleasant consequences if she continued with her lies. Agneta was a head nurse at Alingsås Hospital and a good friend of Irene's.

"The Harbor Police will receive reinforcements and will continue the search of the islands and skerries outside Killevik. The Marines are providing divers. We'll start at Killevik and later widen the search area toward Askimsfjorden."

Irene was startled out of her thoughts by the superintendent's voice. He stood in front of the coastal map making circular motions over the light blue water. Andersson's gaze moved quickly over the group before coming to rest on Hannu Rauhala.

"Make contact with Pathology at lunchtime and try and find out how long the body has been dead. Then you can start going through missing persons' reports filed around the time the body would have been fresh."

Hannu nodded.

The superintendent turned toward the others.

"Everyone except Irene, go out to Skintebo and start knocking on doors. We want to find out whatever anyone observed that may have something to do with the discovery. Has anyone seen similar black sacks or anybody carrying black sacks at odd times? And you know the rest." He stopped himself and sighed deeply before continuing, "Irene and I are going to try and tie up the loose ends surrounding the Angered murder. Everyone has been questioned and the hooligans have confessed, but we have a meeting with the prosecutor later this morning to go through the whole case."

IRENE HAD a great deal of admiration for Inez Collin. They were roughly the same age. Superintendent Andersson had always had problems with the female prosecutor and Irene often thought that the reason was that she was not only a woman but schooled in the law as well.

Inez Collin looked absolutely fantastic, as usual. Today she was dressed in a light dove gray dress with matching shoes. Over the dress she was wearing a sober blazer that was a shade darker than the narrow dress. She had gathered her light hair into a ponytail and fastened it with a large silver clasp. Both her lips and nails were painted a delicious shade of bright red.

It was always easy to work with her and they finished just before lunch. Andersson was in a hurry to leave the room. Maybe he was afraid that Inez Collin would suggest that they have lunch together, thought Irene.

The truth was that Andersson wanted to find out if the pathologists had called. He was too impatient to wait for the elevator and started up the stairs instead. On the way he started to regret his impulsiveness. By the time he reached the Violent Crimes floor his face was flushed and he was gasping like a broken bellows. Slowly, he started to make his way down the corridor while trying to get his blood pressure and breathing under control.

Hannu came out of his office, stopping when he caught sight of his panting boss. He looked at Andersson and assessed the red patches on his face and neck, but as usual made no comment. With difficulty, the superintendent tried to laugh it off. "I guess you shouldn't go in for sports when you're almost sixty."

Hannu smiled politely but a hint of concern could be seen in his ice blue eyes.

"Have you gotten hold of the pathologist?" Andersson asked.

"Yes. Professor Stridner said that they wouldn't be finished before two o'clock."

The color in Andersson's face darkened. "Two! Is it going to take longer to examine that little piece than it usually takes to cut up a whole body?"

Hannu shrugged his shoulders without answering. Andersson took a few deep breaths before asking, "Do you know if they've found anything else at Killevik?"

The response was negative. The superintendent gave Hannu an irritated look and disappeared into his office.

As she entered the corridor Irene heard the last exchange. She smiled at Hannu and said softly, "He's a bit bent out of shape today. First Inez Collin in the morning and then having to go and wait for news from Yvonne Stridner. . . . It's just too much."

Hannu laughed softly. If the superintendent felt uncomfortable around the coolly elegant prosecutor, then he practically had a phobia about the pathology professor, Yvonne Stridner. She was a colorful woman with a great air of authority and competence, one of the most skillful medical examiners in Scandinavia. Everyone thought so, not least the woman herself.

"Maybe we can go and eat in the meantime," said Irene.

"Unfortunately, I've already made plans to meet someone else."

The slightest hint of red could be seen across his high cheekbones. Wow! For the first time in the two years Hannu had been working with them, he was showing signs of an emotional life. Irene's imagination instantly started painting a picture of a romantic lunch date with a secret woman. Or maybe a man? She realized that she had no idea whether Hannu had a live-in girlfriend or a wife, or if he was single. She was insanely curious but at the same time she knew she would never get any information out of Hannu. Maybe one could run an internal investigation? A mean thought, but tempting nonetheless. Without a hint of what was going on inside her head, Irene said lightly, "Too bad for me. I'll see you around two."

The whole thing had been almost too easy. Irene heard Hannu close the door as he left. She stood and peered out the window in her office. Hannu emerged from the police station and walked across the parking lot. He directed his steps purposefully toward a scrubby yellow VW Golf. He opened the door on the passenger's side and hopped in.

Irene recognized the car all too well. There weren't many models from the mideighties still rolling around the streets, but Detective Inspector Birgitta Moberg had one. She took good care of the car and she would never lend it to anyone. There was little doubt that it was Birgitta herself who was driving.

"WHAT THE hell does she mean?! Not done yet! It's two o'clock and she's had all day!"

Superintendent Andersson lost all control when the message came from Pathology. Irene had been the one to take the call and tell her boss the news. He glared angrily and accusingly at Irene. She didn't take it personally because she knew the looks were intended for Professor Stridner.

Andersson stepped up to the window and looked through the dirty pane at Ernst Fontells Plats. Irene understood from his low muttering that he was thinking. After a while he turned to face her and said, "We're going up to Pathology. Stridner must be able to tell us something! Then we'll drive out to Killevik. I want to see where the sack was found."

AS ALWAYS, when he stepped across the threshold of the Pathology Department, Andersson seemed overwhelmed by a strong sense of discomfort. Irene knew how he felt but she acted as though she didn't notice. His sensations certainly didn't improve after the blond bodybuilder of an attendant informed them that the professor was in the examination room. He was familiar with the superintendent's loathing for autopsies and beamed with a charming but provoking smile. His teeth shone white against his sunburned skin. Though he had been working at Pathology for many years, his appearance, together with his neat ponytail, gave an impression of vitality that was entirely out of place in those surroundings. Irene only knew his first name, printed on his name tag: Sebastian.

It was the smell that was the worst. Perhaps it was possible to get used to it if you experienced it daily, thought Irene. But when people like her and the superintendent visited only now and then, it hit them with its full effect.

Andersson stopped just inside the door and, to her surprise, Irene noted that he had pushed her in front of him. So she trotted up to the steel table where Yvonne Stridner was dissecting the upper half of the torso that had been found.

The pathologist looked up over the edge of her magnifying eyeglasses and knit her eyebrows. "What are you doing here?" she asked sharply.

Irene felt impelled to answer since the superintendent was silent.

"We were wondering if you really hadn't discovered anything . . . useful?"

Stridner snorted loudly. "I'll contact you when I'm finished."

"You don't know if it's a man or a woman?"

"No. The pectoralis major, the large muscle in the chest, has been almost completely removed on both sides. It doesn't make sense."

"What doesn't make sense?" Andersson ventured to ask.

"The mutilation of female breasts is usually limited to the breast glands and fatty tissue. But here they have gone deeper and removed the muscle. Consequently, I can't say whether it's a man or a woman. The incisions are elliptical and nearly eleven by seventeen centimeters.[*] It appears as though two female breasts have been removed. Yet I need to look more thoroughly. . . ."

"What's the cause of death?"

"Impossible to say. Find the head and maybe that will provide a lead. In this type of case strangulation is the most common cause of death."

"You don't see any marks on the neck?"

"There is no neck to see any marks on. The head has been removed above the seventh cervical vertebra. All of the internal organs have been removed. No lungs, no heart, no abdominal organs. The chest has been opened all the way up to the throat. The entire sternum has been sawed open."

"How long has the body—or the body part—been in the sack?"

"Can't say for certain. Based on decay it could be anywhere from two to four months. It was very cold in February and March, which is obviously a factor. There haven't been any long periods of warm weather from April up to today either. But we have taken the usual samples and, of course, performed toxicology tests. We'll have the results in a few days and then we can be more certain."

Irene heard the superintendent heading toward the exit behind her. Her brain worked feverishly to come up with an important question she should ask while there was still time. Suddenly, it struck her. "The tattoo. Is it possible to see what the image is?" she asked.

"Yes. It looks like a small upside-down y with a cross stroke where the fork separates and a cross stroke a bit higher up on the shaft. I think it resembles a Chinese character. There is a dragon wrapped around the sign and it's biting its own tail. A very attractive tattoo. Actually a real piece of art, in different colors. See for yourself."

Stridner twisted the limp grayish green chest so that Irene would be able to see the tattoo. It may have been very beautiful, but now Irene was also starting to feel ill. She pretended to examine the tattoo closely before she thanked Stridner and hurried out of the room.

* * *

---

[*] One centimeter equals 0.39 inches, so eleven by seventeen centimeters is about four and a quarter inches by six and three-quarters inches.

THEY TOOK Highway 158 from Järnbrottsmotet toward Särö. It wasn't until they had turned off at Brottkärrsmotet and headed out to Skintebo that Irene broke the silence.

"I think we got a lot of information."

The superintendent mumbled an answer. Irene thought it sounded like "far too much," but she wasn't entirely certain.

"Are we going to have a case review tonight?" she asked, mostly as a means of changing the subject.

"No. Nothing is pressing. We'll take care of it at morning prayers."

Irene drove by Billdal's Park and after a while she turned onto the little road to Killevik. From there they could see the boat that the marine divers were using. It was swaying listlessly in the lightly rolling seas outside some of the smaller skerries a few hundred meters from the beach. Blue-and-white flags marked the area where the divers were working. In the distance they could hear rumbling from the Harbor Police boat as it searched through every single islet and the countless small islands.

"Where are all of our people?" wondered Andersson.

"Supposedly out knocking on doors," Irene answered.

Andersson muttered something unintelligible. He took out his cell phone and started rummaging around in his pockets. He finally seemed to find what he was looking for because his grunting sounded less irritable when he pulled out a wrinkled note. Irene was able to make out the words "Harbor Police" written in red ink. A telephone number was listed below. Andersson dialed the number.

"Hi. Sven Andersson here. Have you found anything?"

He scowled as the person on the other end replied.

"Uh-huh. The divers haven't either . . . ? Oh." He couldn't hide the disappointment in his voice. "Call as soon as something comes up . . . I mean . . . if you find anything. Good. Thanks."

He did his best to sound normal when he ended the call but Irene knew her boss well enough not to be fooled.

Andersson leaned toward the windshield and glared darkly out at the three boulders. For a long time he sat still, staring intently at the rocks in the water. Thin gray veils of clouds hid the sun but the light sifted through and sprinkled the waves with silvery glitter. Seagulls circled low over the water's surface, which reflected the sunlight in silvery white. Andersson was lost in thought and didn't see how beautiful it was. Irene waited for him to break the silence.

"How the hell did the sack get there?"

"I believe in your theory that it was driven between the rocks during a storm. Otherwise we should have found more sacks in the same place or in the surrounding area."

"Where did it come from?"

Irene shrugged her shoulders.

"No idea. Maybe it came from one of the islands."

"Hmm. Styrsö is located straight out. And Donsö. But I don't know how the currents run out here. Maybe it came from Vrångö. We'll have to check the currents although it is quite a way for a sack to float."

Irene nodded. "I'll check on it."

A thought struck her. "I'll ask Birgitta if she has a nautical chart. She sails a lot."

"It's almost four thirty. I'll drive you home. Or is your car parked at the station?" Andersson asked.

"No. Krister took it today. He doesn't get off work until after midnight."

They could only afford one car, but the system they used worked well. The car was always parked in the Police Department's parking lot. It was only a five-minute walk from the stylish pub, Glady's Corner, where Krister worked as master chef. The one who left earliest, usually Irene, would take the car in the morning. If they could ride together they did. The one who worked the latest would drive the car home. For Irene's part, taking the express bus home from Drottningtorget was fairly quick. But the thought of not having to sit on an overcrowded bus was tempting, so she accepted the superintendent's offer of a ride.

They drove back toward Highway 158 through open country that was becoming green. Even though villas and row houses had been built in high concentrations in some areas, there were still parts that were very rural. Irene didn't comment since she knew her boss was not interested in hearing about idyllic natural scenery right now.

"Murders with dismemberments are very uncommon. I've been a crime investigator for almost twenty-five years and during that time we've had three or four cases. I've only investigated one murder-mutilation previously. This will be the second," he said.

"Who was the victim in the first case?"

"A drug addict and prostitute. They're the ones who end up like this. They attract the sickest types. I guess you could call it an occupational hazard. If you happen to be a snake charmer, you have to count on being bitten at some point."

"Such girls feel very abandoned."

Andersson grunted in response. Irene continued. "Was that body also cut open and emptied of all organs?"

"No. A confused bastard had killed her during some extra-heated sex game in his apartment. He panicked because he didn't know how he was going to get rid of the body. So he dismembered her in the bath-tub and stuffed the pieces into three suitcases. Then he threw the suit-cases in a big Dumpster at a building site in the area."

"Did it take a long time to catch him?"

"Four days. He drank like a pig after the murder and went crazy. He stood on his balcony and shouted, 'I was the one who cut her up! I was the one who did it!' After about an hour, the neighbors got tired of it and called us. It was just a matter of driving there and picking him up. He hadn't even cleaned up properly in the bathroom and the hooker's clothes were still lying on the floor." Andersson chuckled at the mem-ory. "But this is something else. Something much worse," he said and suddenly became serious again.

"What do you mean?"

"To murder a human being and then take apart the body piece by piece like a . . . roasted chicken. It's damned disgusting!"

"I agree with you. But we don't know what happened yet. Is this a case of murder or of a necrophile who came across a body and dis-membered it for the sake of excitement. . . ."

Irene stopped herself when she became aware of Andersson's faint moaning.

"Goddamn it! Goddamn it!" he said emphatically.

Irene nodded and decided to drop the subject. Even if both Irene and her boss had worked with murders and murderers for many years, there were still some things that were worse than others.

* * *

BY CHANCE Irene had happened to see the announcement in *GP* a week or so earlier: "Welcome to the Hair Center at Frölunda Torg! We're now open until 8:00 p.m. on Wednesday and Thursday evenings!" She had pounced on the phone and made an appointment. Finally a hairdresser who understood when people had time to do their hair! She had gotten an appointment at six thirty, which suited her. She would have time to make it home and walk Sammie first.

The twins had their own activities after school. Jenny was very musical and played both guitar and flute. She also sang in two choirs. Today, flute practice was on the schedule. Katarina had a good chance of winning this year's Junior National Championship in judo since she had won the year before. Irene herself had become European Champion almost twenty years ago. At that time she was the only woman in Scandinavia who had a black belt, third dan.

Sammie was sitting just inside the door and welcomed her with big leaps of joy. That was the advantage of having a dog, thought Irene. It was happy no matter what time of day you came home.

She barely had time to take off her jacket before the phone rang.

"Irene Huss here."

"Hi, Irene. This is Monika Lind. Do you remember me?"

It took a second for Irene to go through her memory bank to find Monika Lind, but she managed in the end.

"Of course. We were neighbors for a few years. But hasn't it been four or five years since you moved to Trollhättan?"

"To Vänersborg. Five years ago."

Monika Lind's daughter, Isabell, was one year older than the twins. The girls had played together when they were younger, but when the Lind family moved all the way to Vänersborg the contact faded and finally stopped completely. Irene wondered what her former neighbor might want from her.

"It's about Isabell. The police don't care and I have to speak with a sensible police officer!"

Monika's voice broke at the last sentence, and Irene realized, to her consternation, that Monika had begun to sob. Irene tried to use a calming tone of voice. "What is it that's happened? Has Isabell gotten into trouble with the police?"

"No, but she's gone! I've looked for her . . . but no one cares!"

Heavy weeping could be heard again.

"Monika, please. Try and start from the beginning."

It was quiet for a while. Irene understood that Monika was making a real effort to calm down. She started speaking in a shaky voice. "Isabell started her second year in the social studies program in the fall. But she didn't get on well. She has always had a hard time finding her place at high school. She won a beauty contest last summer and after that she wanted only one thing . . . to become a photo model. A photographer here in the city took some very nice pictures of her that cost a fortune . . . but she really wanted it."

Monika Lind became silent again. Irene could hear her breathing and she knew how difficult it must be for Monika to talk about this.

"Everything stopped at Christmas. She refused to continue going to high school. She said that she had picked the wrong track and wanted to start the mass media program in the fall. And she had also had contact with a modeling agency in Copenhagen."

Irene jumped in. "How did she get in touch with the agency?"

"Through an ad. They were looking for Swedish girls who were willing to work in Copenhagen."

"What's the name of the agency?"

"Scandinavian Models. She got in touch with a female photographer named Jytte Pedersen. I actually spoke with her on the phone twice before Bell left. The agency arranged the trip and the apartment and—" Monika's voice broke again and she wept in despair.

"She rented her own apartment in Copenhagen?"

"No. She shares one with two other girls. One from Oslo named Linn and one from Malmö named Petra."

"Where is the apartment located? In what part of Copenhagen?"

Irene had only been to Copenhagen once in her life in the last year of high school. Her memories were a bit blurry, probably due in large part to the good, cheap Danish beer and to the distance from watchful parental eyes.

"It's just next to Frihamnen. Østbanegade is the name of the street."

"You've never visited her?"

"Yes, no. Not her . . . I wanted to go down and visit during the break in February. The disadvantage of being a teacher is that I only have vacation during school breaks. My husband promised to take care of Elin. . . . You might remember that I was pregnant when we moved to Vänersborg. Isabell has a little sister who is almost five. Rather, a half sister. But then Bell didn't want me to come because they were busy renovating the apartment. Then I wanted to come over Easter but she said that she had so much work. She was going to travel to London for some photo shoots and so on. Increasingly I got the feeling that she didn't want me to come. The girls didn't have a phone in the apartment so Bell would always call us. I wrote at least once a week."

"How often did she call?"

"Usually once a week. A few times it might have been ten days between calls."

"When did you last hear from her?"

"She called one evening in the middle of March. Janne answered the phone. I had parent-teacher meetings."

"What did she say?"

"Not very much. As I said, it was Janne who answered the phone."

"How is the relationship between Isabell and your husband?"

A loud sigh could be heard. "As you know, there were already problems when we were living in Fiskebäck. Bell was eleven when Janne and I met. Because contact with her father had been irregular since the divorce, it had only been the two of us for five years. And then Janne came and got between us. You must remember all of the times she ran away and came to your house and you weren't allowed to say where she was because she wanted me to worry."

"You don't think it could be something like that this time? She is staying away so that you'll start to worry. . . ."

"That's exactly what the police in both Sweden and Denmark want me to think! They don't believe that she's disappeared!"

"She's disappeared? What do you mean?"

"She isn't in Copenhagen! All of April went by and I didn't hear anything from her. The Thursday before Walpurgis Night Eve I took the day off and went down to Copenhagen. First I went to Bell's address. You have no idea what a seedy-looking hovel it was! A big dirty apartment building next to Søndre Frihavn. I went up the stairs to the landing where Bell supposedly lived but there was no apartment with three girls as roommates. Of course I knocked and asked all the tenants who were home. No one had seen or heard anything about those three girls."

Monika paused. "Finally, I got ahold of a phone book and started searching for modeling agencies and photographers. There's no modeling agency called Scandinavian Models, and there's no photographer named Jytte Pedersen. I went to all of the photographers and agencies I could find. I had a picture of Bell with me that I showed them. None of the photographers had seen her. Then it was the weekend so I went home. But I reported Bell as missing to the Danish police before I left."

Her voice cut off again and Irene had to wait a long time. In the meantime, she jotted down notes on a pad hanging on the wall by the phone.

Monika snuffled and continued in an unsteady voice. "They were . . . laughing! They didn't think it was alarming that a seventeen-year-old had disappeared in Copenhagen. According to them, that kind of thing happens every day. Young girls run away from their parents in order to experience the big city. Apparently completely normal! They said that all the police could do was post a description and see if she popped up in connection with some other case. They practically told me to my face that they weren't going to do anything!"

And what could they do? Send out patrols to look for Isabell from Vänersborg? Irene realized that it wouldn't be a good idea to even suggest such a thought. Instead she asked, "Have you contacted the Swedish police?"

"Yes, on May 2, last Sunday. They have the same outlook as their Danish colleagues."

Irene thought hard. "You said that Isabell called. Did she ever write cards or letters?"

"No. She was never much for writing."

"Try and remember what she said. About the apartment. About the other two girls. About working as a model . . . everything!"

"She said the first names of the girls she was sharing with were Linn and Petra. She mostly talked about all of the new friends she was meeting. There were people from all over the world. There was an English boy named Steven and an American named Robin. The girls usually went out together and then they met tons of people. Of course there were a lot of other models. One friend's name was Heidi. Then she talked about how it was fun but difficult to be photographed."

"You don't know any of the last names of the people she mentioned?"

"No. She said that she had bought a lot of clothes. She and the other girls would go out on the town and shop. She has always been crazy about clothes, and now she is earning quite a bit. If I know her, she is spending all of it on clothes and makeup."

"How did she describe the apartment and the building?"

"As being very nice and pleasant."

"But it didn't match the reality."

"No."

"Has she said anything else that you later found to be a lie?"

"Not that I can think of."

Irene chose her words carefully before she said, "Unfortunately, the situation is just as both my Swedish and Danish colleagues have said. There isn't much the police can do as long as there is no clear indication of a crime unless she shows up in connection with some police investigation. But you can always hire a private detective."

"That would be too expensive. But maybe that's what I'll have to do. What do you think has happened to her?"

"It's difficult to say. One possibility is that she is in hiding of her own free will for some reason. Another is that she isn't in Copenhagen anymore. Isn't there a chance that she went to England again?"

"But she should have called!"

"Yes. That's what's worrisome, that she hasn't. I think you should ask the police you contacted here in Sweden to register her with Interpol."

Monika thought this over. Irene had no more to say, so she just waited.

"Will you call if you come up with something?"

"Of course. Can I get your numbers at home and at work?" Irene wrote down the information on the notepad. She didn't entertain much hope of needing to use it in future. There wasn't a lot a detective inspector with a full-time job in Göteborg could do.

THE HAIRDRESSER had cut off too much. When she revealed the results to her husband, his comments confirmed her fears.

For the last seventeen years he had viewed her hairstyle intensely and critically. Now he raised his hand in greeting and said, "Howdy, Bob."

Naturally, she felt offended but at the same time she had to admit that she should have stopped the woman sooner. Irene decided that it was the hairdresser's fault. She had placed a picture of a young and fresh-looking model in Irene's face and said, "Look at this. Just your style. Tough but still feminine. A bit sixties retro, if you remember the Twiggy cut. Easy to take care of. And then we'll just add some darker red-brown highlights."

If Irene remembered the Twiggy cut . . . every girl's ideal at the end of the 1960s. She had been nine or ten years old. Without saying anything to her mother, she had made an appointment with the ladies' hairdresser at Guldhedstorget. The sweet-smelling plump hairdresser with bright red lipstick had wondered in a friendly way if Irene really was determined to cut off her long hair. Irene had declared that she was. And she also wanted to look like Twiggy. Perhaps the hair became Twiggylike, but not the rest of Irene. No one would ever mix them up—not then and not later.

And now she had gone and done it again.

With a sigh, Detective Inspector Irene Huss looked at her reflection in the hallway mirror critically. She saw a tall slender woman, dressed in black pants and a light blue V-neck cotton top. Her hair was very short but the color was nice. Her usual dark brown hair had a deep red luster. All of the gray streaks were covered, and in the hall light she looked younger than her forty years. If she didn't step too close to the mirror.

With a hefty pull, the outside door was thrown open and her twin daughters tried to squeeze through the doorway at the same time. When the argument over who was going to take the last coat hanger was sorted out, the girls turned to their mother.

"We've been and looked at them. It's him," said Jenny.

"Without a doubt," Katarina agreed.

As one, mother and daughters moved to the kitchen where the two male members of the family were gathered. Since Krister worked as a master chef and cooked both as a career and a hobby, he had started on their late dinner. Sammie was sitting next to him expectantly, completely concentrated on his master's activities. A tasty morsel might fall on the floor.

"Katarina and Jenny have been to look at them. No doubt that Sammie's the father," said Irene.

"Then the ill-tempered shrew was right when she called and scolded us," Krister remarked.

"Of course she was angry! Her purebred poodle had gone and pleased herself with a terrier! But she only has herself to blame. You don't let a bitch in heat out in the yard in a neighborhood with row houses. Not with the low fences we have here. She even complained to me that the bitch is an international champion," Irene informed them.

"So, Sammie, you've been consorting with a champion," Krister said harshly but with a faint smile on his lips.

If this had been a cartoon, a question mark would have lit up over Sammie's head. He had such a look of wonder on his face as he glanced from one to the other that they felt as though they could almost see it floating over him. Jenny was the one who couldn't control herself and burst out in snorting laughter. The others joined in and soon they were all laughing so hard they were crying. But then Sammie became grumpy. If there was anything a dog with self-esteem loathed, it was being laughed at and made a fool of. With his tail between his legs he left the kitchen and went upstairs to the second floor. There he went into Jenny's room and crawled under the bed.

"There are three of them!" Jenny said. "The cutest ever! Two girls and one boy. They sort of look like Sammie when he was a puppy. But much smaller since they are only three weeks old and also much darker and—"

"Of course! The mother is black," interrupted Katarina.

"Obviously, I know that's the reason why! But the old bag has threatened to put them to sleep if we don't help her find homes for them."

"A mix between a poodle and a terrier doesn't sound entirely successful. Based on looks they will probably be absolutely adorable. But as for temperament and personality . . . I don't know," said Irene, wondering.

"What have you done to your hair!" Katarina burst out. She hadn't noticed her mother's new hairstyle until that moment.

"The newest of the new. Perfect," Irene asserted.

"And you complained when I cut my hair short," said Jenny.

"Cut it short! You *shaved* it off!" Katarina reminded her.

Jenny didn't continue with the discussion about her very short haircut of a few years earlier. Both girls sat quietly and inspected their mother's new look. Irene looked back at her daughters. Twins, but still so different that people often didn't think they were even sisters.

Katarina was the very image of herself at that age. Already one hundred and seventy-three centimeters tall and in good shape. She had Irene's coloring, with dark brown hair and dark blue eyes, and a complexion that took to the sun easily. Jenny was the image of her father or, maybe more accurately, of her aunts on her father's side. To her own exasperation she was the shortest in the family. Since the girls had already turned sixteen, they probably wouldn't grow any more. Jenny's hair was golden blonde, she had light blue eyes and a fair complexion that was very sensitive to the sun. She usually whined about how unfairly fate had affected her looks compared to those of her sister. The truth was that Jenny was beautiful, but she just couldn't see it herself.

In order to put a stop to the daughters' critical staring, Irene asked, "What's for dinner?"

"It's Wednesday. Vegetarian. I'm making a Thai vegetable stew with coconut milk," Krister answered.

Irene sighed inside. Even though they had eaten vegetarian meals three days a week for almost two years, she still had a hard time getting used to such different food. It started when Jenny decided to become a vegan and Krister felt he needed to lose at least twenty kilos.* The family changed eating habits. Jenny ate vegetarian dishes on the days when the rest of the family gorged on poultry, fish, and meat. Krister hadn't lost his twenty kilos, but he was at least under a hundred. Because he was so tall, he didn't give the impression of being heavy, just robust and impressive. But Irene knew that his knees had started protesting against all the extra weight. This kept him from going on long walks with Sammie, but he did swim almost two thousand meters every week at the Frölunda community center pool. He would turn fifty

---

* One kilogram or kilo equals 2.2046 pounds, so twenty kilos is about forty-four pounds.

this fall. Irene didn't hold out much hope that he would become thinner or have more energy; instead, she realized that she would have to satisfy herself with the changes in eating and exercise habits he had already made.

Chapter 3

THE SEARCH AREA HAD been widened every hour and the radius from Killevik continued to grow, but so far no one had made any new discoveries.

Superintendent Andersson tried to reach Pathology. Professor Stridner sent a message that she was busy and would get in touch as soon as she had time. Hannu was plowing through the register for persons who had been missing since New Year's. He still hadn't found any promising leads. None of this improved the superintendent's frame of mind.

"We are standing here twiddling our thumbs. Someone must be missing this person!" he burst out.

Irene tried to calm him down. "It's barely been two days since we found the sack, and the public isn't aware of the tattoo. It might provide a clue to the victim."

Andersson reflected as he rocked back and forth on the soles of his feet. Finally he cleared his throat with difficulty. "The tattoo . . . my line of sight was disrupted, I didn't get a good look. What was it a picture of?"

Since he had been standing several meters away from the examination table it was quite understandable that he hadn't been able to see the tattoo. Tactfully, Irene refrained from pointing this out and turned to the remaining colleagues in the room. "Stridner believes that it's a Chinese character encircled by a dragon biting its own tail. It wasn't very easy to see since the dog had bitten right on the tattoo and the body was decomposing . . . you know. But she described the character as an upside-down y, with two cross lines on the stem—one at the fork of the y and the other a bit higher up on the stem. The dragon is tattooed in several colors, and according to Stridner, it's a real work of art."

"I don't think it's an ordinary tattoo. I don't think just anyone did it," said Birgitta.

"Find the tattoo artist in order to find a trail to the victim," added Fredrik Stridh.

"The best thing would be if we had a photo of the tattoo so that we could show it to all of the tattoo artists in Göteborg," said Jonny.

"You don't want to walk around with a picture of what it looks like right now. Believe me!" Irene assured him.

She thought for a bit before she asked, "Could we arrange to have a drawing instead of a photo? A drawing would be much clearer."

Andersson brightened and nodded. "It's a good idea. I'll try and arrange it."

He turned toward Fredrik. "How is it going with last night's stabbing?"

"The victim has been identified as Lennart Kvist; in drug circles he's known as Laban. He's a guy who has been in trouble for years and has a lot of drugs on his conscience. It was probably the result of some argument over a deal. A witness heard loud cries for help from behind Flora's Hill. He called the police on his cell phone. The patrol found Laban's dead body in the park. On the ground under him there was a open bag full of ready-to-sell heroin. Most likely the culprit is a client who hadn't gotten the credit he wanted."

"Did the witness see anyone running from the scene?" asked Andersson.

"No. The murderer probably disappeared in the direction of the Big Theater via the park; he may have gone along the canal."

"OK. You and Birgitta are in charge of that investigation. Get in touch with Narcotics if you haven't already done so. Irene, Jonny, and Hannu will continue with the murder-mutilation case. We'll meet this afternoon around five."

SEVEN TATTOO artists had placed advertisements for their services in the Yellow Pages. It was possible to get piercing done at some of the places. Painful treatments, which people subjected themselves to voluntarily, thought Irene. Personally, she hadn't even dared get her ears pierced.

"There's no point in running around to tattoo parlors before we have a picture to show them," said Jonny.

"I'll find out if Andersson has found an artist and if Stridner has called yet."

Irene needed to stretch her legs a bit. Neither she nor Jonny had any good ideas when it came to the continued investigation. They needed a way to trace the victim's identity.

On the way to Andersson's office she ran into Hannu. He politely held the door open and she curtsied jokingly as she passed through it.

"Do you have to make a fuss about just walking through a door?" the superintendent said sourly.

There was a distinct feeling in the air that nothing of importance had occurred. Irene hurried to ask her question.

"No. No artist. And Stridner hasn't—" He was interrupted by the ringing of the telephone. He quickly grabbed the receiver. "Superintendent Andersson. Yes. Oh? Hmm." Andersson listened to the voice on the phone. From his stiff facial expression and the chattering voice that could be heard, the two listeners could tell he was speaking with Stridner herself. The superintendent's sulky expression was slowly replaced by one of surprise. He hemmed and hawed monosyllabically before he managed to interrupt the sharp voice on the other end of the line.

"We have a slight problem. We need a drawing of the tattoo . . . no, preferably not a photo . . . drawing, yes . . . would be a bit clearer. Oh, really? Great!"

With the last sentence he brightened up and gave both his inspectors a triumphant look.

"Thanks a lot."

He put down the receiver and unconsciously rubbed his hands together with satisfaction.

"Stridner will arrange for the sketch. One of the autopsy assistants is working on a degree in art. He's there today. They'll send the picture over when it's finished."

"Do they know if the victim is a man or a woman?" asked Hannu.

"A man. They did a chromosome test."

Without changing his expression, he took away the top pages in the pile of missing persons information he was carrying.

"That leaves three," he said.

"Stridner has also measured the skeleton. She says that the victim is a rather broad-shouldered man between twenty-five and thirty-five years of age, and between one hundred and seventy-five and one hundred and eighty-five centimeters in height. The body hair that was left on the chest was relatively dark. The man probably had dark hair, but not black according to Stridner."

"A foreigner?" suggested Irene.

"Maybe. But he wasn't dark skinned and didn't have black hair. Probably brown to dark brown hair."

Hannu flipped through his papers and placed yet another page farther back in the pile. "That leaves two," he said calmly.

Irene could not contain her curiosity and asked, "Was it a man you weeded out?"

Hannu nodded. "Seventy-two years old. White haired. Heavy. One hundred and sixty-seven centimeters. Disappeared in Hindås in January. It's not him."

"Hardly. But which ones do you have left?" Andersson interrupted impatiently.

"Steffo Torberg. Thirty-two years old. Disappeared during a furlough from Kumla, March 13. In prison for seven years for bank robbery and manslaughter. He had one year left and had handled all of his furloughs excellently up till then. We know that he took a train to Göteborg to visit his family. Has two children down here with his ex-girlfriend. All traces disappear at the Central Station."

"Didn't he have some connection with a motorcycle gang?"

"The Brotherhood."

"Not the best guys to have problems with? Did he?"

"Not that we know of."

"Description?"

"One hundred and eighty-three centimeters, weighed about one hundred kilos. In good shape. Shoulder-length thick dark hair. Not black. Dark brown."

"Tattoos?"

"Tons. Over his entire body."

The superintendent sighed. "He probably looked like a comic strip."

"Probably."

To Irene's surprise, Hannu winked mischievously in her direction. Was he teasing the boss? She wasn't sure, since he immediately returned to his neutral tone of voice.

"The next one has several tattoos and piercings."

"Piercings? Damn!" Andersson said emphatically.

"He's too young. Twenty-two years. Pierre Bardi. Has lived in Sweden for three years. The whole time in Stockholm. Disappeared March 22 after a fight with his live-in girlfriend. Pierre packed his bags and said that he was going back to Paris. He took his passport, two suitcases, and left. No one has seen him since. In Stockholm or in Paris.

"Description?"

"One hundred and seventy-six centimeters, in good shape and good health. Shoulder-length dark brown hair with blond highlights. Large tattoo on the left shoulder blade, right shoulder, and above the left nipple, though no dragon. Piercings in the nipples, through the top of the penis, in the right eyebrow, and in the tongue. Several gold rings in both ears."

Andersson knitted his eyebrows in concentration. Finally he shook his head. "No. It isn't either of them. Our body part only has one tattoo. He certainly could have had rings in his nipples, but we don't know anything about that since the entire chest muscles are missing."

Hannu nodded in agreement.

"So who is the victim? Could it be a foreigner nobody misses? A sailor?"

"No sailors have been reported missing during the last six months," Hannu said calmly.

"Whoever he is, no one has reported him missing," Andersson stated.

"We may have to publish the picture of the tattoo in the papers," Irene suggested.

Andersson muttered to himself for a moment before he answered. "Maybe so. We'll wait another day or so and see if we find more pieces of the victim."

TWO MORE sacks were found that afternoon by a dog patrol searching the coastline south of Killevik. In a small overgrown bay, an old leaky skiff, turned upside down, was lying a few meters from the water. The dog instantly started for the boat, struggling to get to it. The two policemen carefully turned the skiff on its side. When they saw the sacks, they called in backup from Technical and from the Violent Crimes Unit.

The technicians were already hard at work when Irene and Jonny arrived. Svante Malm stopped photographing in order to greet them.

"Appears as though they belong to the same body we found the day before yesterday," he said.

"What's inside the sacks?" asked Irene.

"The lower part of the abdomen in one and the thighs in the other."

The technician got back to his work with the camera.

Irene and Jonny walked around the discovery site. They had to watch where they put their feet because of the treacherously slippery stones and boulders. It was a gray and overcast afternoon, and the low-lying clouds warned of rain for the evening. Appropriately, a gloomy light shone over the ocean and the police officers on the beach. Beach grass was growing thickly around the skiff.

"Good hiding place," Jonny pointed out.

"Yeah. No one comes here to swim. It's too overgrown," Irene agreed.

"Was the sack with the upper body also deposited here?"

They looked around, trying to answer the question. Finally Irene said, "No. It couldn't have been under the skiff. There's no chance that it could have washed out during high tide."

"So then, there are more hiding places."

"Yes, but probably close by. How far is it from here to Killevik?"

"As the crow flies I would guess four hundred meters."

"It's easy to get here by car."

They looked up toward the little gravel road that followed the coastline in a north-south line.

"You can get all the way down to Kungsbacka on these roads," said Jonny.

"It's just a matter of continuing to search along the ocean and the smaller roads."

"IT'S AFTER six. Go home. You aren't working this weekend. Fredrik and I are on duty," said Birgitta.

"But you have the murder behind Flora's Hill," Irene objected.

"We've actually gotten a tip that Fredrik is checking out. It may be a jealousy killing. That wasn't what we would have suspected would happen to Laban. Apparently, he had been together with a relatively young girl. Since she is a drug addict and he was a dealer they had a lot in common. Supposedly, the girl's ex went around telling the world what he was planning on doing to Laban when he got his hands on him. Stabbing him to death was the least of it. We only know the ex's first name. Robert. Apparently, he is also her pimp."

"Has Fredrik gone to talk to Robert on his own?" asked Irene.

"No, he's just going to get a fix on his whereabouts. Then we'll bring him into the station for interrogation. If we're lucky we can pull him in over the weekend. So the investigation of Laban's murder is going forward. But I don't think anything will happen with the murder-mutilation case in the next few days. Pathology is going to look at the pieces and that usually takes a while. Are they going to continue searching with dogs over the weekend?"

"Yes, and the Harbor Police are searching the coast. Hannu has gone through the register but there isn't anyone reported missing who matches our victim. Actually, there isn't a lot we can do right now."

IRENE UNLOCKED the door to her old Saab 99:a. It was twelve years old and was affectionately cared for by the Huss family. They might be forced to buy a new car at any time, and every day that this was put off was valuable. Irene felt lighthearted even though it was raining heavily. Krister had his usual Friday off and she knew that meant good food and good wine. It would have to compensate for his having to work the rest of the weekend. That was the way it went when you were married to someone in the restaurant business. And, for that matter, to someone who worked as a police officer.

"DEAR, COULD you take Sammie out for a walk? The food isn't quite ready yet." Krister's voice could be heard from the kitchen.

Judging by the smell, the food was coming along nicely. Irene suddenly realized how hungry she was. Sammie came down the stairs calmly. He had taken a nap before supper and, just to be different, had slept so deeply he hadn't heard his mistress come in. But he woke up when he heard the words "out" and "Sammie." Then he knew it was time for a walk.

Irene put on her rain clothes since it was bucketing down outside. Even when it poured in the spring it never got dark. Despite that, Irene didn't see anyone until the woman and her dog were almost on top of her. She suddenly became aware of movement out of the corner of her eye. Before she had the chance to turn, she heard a piercing voice say, "Have you found a home for the puppies yet?"

Sammie became excited and threw himself at his black girlfriend. She was reserved but nothing compared with her mistress. The elderly woman looked as though she had just drunk a bottle of vinegar.

Furious, Irene didn't make any attempt at being friendly. "No. I've worked late every evening this week. Police officers usually don't have time to have a dog, and the others I meet in my line of work aren't allowed to have them. They are forbidden both in holding cells and prisons.

"Actually, it takes two people to care for a child and that goes for dogs as well. We'll get in touch if we hear of anyone who is thinking about get- ting a dog, but you also need to do your part. Put in an ad, for example."

"That costs money. If you had any idea what I've had to pay for the vet and food . . ."

"Even if they're mixed breed, you'll still be paid for them. We aren't going to request a stud fee. A healthy mixed-breed puppy costs fifteen hundred SEK."*

The pursed look on the neighbor lady's face lessened a bit.

"That much?"

"Yes. Purebred wheaten terriers cost about seven thousand SEK."

"That much!"

She was a really boring person to talk with. Irene had to end this conversation before her entire Friday evening was ruined.

"You'll have to excuse me but I have food in the oven. We'll get in touch as soon as someone who is interested shows up," she said.

THE FOOD was exquisite. Salmon filet baked on a bed of coarse salt, saf- fron sauce, lightly steamed sugar peas, and a green salad put Irene in a good mood again. Krister had bought a new wine that they were trying.

"Somerton. Australian. Comes in red as well," he said.

"Fantastic with the salmon." Irene was no expert but she had learned a great deal from Krister over the years.

---

* SEK refers to Krona, the basic unit of money in Sweden. One Krona equals 0.128085 dollars, so fifteen hundred SEK is about $192.

"Where are the girls?" she asked.

"Jenny was going to a try out with a band. Katarina was picked up by that kid, Micke. Apparently, he was allowed to borrow his father's car."

"As long as he drives carefully. Where were they going?"

"To a party in Askim. A classmate of Micke's has a birthday."

"Did Jenny want to be picked up somewhere?"

"No. Pia's parents were going to drive them."

"Good. Then we can open another bottle."

THE PHONE rang just before three o'clock. Half awake, Irene heard Krister answer. Then he sat up straight and swung his legs over the edge of the bed.

"I understand. I'll come as soon as I can."

Heavy with sleep, Irene mumbled, "What was that about?"

"It was Sahlgren Hospital. Katarina and Micke were in an accident. They aren't seriously hurt but they had to be patched up at the emergency room. It was Katarina herself who called. She wants to be picked up. Micke has to stay overnight for observation. It seems he had a head injury."

Irene started to come out of her wine-induced sleep. Her heart began to race and, suddenly, she was wide awake. Her daughter had been injured. She quickly got out of bed but then had to sink back down when the floor started moving under her feet. She had probably consumed a bottle and a half by herself, far too much when she was tired to begin with.

Krister said, "Stay here. I'll go get her. She was able to call so she can't be hurt that bad. There's no reason to wake up Jenny. She may wake on her own when we come home."

He patted Irene on the cheek and dressed. Irene lay down again but now she couldn't relax. She was wide awake. That something horrible could happen to your kids when they were out on their own was every parent's worst nightmare! Monika Lind and Isabell, who was missing in Copenhagen, came to mind.

She wrapped herself in her bathrobe and went down to the kitchen. With a heavy snore, Sammie rolled over into the wonderfully warm hollow in the bed that she had vacated.

It would have to be a cup of instant coffee. She warmed the water in the microwave, and while she waited found a package of old rice cakes. When the coffee was ready, she sat at the kitchen table and chewed listlessly on one of the dry cakes.

Jenny was home, at least. She had been very satisfied with her evening's performance. The audition had turned out even better than she'd expected. They had asked her to come back and rehearse with them. She had been very excited and had bubbled with enthusiasm as she sat on the end of their bed telling them about the band. Polo, that was the name. Irene was pretty sure that Jenny had said Polo.

Irene had barely had time to finish her coffee when Jenny came downstairs.

"What's happened to Katarina?" she asked, and yawned.

How did she know anything had happened to her sister? Was it an example of the telepathic contact twins were said to have in certain situations? But wasn't that only for identical twins, thought Irene.

"I dreamed that Katarina was sad and in pain. And then she had a bandage on her face," Jenny continued.

Irene tried to hide her surprise. "Pappa has gone to get her at the emergency room. She and Micke were in an accident. It can't be that bad since she's allowed to come home."

The last sentence was mostly to comfort herself. Jenny filled a glass with apple juice and fixed herself a sandwich while they waited.

When they heard steps at the outside door, both of them jumped up and rushed out into the hall. Krister opened the door and let Katarina in. She had a large bandage over her right eyebrow.

Krister smiled broadly. "Everything's fine. She has a bruised shoulder and a few stitches above her eyebrow."

ON SATURDAY afternoon the Huss family ate a late breakfast. The mood around the breakfast table was uneasy. Katarina complained about pain in her shoulder and neck muscles, but otherwise she felt pretty good.

"How did the accident happen?" Irene asked.

"We were going through an intersection and we had a green light. Then that idiot came and drove right into the side of Micke's car. Or rather his father's car. It's almost new. His father is going to go insane!"

"Was Micke drinking at the party?"

Katarina tried to shake her head fiercely but stopped herself and with a small whimper rubbed the side of her neck.

"No, he had Coca-Cola because he's scared to death about his new driver's license. And the car—"

"What about the driver of the other car? Was he sober?"

"Don't know. I was looking out the window on my side of the car and didn't see him when he drove into us. There was just a *wham* on Micke's side of the car. Afterward I was probably in shock and . . . like gone, kinda. I don't even remember what the other driver looked like. He was bleeding from his forehead like a pig. Apparently, he hit the windshield with his head. I don't think he was wearing a seat belt."

"Who called the ambulance?"

"I did. Micke had his cell phone with him, so I called."

"What time was it when the accident happened?"

"Just before one o'clock."

"The nurse at the emergency room thought that we should make an appointment at the clinic and have a doctor look at Katarina's neck and shoulder. There's a risk of whiplash in these types of accidents," Krister said.

"What about my training for the National Championship?!" Katarina burst out.

Irene understood how Katarina felt but also realized the injuries could worsen if she started training again too soon.

"You can't start training before the pains in your throat and neck are gone," she said sternly.

"Good-bye, National Championship," her daughter retorted drearily.

Chapter 4

"WE WON'T GET ANYTHING from Stridner until tomorrow, and we still don't know who the victim is," Superintendent Andersson said on Monday morning.

All the officers were there with the exception of Birgitta Moberg and Fredrik Stridh, who were busy interrogating Robert Larsson about the murder of Lennart Kvist. Before they entered the interrogation room, Birgitta had told Irene, "Narcotics says that he's a real bad guy but he hasn't been arrested in the last seven years. Before that, they had him up for possession and bootlegging. He was interrogated in an assault case but they were never able to prove anything. The witness was frightened into silence. He owns a strip club down by Masthuggskajen called Wonder Bar. The last few years he has expanded into prostitution and right now he is the object of an ongoing investigation into pimping. He doesn't know about it; one of his girls probably squealed. It isn't a good idea to rough up your source of income. It might be that girl Laban was with, but that's just speculation on my part. I don't know anything for certain."

"Did Robert abuse her?"

"Yes, apparently quite severely. But it's the drugs that have really hurt her."

Irene peered into the interrogation room and a glimpse of the suspect being questioned gave her a strong feeling that breaking Robert Larsson wasn't going to be easy. He was around thirty, quite tall, and very muscular. His well-trimmed hair was light; long blond hairs covered his powerful arms all the way down to his fingers. His elegant shirt was nonchalantly unbuttoned at the neck and showed a tight carpet of thick golden hair on his chest and climbing up his neck. A heavy gold chain glimmered in the opening. It would have been easy to call him a blond gorilla, but no one who saw his face would have done so. That face could have been used in a shaving commercial. His eyes were a cold, intense blue, and his heavy eyebrows had a slight arch that harmonized well with his straight nose. He had a dimple on the point of his chin, which was covered with heavy reddish blond stubble. His smile was relaxed and charming.

Birgitta and Fredrik took turns asking Robert questions. He reclined in the creaking chair, smiled faintly, and said in a low tone of voice, "Why are you asking me this? I want to speak with my lawyer."

He cast a preoccupied glance at his heavy gold Tag-Heuer, demonstrating that he was starting to tire of the bullshit that was taking up his precious time.

Irene closed the door and went to work on her own investigation. It was at a complete standstill. They hadn't found any new sacks, no new information had come in that would lead them to the victim's identity, and there were no new witness accounts from the people around Killevik about events that could be connected to the black sacks.

Nothing happened during the whole morning. Irene went through a lot of paperwork that had been lying around. She became stiff from sitting for so long at the computer, so she took breaks and went in to chat with colleagues. The truth was that she felt lonely in the office she shared with Tommy Persson. She called him at home to find out how he was doing.

"I'm OK, thanks. It feels good as long as I don't do any high jumps," he replied.

"Then maybe you can come to work?" Irene said, hoping.

"Well, I don't think I can quite keep up with you yet. The hernia was pretty big. They've done quite a job."

"They didn't take out your appendix since they were already inside?" Irene asked teasingly.

"No. The surgeon was sober."

After an uninspiring Sausage Stroganoff for lunch in the employee dining room of the nearby building, Irene became restless. She considered heading up to Pathology. Professor Stridner probably wouldn't be happy but she might let a bit more information slip about the victim. That was what was so frustrating about this investigation—the lack of information.

YVONNE STRIDNER was in the process of inspecting Friday's findings. The smell was just as nauseating as it had been during Irene's first visit, but she braced herself. She walked up to the examination table with determined steps. When she saw what was lying on it she regretted this but it was too late. Professor Stridner had already lifted her head and seen her.

"It's you again?" she said.

Irene tried to steady her voice when she replied. "Yes. I'm one of the officers working on the investigation."

Stridner nodded. She cut off a piece of the gray flesh and placed it in a labeled test tube. "Just in case," she muttered to herself.

Irene looked at the lower part of the abdomen, which was lying on the shiny steel surface. The genitalia had been completely removed. No intestines could be seen within the open abdomen. It was just as empty as the upper half of the torso had been. The thighs had been cut off at an angle just below the groin. Stridner looked up from her work.

"I'm almost done. You can go into my office."

Relieved, Irene obeyed.

"THIS IS unusually nasty. We're dealing with a very gruesome type of murderer, who is probably a sadistic necrophile," Stridner opined.

They were sitting in her workroom, one flight up. The professor was enthroned on an expensive leather armchair, and Irene was sitting on a lumpy and uncomfortable plastic-covered visitor's chair. It didn't matter to her. The main thing was that the pathologist seemed ready to speak to her.

"As you have seen for yourself, all of the internal organs are missing. The chest and buttock muscles on both sides have been cut away and, moreover, the genitals and the rectal opening have been removed. The pubic bone shows signs of substantial trauma. The arms and legs were probably sawed off with a circular saw or similar tool. There is a plenitude of bone splinters in the surfaces of the cuts that point to this. The head was removed between the third and fourth vertebrae. Again a circular saw was used. The separation was not carried out with any great anatomical knowledge: rather, the parts have just been sawed off. But then we have the removal of the body's internal organs."

Stridner interrupted herself and looked earnestly at her dark computer screen. For a short while her thoughts seemed to be very far away.

"The incision is a standard autopsy incision and was started at the upper part of the breastbone descending to the pubic bone. The navel is not involved; rather, the incision makes a little curve around it, which is standard in autopsies. Another thing that makes me think about someone familiar with autopsy procedures is the complete removal of all organs inside the abdominal membrane and the removal of the pelvic organs. This is seen during completed autopsies."

Again she stopped herself before she caught Irene's eye and said with her sharp voice, "However, the removal of the outer musculature and genitalia is *not* common autopsy procedure!"

"So you think that the murderer is familiar with autopsies?"

"Yes. Or a very skilled hunter. The organs were removed in a highly professional manner."

"But the head, arms, and legs were not removed in a professional manner?"

"No. Anyone could have done that with a good circular saw."

She stopped herself and took a deep breath. "But this isn't just anyone."

"What kind of person is it?"

"A ghoulish person. He's looking for a dead body—in order to do that, first he has to kill. And he does."

"He. You're saying he. Can't it be a woman?"

"I've been reading the current literature."

Stridner rose and went to the bookshelf that covered the wall behind her. She took out a bundle of books and set them down on the desk with a thud.

"I've skimmed through these over the weekend."

Irene could make out the titles of the top two volumes: *Der nekrotope Mensch* and *Sexual Homicide: Patterns and Motives*.

"You asked if it could be a female killer. The answer is, with almost complete certainty, no. There are hundreds of case studies of necrosadistic mutilation in the literature and in not a single case has the perpetrator been a woman. Perhaps an accomplice, but it's unlikely."

Stridner was quiet while she straightened her green-framed glasses on the thin bridge of her nose.

"When I was examining the upper portion of the abdomen I began to suspect that we were dealing with a necrosadistic murderer. There are two types of murderers who dismember. The first wants to get rid of the body and remove all traces of his and the victim's identity. The other wants to have a dead body in order to satisfy himself sexually during the dismemberment by defiling the dead body. There are no similarities between these two types of murderers."

She tapped meaningfully on the pile of books and paused dramatically before continuing.

"One thing is very unusual—namely, that the victim happens to be a man. That is rare. Almost without exception it's men killing women. There are, however, a few deviations. I found a pair of brothers in the USA who had murdered over thirty young men. They had subjected their victims to standard sadistic necrophiliac dismemberment and later buried the bodies on their ranch. Certain parts of the outer musculature were missing from the bodies. In the brothers' freezer, these body parts were found, well preserved. Mostly, the buttocks. Cannibalism is not unusual with this type of murderer."

"It sounds like an American horror film," said Irene. The persistent feeling of nausea she'd had in her stomach since she arrived at Pathology was increasing.

Stridner continued, "I'm very concerned that this sort of victim has been found here. Thankfully, this type of murder is unusual. It means that the type of murderer is also very unusual, but when such a murderer starts killing, the risk is high that he will kill again."

"He isn't satisfied with one victim?"

"No. Dismemberment and the defiling of the body fulfill his fantasies and keep his anxiety in check. He feels good after his exploit. He wants to have that sensation repeated."

"Is he fully aware of what he has done?"

"Yes. Just as he is aware that he can do it again. Whenever he wants."

Irene started to understand why this case had affected her so much from the beginning. Instinctively, she had sensed a merciless killer's presence. A type of murderer she wasn't accustomed to. Nor was anyone else at Violent Crimes in Göteborg, for that matter.

"Is he mentally ill?"

Stridner drew her eyebrows together and focused on Irene while she thought.

"Not so that one can label him with a psychiatric diagnosis. Often these murderers seem relatively normal. I say relatively because if you take a closer look at them, they have certain personality traits in common. Usually, they are lonely people. They are pleasant and polite when you speak with them but they don't invite any deeper friendship. They rarely display their violence; it is buried deep within. They have rich fantasy lives that are fed by violent pictures, films, and books. Frequently, they start on their paths with sadistic acts performed on animals. Their sex lives are often odd. Commonly, they are impotent, but they get their release through masturbation during the rites they enact with the dead bodies."

Irene thought fast. "Have I understood you correctly? Are you saying that our murderer is probably homosexual?"

Stridner shook her head. "Not necessarily homosexual. Sexually ambivalent. As I said, their sexuality is often odd. Outwardly they can almost seem to be asexual. There can be hints of homosexual interest, but usually fetishism or, for example, transvestism interests them. They are sexual seekers. It is only when they start performing rites with dead bodies that they attain an outlet for their fantasies and feel well. They need complete power over a dead body. No one is as vulnerable as a dead human being.

"May I ask a big favor of you?" Irene asked.

"Depends. What is it?"

"Would you be so kind as to come down to Violent Crimes tomorrow morning? We have a meeting at eight o'clock. It would be helpful if my colleagues could hear what you just told me."

"Can't you repeat it?"

"No. I'm going to forget half of it, and I can't answer the questions that I think we will have. We have no experience with this type of murderer. But you know a great deal."

"Well, since it's an extraordinary case, I'll be there tomorrow at eight o'clock."

Irene thanked her, rose, and started for the door. She was stopped by Stridner's voice. "I will have the drawing of the tattoo with me tomorrow. It's supposed to be finished today."

AT EXACTLY eight o'clock on Tuesday morning, Professor Stridner started her case review. All the officers in Superintendent Andersson's investigation team were present, as was the superintendent himself. The fact that Stridner had come in person to brief them showed how seriously she was taking this case. They listened to the medical examiner with increasing concern. The portrait of the murderer was becoming clearer but none of them could see who the individual in Stridner's terrifying picture might be.

When she asked for questions, Birgitta raised her hand.

"Why has the murderer cut away the breasts in circular form? Just as if they were female breasts?"

"Ellipses. This probably has to do with the sexual ambivalence of the murderer. We don't know exactly how he thinks during the dismemberment process, just that he finds an outlet for his strong inner feelings and fantasies. Objectively, what one sees with the victims is that the violation always affects the breasts, rectum, and genitalia. Always."

"Why?"

"It has to do with power. The power to efface the sex. Complete power to annihilate the victim's humanness."

"Damn!" Andersson said.

Irene asked, "What is known about the victims? Is a particular type of person selected?"

"Women are often the victims, but there are exceptions. Yesterday, I told you about the brothers in the USA who had murdered and dismembered more than thirty young men and buried them on their ranch. When the men were identified, it turned out that most of them were homosexual prostitutes. Even among females the victims tend to be prostitutes. This isn't because the necrosadistic murderer is drawn to prostitutes. The killer isn't attracted to any one type. He wants a dead body. The easiest thing is to pay a prostitute and take her, or him, to a secluded place. There the murderer can carry out his real intentions: kill and dismember."

Fredrik Stridh raised his hand. "How common is this type of murderer?"

"Very rare. We've only had a handful of cases in Sweden during the twentieth century. Murder-mutilation as a phenomenon is more common. During the last thirty years we have had about ten. But these were dismemberments where the body needed to be disposed of. They weren't defiled in the same brutal way. For reasons of practicality, the extremities and the head were cut off so that the pieces could be stowed in sacks or suitcases, quite simply as a means of getting rid of the body and hindering identification."

"So practical . . . I feel ill," Birgitta mumbled to Irene.

Irene nodded in agreement.

Andersson looked meditative, but Stridner was the one who broke the silence. "Tomorrow I'm going to London for a large medical examiners' conference. I could ask around about similar cases among my colleagues."

"That . . . that would be great," Andersson stammered.

Stridner opened her elegant briefcase and took out a large envelope.

"The picture of the tattoo."

She held it out to Andersson.

"Thank you very much," he remembered to say after a while.

But it was too late. The clicking of Stridner's heels could already be heard disappearing down the corridor.

THE DRAGON'S red mouth was wide open and long razor-sharp teeth coiled around the end of its own tail. The eyes glowed like sparkling emeralds. The claws were wide open and ready to drag the intestines out of anyone who came too close. The entirety of the powerful and agile body was covered by red, blue, and green armored scales. The dragon curled itself in a protective circle around the mysterious character.

An upside-down y, Stridner had said. Or maybe it was more like an upside-down fork with two cross strokes over the stem, one exactly at the split in the fork and the other at the middle. The investigation team was in agreement that it was probably a Chinese character. Just to be sure, Hannu had been directed to contact Göteborg University in order to try and find someone who was skilled in Chinese characters or to consult the Chinese embassy.

"Make copies on a color copier. Then you can start visiting the tattoo artists in town. But don't come back with a ring in your nostril! Ha ha!" Andersson joked.

None of the others thought that it was particularly funny, but they smiled politely and assured him that they wouldn't be tempted.

Birgitta and Fredrik were still working on the investigation of the murder of Laban. Robert Larsson had come up with an alibi. Two of his girls working at Wonder Bar had assured them they had been in the Jacuzzi with their employer at exactly the time of Laban's demise. Since no witness had turned up to contradict them, it would be difficult to hold Larsson.

Jonny, Irene, and Hannu divided up the seven tattoo artists in Göteborg among themselves. Irene drew Tattoo Tim on Nordenskiöldsgatan and MC-tattoo on Sprängkullsgatan.

Since MC-tattoo was the closest, Irene decided to start there. She found a parking spot by Hvitfeldtsplatsen. Without hurrying, Irene strolled across the bridge over Rosenlundskanalen. The big blossoms on the large chestnut trees stood straight up on the branches like unlit Christmas tree candles. A cascade of colorful bulbs were spread out underneath the tree. It struck her that she was only a stone's throw away from Flora's Hill. Laban had died when the area around the canal was at its most beautiful. But Irene doubted that was any comfort to him.

Personally, she felt in great need of comfort as she closed in on MC-tattoo. Two heavy motorcycles were parked outside. In the last few years she had developed a phobia. Not without good reason since she had had a very unpleasant run-in with the Hell's Angels. It had put her in the hospital and left deep psychological wounds. She thought that she had gotten over her fear, but when she saw the shiny machines outside the tattoo parlor, she wanted to turn and run. It took great self-control to open the door and step inside.

A fiery humming buzzed in the air. A thin man with a shaved head was sitting, concentrating, as he marked the shoulder of another man, whose upper body was bare, with a small color drill. The humming stopped in the same instant that the door slammed shut behind Irene.

"Hey, there. Will it be a little rose on your ass or a butterfly on your tit?" said the skinny one.

The subject laughed and his friend in the visitor's chair joined in. Since the tattoo artist's work area was illuminated by a strong lamp and the room was for the most part dark, Irene hadn't seen the man in the corner when she came in. But when she heard his laugh she peered into the darkness, then let her gaze roam back to his friend. Her mouth became parched.

Each of them could have kept a seasoned investigator awake all night just based on looks. They were heavy, bordering on fat. But under the fat, one could sense many hours of work with bars and weights. The one who was being furnished with a new tattoo had put his long hair into a ponytail, probably so that it wouldn't be in the way of the tattoo artist. His shoulder must have been the last spot on his body that wasn't yet tattooed, Irene thought. From his fingers, up his arms, and over his entire upper body, he was covered with tattoos, a variegated map of everything from graffiti to sophisticated pictures in different colors.

The nicer tattoos interested Irene. She straightened and tried to sound official. "No, thanks. I'm not here to get tattooed."

She pulled out her police identification and waved it in front of the tattoo artist's nose. "Detective Inspector Irene Huss."

The big man on the visitor's chair said, "That name sounds familiar . . . but I'll be damned if I know from where."

"I don't think so. We haven't met," she said shortly.

Inside, her pulse was racing so fast her ears were buzzing. Quickly, she said, "I'm here to ask a favor. It's about the murder-mutilation in Killevik. We don't know who the victim is but he has this tattoo on his right shoulder. Do you know who might have made it? Or maybe who the man is?"

Now all three of them were paying attention to her. She held out the picture of the dragon tattoo to the tattoo artist. He carefully took it by one corner. It wasn't until then that Irene saw he was wearing plastic gloves. He studied the color copy for a long time without saying anything. Irene nervously let her gaze roam over the walls, which were wallpapered with different tattoo themes. Most of them seemed to feature eagles, skulls, and American flags.

"A real master has done this one," the tattoo artist finally said. "A damn good work of art!" he added. His voice revealed sincere admiration.

"Who could have made it?" Irene asked.

"No idea. I don't think that it was done in Sweden."

"Why don't you think so?"

"The subject. The sign in the middle. It doesn't look Swedish. The dragon is so . . . Asian. Is the guy Asian?"

It took a second before Irene understood that he was talking about the victim. "No. A dark-haired European," she answered.

The tattoo artist took a thorough look at the picture before he handed it back with a shake of his head.

"Sorry. The only thing I can say is that it takes time to complete a tattoo like that. It isn't something you do during a coffee break."

"Like the shit you're scratching on me?" asked the man in the tattoo chair.

All three of them let out a roar of laughter. Irene took the opportunity to put away the picture and leave. Just as she opened the door and was about to step out onto the sidewalk, she heard the man in the visitor's chair exclaim, "Damn! Now I know who she is! Do you remember that row out in Billdal for—"

Quickly, Irene closed the door and hurried toward her car.

Tattoo Tim was closed. The parlor never opened before one o'clock according to the piece of cardboard taped on the inside of the glass door. On the other hand, it didn't close before nine. Irene decided to eat lunch before she met Tim.

On Linnégatan there were all sorts of cozy restaurants. Irene decided on a little Italian pub. While she was waiting for the food at a table by the window she looked out at the heavy traffic on Linnégatan and the new houses built in Art Nouveau style on the other side of the street. Elegant shops were located on the ground floors.

The fresh pasta came with a ham and cheese sauce that smelled wonderful. A crisp salad and an ice-cold light beer completed her meal. She had declined the waitress's suggestion of a drink before the meal. She'd felt strongly tempted for just a second, but then thought better of it. An investigator couldn't go around breathing alcohol fumes on the people she was trying to interrogate. It didn't instill confidence.

She had lingered over coffee and had several refills so it was almost one thirty when she arrived at Tim's tattoo parlor again.

A girl in her early teens was sitting with her mouth wide open. A young man with dyed black hair down to his waist had a firm grip on her tongue, which he'd wrapped in a piece of cloth. With a large tonglike instrument, he punched a hole in the tongue.

"Aaggg," said the girl.

The man let go and gave the girl a hand mirror. She held it in front of her face and stuck out her tongue. A round glittering silver ball was located a little way in on it.

"Aagsome," the girl said, delighted.

"Cool," the young man agreed.

A few bills were exchanged and the girl sailed out through the door. Now Tim noticed Irene, who had been watching him.

He was short and skinny. On his feet he wore heavy black leather boots that must have added several inches to his height. His black leather pants were snug around his skinny thighs and held up with a wide belt. It was a good thing the pants were tight or they might have been pulled down by the weight of the belt. It was decorated with large pointy rivets and had a skull for a buckle. His leather vest was also heavily supplied with metal rivets. Under it, he was wearing a dirty T-shirt that bore the words "Fuck you." His arms were covered in tattoos, and what could be seen of his neck was adorned by them. An Indian band in red and black was tattooed across his forehead. He wore at least ten rings in different sizes in each ear. At angles in his eyebrows he had inserted several silver rods that seemed to be held in place by small silver plates on either side of the insertion points.

But it was his mouth area that took Irene's breath away. It looked as though he had an extra mouth of sharp spikes surrounding his real mouth. Anyone who was tempted to kiss him for the sake of adventure might have to reconsider.

"What do you want?" he asked.

"I'm Detective Inspector Huss. I'd like to ask you something."

She started to take out the picture of the dragon and the character when his husky voice rose to a falsetto and he shouted, "Get out! This is my store. Out!"

"Why? I just want to ask for your help."

In order to pique his curiosity, she added, "It has to do with a murder."

He didn't take his eyes off her but he didn't say anything. Encouraged, Irene said, "You've probably heard about the body parts we found at Killevik. We don't know who the victim is, but it's a man, and he has this tattoo on his right shoulder."

She held out the paper to Tim, who willingly accepted it. He was startled by the image. After a long inspection he said, "Damn fine work."

"Could anyone in Göteborg have made it?"

He shook his head. "Hardly."

"I spoke to the guy at MC-tattoo. He said that the tattoo appears to be Asian. Do you think so, too?"

"Exactly. Japanese."

Irene was surprised.

"Not Chinese?"

"No. It's Japanese."

He handed the paper back and his body language said that the audience was over.

"THE TATTOO is unusual and very well done. This kind takes several days to do and was probably not done in Sweden. The theme is Asian and one of the guys said probably Japanese. Have I forgotten anything?" Superintendent Andersson summed up.

The superintendent, Irene, Jonny, and Hannu were sitting in Andersson's office. It was almost five o'clock and they were going over what the day had provided in terms of new information.

"The character is Japanese," said Hannu.

"Are you sure?" asked Jonny.

The others looked at Jonny reproachfully. Only he would question Hannu's information. If Hannu said that the character was Japanese, then it was.

"Yes. It's the sign for 'man.' "

"Man," the superintendent repeated thoughtfully.

"Why would you tattoo the sign for man?" asked Irene.

"He might have been so feminine that he was forced to. Like product information. At least for Japanese." Jonny grinned.

Irene had grown very tired of Jonny's ridiculous jokes a long time ago. She ignored his remark and continued, "But the dragon is special and well drawn. It should lead us to more information."

She felt elated. The tattoo could bring them a bit closer to discovering the victim's identity. Or could it? When she thought about it she became uncertain. They didn't know who the man was or his nationality. They didn't know where the tattoo was made. They didn't know where or how the victim had died. The thought of *not wanting* to know flew through her brain for a second, but naturally she did want to know. She was, after all, a police officer.

"One of the parlors I went to thought that the dragon could have been drawn in Copenhagen or London," said Jonny.

"Otherwise, it was done somewhere in Asia," the superintendent said gloomily.

"But we know that the man wasn't Asian. Maybe that points to its not having been made in Asia," Irene objected.

"The way people get around these days, we can't rule anything out," said Jonny.

Andersson thought for a moment before he said, "I think it's time to release the picture of the tattoo to the papers. They'll get it tonight, so it will appear tomorrow. Someone may recognize it since it's so unusual."

"It's strange that no one has missed him. A young man in his prime," Irene said.

"He probably isn't Swedish," Jonny added.

"We should send the dragon out via Interpol. He may have been reported missing in another country," Andersson said. "I'll contact Interpol tomorrow afternoon if the papers don't draw a response."

Before Irene went home for the day she made a call to Tommy to see how he was doing. His ten-year-old daughter answered. "Persson."

"Hi, Sara. It's Irene. Is your pappa home?"

"No. He's walking around the neighborhood to exercise a bit."

"Is he having a hard time walking?"

"Yeah. He's stiff. Oh! Is it true that Sammie's a father?"

"Of course. Three of them. One boy and two girls."

"Oooh! How old are they?"

Irene had to think. At the same time an idea started to take shape. "The puppies are almost five weeks. They are sooooo adorable!" she replied.

"Can I come and see them? Can I?"

"Of course. Bring your father now that he's off work and come over when you can. But telephone first. The puppies are with their mother so we have to call her family and see if they are home."

They said good-bye and hung up. Irene felt slightly guilty, since Tommy was her best friend. But she had to find good homes for the puppies, she told herself, in order to clear her conscience.

* * *

"I ACTUALLY think that Lenny will take one of the puppies," said Krister.

It was late at night, and they had already crawled into bed. Lenny was a cook at the restaurant where Krister was master chef.

"Doesn't Lenny already have a dog? A fox terrier?" Irene asked.

"Yes. Or no. It died a month ago. The kids are having a difficult time. And it would be good for Lenny and his wife as well. They had decided to buy a new one and then I suggested one of Sammie's puppies. It seems as though they are interested, and it isn't a problem that they are mixed breed."

Irene was hesitant at first to tell about her attempt at finding a home for one of the puppies. In the end she decided to confess. "I, too, have planted a seed."

"Really? With whom?"

"Sara. Tommy's middle daughter."

"He's always said he didn't want a dog! Now he'll be upset."

"Just wait till he sees them. They're absolutely wonderful!"

"Aren't all puppies?"

"Exactly. That's why we need to get them here as soon as possible to see them while they're so little."

Krister laughed and moved over to his wife's side of the bed.

Chapter 5

THE PICTURE OF THE tattoo appeared on the front page of all the newspapers. Every time the phone rang, Irene's pulse sped up.

But at the end of the day not a single useful tip had come in. Just the usual array of idiots who always called as soon as the police asked for help through the media, had responded.

"I was the one who dismembered the man. Oh, you recognize me? Of course, I was the one who shot Olof Palme!" or "My neighbor killed that poor man. He has drinking parties late into the night so no one in the building can sleep! Sometimes they fight in there. He dismembered one of his drinking buddies. Believe me. What am I basing my accusations on? He looks deceitful!"

It became tiring to listen to this sort of report but everything had to be noted and checked out.

Some members of the group ran into other obstacles. The witness who had reported Robert Larsson's threats backed down. Suddenly, she hadn't heard him express any threats toward Laban. The witness's own injuries had occurred when she "fell down the stairs." That was the same story she had given when she arrived at the emergency room. And she had made up the stuff about Robert taking the largest portion of her income from prostitution. She just wanted to get back at him because she was angry and jealous.

Despite heavy pressure during the interrogation, she didn't change her new story. No one doubted that she had been threatened, even though the police had tried to protect her within the limits of their resources. A messenger had gotten to her.

The entire case against Robert Larsson burst like a popped balloon. Nothing could be proved without witnesses. And no new witnesses from the evening Laban was killed had surfaced. No one had seen a thing! Larsson was already out of jail and now they had to drop the investigation of him and his business dealings.

"You'll have to take him like they took Capone," said Superintendent Andersson.

"Al Capone?" Fredrik asked stupidly.

"Who else? He was convicted of tax evasion. That's the problem for the bosses in the drug and sex business. Business is too good and brings in too much profit. It's hard to launder all the money."

"The sex industry brings in more money than the drug trade in the USA. And the risk of jail time is a lot lower," Birgitta put in.

"Why is there less risk?" Irene asked.

"No one wants to mess with it. Everyone has a skeleton in the closet, and we know how the Americans are as soon as it comes to sex. As soon as the smallest sex scandal involving some celebrity or politician comes out, they are horrified and go through the roof," said Birgitta.

"Everything should be nice and neat on the surface. Everyone pretends not to know what lies beneath," Irene agreed.

Fredrik had been sitting leaning back in his chair, blankly staring at the ceiling. Now he sat up and said with his usual energy, "I'm going to talk with Annika Nilzén in Narcotics again. We might be able to get some help from Financial Crimes if they'll keep an eye on that slimy Robert's finances. The money is laundered through the club."

"Definitely," Andersson agreed. He sat absentmindedly folding an origami paper swallow. Irene noticed that the paper was one of the copies of the tattoo.

"Should we contact Interpol now?" she asked.

Andersson nodded. He tried to straighten out the paper again but the folds were too sharp. Luckily there were more copies.

"I'll send out a query about the tattoo. Then all we can do is wait."

"Tomorrow is a holiday, Ascension Day. Probably no one will call us. Friday is a working day between holidays and our colleagues in Europe are probably also on holiday. Then it's the weekend. So it looks like nothing will happen before Monday," said Birgitta.

She turned out to be right. Nothing happened before Monday, but then everything happened at once.

NO MORE sacks were found along the coast. The decision was made to continue looking for another two days before the search was called off. Two weeks would have to do. Andersson had absolutely nothing new on the Monday morning after the Ascension Day weekend. He sent everyone off to work on their own.

Irene was happy that Tommy was back at work even though he still walked stiffly. When he arrived at the office they shared he said, "Sara apparently talked with you about Sammie's puppies."

Irene tried to sound innocent. "She asked if it was true that Sammie has become a father and . . ."

"And you immediately invited her to come and look at them."

Irene didn't answer. He knew her all too well.

"We actually had a family meeting about it. With four votes to one, the Persson family has decided to come over to your place and look at puppies."

Irene could hardly believe her ears. With four votes to one, the Perssons were practically dog owners already! She tried not to show her excitement and instead said in a neutral tone, "When do you want to look at them?"

"Tomorrow night."

"I'll call the dog's owner and see. There's actually a friend of Krister's from work who's also interested. . . ."

"I just want to point out that *your* friend from work is not interested. Due to pressure from young children, you have made his family interested. There's a big difference."

Boy, did he sound sour, but not without good reason, Irene admitted to herself. She was saved by the ring of the telephone. She barely had time to lift the receiver before she heard Yvonne Stridner's sharp voice. "This is Professor Stridner. I obtained some interesting information in London."

It took a few seconds before Irene remembered that Stridner had mentioned a symposium in London during their last meeting.

"Good. Nothing has happened here."

"I know. But I have a good lead. I made a presentation at the symposium about signs that reveal whether the cause of a death is murder or suicide. A very much appreciated and well-attended presentation and . . . in any case, I asked if I could take a few more minutes of their time and took the opportunity to describe what our torso has been subjected to. Of course, most of the colleagues had heard about this type of murder but very few of them had seen such a complete removal of organs and desecration of the body. Everyone thought it was very interesting. Afterward, an old friend and colleague came up to me. His name is Svend Blokk, and he is a professor of forensic medicine. He works in Copenhagen at the state hospital."

At this point, Stridner was forced to catch her breath, and Irene squeezed in a question. "Excuse me, but what is a torso exactly?"

"You don't know?! It's the body without arms, legs, or a head. Just the trunk. In any case, Svend said that they had had a very similar case two years ago. I say similar, but there is one difference. Their victim was a female prostitute."

"Did he mean that the dismemberment process was the same?"

"Identical."

Irene thought feverishly before she asked, "Did they find all of the parts of that corpse?"

"No, but Svend was a little vague. He wasn't in charge of the forensic investigation. He also said that despite a massive search effort they never found the murderer."

Stridner gave Irene Blokk's address and telephone number. After hanging up, Irene started telling Tommy about her conversation, but he interrupted her. "Save it for the others. Andersson has put me on the Jack the Ripper case. He's been at it again. The fourth victim is in central Göteborg. This woman is also young. She was going to stay at her parents' after a party. The assault occurred in the stairwell leading to their apartment on Vasagatan."

"I didn't know that. When?"

"Around 2:00 a.m. on Saturday night."

"Was the victim able to provide a description?"

"Yes, and it's close to the three previous ones. Swedish-speaking man of medium height with a nylon stocking over his face. Two of the women have described him as having a slender build, and the other two said he was of a normal build."

"The same method?"

"Yup. Rape, under threat from a knife. Afterward he cuts the woman on the stomach and thighs. Not life-threatening injuries but she's scarred for life."

"Why wasn't there anything in the papers?" Irene wondered.

"The psychologist thinks that that is why Jack does what he does. In order to get attention."

"But if they don't write about him, there is a risk that he'll become more violent and maybe kill his next victim. I think we need to send out a warning to all women who are out and about in Vasastan around midnight on the weekends."

"The powers that be are making a decision about that. Meanwhile, I'll hack away at the investigation."

"Do you think he would be capable of something like the murder-mutilation out by Killevik?"

Tommy thought about it.

"No. I think he has a block that keeps him from killing his victims. He only wants them to suffer and be marked. If he kills them, they won't be able to tell anyone what a horrible thing they've experienced."

Irene rolled her eyes. Just suffer . . .

The tattooed torso couldn't speak but the remains bore witness to a rare, dangerous, and macabre murderer who was waiting to strike again. The message was clear.

THE DAY was filled with routine duties. Irene was able to contact the puppies' owner and arranged with her to see the small creatures the next evening around six.

Irene had just started putting on her coat when the superintendent came steaming into the room. His face was blotchy from excitement. "Copenhagen has called!" he puffed excitedly.

"Has Stridner's professor friend come up with something new?" Irene asked.

"No! Not the professor. The police! Our colleagues have called us!"

"What did they say?"

"The dragon isn't a tattoo! It's a sign!"

Irene met her boss's eyes. Did he look a bit confused?

Andersson saw what Irene was thinking and he tried to collect himself. "So then. Criminal Superintendent Beate Bentsen called from Copenhagen. She said that she recognized the image in the picture we sent out. It's a shop sign."

Irene felt a tingle inside. This finally felt like an opening.

"What kind of store is it? An Asian food store?"

Andersson blushed with embarrassment. "It . . . I don't know. I have a hard time understanding Danish over the phone but this is what I did get." He was thinking. "Someone should head down to Copenhagen. We should talk with the coroner in Denmark who examined the dismembered corpse of the prostitute and with Bentsen. And of course take a look at the sign. Maybe it will provide a clue to our torso's identity."

Irene nodded.

"Good. You leave tomorrow."

"Tomorrow! But—"

"You don't need a passport to go to Denmark. Why don't you give Bentsen a call." Andersson pulled a wrinkled note out of his pants pocket and held it out to Irene.

She took it with the feeling that she had just walked into a trap.

BEATE BENTSEN sounded very obliging though a bit stressed. She excused herself by saying that she was participating in a training course for police commanders that would last the rest of the week. The classes met until four o'clock; after that she could see Irene. It suited Irene perfectly. She had some things she wanted to do before she left.

First she called Monika Lind in Vänersborg.

"Hi, Monika. This is Irene Huss."

"Have you found anything?"

"No, we haven't found her. But I'm going to Copenhagen tomorrow on a different case. I thought I would take a look around. Do you have a recent picture of Isabell?"

"Several. They were taken six months ago."

"Does Janne still have his computer company?"

"Yes."

"Can you send a picture over to me?"

"No problem."

It would take about half an hour before Irene had the picture. She used the time to make some phone calls and take care of practical matters. She printed out a map of Copenhagen and booked a hotel on the Internet. It turned out to be the Hotel Alex on H. C. Andersen Boulevard. According to the map, it was centrally located and not far from Vesterbro, where Superintendent Bentsen worked.

Everything was ready when the soft-toned studio picture from Vänersborg arrived. Isabell's hair was shoulder length and thick but blonder than Irene remembered. There was a lot of makeup around the eyes as well as on the pouting mouth. The facial features were clean with a slight hint of a snub nose. Isabell was cute in a Barbie doll–type way. Irene printed out the photo. She was impressed by the focus and the good reproduction of the picture.

There was a short message from Monika:

Bell was born on February 7, 1982. She is 172 centimeters tall and weighs about 56 kilos. She got braces when we moved to Vänersborg. That's why she doesn't have the gap in her front teeth anymore. The picture was taken just before Christmas. I think it is a good likeness. Please, Irene, find her!

Many greetings,
Monika L.

Irene felt a twinge. She hadn't meant to give Monika false hope that she would actually find Isabell, but she would try.

"COPENHAGEN? OK. I'll take care of the puppy showing," Krister sighed.

They were sitting in the living room, drinking coffee after dinner. Irene had curled up at the end of the sofa with her knees tucked under her. She had already packed the things she would need for an overnight stay. Everything had easily fit in her dark blue police bag.

"How are you getting there then?" her husband asked.

"I'm borrowing one of the cars from work and driving down to Helsingborg. Then I'll take the ferry over to Helsingör. I'm counting on it taking about four hours to Copenhagen. It might be five because there may be a delay if I have to wait for the ferry."

"Will just you be enough?"

"Yes. I'm just going to talk with Danish colleagues and a medical examiner. This is the first concrete lead we've had to the victim's identity. And maybe the murderer's as well."

"Are either of them Danish? Or both?"

"Don't know. Maybe."

"About the puppy showing . . . I'll talk with Lenny and see if his family can also come and look tomorrow. I think it would be practical considering how crabby the lady is. One has to say in Sammie's defense that you don't pick your in-laws. It was the black beauty he fell for, not her owner."

"In-laws! I haven't called your mother-in-law for a week!"

Irene hopped off the couch in order to repair her daughterly negligence.

Mamma Gerd didn't answer. Irene let the phone ring about ten times before she gave up. She went out to Krister filled with concern.

"Mamma isn't answering. Do you think something's happened? She is almost seventy-three. . . ."

Krister thought for a moment before he said, "But wasn't this the week she and Sture were going to go on a wine trip to the Moselle Valley?"

Irene had totally forgotten about it. Mamma and her significant other had been planning the trip all winter. A group from the association for retired persons they both belonged to were going.

Maybe someday trips as a retiree would be her chance to see a little of the world. Until then, a trip to Copenhagen for work would have to do.

Chapter 6

A PALE SUN MADE some brave attempts at breaking through the clouds but it gave up around Varberg. It drizzled the rest of the way down to Helsingborg. Even though the spring had been rainy and cool so far, the farther south she drove, the greener it got. The chestnuts were blooming magnificently in Helsingborg but the detective inspector from Göteborg could not enjoy the splendid blooms. She was busy trying not to get lost. The city was bigger than she had thought and to add to her misery there were several ferry lines to choose from. Randomly, she chose HH-Ferries. She paid for her ticket, drove up, and joined the waiting line of cars. The ferry had just docked and cars were in the process of driving off it. She was allowed to embark after just ten minutes.

It felt good to stretch her legs. Irene walked around and inspected the boat. The ferry was relatively small, and the shipping company had to be Danish since all the signs were in Danish. She wasn't tempted to stay on deck because of the weather, so she went inside when the ferry left the dock. She ended up in the cafeteria and decided to get a sandwich and a cup of coffee.

The sandwich was enormous. Somewhere under the layer of roast beef and pickles there must be a slice of bread, she hoped. It was a clear sign that she was on her way abroad, to a more hedonistic land.

Soon the feeling of being in another country grew stronger when Irene went to the bathroom. A yellow plastic tub hung on the wall next to the mirror over the sink. On the tub there was a broad label: USED SYRINGES. So nice to have a special place to discard them, Irene thought sarcastically.

They arrived in Helsingör after twenty minutes. With a silent prayer that the rattling car ramp was more stable than it looked, she drove off the ferry just after one o'clock and followed the signs for Copenhagen. After having made her way through heavily trafficked side

streets, she finally reached the highway where there was much less traffic. The first twenty-four miles passed without difficulty, but the closer
to Copenhagen she got, the tougher things became. Traffic became
more congested, the signs were too small and hard to find, the lane des-
ignations weren't logical, and cyclists came from every direction like
projectiles. She had never driven in Denmark before and wasn't used
to traffic in a big city. Finally, Irene realized that she needed to stop at
a gas station to buy a decent map.

She bought an ice cream and a map. While she was eating the ice
cream she tried to memorize the best route. Finally she had it: Øster-
brogade down to Sortedams Sø, then a right turn and drive along the
water on Øster Søgade, which turned into Nørre Søgade. Where it
ended was where she was supposed to turn left and come out onto H.
C. Andersen Boulevard.

It didn't look that complicated on the map, but the reality was
something completely different. Her blouse was sticky with sweat
when she finally stopped outside the Hotel Alex, where you were
only allowed to park for five minutes. Irene went in and asked the
receptionist where the car could be left. The friendly, smiling young
woman explained that, for the most part, it was fine to park anywhere
there was a free spot. She recommended that Irene try the side street
next to the hotel, Studiestræde.

Irene drove around the large block and came onto the side street.
There was only one free space, almost right in front of the entrance to
the bar Wild Strip. In English it was advertised as a "Nude show" and
in Danish as "Dance that's the very barest." She didn't care so long as
she had a parking spot.

She took her bag and went to check in. The friendly receptionist
handed her a message from Beate Bentsen, which she decided to wait
to read.

The room was clean and newly renovated. As luck would have it,
the window faced Studiestræde. She could even see her car if she
leaned out. She didn't have to worry about having her night's sleep
interrupted by the traffic. The noise level through the well-insulated
windows was surprisingly low. She succumbed to the temptation to lie
on the inviting bed. It was wonderful to be able to stretch out. Her
muscles were tired and stiff from sitting still in the car. She decided to

walk down to Station One at Vesterbro. She pulled out her map of Copenhagen and judged that it would be a brisk fifteen-minute walk from the hotel to Halmtorvet.

The message from Beate Bentsen took a while to decipher since it was handwritten and in Danish. In the end, Irene understood that Superintendent Bentsen did not have time this afternoon as she had promised. She apologized profusely and hoped to be able to take Irene to dinner at seven at Restaurant Vesuvius of Copenhagen. The directions were simple: straight across the street from the hotel entrance and then at an angle to the right. But Bentsen would send Inspector Peter Møller to pick up Irene at exactly three o'clock. According to the superintendent, he was familiar with the investigation and with the area around Vesterbro.

Irene looked at the clock. Peter Møller would be there in less than twenty minutes. She told herself to get up and change.

She was awakened by the ringing of the telephone and found herself standing at the side of the bed before she was fully awake. A soft female voice told her in Danish that Inspector Peter Møller was asking for her.

"Goodness! Tell him I'll be there in five minutes."

She was out of her clothes before the receiver had come to rest in the cradle. The shower was short and hot. The jeans she had had on during the day would have to remain on the floor. She pulled out her new dark blue linen pants, clean underwear, and an ice blue colored tennis shirt. She exchanged the worn-out tennis shoes for black loafers. Maybe it would have been more elegant if the shoe had had a bit of a heel to go with the nice pants, but if you were one hundred and eighty centimeters tall without shoes, you don't wear heels. Irene had never even learned to walk in heels. A short pass with lipstick would have to do as a means of freshening up her makeup. On the way down the stairs she twisted her arms into a new trench coat-style jacket. It was blue, the color of her eyes.

A slender young man stood leaning against the reception desk. He had short blond hair. He must have heard her steps on the stairs because he turned in her direction. His light blue eyes passed over her appraisingly. She saw that he was older than she had first thought, at least thirty-five. He smiled pleasantly and walked toward her with his hand extended.

"Irene Huss, I presume?"

"Yeah. I mean . . . yes."

"Inspector Peter Møller."

They shook hands and he motioned in the direction of the street. "The car is outside."

He walked in front of her and held the door for her. When they passed each other, Irene noticed that he smelled of good aftershave and that she was just a hair taller. He was also dressed in civilian clothes, a short light brown suede jacket and light tan chinos. Peter Møller walked up to a dark wine red colored BMW, the newest and largest model, and opened the door for Irene. When they were sitting in the car, Irene said, "The police certainly have nice cars here."

"It's my own," said Møller.

A short silence followed and Irene decided to leave the topic of cars and move on. "I'm sorry that you had to wait. The ferry took some time. . . ."

She left the sentence unfinished on purpose. Møller turned his face toward hers and smiled charmingly.

"I expect that sort of thing when I'm picking up a lady," he said.

Knowing that Denmark had had weather as bad as Sweden's during the spring, Irene concluded that his dark tan resulted from a trip abroad. It could just as easily have been acquired on a tanning bed at home but something about Møller's manner told her that his tan was genuine. It would have to do as a conversation opener.

"Have you had good weather here in Denmark? You're so dark."

He laughed softly. "No. I've been to a place with guaranteed sunshine."

"Wonderful!"

"Yes. But a bit too warm. Have you been to Copenhagen before?"

"Twenty years ago."

"Then it was about time for you to come back." Møller smiled.

He quickly became serious and asked, "Do you want to drive out to Hellerup now or later?"

"Hellerup?"

"That's where the sacks with the body parts of Carmen Østergaard were found."

"When was that?"

"June 1997. Almost two years ago."

It was a good thing he added that it had been almost two years ago; the number ninety-seven, uttered in Danish, was completely incomprehensible to Irene's ears.

"I think we can drive out there later if it's necessary. It feels more important to see the sign with the dragon."

"You'll get to see that in just a second."

They drove down a wide street that, according to the signs, was Bernstorffsgade. Peter Møller turned into a parking lot behind a box-like building of gloomy brown brick. He didn't have to tell Irene that they had parked behind the Police Department. All police department buildings built during the sixties and seventies appeared to have been designed by the same deeply depressed architect.

"Come. We'll go and look at the sign right away," said Peter.

They left the parking lot and started walking along a small, quiet street lined with dreary-looking houses. The dirty building fronts, rotten doors, and windowsills with chipped paint gave the whole street an atmosphere of gloomy decay. The dirty gray weather added to the unpleasant impression.

The houses farther down the street were covered with scaffolding and plastic fabric. Under the fabric, the harsh buzzing of a high-pressure sprayer could be heard.

"Nice that they are renovating the old buildings," said Irene.

"They are trying to sanitize the shacks. Get the houses in order and raise the rents so that the rabble can't afford to stay there. These old houses are in an attractive central location."

"Something similar has been done at home in Göteborg. Has it been successful here?"

"The poor are driven away, farther out into the suburbs. They are the drug addicts and the street prostitutes. We don't get rid of the others as easily. They have far too much money."

"Sex is a profitable business," Irene concluded.

"Exactly. Do you know anything about Vesterbro?"

"No."

"It's known as Sin Central in Copenhagen. It used to be Nyhavn but now only millionaires and people of culture can afford to live there. Upscale bars and restaurants have opened, pushing out all but the most discreet sex operations. But if you want sex, you come to Vesterbro and, above all, to the area around Istedgade. Everything can be found here. Absolutely everything!" As confirmation, a porn movie store popped up advertising "Here you can get the video you didn't think existed!" Peter continued walking as though he hadn't noticed.

"Are we on the way to Istedgade?" Irene asked.

"Yes, to one of the cross streets. We're almost there."

A sex shop on the corner in front of them had thin gauze underwear with strategically placed holes hanging in the display window. As a counterbalance, there were more substantial items in leather but these also seemed to be made of thin straps and holes. It was probably a good thing they were well equipped with rivets so that they sort of held together. In order to embellish the display further, whips and handcuffs hung from the ceiling. Dildos in various colors and sizes lay on the floor of the display window. A large one in black rubber was almost as long and as thick as Irene's forearm.

Bewildering pictures came to mind: A man was whipping a woman in see-through red underwear after first having chained her with handcuffs to the bedpost and then taken the black rubber dildo . . . What kind of people would have to subordinate other people in order to get some enjoyment? Was it power over another person that gave them a boost? Pictures, and mechanical procedures with sex toys, provide a quick release. Warm and sensual relationships are more difficult and take longer to build. Most of all, they required emotional engagement. Masturbation is easy; relationships, difficult and time consuming.

Suddenly she became aware that Peter Møller was talking to her. With a great deal of effort she abandoned her train of thought.

"Pardon me. What did you say?"

"Are you going to buy anything?" Peter teased.

Irene felt her throat tighten with rage but she managed to sound relatively calm when she answered, "No. There's nothing here that I want. I get depressed when I see this sort of thing."

"It's just for fun. Casual sex toys—"

"No! It cannot be fun to have that huge rubber dick shoved in! It must hurt terribly!"

She stopped herself and tried to calm down. Møller looked at her in confusion. With great control she said, "You may not understand this, but there is no *casual* sex in this display window."

Peter Møller didn't answer. He looked completely unsympathetic and shook his head slightly. Maybe he thought his colleague from Sweden had taken a dose of prudishness? He could think what he wanted.

They crossed Istedgade and walked one block up the street of sin.

"Here it is," said Peter Møller. He stopped at the corner and pointed at a cross street. The street sign said Colbjørnsensgade. Irene took a few steps before she stopped short.

A large enameled sign hung on the wall over a store. It was almost three square meters in size. The Japanese character for "man" was encircled by a terrifying dragon. The background was light blue, which effectively contrasted with the colorful dragon. Every scale on the monster's body glittered in varying colors. The horrifying mouth with its razor-sharp teeth was wide open, and the whole monster pulsated with restrained power.

But the sign was not hanging over a store for Asian food. On the display window it said, "The Best Gay Place In Town."

"A gay sex store," Irene said. She couldn't help letting out a deep sigh. Møller glanced at her but didn't say anything. They walked up to the shop's window.

Things were also hanging from the ceiling in this display window. They looked to Irene like Barbie's fiancé, Ken, but when Peter and Irene came closer, Irene realized her mistake. These boy dolls were not intended for little girls; they were supposed to be used by boys and grown men. The dolls were dressed in different outfits but their pants were pulled down to their knees, in order to show that they were well endowed. A human-size display doll stood on one side of the window. The uniform he was wearing looked surprisingly like a real police uniform and he was holding a bunch of handcuffs in both his hands. Across from the police doll hung a porcelain urinal. Along the edge there was a whitish liquid that was apparently supposed to represent semen. Dildos, videos, and magazines lay on the floor. One of the covers caught Irene's eye. The magazine was called *Fist*, which would have been *Knytnäve* in Swedish. The picture showed two male hands spreading apart the buttocks of another man.

"This is sick," Irene said loudly.

Møller shrugged but didn't comment. Irene turned toward him and caught his gaze.

"Have you or anyone else from the police been here and spoken with the owner about the sign and the connection to our murder-mutilation case?"

"No."

"Then we have to go in and find out if he knows anything."

Møller sighed. "We probably should. Then you'll get to meet Tom Tanaka."

"Who's that?"

"The owner."

Again he went first and held the door for Irene. His courtesy pleased her. He was polite and well mannered but unaccustomed to being so, in Irene's opinion. She stepped into the gay shop with an uneasy feeling in her stomach.

Everything she had anticipated was on display. Leather clothes, leather corsets, leather scrotums, whips, and rubber clothes were hanging everywhere. There were neat shelves lined with videos and magazines and sex toys of whose purpose she had no idea. Two men were standing close together over a leather corset, talking, but they stopped when Irene made her entrance. They weren't relieved when Peter Møller appeared right behind her. Suspiciously, they observed the police officers' progress to the store counter. Tom Tanaka was enthroned behind it.

Whatever Irene had expected, this man surprised her. He was almost two meters tall and probably weighed over two hundred kilos. He looked like a sumo wrestler, and wore his hair in the characteristic style with small hard knots of hair at his crown. To Irene's relief, he was not wearing the diaperlike pants in which sumo wrestlers compete; instead his huge body was covered in black silk pajamas.

Irene's undisguised surprise must have been obvious because Tom Tanaka made a hint of a bow and said in English with a strong American accent, "If you're surprised to see me here, it's nothing compared to how I feel about seeing you."

His voice was very deep and his tone ironic. Irene couldn't keep from smiling.

"Good day. My name is Irene Huss. I'm a police officer from Göteborg,

Sweden, and I'm investigating . . . a crime. May I ask a few questions?" she said in her broken English.

Tom Tanaka looked at her without expression through dark eyes embedded in the huge rolls of fat on his face. Irene didn't believe that the man in front of her was an out-of-shape, harmless mountain of lard. Fighting with a sumo wrestler was like running right into an oncoming steam locomotive traveling at full speed.

The Japanese man nodded slightly. In a deep bass he rumbled, "Emil."

The door behind Tanaka opened almost instantaneously, and a tall, ruddy young man stuck out his head and also answered in English, but with a heavy Danish accent, "I'm almost done eating—"

He stopped himself when he became aware of Irene and Peter. His gaze locked onto Peter but quickly shifted. Irene suspected there had been a hint of recognition. Emil swallowed hard several times, and his prominent Adam's apple yo-yoed up and down his thin throat.

"Will you take over the store while I'm speaking with the police officers?"

Emil hurried to finish chewing. He slipped through the door and stood behind the counter as far away from the arm of the law as he could get, nervously pulling at his red goatee.

With a massive hand Tom Tanaka gestured toward the door. They passed through a small windowless employee lounge with soft lighting and two comfortable black leather recliners. Tom Tanaka went over to a heavy door and unlocked it.

Inside there was a huge, very modern kitchen done in white, black, and stainless steel. The floor was laid with wide polished boards of cherrywood. A strong smell of fried fish hung in the air. On the other side of the kitchen Irene glimpsed a sizeable room like a living room. She heard the sound and saw the color flickering from a TV. Between the kitchen and the living room there was a small hallway.

"I live here," Tanaka said simply.

"So you don't have far to go to work," Irene tried to joke.

"True," the Japanese man replied.

He led the way through the kitchen and then headed to the right. The floor beams creaked under his considerable weight. He opened a door and preceded them into the room. There was no other option since neither Irene nor Peter would have been able to squeeze past him.

"My office," said Tanaka.

This room was also large. A pleasant smell of expensive cigar smoke encircled the visitors. The room was sparsely furnished in Japanese style. The desk was made of black shiny wood, and the black leather desk chair had obviously been specially constructed to hold Tom Tanaka's colossal body.

Along the short side of the room there was a glass cabinet containing knickknacks and prize buckles. Irene observed, "You must be a good sumo wrestler."

One of the corners of Tom's mouth twitched and Irene took it to be an amused smile.

"*Was* a good sumo wrestler. I'm retired."

Irene looked at him, surprised. He couldn't be older than she was.

"We retire at age forty."

She didn't know why she volunteered, "I've also worked with Japanese wrestling—jujitsu."

Tanaka didn't respond. He pointed at two cloth-covered chairs next to the desk.

"Please," he said.

Irene and Peter Møller sat. Then Irene realized that Møller hadn't said a word since they'd entered the store. She looked at him but he remained silent so she started talking about the dismembered male corpse they had found in Sweden. She emphasized that the only clue they had to the man's identity was a dragon tattoo, and raised her gaze over Tanaka's head to look at a silk painting that was evidently the original of both the sign and the tattoo.

There was one important difference: there was no sign for *man* on the painting. Instead, a pointy mountaintop could be seen. Irene recognized the holy mountain, Mount Fuji. She said so and Tanaka nodded.

"Colleagues here in Copenhagen contacted us when we sent out the picture of the tattoo via Interpol. That's why I'm here. Do you know who the man might be?"

"No. No idea."

"You don't know of anyone who has had a tattoo done based on your sign or this painting?"

He shook his head in denial.

"I've had the store for less than two years. I inherited it from my cousin. He was the one who started it, years ago. Maybe the tattoo was made during his time. The idea for the sign and for replacing Fuji were also his," he said.

Irene thought a moment, then asked, "Do you know of any tattoo artist in the area who is especially skilled?"

"A master? No."

They rose at the same time, and Tanaka led the way. At the kitchen door he stopped with his hand on the door handle and turned to Irene.

"Keikoku. Uke. Okata?" he asked softly.

He warned her of enemies and asked if she had understood. She didn't know the Japanese language but these words and expressions were used in martial arts. In a calm voice she answered, *"Hai."*

Tanaka let them out through the shop, which now contained many more customers. With a neutral "good-bye," he closed the door after them.

"What was it he said in Japanese?" Møller asked when the door shut behind them.

Irene concluded that he hadn't understood Tanaka's warning. She didn't know anything about him, and he, too, might have been familiar with Japanese martial arts. But she was willing to take the risk.

"He asked if I remembered any terms from jujitsu," she said indifferently.

They walked back to the Police Department in silence.

"This is Inspector Jens Metz."

Peter Møller introduced Irene to the heavyset, reddish blond colleague in an office that smelled like stale smoke. Jens Metz looked so typically Danish that Irene had to hold back a giggle. Instead, she gave him a friendly smile and let her hand be encircled by his sausage-like fingers. He wasn't in Tanaka's class, but he was heading in that direction. Irene guessed his age to be somewhere around fifty-five.

"Welcome to Copenhagen. But the reason could have been more pleasant." Metz smiled with nicotine-stained teeth.

He appeared to be friendly and efficient. Out of nowhere he magically made three steaming cups of coffee appear on the desk. This sort of thing always earned bonus points in Irene's coffee-dependent existence. That the coffee tasted like it had been brewed from crushed pieces of vinyl was a completely different matter. One can get used to Danish coffee, Irene tried to tell herself.

Jens Metz tapped a pile of thick folders that was lying on the table.

"Here is the material from the case of the murder-mutilation of Carmen Østergaard. You'll get to meet the medical examiner tomorrow at eleven o'clock. One of us will drive you there," he said. And he briefly went through the investigation of the dismembered corpse that had floated onto the beach in Hellerup. The first sacks had been found on June 3, 1997. Two more sacks were found the day after. The head, limbs, and the intestines were never found. Both breasts, including the musculature, along with the buttocks, were gone. The outer genitalia and the rectal opening had been removed. The victim had extensive bruising on her pubic bone as a result of extremely brutal force.

"She was as empty as a watch case," Metz commented.

"The dismemberment sounds strikingly like that of our corpse," Irene observed.

"You'll get more details about it from the pathologist tomorrow. We didn't know who the victim was, but two days later, on June 5, a man named Kurt Østergaard reported that his wife, Carmen, was missing. He hadn't seen her since the last week in May. He started missing her then since she was his source of income. Both of them were on heroin. We could rule out Kurt as the murderer pretty quickly. He wouldn't have been able to hold a knife in the shape he was in. Actually, I heard that he died last winter of an overdose."

Metz caught his breath, wet his index finger, and turned the page. "At the time of her death, Carmen was twenty-five years old. She had been a prostitute for four years, the same period during which she had been married to Kurt and hooked on heroin. Her mother was Danish and her father Spanish. The girl was a souvenir from a hitchhiking trip to Spain. Many of us in the district knew Carmen, since she lived here in Vesterbro. The mortician established that she was HIV positive. She probably wasn't aware of it since she wasn't registered anywhere for testing. We interrogated Kurt but he couldn't give us any information. Carmen never told him about her customers; she just gave him money."

Metz looked down at the papers and continued, "We interrogated all the prostitutes in Vesterbro. A lot of the women had been threatened by customers during that time, with everything from strangulation to assault. But nothing sounded like the murderer we were after. Sometimes Carmen hung out with two other prostitutes. They talked with each other in between clients and ate together. Carmen supposedly talked to one of them in a café about a police officer who had frightened her in the days before she was killed. A customer who paid well but had strange requests and was also a cop. Carmen never said what in particular the police officer wanted. Before they left the café, Carmen allegedly said, 'The policeman or the doctor will be the death of me.' Her friend asked her if she had to see them again and she just said, 'Yes. Money and drugs.'"

"Did any of the other prostitutes know anything about a suspicious policeman or doctor?"

"One broad talked about a strange doctor and another started talking about a policeman. But she was high on God knows what. When she started to come down, she denied everything and claimed that she had made it all up. We never found any evidence that these two characters existed."

"Did you ask the girls at the bordellos?"

Both Møller and Metz smiled. It was Metz who answered. "Do you realize how many nightclubs, escort services, strip bars, and so forth there are in Copenhagen? Not to mention all of the girls at these places? And boys, for that matter."

He paused, then said, "Since Carmen never worked at a place like that—she worked the street—we only asked the girls on the streets. The papers printed a lot about the murder. Had any of the girls at the clubs experienced something terrifying, they could have gotten in touch with us. But no one did."

They didn't dare to because they would lose their jobs, Irene thought, but she didn't say anything.

"It's the whores on the street who are addicted to drugs who fall victim to the most gruesome violence. At least in the clubs they have some degree of protection," Peter Møller added.

"Mmm. We worked the whole summer on this case but during the fall we had to shut it down. It was at a complete standstill. No new witnesses and, thankfully, no new murders."

"Until now. In Göteborg," said Irene.

"Yes, it's really strange. If it hadn't been for the tattoo, I would have said that there was no way there could have been a connection, even if the dismemberments were identical and extreme. But the sign is located here in Vesterbro. Everyone at the station has seen it," said Metz.

Møller started talking about their visit to the gay sex shop. Irene noticed that he didn't mention Tom Tanaka's short sentence in Japanese. She hoped he had forgotten about it. He finished up with his own theory about the tattoo, "I think the victim in Sweden had taken a photo of the sign. The tattoo looks like the sign and not like the painting in Tanaka's office."

Irene nodded.

"That's not impossible. We have to find the tattoo artist," she said.

"But if the tattoo was based on a souvenir photo, it could have been made anywhere in the world," Metz pointed out.

"That's true but we have to begin somewhere. I'm going to start in Vesterbro," said Irene.

She unfolded the picture of Isabell Lind and put it on the desk in front of the two Danish crime investigators. "At the same time, I'm thinking about trying to locate this girl. She's the daughter of a friend."

She briefly went through the story about Isabell. Møller and Metz examined the picture thoroughly while she was talking. When she was finished, Metz said, "I understand why the mother didn't find a photographer or agency for photo models that recognized her. You'll probably find her in one of the clubs. Usually they call the girls at these establishments hostesses or models."

"Scandinavian Models . . . I think it must be an escort service," said Peter.

Metz gave the picture back to Irene. With a big yawn, he stretched his arms out and straightened his back. "My friends, it's almost six o'clock, and I want to go home to my dinner. See you tomorrow morning at eight o'clock."

Peter and Irene went into the corridor. He walked beside her in silence. Finally he said, "And you . . . where are you going to eat dinner?"

"Superintendent Bentsen has invited me to a restaurant not far from my hotel."

"Good . . . I mean otherwise I would have asked you . . . but as you've already made plans with Beate . . ."

The relief in his voice couldn't be missed, and Irene was just as relieved. There was a reserve about Peter Møller that was difficult to overcome and she didn't feel particularly motivated to try. She didn't have that kind of time here in Copenhagen. There were other more important people to focus on.

Møller drove her back to the Hotel Alex. The traffic was heavy but he was accustomed to it and navigated skillfully. He parked quickly in front of the hotel entrance. Before Irene got out he offered, "I can pick you up here tomorrow at a quarter to eight."

"I'll definitely say yes to that."

They took leave of each other. In the reflection of the door's glass she saw the elegant BMW engulfed by the flow of traffic as it disappeared.

When Irene asked for her room key, to her surprise, she was given an envelope by the receptionist. It was made of thick white linen paper and was glued securely shut. She resisted the temptation to open it in the elevator. In her room, with equal parts curiosity and impatience, she tore open the envelope. It contained a stiff white card with the message:

Please come at 10 p.m. Important!

T. T.

Tom Tanaka. He wanted her to come to his place tonight. It was important. With some trepidation she remembered his words, *Keikoku. Uke. Okata?*

AS THE clock struck seven, Irene stepped into Restaurant Vesuvius. She had to revise her misgivings about having been invited to a pizzeria. Obviously they served pizzas but they were the size of mill wheels and smelled wonderful. The restaurant was big and packed with customers. In broken Danish a dark-skinned, harried young man asked if he could help her.

"I'm meeting Beate Bentsen here," said Irene.

The man bowed and led her into a smaller room with about ten tables. The walls were decorated with black-and-white photos and posters from Italian films. Under a large picture of a young Sophia Loren sat Beate Bentsen. The actress smiled seductively straight into the camera with her bare arms stretched over her head and her hands clasped behind her neck. The ideal of feminine beauty changes, Irene thought, when she noticed that the film star had small tufts of hair in her armpits.

The waiter politely pulled out the chair for Irene, placed a menu in her hands, and quickly disappeared.

Irene shook hands with the superintendent. To Irene's surprise, Beate Bentsen's slender hand was ice-cold despite the warmth of the room. Irene judged that the woman sitting across from her was a few years older than she was but tall, attractive, and in good shape. She had twisted her coppery red hair into a bun but a few stray wisps had gotten loose and curled around her forehead and ears. The linen dress suit she was wearing was a sober tan. Under its jacket she wore a low-cut silk top in light green that perfectly matched the eyes behind her black-framed eyeglasses.

"Forgive me for not being able to meet you this afternoon. But I assume that Peter and Jens took good care of you," Beate began.

"They have been great."

"Good. Maybe we should order before we talk."

With a hint of a nod she called the waiter over. Irene understood that Beate was one of the regulars. Irene ordered saltimbocca à la romana and a large beer, and the superintendent ordered a seafood dish and a glass of white wine.

While they were waiting for the food, Irene told Beate what had transpired during the day but she didn't mention Tom Tanaka's warning or that he wanted to meet her later that evening. Beate sat and observed her and sipped her wine. Sometimes she nodded as if confirming something she had already suspected.

When Irene had finished she said, "It'll be difficult to find the person who made the tattoo. It may not have been made in Copenhagen. But the similarities between the dismemberment of Carmen Østergaard and the male corpse in Göteborg are remarkable. I participated in the investigation as an inspector; I've since been promoted. We've never seen anything like what Carmen was subjected to, even here in Copenhagen."

"Then you're familiar with the witnesses' reports that Carmen had spoken about a policeman and a doctor?"

The superintendent said, "It was in all of the papers. Someone leaked it to the media and was well paid. As usual."

"A doctor would be able to completely empty the body."

"Yes, the pathologists picked up on that as well. But there were some complicating factors. You'll find out more from Blokk tomorrow. He's a pleasant fellow."

Irene remembered that the name of Professor Stridner's friend and colleague was Svend Blokk.

The food came and the delicious smells made Irene realize how hungry she was. Her veal with Parma ham and noodles in a white wine sauce was wonderful. They concentrated on the food for a long time. When they were almost done, Beate said, "Tomorrow you can read through the investigation file on Carmen. You can make copies of whatever you think is important. The same thing goes for the autopsy report itself. You'll get that from Blokk. And you—"

She was interrupted by the first bars of "The Marseillaise." It took a few confused seconds before it occurred to Irene that it was her cell phone that was blaring. Blushing, she dug through the pockets of her coat, which hung next to them on the wall.

"This is Irene."

"Hi, Mamma. It's Jenny. The dog sitter has the stomach flu. Who can take Sammie tomorrow?"

"Goodness . . . I don't know. I'm sitting at a restaurant eating dinner right now. Can I call you in an hour? Are you at home?"

"Sure."

"Sounds good. Bye for now, sweetie."

She hung up and started mumbling an apology. Beate Bentsen stopped her. "I know how it is with kids. How many do you have?"

"Two. Twin girls who are sixteen."

"My son is twenty-two."

They nodded in motherly understanding, raised their glasses, and drank the last few drops. Irene had an idea and dug through her other coat pocket. She pulled out the picture of Isabell Lind and set it in front of the superintendent. Briefly, she went through the story about the missing girl. Summing up, she said, "Peter and Jens think that Scandinavian Models might be an escort service and that Isabell is working as a prostitute."

Beate studied the picture before she answered.

"Unfortunately, it's quite likely. Copenhagen lures hordes of young girls, consumes them, and spills them onto the trash heap after a few years. They often come here with the dream of making a career in the theater or as photo models. The reality is something completely different."

"Have you heard of Scandinavian Models?"

"No. There are countless places like that. Usually they disappear after a while or change their name and owner. It's impossible to keep track of all of them."

"Where do I look for a list of porn clubs, strip bars, escort services, and the like?"

Beate laughed hoarsely and lit a cigarette at the same time. She lifted the extra-long filter cigarette that was already glowing, gesturing toward Irene, and asked, "You aren't offended?"

Irene shook her head.

"I just remembered that the Swedes are so touchy when it comes to smoke. Do you smoke?"

She held the pack out to Irene, who politely declined.

The superintendent inhaled greedily and peered at Irene through the smoke. "A list where you may find Scandinavian Models? I would suggest that you look in the tourist guide in your hotel room. There are usually advertisements in the back for . . . everything. The worst places aren't allowed to advertise, but people find their way there anyway."

Neither of them wanted to have dessert. They ordered two cups of coffee. It was almost eight thirty when they finished. Irene excused herself by saying that she needed to call home.

Beate remained sitting there, smoking a newly lit cigarette, as Irene walked out into the drizzle.

"IT'S BEEN taken care of. Mrs. Karlsson across the street is going to take him on a walk around lunchtime. The kids have chicken pox and are at home," said Jenny.

"Can she leave them to go out with Sammie then?"

"It's fine. The kids are doing pretty well now. When are you coming home?"

"Tomorrow night. How are things with Katarina?"

"She has pain in her neck and is stiff. But she has an appointment tomorrow at the clinic."

"Good. I'm turning off the cell phone tonight. If there is an emergency you can call the hotel."

After sending extra hugs and kisses, Irene hung up. At least things were sorted out with Sammie. Now her own evening rounds would start.

"COPENHAGEN THIS *Week—May 1999*," it said on the thick tourist guide on the desk. The cover was illustrated with a badminton player against a lime green background: healthy and sporty. Irene quickly flipped past the museums and cultural attractions to the pages farthest back. A black page with some stars and a half-moon announced, "Copenhagen After Dark."

Color pictures of naked young girls were lures to tourists. The businesses were called go-go bars, nightclubs, sauna clubs, escort services, and other creative euphemisms but it was obvious that young girls were for sale and, in some of the ads, boys. None of the pictures showed girls who looked older than twenty-two. They stood sticking out their breasts and tilting their hips, either wearing thongs or, in some cases, totally nude.

She found the advertisement for Scandinavian Models on the last page. The illustration was in black and white and showed a group of four girls standing tightly together with their arms around each other. They smiled invitingly at the camera with pouting lips, wearing only thongs and short T-shirts on their upper bodies that barely covered their nipples. Their names appeared above their heads: Petra, Linn, Bell, and Heidi. Bell was Isabell Lind.

"This is an actual photo of our models you will meet here in Copenhagen—guaranteed or your money back!" the advertisement proclaimed.

Irene felt her stomach knot. The pouting girl in the picture who was selling herself had been her daughters' playmate.

With great effort she forced herself to continue reading. "We are always ready to visit you. Or, alternatively, you are welcome to visit us at our luxurious, newly built, one hundred percent safe and discreet studio. We are located in the beautiful central Nyhavn area of the city." The address was Store Kongensgade.

After searching for a long time on the small map in the tourist guide folder she found the street. The letters were tiny and blurred. Could it possibly be time to get reading glasses? Nope, that was for old ladies. But Irene had to turn on the desk lamp and hold the map close to the light with arms outstretched in order to make it out.

Store Kongensgade was located past Kongens Nytorv. It was in exactly the opposite direction from Vesterbro if one walked from the hotel. She would have to go to Tom Tanaka's first and then visit Scandinavian Models. It was difficult to say which of the visits would be most uncomfortable.

First, she needed to be able to move around unnoticed in the Copenhagen night. That's easier said than done when you're a woman who is nearly six feet tall.

Irene removed all of her makeup. A few passes through her hair with a wet comb gave her an androgynous hairstyle. She changed to jeans and tennis shoes and decided to put on the trench coat instead of her short jacket, partly because it was a unisex model and also because it was still raining outside. The weather was perfect for her hair, which was supposed to look flat and boring. She inspected herself in the mirror on the inside of the closet door. No one was going to notice her.

She left the hotel and disappeared into Copenhagen after dark.

It had stopped raining. Instead, a cold, raw wind swept in from the ocean. Irene wished that she had brought along a pair of gloves, but that wasn't something you thought about when you were packing your luggage in the middle of May. She shoved her hands deep into her pockets and turned up her collar for protection. There were a lot of people out and about near Tivoli, Copenhagen's world-renowned pleasure garden. The many bars and restaurants were already full and looked inviting to one who happened to be walking outside in the grim weather.

The closer to Colbjørnsensgade she came, the less she felt tempted to go inside one of the establishments. The signs now offered go-go girls, stripteases, and "the best sex show in town." It wasn't that she was a prude or had never been exposed to what the sex industry had to offer. After almost twenty years as a police officer she had seen everything, but not all at once. That was what nauseated her about this area, not least the hard-boiled marketing and the contempt it showed for mankind.

The red-faced men who bellowed and pranced through the doors, or slipped in, in an attempt not to be noticed—what was their view of women? And how did these women see themselves? Did this exploitation affect the self-esteem of other women? Was she affected?

She stopped and thought about that last question. Yes, she felt violated and degraded as a woman. The feeling actually surprised her, but that was what she really felt. She thought about her two beautiful and headstrong daughters. Was this what they would be reduced to in the eyes of many men: fuck objects?

Irene felt anger rise inside her; the last steps she took to Tom Tanaka's gay sex shop had extra length and force due to her anger.

Maybe it was the power of that rage that made her yank open the shop door more vehemently than she had intended. Everyone in the store turned in her direction. More customers were there now than had been earlier. Tom Tanaka stood behind the counter with Emil at his side. She walked across the floor of the shop and said hello to them. The young man quickly looked away. Nervously, he rubbed his goatee and mouth with his forearm. In one hand he was holding a ham sandwich and in the other a can of Coca-Cola. Irene saw him try to chew and swallow at the same time.

Irene and Tanaka went through the employee lounge. He opened the door to the apartment and gestured for Irene to enter. Without saying a word, he walked toward his office, then invited her to sit on one of the chairs. The good cigar smell felt almost home like.

"A beer or a whiskey?" he asked.

Irene hesitated at first, but then said, "A beer, thanks."

He bent and, to Irene's surprise, took two chilled beers out of a little minibar in his desk. There were glasses there as well. He filled one and pushed it toward her. Tanaka raised his open bottle and clinked it against hers in a toast. The beer was amazingly refreshing and she agreed with the slogan that a Tuborg tastes best "every time."

Tanaka set his bottle down on the desk and focused his black eyes on her. "Inspector Huss. I must be able to trust someone. You aren't a police officer in Copenhagen and that's why I'm willing to trust you."

Irene lowered her head but didn't say anything for the simple reason that she didn't know what she should say.

"I'm pretty sure I know who the murdered man in Göteborg is. His name is Marcus Tosscander."

Tanaka had difficulty pronouncing the last name. He held out a business card to Irene, which read:

Tosca's Design
Marcus Tosscander, Designer

in dark blue letters on a card of linen-paper. Simple, nice, and of the highest quality. The address and telephone number for Tosca's Design were listed farther down on the card.

"Kungsportsplatsen in Göteborg," Irene said aloud.

She looked up from the card and met Tom's gaze.

"Why do you think it's his body we found?"

"The tattoo. He was allowed to borrow the painting from me and take it to Copenhagen's most skilled tattoo artist, whom I recommended."

"What's his name?"

"It's a she. Woon Khien Chang. Her father is a Chinese tattoo artist in Hong Kong. Woon was trained by her father."

"Can you give me her address?"

"Of course. It's no secret. But you can't tell your Danish colleagues that you learned about her from me."

"Why not?"

Tanaka hesitated before he started to tell her the story. "Marcus came into my shop for the first time at the end of January. It was . . . I don't know how I'm going to explain . . . it was like the whole store lit up. He was so beautiful and radiated warmth around him. He came up to me and said, 'Hi, Tom Tanaka, I'd like to speak to you.' He knew my name before he came into the store. I didn't think much about it, but after the visit from you and the Danish policeman yesterday, I started thinking and I then remembered."

Tanaka paused and watched Irene as she took notes on a wrinkled pad of paper. Marcus Tosscander. Finally they had a name to go with— the torso.

"I was both happy and surprised that he wanted to meet me. We came in here. It was easy to talk with him. His English was perfect. Suddenly he asked if he could borrow my silk painting because he wanted an unusual tattoo as a souvenir of Copenhagen. Apparently he had seen the sign outside the shop and fallen for it. I still don't know why I agreed to lend it to him but I did. And I gave him Woon's address."

He fell silent. When he started speaking again, Irene heard a sorrowful undertone in his voice.

"After every visit to Woon he would return the painting. It took two weeks to complete the tattoo. He couldn't go to her every day because he didn't have time since he had several large projects here in Copenhagen. He continued to come to see me even after the tattoo was finished. He would always come and go by the back way. I'll show it to you later because you're also going to use it."

"When was the last time you saw him?"

"February 28. It was a Sunday. We ate dinner here in my kitchen and he told me that he was going back to Göteborg to get his summer clothes. It seemed as though he was seriously considered moving here. He said that it was mainly for my sake."

His voice broke after the last sentence. Tanaka lowered his heavy head to hide his tears and sat in that position for a long time. Then lifted his head and looked at Irene with a furious glare.

"He left on Monday, March 1, and since then I haven't heard from him. Now I know why. That's why I'm telling you, a Swedish police officer whom I trust. You have to catch the murderer!"

"Why don't you want to talk to the Danish police?"

"Marcus moved to Copenhagen just after New Year's. He was living with a . . . friend. This friend was a police officer. Marcus was always talking about *my little policeman*. The officer wasn't allowed to know anything about us as long as Marcus was living with him. Sometimes I got the feeling that he was afraid of that officer. He often said, 'He's almost worse than my doctor in Göteborg.' "

"Wait a second! Did he really say 'worse than my doctor in Göteborg'?"

"Yes. Word for word and on several occasions. I read it as though the officer and the doctor were jealous. Maybe of each other. But maybe Marcus meant something else."

The officer and the doctor had shown up again. But Carmen Østergaard was a woman and Marcus a man. Was it the same officer and doctor? A coincidence? How did all of this fit together?

"Do you know the officer's name?" Irene asked.

"No. He didn't want to tell me. 'You would be surprised. It's best that you don't know,' he said when I asked. But one time it slipped out that the officer had a connection to Vesterbro. 'We have to be cautious,' he said."

"You got the impression that the officer worked in this district?"

Tanaka considered. "I don't remember every word. But that he had some connection here was very clear."

"Do you know where the officer lives?"

"No. Just that it was somewhere around the Botanical Gardens."

"Do you know how old Marcus was?"

"Thirty-one."

"Do you know anything about his family and friends in Göteborg?"

"No. Nothing. We talked about almost everything but that."

"What did you talk about?"

"We had a lot of things in common. Trips, for example. Marcus loved to travel. We had talked about going to Japan in the fall. . . ."

Tanaka interrupted himself and stood abruptly. He said, "Here is my cell phone number. Only a handful of people have this number. You can reach me around the clock. Call immediately if there's anything you can tell me."

Irene took the note. Tanaka bowed to her and she bowed back. She appreciated the respect and trust Tom Tanaka was showing her.

He led her though the small corridor and into a huge bedroom. The scent of expensive male cologne was prevalent. The room was dominated by a huge bed without covers, made up with black silk sheets. The walls were white plastered and displayed two large framed photographs. Both were studies in black and white of naked young men. On one of the walls there was a door. Irene noticed that it was supplied with both a keypad lock and a heavy-duty burglarproof lock. Tanaka unlocked both locks and opened the door. Behind it there was a little landing and a flight of narrow stone steps.

"If you need to meet with me, call me. We'll make an appointment and I'll open the door for you."

Again they bowed to each other. Irene pushed the glowing button for the stairwell lighting and went down the little half flight of stairs. She opened a door to a small, dark courtyard. The smell of food from a restaurant on the other side of it was nauseating, as was the odor rising from the piles of trash lying against the wall. The scratching and rustling from inside the piles implied that there were inhabitants of the trash pile who were happily living the good life.

As Irene hurried across the courtyard toward the entrance to the street, she saw ashes from a cigarette float to the ground.

Someone was standing just inside the doorway.

She turned around but the door she had used to enter the courtyard had locked behind her. The restaurant didn't have a back door. She would have to confront the person who was waiting in the darkness. She didn't know if the person was armed, but would have to assume so.

She started toward the street entrance. She was close enough to hear suppressed breathing as she passed someone in the shadows. When she was about to take the last step into the street, a man jumped out and stood in front of her, blocking her path. The streetlight outside reflected on a knife blade and glimmered faintly on his shaved head. He had been standing outside; that meant there were two of them.

Without turning her head, Irene shot her arm out to the right like lightning, straight to where she knew the other one had to be standing. She got hold of a thick jacket and pulled so hard that her assailant stumbled in front of her. With a thump, his club hit the wall instead of landing on her head. She quickly changed her hold and took a firm grasp of his neck. She could feel more than see that he also had shaved his head. She rammed it into the stone wall with a hollow thud. He crumpled to the ground with a faint grunt.

The man with the knife stepped over his fallen accomplice. He stood in the dimly lit doorway and made a jab at her stomach with the knife. She blocked this attack and grabbed his wrist. Quickly, she stretched out his right arm and moved in a half circle to the right. With an iron grip she held the arm with the knife straight up and at the same time she aimed a kick at his stomach. *Mae-geri.* All the air went out of him. Before he had the chance to catch his breath she put her left arm around his throat and twisted while still holding his right arm straight out. When he was lying on the ground it was easy to push her lower leg against his throat and bend his elbow backward over her thigh. It must have been unbearably painful. He let go of the knife.

So that he wouldn't recover his courage and decide to come after her, she aimed a hard kick at his ribs, not to break them but to inflict pain. Based on his scream, he wouldn't have an interest in pursuing her any time soon. She took the knife with her when she hurried from the scene. The last she heard was one of them wailing in a broad southern Swedish accent, "That was no damn fag!"

"What was it then?" the friend whined.

"Damned if I know!"

Apparently they were two thugs who had ridden the ferry from Sweden to take part in the popular sport of gay bashing. Irene had investigated similar cases a few years before. Some of the victims still had deep scars. She felt satisfied. The knife she had taken from the skinhead turned out to be a stiletto. With a soft click the knife blade slid into the shaft. The weapon fit easily into her pocket.

She jogged up toward Istedgade. If she was going to make it over to Store Kongensgade and visit the girls at Scandinavian Models she was probably best off taking a taxi.

After just a minute or two she found a cab, got in, and caught her breath. When she gave the older taxi driver the address he said, "A whole night out on the town by yourself?"

He could think what he wanted. She looked out the window and pretended not to understand.

It was unbelievably tiring always having to strain to understand Danish, not to mention Tom Tanaka, who spoke to her in English. Until now she had managed pretty well, but it wasn't always easy. Especially when people spoke Danish quickly.

But Tom Tanaka spoke very good, clear English. Maybe he was extra pedagogic when he was speaking with her. How was it that he, a Japanese, was so fluent in English? At least he seemed to be, to her. Had he lived in the USA? She would have thought someone in his field would have stayed in Japan, where sumo wrestlers were practically treated like gods. Did his leaving there have to do with his sexuality? Possibly.

Finally they had a probable name for the poor victim at Killevik. Marcus Tosscander, thirty-one years old and a designer. It struck her that she had forgotten to ask what he designed, but that would be answered now that they knew his identity.

The two who had attacked her by the doorway—could they have something to do with the investigation? When she thought about it in the peace and quiet of the backseat of the taxi she ruled out that possibility. It was probably a coincidence.

They drove along the wide boulevards, passing brightly lit houses. Her eyelids felt heavy and she realized how tired she was.

The taxi driver signaled and turned over toward the sidewalk. "There. So here we are at the next bit of entertainment," he said.

"Would you mind waiting with the car? I'm just going in to ask after someone."

"Yes, but you'll have to pay for this ride first."

Irene paid, and the taxi driver promised to wait for five minutes. If she didn't return by that time, he would leave.

She opened the car door and was just about to step out when she stopped herself and slowly sank back into the half darkness of the car. A man came by, walking briskly and stopped in front of the door to the building where the Scandinavian Models office was located. With his index finger he followed the list of the building's tenants. Apparently, he found what he was looking for. Without the slightest hesitation, Detective Inspector Jens Metz went up the half flight of stairs. Irene saw his broad back disappearing through the landing door.

She sat in the taxi for a good ten minutes. Finally she had had enough of the taxi driver's knowing mutter. "Oh. We were shadowing the unfaithful husband. That's what we were doing!"

She got out of the cab and walked to the entrance to the building. On the list of tenants, Scandinavian Models was located on the first floor. She pushed the brass button next to the little sign. The lock buzzed and then she opened the heavy door.

On the middle of the first-floor landing there was a door with a shiny brass plate saying WELCOME TO SCANDINAVIAN MODELS. At a quick glance it could just as easily have been the entrance to a lawyer's office.

After Irene's second ring the door was opened by a girl who, according to the picture in the tourist guide, was Petra. She was blonde and had on heavy makeup, but still barely looked twenty. Even though she didn't have the super-short T-shirt on, her sheer see-through blouse was just as revealing. Her black leather miniskirt was a centimeter away from being just a wide belt.

She jumped when she saw Irene. A quick look of fear came into her eyes. Irene understood. What strange requests and desires might this tall woman have? Before Irene had time to introduce herself, Petra said curtly, "Have you made an appointment?"

She spoke broad southern Swedish.

"No. I'm a Swedish police officer and I'm looking for Isabell Lind. She's also known as Bell."

Petra grew pale under her makeup and pressed her lips together. Her gaze wandered around the newly painted stairway, which was marbelized in a sober light gray. There was no one there who could help, and her nervous gaze returned to Irene.

"Bell . . . Isabell isn't here," she finally said.

"No? Where is she?"

"Out. With a client."

If they had been at home in Göteborg, Irene could have asked to come in to search the office. Now she was in Copenhagen, where she didn't have any authority. But Jens Metz did. She hadn't seen a trace of him since he'd entered these the premises. He must be inside somewhere. What was he doing? Was he helping her inquire after Isabell? Or had he decided to become a customer?

"Do you know when Isabell will be back?"

Petra shrugged. Irene decided to push a little harder.

"I'm not here on police business. I'm an old friend of Isabell's and of her family, and it's the family that needs to get in touch with her for important private reasons, you understand."

With the last sentence she lowered her voice and sent Petra an imploring look. The girl looked confused and seemed not to know what to say. Irene took out her wallet and fished out a calling card. Under her name she wrote:

Hi Bell! Contact me at Hotel Alex or call my cell phone number, which is on the card. It's important that we speak with each other.

Irene

She handed the card to Petra, who took it reluctantly.

"Could you please give this card to Isabell?"

Petra nodded sulkily and closed the door.

Irene stepped into the shadow of a parked truck and kept an eye on the entrance to the building for another half hour. Jens Metz didn't emerge.

Chapter 7

THE RINGING OF THE telephone woke her from a deep sleep. At first she didn't have the faintest idea where she was. The telephone kept ringing. After a while she managed to find the receiver and answer. A faint female voice speaking English informed her that it was time to wake up. It was six thirty. Irene sank back into the pillow with a groan. Her body was sore after the last night's skinhead fight. Sleep hung treacherously in her eyelashes, and forced her eyelids to close. . . . She sat up in bed with a jerk. It was best to get up now, otherwise Peter Møller would have to wait for her again in the reception area.

She felt more awake after a long hot shower. She put on her light yellow Björn Borg T-shirt and the blue linen pants. Together with the blue trench coat it would definitely say *I'm so happy that I'm Swedish, ho ho!* but she didn't have any other clean clothes.

She called home to her boss on her cell phone. Superintendent Andersson sounded like he had just awakened but livened up a bit when he heard that it was Irene.

"I have a good tip about the victim's identity. His name is Marcus Tosscander, thirty-one years old, and he was a designer with an office on Kungsportsplatsen. He was working in Copenhagen just before he disappeared and he had exactly the same tattoo as—"

"Wait! I don't have pen or paper."

She heard him rustling around, looking for something to write on. When he returned she gave him all of the information she had on Tosscander. Andersson sounded very pleased until she declined to tell him how she had gotten the information.

"Why can't you tell me? Is the informant reliable?"

Irene didn't have any difficulty picturing her boss's reaction if she described her informant: a former sumo wrestler who was gay, dressed in black silk pajamas, and owned Copenhagen's largest gay sex shop.

"The informant is very reliable. You have to trust me when I say that the whole thing is complicated. A police officer and a doctor showed up in the investigation into the murder-mutilation of the female prostitute here in Copenhagen two years ago. The peculiar thing is that, according to the informant, there were also a police officer and a doctor in Marcus Tosscander's life prior to his disappearance. If so, it's an amazing coincidence. The police officer seems to have a connection to Vesterbro. Which means it could be one of the colleagues I'm working with right now. I absolutely cannot tell them what I've found out in case it is one of them."

"A police officer! I don't believe it for a second!" Andersson cleared his throat a few times before he continued. "Irene. You . . . watch out. Don't take any risks. If it really is like you say, it may be dangerous."

His voice revealed sincere concern. Irene realized that she wasn't going to be able to tell the whole truth about what she had been up to the previous night.

"I'll take care of myself. Today I'm just making copies of the reports from the investigation into the murder of Carmen Østergaard and then I'm coming straight home."

"Good. Call if anything comes up."

"OK. Good-bye."

When Irene opened the curtains, she could see, to her joy, that a pale sun was actually shining on the side of the house across the street. Encouraged by this, she went down into the hotel's cafeteria and ate a delicious Danish breakfast. She discovered to her pleasure that their coffee actually tasted quite good.

Satisfied, she went up to the room and packed the rest of her things in her bag.

Peter Møller showed up just as she was in the process of checking out.

"Good morning! Everything OK?" he asked and fired off a sunny smile.

He reminded Irene of Fredrik Stridh. Both were types who always looked bright and fresh even if there was no way they could be. This was an enviable quality that she suffered a regrettable lack of. If she had only slept five hours, as she had the night before, that's exactly how she looked in the morning. She carefully applied her makeup and gave Møller a wide smile in return. With any luck, he would buy it. If he thought that his colleague from Sweden looked a little worn-out early this morning, let him think she had plundered the minibar in her hotel room out of loneliness. None of the Danish colleagues would learn of her private reconnaissance work around midnight.

"Morning to you, too. All's well?" she said.

Møller took her bag before she even had time to reach for it. With his other hand, he held the door open for her as usual. Polite and well mannered but difficult to get any real understanding of, thought Irene. Maybe *he* was the officer? Resolutely she forced the idea away. She might become paranoid if she started thinking along those lines.

IT WAS time consuming to read the reports of the interrogations in Danish. Irene had to skim through the text and try to pick out the things that seemed important. There was a risk that she might miss something essential but she comforted herself with the fact that the copier was new and efficient. She was delighted when she found the witness reports on both the police officer and the doctor. Unfortunately, the interrogator hadn't pushed very hard during these interrogations so the material was quite slim. One of the prostitutes had fallen into the hands of the policeman; the other had encountered the doctor.

Christine Ehlers, twenty-four years of age, a junkie and street prostitute since she was a teenager, stated that she had been threatened by a man about a week before Carmen Østergaard was murdered. He had picked her up in a car and driven her to the back lot of a house that was going to be demolished. She didn't remember the make of the car, but described the car as being big and new. When he had stopped the car he had taken off his dark overcoat. Under it he was wearing a police uniform. He started to hit her in the face and called her a whore, a slut, and the like. He got a powerful stranglehold on her and she wasn't getting any air. In a panic, she managed to knee him in the crotch. Apparently, it hit hard where it was supposed to, because he released his grip and Christine managed to run away.

Because she was under the influence of heroin at the time and in shock after the event, she couldn't give a description of the assailant. The only things she remembered were that he seemed to be young and relatively tall and skinny. He had spoken Danish without an accent. Stubbornly, she maintained that he had been dressed in a police uniform, hat included. She didn't remember if he had had the hat on from the very beginning when he picked her up, or if he had put it on later. It was the dark blue dress hat, not the white summer hat.

Anne Sørensen was twenty-five years old and had been a street prostitute for a few months. Earlier, she had worked at a club but was thrown out when her drug addiction became too obvious. Just before Walpurgis Night 1997, she had been picked up by a customer traveling in a car. She also didn't know the make of the car, but she remembered that it was red and very stylish. He had also driven to an abandoned back lot behind a house about to be demolished and he had spoken Swedish. He had told her that he was a doctor when they were in the car. When she had asked what kind of doctor he was, he hadn't answered.

After parking the car in the dark lot, the man had taken out a black bag that had been lying in the backseat. He took out a filled hypodermic needle from the bag.

"I want you to take this first so that you will be in good shape," he said.

Anne had become suspicious. She tried to worm her way out of it by saying that she had already taken some earlier in the evening and it was too soon for another hit. Then the man had become furious. He had screamed and threatened her: "If you don't take the shot, I'll beat you to death anyway!"

The last bit had scared Anne enough that she had come to her senses. She understood the man had decided to kill her and fear gave her enough extra strength so that she managed to knock the needle out of his hand. Somehow she got the car door open and managed to leap out. She escaped by running from the scene.

Both women knew who Carmen Østergaard was but neither of them were closely acquainted with her.

Irene leaned back in the borrowed desk chair. The girls' stories were fairly similar. The back lots could be the same; however, one assailant presented himself as a police officer and the other as a doctor. And the doctor had spoken Swedish while the officer appeared to be Danish.

Marcus Tosscander had lived with a Danish police officer and he knew a doctor. "He's worse than my doctor in Göteborg," he had said to Tom Tanaka when he'd spoken about the police officer. A Swedish doctor who lived in Göteborg.

The telephone on the desk started ringing. She answered since no one else was in the room. "Detective Inspector Irene Huss," she said slowly.

She tried hard to speak extra clearly, in case the person calling had a hard time understanding Swedish.

"Wonderful that I got hold of you!" It was Yvonne Stridner.

It was unnecessary to add the last part. No one else trumpeted on the phone like the professor.

"Have just spoken with Svend Blokk. There were certain details about the dismemberment process of our body that I wanted to compare with their murder-mutilation from two years ago. He mentioned that you were going to meet him today to pick up detailed autopsy reports. You don't need to. I'll take care of it directly with Svend. But I can say right now, it's the same mutilator."

Irene could only say, "Thanks."

Maybe it wasn't the right answer, or Stridner misunderstood, or maybe she just wasn't listening.

"No problem. It's no extra trouble. You take care of the police work, and I'll handle the pathology. But isn't it remarkable that this type of murderer is operating in both Göteborg and Copenhagen? There is some distance between the cities, at least 180 miles. And Öresund is in between."

At that moment, Irene realized that the professor was wrong. It wasn't at all remarkable since they were probably dealing with two murderers. A Danish police officer and a Swedish doctor. It could, of course, also be someone who commuted between the two cities, but the few descriptions that existed indicated there were two murderers.

Stridner was saying something else into the receiver. In order to cover her lapse, Irene mumbled something inarticulate in a tone of agreement.

"Wonderful! Then we're agreed," Stridner said.

A click indicated that the professor had hung up. Irene did the same and wondered what she and Stridner had agreed on.

Irene was busy with the copying until almost twelve o'clock. Then Jens Metz opened the door to the office and stuck in his round face.

"Are you coming to lunch?"

"Yes, thanks. I'm finished now."

"You're efficient," Metz commented, smiling jovially.

He hadn't said a word about his visit to Scandinavian Models. Maybe he would do so during lunch? She would wait and see. She gathered up her papers and put them in her bag. It became considerably heavier but she wanted to take them along. She hoped to drive home directly after lunch.

Peter Møller kept them company. They ate lunch at a very smoky pub behind Tivoli. All three ate beef patties fried with onions, served with potatoes. Møller and Metz each had a large beer. Irene declined with the excuse that she would be driving.

"The alcohol will be gone before you get to Helsingborg," said Metz.

"Stupid to take the risk." Irene smiled. In order to change the subject, she said, "You'll have to give my best to Beate Bentsen and thank her for being so accommodating. Not to mention a big thanks to the two of you for all your help."

"Don't mention it," said Metz and raised his beer glass.

Mostly to have something to say, Irene said, "Not to be nosy, but what does Mr. Bentsen do?"

Metz laughed. "There's never been a Mr. Bentsen."

"But she talked about a son," Irene said sheepishly.

"Yes, you've already met him," Jens Metz grinned.

Irene caught the warning look Peter Møller sent his colleague, but Metz didn't. He was fully concentrated on his beer glass. When he finally managed to tear it from his lips, Irene continued, "I've met Beate Bentsen's son?"

"Of course! Emil, who hangs out at Tom Tanaka's. Emil Bentsen. Peter said that you met him in the store yesterday."

You could have knocked Irene over with a feather. Jens Metz wrinkled his forehead and looked uncertainly in Peter Møller's direction.

"Didn't you tell her about it yesterday?" he asked Møller in an irritated tone.

Møller sighed before he answered, "It didn't have anything to do with her investigation."

He was right about that. But it wasn't unimportant if one happened to have the remaining information that Irene was in possession of but which her two Danish colleagues weren't aware of. She had to speak with Tom Tanaka again before she left.

Just then notes of "The Marseillaise" fluted out of her coat pocket. "Irene Huss," she said into the cell phone.

It was quiet on the phone, but she could hear someone breathing. "Hello?" she said.

"It's . . . it's Petra. At Scandinavian Models. Bell . . . Isabell is gone." Irene felt her heart skip a beat. "Wait a moment," she said.

She took the Nokia from her ear and smiled at Metz and Møller. "Excuse me. It's my daughter. Personal problems."

She got up from the chair and headed for the women's bathroom. Once there, she put the phone back to her ear. "Hi, Petra. Are you still there?"

"Yeah."

"You said something about Isabell being gone?"

"Yes. She hasn't come back from . . . a job. . . ."

"How long has she been gone?"

"She left here around eleven last night."

"Where did she go?"

"To the Hotel Aurora."

"You know this for certain?"

"Yes. We write down all of the orders in a logbook. Bell was supposed to be at the Hotel Aurora before eleven thirty."

"Do you know who asked for her?"

"I didn't take the call, but it says here that the customer was Simon Steiner."

"The request was made by telephone?"

"Yes."

"Do you know where the Hotel Aurora is located?"

"The address is listed here. Colbjørnsensgade. It's in—"

"Vesterbro. I know."

Irene had been in Tom Tanaka's apartment behind the gay sex shop on the same street, at about the time Isabell should have arrived at the hotel. More accurately, it was probably just before Irene's encounter with the skinheads. Her brain was working in overdrive but she couldn't get her thoughts in order. Finally she asked, "Could Isabell have stayed with the customer overnight and overslept?"

"No, we never stay the night with a customer."

"Have you called the police here in Copenhagen?"

There was a long silence before Petra answered. "No. A man came yesterday asking after Bell. He said that he was a police officer and showed his police ID . . . but Bell had already left, and then you came. But you gave me the card with your name and cell phone number, so I thought . . ."

"Petra. I'm really grateful that you called and told me about this. But I don't have the ability to do anything here. A Swedish police officer has no authority in Denmark. I would suggest that you call the police in Vesterbro and report that Isabell never came back after an appointment at the Hotel Aurora. Only a Danish police officer can search the hotel."

Petra said, "Do you think I could leave it as an anonymous tip?"

"Yes, but there's a risk that they will dismiss it as a prank call. Another option is for you to call the hotel. Have you done that?"

"No, but maybe I should. . . ."

"You can start with that. By the way, did the man looking for Bell yesterday really say that he was a police officer?"

"Yeah . . . they do that sometimes . . . say that they want to inspect . . . you know . . ."

In order to get a free pass, thought Irene. Loudly she said, "Hey, I have to run now. I'll call you in two hours and see if you have come up with anything. And please call my number if Isabell happens to show up."

"OK. Bye."

When Irene had hung up, she felt her stomach flutter with worry. What had happened? Was it really a pure coincidence that she and Isabell had been on the same street at the same time in this huge city?

An ice-cold chill ran down her spine. It felt as though an invisible hand was maneuvering her as if she were a marionette. Someone was playing a cleverly calculated game. Right then, she would have given almost anything for a glimpse at the script.

Could Tom Tanaka be responsible for Isabell's disappearance? But she hadn't mentioned Isabell to him. The only ones she had spoken with and shown the picture to were Beate Bentsen, Jens Metz, and Peter Møller. Three police officers.

Tanaka had said that he trusted her, and in turn, it now seemed as though he was the only one she dared to trust.

She got out Tom Tanaka's calling card with his cell phone number. There was one ring before he answered. "Tom."

"Hi. This is Irene Huss."

"What's new?"

It took a confused second before Irene understood what "What's new?" meant. Stammering, she started to explain. "No. I don't have any . . . news. But I need to ask a few questions. Is that OK?"

"Depends on what kind of questions."

"Are you alone now?"

"Yes."

"It's about Emil. How long has he worked for you?"

To Irene's surprise, he let out a short laugh. "Emil doesn't work for me. He's more like a volunteer."

"Volunteer? What do you mean?"

"He has been hanging out in the store ever since I took it over. Sometimes he buys a few things. But mostly he just hangs out. We have gotten to know each other over time. Little by little, as it turned out, he started helping here."

"Does he have any other jobs?"

"He studies law."

"Do you know anything about Emil's parents?"

"Not a thing. Doesn't interest me. Why are you asking about Emil?"

"His mother is Beate Bentsen. She is the superintendent of police in the Criminal Division. A police officer with connections to Vesterbro . . . she works there."

It became quiet. Irene heard Tanaka's heavy breathing. When he finally took a deep breath and then exhaled, there was an explosion in the receiver. "Damn! Shit!" Then he said in a normal voice, "When are you going home to Sweden?"

"Now. I've just had lunch with my colleagues. Some other things have come up that I'd like to ask you about."

"Can you stop by on the way?"

"I'll try. We're behind Tivoli now so it isn't far to walk to you. I'll call on the cell when I get there. You want me to take the back way, don't you?"

"Yes."

Irene ended the call. She quickly touched up her lipstick before she went out again to her male colleagues.

They were in the process of paying. Irene smiled apologetically. "You can't be away from home one day without the whole house falling apart—at least it seems that way. Naturally, I'll pay for myself."

She pulled her wallet out of her pocket but Metz waved it off.

"Not at all. It's on us. You can treat us when we come and visit Göteborg."

"Of course. Thanks a lot."

The police officers said good-bye to each other outside the pub. Irene and the men went in separate directions. She walked up Bernstorffsgade. She should have taken a right at the large intersection in order to get to her parked car on Studiestræde. Instead, she turned left and followed Vesterbrogade for about one hundred meters, and then turned onto the next cross street, which was Helgolandsgade.

The closer she got, the more hesitant she became. She would hardly be attacked in broad daylight, but the memory of the assault half a day earlier suddenly felt very tangible. She peered into the half darkness of the doorway before she sneaked into the courtyard. Everything was fine. She pulled out her cell phone and dialed Tom's number.

"Tom."

"It's Irene. I'm in the backyard."

"OK. I'll come down and open the door."

Tanaka's heavy, shuffling steps down the short half flight of stairs could be heard clearly. When he looked at her his massive upper body and face filled the entire glass pane of the door. With a faint smile he greeted her and opened the door.

"Thanks for taking the time to come," he said.

"Good that you could meet with me," Irene replied.

"No problem. I don't start until six today. Ole, my real employee, is working now."

Laboriously, Tom Tanaka started to climb the stairs. His labored breathing echoed in the stairwell. He politely held open the heavy

door for Irene and she stepped into his bedroom. It looked the same as
it had last time. The bed was neatly made with black silk sheets. Tom
had changed into a dark blue silk outfit, pajamas like the black ones he
had been wearing the day before.

He showed her into his office.

The sparsely decorated room was soothing. Irene sat on one of the
cloth-covered chairs and Tom in his special chair behind the desk.
Without asking if she wanted any, he bent and took two cold Hofs out
of the minifridge. Just like last time, Irene got a glass while he drank
directly from the bottle.

"Marcus designed this room for me. Like the kitchen. It was finished
last month. He never got to see the finished product," he said.

"Was he an interior designer?"

"Among other things. He designed most things. Window and shop
displays, fabrics, and all kinds of things. The big job that brought him
here to Copenhagen was furnishing a gay bar on one of the cross
streets to Ströget. A new and very popular place. It was unbelievably
successful and he quickly got new jobs."

"I've informed my colleagues in Göteborg of your information without naming you as the source. Now the investigation at home will
really get going thanks to you."

"It's the least I can do for Marcus."

Irene thought through what she should say about Isabell. She
decided to start from the beginning, with Monika Lind's phone call. In
her broken English she tried to explain as clearly as possible. Tom listened. Sometimes he nodded almost imperceptibly.

When she came to the previous day's skinhead attack, Tom sat up
straight in his chair and looked at her sharply. The next moment he
relaxed, and, to Irene's surprise, he started laughing. The laughter
rolled up out of his broad chest and rumbled out of his mouth.

"You! That was you!"

When he had finished laughing, he said, "I heard about it this
morning. A police officer found two beat-up skinheads on Helgolandsgade. They said that a transvestite had robbed and beaten
them."

Tom stopped again for a new round of laughing. Transvestite! Irene
didn't think that was so funny.

"I have to admit it didn't cross my mind that it was you. Even though I knew you practice jujitsu. But this seemed more violent."

"It was more violent. Jujitsu and a bit more," Irene answered.

Tom shook his big head and chuckled to himself.

Irene felt time was running out and quickly returned to the subject of Isabell's disappearance from the Hotel Aurora on the same street as Tom's store. He became serious and thoughtful.

"It's a strange coincidence. But Marcus's murder and the terrible thing that has happened to him can't have anything to do with the girl's disappearance."

"No. I don't think so either. But the coincidence worries me."

He let his gaze rest on her for some time. "There is a connection," he said finally.

"What?"

"You."

He said the very thing she had been thinking. Again she was gripped by the feeling that someone was standing in the wings and playing a game with her.

They sat quietly for a while looking at each other. Tom broke the silence. "I know someone at the Hotel Aurora."

He pulled out his Rolodex and let his index finger slide over it. Irene hadn't noticed until then that he had on blue nail polish. He definitely hadn't worn it yesterday. Maybe he had put it on to match the blue silk outfit. Apparently he found the number he was looking for because he pushed a button and the machine dialed. Irene could hear several rings before anyone answered.

"Hi. Tom speaking."

The voice on the other end broke out into a long tirade that Tom patiently let go for a while. Finally he interrupted brusquely. "I know. It's been a while. But I'm calling to ask you for information. A friend of mine is concerned. Word has it that a young Swedish girl may have disappeared at the Aurora . . . yesterday around midnight . . . tall and blonde . . . yes, an escort service . . . she's called Bell."

He pulled the receiver from his ear and asked, "What was the customer's name?"

"Simon Steiner."

"Apparently a German. Simon Steiner," said Tom.

He sat quietly for almost two minutes before the jabbering started again on the other end of the line. Tom nodded a few times and hummed. Irene thought she heard a faintly surprised tone in his voice. After a few words of thanks and an assurance that they would see each other again soon, Tom put down the receiver.

"That's remarkable. My contact says that there isn't and hasn't been any Simon Steiner at the hotel. But maybe he gave the escort service a false name. And it doesn't seem as though anyone has seen Isabell either. He will ask the night porter when he comes in later tonight."

"I can't say that I'm relieved. Now I'm really worried. Where can she be?" said Irene.

"No idea. Could she have been led into a trap?"

"Possibly. But why?"

Tom looked at her. Slowly, he said, "We'll have to go back to what we said a little while ago. The connection between the murder of Marcus and the girl's disappearance. *You*."

Irene's throat became completely dry despite the fact that she had just taken a sip of beer. When she finally got a few words out, her tongue grated against her palate like sandpaper.

"Me? What do you mean?"

"The way I see it, little Isabell was alive and well until you showed up and started asking about her. Someone found out and decided to send you a warning. Kidnap her . . . maybe something worse. But I don't think it's because of Isabell or her profession. It has to do with the real reason you came to Copenhagen. The murder-mutilations."

"There are only three people here in Copenhagen that I've spoken to about Isabell."

"Three police officers."

It wasn't a question but a statement. Irene nodded. Tom fished a little notebook out of a desk drawer and said, "Can I have their names?"

Irene gave them to him. Tom wrote them down and then looked at the paper for a long time before he said, "No. The names don't say anything to me. Except Bentsen, of course. Emil Bentsen's mother!"

He snorted loudly, Something told Irene that Emil was going to get an earful next time he saw Tom.

"It seems as though 'Simon Steiner' has taken Isabell somewhere, and Copenhagen is enormous. I promised to contact her friend Petra at Scandinavian Models. The best thing is to convince her to report Isabell's disappearance to the police," said Irene.

She cast a glance at the clock and realized that it was time to go. She had almost five hours of driving and a ferry ride ahead of her. They each rose at the same time. Tom led her out of the workroom, through the short corridor, and into the bedroom. He stopped in front of the door with the safety locks. They took each other's hands and Tom said, "We'll stay in touch by cell phone."

"Yes. Thanks for all the help."

"No problem."

THE CAR was parked outside the strip club where she had left it on arriving in Copenhagen. There were barely fifteen minutes left on her twenty-four-hour parking ticket. Had she really been gone only one day? It had been an intense and eventful one. Now she just wanted to get home.

It was easier to find one's way out of Copenhagen than in, but somewhere before Hellerup she must have taken a wrong turn because the road suddenly became narrower. The big dirty brick houses disappeared and were replaced by low white rental houses made of stone-covered white plaster, interspersed with a well-cared-for-villa here and there. The rental houses disappeared and were replaced by larger and larger residences the farther north she drove. On the right side of the car she saw water and she understood that she had ended up on Strandvejen. High walls and hedges enclosed parklike yards. What could be seen of the stately houses was impressive, which was obviously the point.

After a few kilometers Irene realized that the road she was traveling on was a border, economically speaking. The houses on the right side of the road, the ones with beachfront property, were much more impressive than the ones on the left side. Something told Irene that were they to sell the row house in Fiskebäck, they wouldn't have enough to buy even a cabin on the left side of Strandvejen.

She decreased her speed and enjoyed the ocean view and the floral splendor of the gardens. The scent of seaweed mixed with the first lilacs of the season streamed in through the lowered window.

THE CROSSING was quick and uneventful and Irene had time for two cups of coffee.

Before the ferry put in at Helsingborg, Irene called Scandinavian Models as she had promised. To her relief, Petra answered.

"Hi, Petra. It's Irene Huss. Have you heard anything from Isabell?"

"No, but it's so damn strange. . . . I called the hotel and they said that no one named Simon Steiner had stayed there. And no one has seen Bell either. But it says in the logbook—That's what we call it, the logbook—it says Simon Steiner. Of course he could have made up a name."

Petra sounded more angry than upset. She had probably been insulted when her information had been questioned by the Hotel Aurora.

Irene tried to sound friendly and firm. "That sounds odd. What if she's been kidnapped? I think you should report her missing to the police. Or have you already done that?"

"No."

"I think you should do that. For Isabell's sake," Irene urged.

"OK. I guess there isn't anything else to do." Petra sighed and hung up.

Worry creased Irene's brow. Was it really possible that Isabell's disappearance had been caused by her visit to Copenhagen? Or was Isabell hiding of her own free will because somehow she had found out that Irene was asking about her? She hoped that was the case. Then Isabell might show up at any time.

Just before eight that evening Irene turned into the row-house parking lot. When she stepped out of the car and stretched, her joints and muscles popped in protest.

As usual, Sammie was the first who threw himself at her in greeting. To her disappointment, he was also the only one. After having refreshed her memory at the calendar in the kitchen, Irene realized that Krister was working late and the twins had extra practice for basketball. But the girls should be home at any moment. And how could Katarina play basketball with her injured neck? Not to mention the Junior National Championship in jujitsu.

She discovered a note on the refrigerator door.

Hello, dear!
There is some vegetarian lasagna in the fridge. Just need to heat it. Do

you remember our neighbor Monika Lind? She called around three and wanted to talk to you. She said that you have her number.

Your strategy worked! Tommy and Agneta (mostly Agneta) are taking one of the girl puppies. Lenny is taking the other girl. The lady is threatening to drop off the male puppy with us if we don't find anyone who wants him.

XXXXXX
Krister

A sigh and a soft growl from the kitchen door made Irene turn around. Sammie was standing in the doorway, his head tilted a bit to the side. His brown eyes were expectant. Of course his mistress wanted to go on a really long and restorative walk, didn't she?

Chapter 8

ISABELL WAS GONE. IRENE had searched the entire house. She had walked through all the dark and never-ending corridors and looked through all the dilapidated rooms. Dust and spiderwebs whirled up with every step she took. Her feet felt heavier and heavier but she forced herself to continue, pushed by the strength of her despair. It was up to her to find Isabell before it was too late. Because it was her fault that Isabell was gone. Bell was just a little child and now Irene had lost her. The temperature was rising in the gloomy house. Time was running out. Irene felt panic grow inside her. The ceiling started sinking and the walls of the corridor bent inward. Soon the whole house would implode. Everyone who was in the house would be crushed and die. Desperate, Irene tried to yell Isabell's name but she couldn't get out a sound. Suddenly she felt the floor moving and realized that it was too late.

IT WAS Sammie who had jumped up on the bed and made it move. Irene was bathed in sweat and she felt her heart pounding in panic after the dream. The numbers on the dark clock face showed 3:37. Krister was lying next to her, snoring peacefully. Sammie had laid down at the foot of the bed on his back, with his paws in the air. He was already asleep. At least he was pretending to be, in case his mistress tried to get him off the bed.

Irene went into the bathroom to drink some water and to try and slow down her heart rate. Her sweat felt sticky on her naked body. After a while she began to feel chilled. She went into the bedroom for her bathrobe and wrapped herself in the soft terry cloth, then padded to the kitchen barefoot, and sat down with a glass of cold milk.

The kitchen window faced east. On the horizon the sun was in the process of painting a beautiful dawn in pastel colors of pink and turquoise. The few moonbeams that remained glittered like golden ribbons. It was going to be a beautiful day.

Irene had a hard time forgetting her dream, which she didn't have any difficulty analyzing. She had a guilty conscience and was worried about what might have happened to Isabell.

The telephone conversation with Monika Lind barely six hours earlier had been tough. It was difficult to say that she had located Isabell without having had the chance to meet her before she disappeared again. The worst had been talking about Isabell's work. Monika was brokenhearted when she understood that Isabell was a prostitute. The thought had never crossed her mind. She had bought the idea hook, line, and sinker that her beautiful little daughter was struggling to become a famous photo model; she couldn't accept the truth. Maybe she also felt ashamed. Toward the end of the phone call, Monika had become aggressive and started questioning Irene's information. Maybe Irene had seen the wrong picture in the tourist guide? Maybe it wasn't Bell after all! Even if the escort service was called Scandinavian Models, couldn't there be other agencies with the same name? Why not a serious modeling agency? Yet in the end, Irene made her see reality. The girl who had disappeared was Isabell and no other.

Irene hadn't said a word about the suspicions she and Tom Tanaka had. She still had a hard time believing that her appearance in Copenhagen had started a domino effect that led to Isabell's disappearance. It seemed too far-fetched.

She decided not to mention Tom's identity to anyone. She trusted him completely but her boss and colleagues never would. They would make fun of him and question his credibility. But Irene had faith in him, because he had truly loved Marcus Tosscander. Now they had to find out who Marcus really had been. It appeared that he had had many dangerous acquaintances.

IRENE GOT to start Thursday's morning prayers with a report of her doings in Copenhagen. A censored version.

"Good work in Copenhagen. It seems as though it could be some of Marcus Tosscander lying in the sacks," said Superintendent Andersson.

Jonny interrupted him. "What's this funny stuff about not being able to tell us how you got the information?"

He looked at Irene. She had known the question would come and she wasn't all that surprised about who had asked it. "I have guaranteed complete confidentiality to my informant. No one but me knows his identity. Those were the conditions I agreed to in order to get the information. The main thing is that we finally have a name to start with," she answered.

Jonny began to object but the superintendent was ahead of him.

"Exactly. Hannu and Jonny worked on it all day yesterday. Everything points to the torso really being Tosscander. Hannu can begin."

Hannu nodded slightly and read from his notepad: "Marcus Emanuel Tosscander was born March 8, 1968, in Askim Parish. He would now be thirty-one years old. The mother died ten years ago. The father is a retired senior physician. No siblings. Educated at the College for Art and Design for five years. Started his own design firm as soon as his education was done. Moved the business to the offices at Kungsportsplatsen four years ago. According to his tax declarations for the last five years, his company has done very well. The company has declared profits in the millions, and personally he has taken out five hundred thousand in salary each year. Lives on Jenny Lindsgatan in Lunden. Unmarried. No children. Drives an imported red Pontiac, 1995 year model."

Had he actually thought of checking the car registration as well? thought Irene. But by this time she knew Hannu and realized that he had. Where was the car now? Marcus had probably taken it to Copenhagen.

"Jonny contacted the father yesterday," Andersson said to Irene.

Jonny got ready to take over: "I drove out to Pappa Tosscander's after lunch yesterday. He didn't want to meet with me earlier because he was going to be out golfing. This despite the fact that I told the old man it had to do with his son when I called him in the morning. Golf was more important. He lives alone in a damn big shack by the ocean right next to Hovås golf course. But I understood that the old man and his son don't have any contact at all. He seemed like he didn't want to know anything about Marcus. He said several times, 'My son lives his life and I live mine.' "

"Had he heard anything from Marcus during the past few months?" asked Irene.

"From what I understand, they haven't spoken with each other since Marcus moved to Copenhagen."

"But he moved at New Year's!" Irene exclaimed.

"Yes. But apparently that's the way it is."

"Strange not to have any contact with your only son for five months. . . ."

Irene stopped herself. Marcus had said to Tom Tanaka that he might be moving to Copenhagen for good. Had that decision been based on a break with his father? Yet another thought struck her. The father was a doctor. In Göteborg. She decided that she would try and talk with him when she had a chance.

"Has anyone reported Marcus missing?" Birgitta asked.

"No," answered Hannu.

"It could be that the publication of the tattoo drawing confused people here in Göteborg. Marcus Tosscander had it done in Copenhagen before he disappeared. Apparently no one here saw Marcus's new body decoration," said Irene.

"You mean that even if people had missed Marcus, no one would put his disappearance together with the discovery of the body parts out at Killevik? But where do people think he is? He can't have been in contact with anyone since the end of February or possibly the beginning of March," said Birgitta.

The superintendent cleared his throat and started showing signs of wanting to say something.

"Even if we're almost certain that the victim at Killevik is Marcus Tosscander, I want to wait to release his identity to the media. We'll collect all the information we can in the next few days and maybe we'll release his name after the weekend."

"It's a long weekend, Pentecost. That won't be until Tuesday. Five days," said Hannu.

Irene agreed. Five days felt like way too much time to wait. But she could understand the superintendent's unwillingness to be hasty. There was a microscopic chance that the victim wasn't Marcus Tosscander. A mistake like that could be disastrous. They had to have watertight proof that it really was him.

"Has anyone been to his office or his apartment?" she asked.

"No. I was thinking that you should start there today," said Andersson.

IRENE SPENT several hours writing up the report on her trip to the other side of Øresund. It was difficult since she constantly had to think ahead and make sure that she didn't write too much. Meanwhile, Jonny and Hannu were chasing after permission and keys so they could enter Tosscander's residence and workplace.

By lunchtime everything was done.

"We'll take a look at the office first. It's the closest, and then we'll have time to eat lunch before we head over to Lunden," said Jonny.

Hannu and Irene nodded.

The offices of Tosca's Design were located on the second floor of a house between Kopparmärra and the canal. A house telephone and key-pad lock were supposed to keep unwanted visitors outside, but since the police officers had keys, access wasn't a problem. Wide marble steps with massive balustrades stretched upward in the light yellow stairwell. There was no elevator. Apparently, Marcus Tosscander didn't have any handicapped clients, unless they used the telephone or Internet.

TOSCA'S DESIGN, it said on the enamel sign, in elegant dark blue writing against a white background. Hannu had keys to the ASSA deadbolt lock and the burglar alarm.

A stale smell of stagnant, dust-filled air hit them when they opened the door. It seemed as if no one had been here for months. Hannu turned on the light in the long windowless corridor.

The door to the right led into a small room with a glass wall facing the corridor. It had probably been intended as a switchboard operator's or secretary's room but Tosscander had made it into a comfortable room for visitors. The window was large and uncurtained, evidently in order not to block the magnificent view of the canal. A brown buffalo hide on the floor covered almost its entire surface. There were two circular-shaped recliners with backrests and seats upholstered in light brown leather. The frames were made of steel. One of the shorter walls was completely covered by books and glossy interior design magazines.

A large watercolor in sober colors hung on the opposite wall. It showed small houses crouched near the foot of a large mountain. A windstorm was whipping snow over the sea and around the corners of the cottages, but warm light glimmered from the little windows. Irene was captivated by the picture and stepped closer in order to be able to read the signature. The artist was Lars Lerin, but the name didn't mean anything to her.

Straight across the hall was a bathroom. The drains smelled; all of the water had long since evaporated. The door next to it led to a small pantry, a miniversion of Tom Tanaka's kitchen. Everything was there: the cherry flooring, black-and-white painted drawers and counters, the remaining furnishings in stainless steel. The view from this window was not nearly as striking as the one from the visitors' room; it faced the front of the house across the street.

The other corridor doors concealed a cleaning supplies closet, a small wardrobe, and a little office storage area for paper and binders.

The remaining door on the right side led into Marcus's large workroom. The tall bare windows let in generous sunlight. It was warm and stuffy. Irene opened the windows and admired the beautiful view over the glistening water in the canal. The chestnut trees on the other side were in the process of blooming. A multicolored carpet of different bulbs was spread beneath them, a bounty of wasteful splendor, but soon their bloom would be over.

She turned and examined the room. The floor was original and had been sanded and varnished. The walls and ceiling were white. Next to one of the windows was a large desk bearing a computer, telephone, and drawing board. The wall behind the desk was covered by a bookcase. Binders and rolls of sketches were crammed onto its shelves.

An enormous table stood before the other window. Now it was empty but it seemed to have been Marcus's worktable. Paintbrushes, pens, India inks, and chalks were crammed onto a little side table.

Drawings of interiors, sketches of large display windows, various fabrics, and color samples hung all along the walls. A very creative person had worked in this room.

They each put on cotton gloves and started systematically going through the room. When every box and binder had been looked through, Hannu said, "I haven't seen a client list."

Everyone looked at the computer. Hannu turned it on. It demanded a password.

"How about trying *pansy* or *asshole buddy?*" said Jonny.

He laughed at his own wit, but he laughed alone. Hannu tried "Tosca's," "Tosca's Design," "design" and the like but without success.

"We may as well go and eat. Maybe we'll have better luck at his apartment," said Irene.

* * *

THE VIEW at this elevation was fantastic. They looked out over Olskroken and Stampen and off toward Heden, with Ullevi in the foreground. When they had had enough of the scenery, they turned around. The old house was built in country manor style. Marcus Tosscander had a corner apartment on the top floor.

"That kid knew how to arrange awesome views," said Jonny.

They could only agree.

They mounted the narrow steps. The walls along the stairwell were newly painted in an old-fashioned pink. The stairs, doors, and handrails were light gray, creating a cheerful but subdued impression. Irene thought that Marcus might well have had a hand in choosing the color scheme.

On the top landing there was the nameplate for M. TOSSCANDER on one door and for G. SVENSSON on the other.

They entered Marcus's apartment and Irene's suspicion was confirmed. The walls in the front hall were painted in the same pink as the main stairwell. All four doors in the hall were painted light gray. The kitchen was to the right of the entrance. It also featured black and steel but Marcus had used a light-colored wood for cabinets instead of white. The same wood was used for the flooring.

Something struck Irene. "Check the flowers. They seem to be fresh, and it doesn't smell stuffy and dusty in here like it did in the office," she said.

This window was also curtainless. Marcus had trained a yellow creeper to climb along strings on one side of the window, and a flowering wax plant covered the other side. Irene stepped up to the window and looked out. The kitchen faced a thickly foliaged courtyard filled with plants and even a lilac bower.

They peered into the little bathroom, which contained a large bathtub on lion's-paw feet. The floor and walls were completely covered in dark blue tile. Here and there were interspersed tiles with a half or full moon or a star. The ceiling was also painted dark blue and Marcus had stencilled different constellations on it. Irene recognized some of them, but only knew one of the names, the Big Dipper. She imagined lying in the tub with some candles along the edge and looking up at the starry sky. . . .

None of them heard the door open. A sharp voice called out behind them. "Who are you? What are you doing here?"

The three officers turned to look at the owner of the voice. She stood in the middle of the hall, the light from a lamp reflecting from her white hair. The skinny little lady did not inspire fear but the angry expression on her face testified to her feistiness.

"We're police officers," said Jonny. They showed their badges to her.

Most of the anger melted from her face. "Is that so? But what are you doing in Marcus's apartment?" she asked sternly.

Irene chose her words carefully. "We suspect that Marcus is missing. Who are you?"

"Is little Marcus missing? I've begun to fear that myself these last few weeks. It's been two months since I've heard from him."

"Are you looking after his apartment?"

"Yes. I live in the apartment next door; my name is Gretta Svensson."

"We are Crime Inspectors Irene Huss, Jonny Blom, and Hannu Rauhala."

The hostility had vanished from the old lady's face and been replaced with a look of deep concern. "What has happened to little Marcus?" she said.

"We aren't sure yet but his friends in Copenhagen also said that Marcus hadn't been in touch for two months. When did he say he'd be back?"

"No exact time. It depended on how things went in Copenhagen. If things were going well he was going to stay, and if they didn't work out, he would come straight home. What I understood from his call was that things were going very well for him there. I assumed he had gotten a lot of work since he's so talented."

"Has he sent you any letters?"

"No, Marcus always calls. He's so sweet and thoughtful. Could anything have happened to him?"

"We know nothing for certain. But the possibility is always there when someone disappears."

It was just as well not to give Gretta Svensson false hope. She would find out from the mass media in five days.

"Mrs. Svensson—" Irene started but was interrupted at once.

"Ms."

"Ms. Svensson. Will you be home during the next few hours?"

"Yes."

"May we come in and speak with you when we are done looking through this apartment?"

"Of course."

"Good. We'll stop by in a bit."

Gently but firmly, Irene showed Ms. Svensson out of Marcus's apartment and closed the door.

Jonny and Hannu had already gone into Marcus's bedroom. Lots of splendid houseplants stood in the window. The walls were painted a shade of terra-cotta. Near the ceiling there was a wide patterned border in black, white, and different shades of brown. The flooring was dark brown varnished wood. There was only one piece of furniture in the room, a circular bed that had to be at least ten feet in diameter. The bedspread was black silk, and Irene was willing to bet that the sheets were of the same color and quality. Imaginative African masks decorated the walls, and spears and shields were hung, artistically arranged, between the masks.

"Hello, Africa," Jonny said in a deep bass tone.

He was right. The grotesque masks and shields felt threatening to Irene. She had the irrational feeling of being watched.

The living room provided a striking contrast. The walls were white and the flooring was the same type of light wood as in the kitchen. The sun flooded in. It was probably Ms. Svensson who had lowered the wooden blinds to protect the plants.

"This man has done away with curtains. I think it's really nice," said Irene.

A short windowless wall was completely covered by an overflowing bookcase. Two big white leather sofas stood in the middle of the room, facing each other. A black-and-white cowhide lay on the floor beneath them. The coffee table was constructed of two freestanding triangular pieces of marble, one white and the other black. They could also be put together to make a larger table. The remaining furniture consisted of a large stereo system and a wide-screen TV. Two oil paintings hung on the walls, probably painted by the same artist who had painted the watercolor at the office.

"Nice," said Hannu.

Irene was a bit surprised. He rarely aired his opinions.

They searched the apartment without finding anything interesting except for three photo albums that were on a shelf of the bookcase. One turned out to contain pictures of a single man in various poses and outfits. The heading on the first page was MARCUS TOSSCANDER. He had posed nude for the pictures on the last two pages.

He had been very attractive, with thick dark brown hair, clean and symmetrical facial features, big deep blue eyes, and a beautiful smile. Irene had expected him to be effeminate but his looks were completely masculine. From the nude photos, Irene noted that he was muscular with six-pack abs. He was very sexy.

The two other albums contained pictures taken at parties and on trips. There was a good deal of writing next to the pictures so Jonny, Hannu, and Irene decided to take them back to the station.

Hannu remarked on their failure to find an address book here either.

"We'll have to ask the technicians to come and collect evidence. I assume that the big bathtub might have been suitable for the dismemberment of the body," Irene said, although they had found nothing to indicate it had taken place there, but it was best to go by the book.

There weren't many clothes in the bedroom closets. It looked as though Marcus had taken both summer and winter clothes with him. Odd, since he had left in the middle of winter. Maybe he was counting on staying away till the summer. Then again, the distance between Göteborg and Copenhagen wasn't that far. If nothing else, he had both his office and his apartment to look after. Had he really not planned to return to Göteborg a single time during the spring? Yet that's exactly what he must have done: returned home, only to be murdered and dismembered.

In the beautiful apartment, Irene shivered.

"Only one of us has to talk with the old lady," said Jonny.

"OK, I'll do it," Irene volunteered.

Hannu and Jonny had found two keys in a drawer of the tall dresser in the hall. One of them was marked "Basement" and the other "Attic." They each took a key and on the landing they split up. Jonny unlocked the door to the attic, Hannu went down the stairs, and Irene rang the bell of the door across the hall. It opened at once.

"Did you find anything?" asked Gretta Svensson.

There was concern, not curiosity, in her voice.

"Nothing that tells us where he might be," Irene answered truthfully.

She entered the apartment. The hallway was the same size as the one in Marcus's apartment, but the color scheme was completely different. Deep purple velvet flocked wallpaper revealed that the last renovation had taken place sometime during the late sixties. All the interior doors were painted a dark brown. Gretta Svensson showed Irene into a large living room, the same size as Marcus's. This was not a corner apartment so there was only one window and the room was not as bright. The furniture was a mixture of dark oak pieces and IKEA recliners. The window was framed by thick rose-patterned chintz curtains. The impression was dark and oppressive.

"Please sit down. I'll get the coffee," said Ms. Svensson.

Irene didn't protest because she was longing for a cup of coffee. As she sank down on the pink sofa she noticed that the coffee cups had already been set out. She had never had a chance to decline.

The little woman came flying out of the kitchen with a coffee pot made of glass in one hand and a plate of Marie biscuits in the other.

"I don't have any coffee cake in the house. This was a bit unexpected," Gretta Svensson apologized.

Irene nodded understandingly and inhaled the scent of coffee. The biscuits weren't important as far as she was concerned; the main thing was that she got some caffeine.

"Please start by answering a few routine questions that we always ask people in cases like these," Irene said.

"That's fine."

"Your full name?"

"Anna Gretta Svensson."

"Thanks. Your date of birth?"

"October 19, 1921."

Irene quickly did the math and determined that the woman sitting in front of her was seventy-eight years old. Before she was able to ask another question, Gretta continued. "I was born a few houses down on this street, though that building was torn down many years ago. This house hadn't been built yet. Pappa was a baker and Mamma sometimes helped in the bakery where he worked. It was them and the six of us kids in a two-room apartment. I'm the only sibling left of the bunch. I guess I was what you would call a late surprise."

"Have you always lived on this street?"

"All my life. I've lived in this apartment for thirty-two years because it suits me so well. Before that I had a studio apartment in the house next door for many years."

"What did you work as?" It had nothing to do with the investigation, but Irene was curious.

"A seamstress. The last few years I worked at Gillblad's."

Gretta sat up straight in the little chintz-covered Emma recliner and kept her light blue eyes focused steadily on Irene as she slowly brushed a white wisp of hair out of her face and tucked it behind her ear. "But this isn't about me. Where is Marcus?" she asked.

"If we only knew," Irene sighed.

Gretta looked as though she was preparing to ask another question, but Irene quickly prevented her. "How long has Marcus been your neighbor?"

"Ten and a half years. We celebrated our ten-year anniversary during Saint Lucia. He came over with a bottle of wine and I made some delicious sandwiches. We sat talking and had a wonderful time. That's when he told me about Copenhagen and I promised to look after his apartment."

"Do you often get together over a bottle of wine?"

"Sometimes. He comes over when he thinks I'm feeling lonely. That's the way he is. Very sweet and thoughtful."

Gretta smiled unconsciously when she spoke about Marcus.

"I know that Marcus moved to Copenhagen around New Year's. How often did he call you from Copenhagen?"

"Not very often. He had so much to do. There were always new jobs and . . ." She stopped herself and compressed her lips. Finally she said dully, "He called me twice."

"When was the last time?"

"Wait."

Gretta rose surprisingly quickly and disappeared into the bedroom. After a while she came back with a small blue pocket diary. She nervously skimmed back and forth, then triumphantly she announced, "Here. February 18."

She held out the page. "Marcus has called," it said. The other days were blank.

"I always write down important things."

"Do you remember what he said?"

Gretta's brow wrinkled as she concentrated. "He said that he was getting on very well in Copenhagen and he might come home at the beginning of March, but he would call me beforehand. He didn't. But he may have called when I was in the hospital."

"When were you in the hospital?"

"I was admitted the night of February 27 and came home on March 5. I'd had some intestinal bleeding and it turned out to be a large polyp, which they removed immediately. But I lost a lot of blood so they had to give me transfusions. I got seven bags of blood! Then there were a bunch of tests with—"

"Could Marcus have been home during that time?" Irene brusquely interrupted the health story.

"Yes. Because there was something . . ." Gretta fell silent and looked uncertain. "I went to the emergency room on Sunday night. I had gone in and watered the plants at Marcus's on Friday. As soon as I got home, I went into his apartment because I expected that the flowers would be droopy, but they weren't. They looked healthy. As if someone had watered them."

"Did they look like they had been watered recently? Was there water on the dishes? Was the soil moist?"

"They hadn't been watered that recently. Maybe three or four days earlier."

This was very interesting. If they could prove that Marcus had been home the first week in March, they might be able to pinpoint when he died.

Irene chose her words carefully. "Do you know if Marcus had a girl-friend or another friend whom he often saw?"

"Marcus lived such an active life. There wasn't room for a girl-friend. He used to say that he didn't need one because he had me."

What kind of man had this effect? Tom Tanaka and Gretta Svensson both seemed to feel specially chosen by Marcus.

"Did he have a lot of buddies?"

"Not all that many. Sometimes he would have small parties in his apartment. But never any rowdiness! All of the boys were polite and well behaved."

"Do you know any of their names?"

"No."

Irene couldn't come up with any more questions for the moment. She got up and said, "I'd like to thank you for your help. Is it all right for me to return if I come up with any more questions?"

"It's perfectly fine."

The little woman followed her out into the hall. When she had closed the door, Irene heard the lock rattling as the key was turned.

Jonny had found a box that he carried down from the attic.

"Magazines and films. Gay porn," he announced.

There was only an old bike in the basement. Hannu had returned to the apartment and was looking through the albums they were planning to take back to the station.

"Names," he said and pointed.

A wedding invitation was glued to the top of one of the pages. It was a double card with two gold rings on the outside. On the inside it read:

You are cordially invited to the wedding of Anders Gunnarsson and Hans Pahliss in the Göteborg City Hall on 5/29 1998 12:30. Wedding lunch at Fiskekrogen, 1:30. There will be a party in the evening at our home.
Looking forward to seeing you!

"Pahliss. A name that should be easy to look up," said Irene.

"A wedding. But, damn, it's two guys," Jonny said. The distaste was evident in his voice.

There were several photos next to the invitation, which had evidently been taken during the partnership ceremony and at the lunch.

The two men appeared to be in their thirties. One of them was tall and blond and the other was shorter and had dark hair. It was possible that he was a few years older than his blond partner. Both wore dark suits with bright red bow ties. The roses in their buttonholes were also red. They looked serious in the first picture, in which they were listening carefully to the officiator. Marcus's handsome face could be seen behind the blond man. The next picture was taken from the side, and Marcus could be seen from behind. His light linen suit fit perfectly. The last picture from the City Hall ceremony showed the couple standing outside on the steps and being showered with rice by lots of people. Irene quickly counted forty-three, plus the photographer. She could see Marcus's light-colored suit in the crowd.

The pictures that followed were from the lunch: happy people, toasting and laughing. The newly wedded couple beamed at each other and their guests. Irene noticed that there seemed to be an equal number of men and women in the pictures. There were no photos from the party that evening.

"We'll take a closer look at the albums at the station. And maybe you can start looking for Gunnarsson and Pahliss," she said.

The latter was directed at Hannu, who nodded.

"I THINK it's about time for me to meet Pappa Tosscander," said Irene.

She was standing leaning against the edge of Superintendent Andersson's desk. Jonny was sitting on the visitor's chair, sulking.

"I've talked with the old man. And I don't want to go through that gay porn myself." He made a face at the box that was standing by the inside of the door.

"You don't need to pore over the magazines. Just look through the videos," said Irene. She didn't want to admit even to herself that she felt uncomfortable about watching them. That's why she quickly said, "The possibility that Marcus returned to the city in the first week of March needs to be confirmed. Maybe he contacted his father. We have to ask him. Maybe he has forgotten or he doesn't want to remember."

"Has Hannu found those two guys from the album?" asked Superintendent Andersson.

"No, but he's still looking. And he will locate them," Irene said confidently.

"It's after five. It's almost time to leave," said Jonny.

The phone on Andersson's desk rang. He answered and then looked in Irene's direction.

"Just a second. She's here," he said. He handed over the receiver and hissed, "A Dane, asking for you."

Irene took the receiver. "This is Irene Huss."

"Jens Metz here. We've found Isabell Lind. Dead."

Irene couldn't utter a sound. Her colleagues watched in astonishment as she grew pale and tried to steady herself by grasping the edge of the desk.

"Hello! Are you still there?" Jens Metz's voice could be heard asking.

With great effort, Irene croaked, "I'm here."

"Good. She was found murdered at the Hotel Aurora. The top floor is closed to guests due to renovations. The painters found her in one of the rooms. There are signs that point to our mutual murder-mutilator."

To her own astonishment, Irene felt her knees begin to shake. She leaned heavily against the superintendent's desk and managed to rest her weight on the edge. It felt as if her legs wouldn't hold her.

"Is she . . . is she dismembered?" she finally managed to get out.

"No. None of the parts are missing. But the murder method bears our murderer's signature. She was strangled and abused, the same as Carmen Østergaard and the boy you found. The stomach was cut open but none of the contents were removed, according to Svend Blokk, who performed the autopsy."

"Oh my God!" was all Irene could say.

"We want you to come back to Copenhagen. You know more than we do about Isabell and the investigation in Göteborg. I would also like to ask a big favor."

"What?"

"That you notify the parents. It would be better than if we tried to convey this kind of message over the phone, and in Danish."

Irene knew that he was right but her stomach clenched. She didn't want to face Monika Lind's despair. But she had to.

"OK, I'll do it. But I have to talk to my boss about returning to Copenhagen."

Andersson's expression told her that he also had a good deal he wanted to talk about. The color of his face was ominous, and his expression was grim.

He exploded when she hung up the phone. "What the hell! Who's been dismembered?"

Irene had to go through the whole Isabell Lind story from the very beginning, starting with Monika's phone call. She went to get the tourist guide she had taken from the hotel room with the picture of the girls from Scandinavian Models.

Sven Andersson looked sternly at Irene. "And the only ones you showed the picture to were the three police officers you worked with on the murder-mutilation?"

For a hundredth of a second, Tom Tanaka's heavy image floated in front of her eyes but she decided to keep him out of this. Her instinct was to protect his identity.

"Yes," she said, looking Andersson in the eye.

The superintendent gazed at her for a long time. Maybe he sensed that she was hiding information.

"OK. You are going back to Copenhagen tomorrow. But you are taking Hannu with you."

"That's not possible," said Hannu.

"Geez. You don't have to stay the whole Whitsuntide," said Andersson.

"I'm getting married."

The others stared at him as though he had just revealed that he was the murderer. No one had anything to say.

Irene tried to get her act together. "Oh. I mean . . . congratulations."

"Thanks."

"Who the hell are you marrying?" said Andersson.

"Birgitta."

Of course. Irene's brain finally started working again. She had spied on Hannu and seen him get into Birgitta's car, had thought they might be dating, but in her wildest imagination she hadn't dreamed that it would go as far as marriage.

Andersson gasped for breath. After he managed to get some oxygen, he exclaimed, "Birgitta Moberg, here in the unit? Are you insane? A married couple can't work together in the same unit!"

Hannu met his boss's tirade calmly. "It will only be for about half a year. Then she will be on maternity leave a while and we'll have to think things over."

The silence was heavy. Irene sensed it was a good thing she was sitting.

Andersson's eyes looked like they were about to pop out of their sockets. She worried about his blood pressure, since she knew he didn't always take his medicine.

"Well. This is a pretty kettle of fish! My inspectors, going behind my back and keeping secrets from me. Irene is conducting her own investigations in Copenhagen, and Hannu and Birgitta are getting married—"

He paused before he continued, "Of course, that doesn't have any-thing to do with the job. But it still has to affect work when two inspec-tors are in a relationship. Not good at all!"

"Have you noticed any effect on my work or Birgitta's?" asked Hannu.

A certain sharpness could be sensed in his voice. Andersson took note of it and didn't answer. He just stared sourly in front of him. After a while he turned his chair around to face Jonny and said, "Well. And what kind of secret business do you have going on?"

Jonny looked very puzzled. "None. Not that I know of. None," he answered, stammering.

No, you don't have enough imagination Irene thought.

"Good. Then *you* can go with Irene to Copenhagen tomorrow morning. We can't let her loose on her own because then people start dying like flies!"

It was an immature and unfair comment, thought Irene. But she understood that he was really stressed.

"Actually, I can't go anywhere tomorrow either. As you may recall, I asked for the day off. We are going to Stockholm. My wife's niece is getting married on Whitsunday. A big wedding with a hundred guests and—"

"This is unbelievable!" Andersson began, but he stopped himself. He rummaged around, pulled out the calendar, and found Whitsuntide with his index finger. With a wrinkled brow, he looked at the date. Finally, he came to a decision, saying, "OK. You and Irene will go to Copenhagen on Whitmonday. On Tuesday morning you will offer to assist our Danish colleagues."

"But we were planning on coming home on Whitmon—"

"I don't give a shit about that! You can come home whenever you want! But on Tuesday morning you are going to be in Copenhagen!"

IRENE CALLED home to explain that she had to drive to Väners-borg. Jenny didn't ask what she was going to do there, just noted that her mother would be late, as usual.

The meeting with Monika Lind was just as traumatic as Irene had feared. Based on Irene's expression, Monika must have known that the news could not be good. Or maybe it was just the fact that Irene showed up in person that warned her something serious had happened.

Irene explained without going into detail. Realizing that her daughter had been murdered was terrible enough for Monika. In closing, Irene said, "The information we have at the moment is scanty. On Monday, I'm driving down with one of my colleagues to try and find out more."

Monika's husband was at home and helped Irene comfort her. Unfortunately, the five-year-old daughter was also at home. She watched, wide eyed, as her mother cried. Pretty soon she started crying as well, mostly because her mother was.

Irene contacted the parish priest. Her name was Eva Nesbo and her voice sounded young. Without hesitation she promised to come right away. The doorbell rang after fifteen minutes. Irene opened it and let in a blond woman in a pastor's shirt and Levi's. She apologized for her attire, but she had dropped what she was doing and come right away. Briefly, Irene brought the young minister up to speed on what had happened.

On the way home, Irene felt as if a large black hole was opening up inside her. She had vented her sorrow and despair indirectly. Yet even though no one would ever blame her for Isabell's death, she blamed herself. If she hadn't clumsily gone around Copenhagen looking for Isabell at the same time she was chasing a terrifying killer, Isabell would still be alive. How had the murderer found out about her private investigation? Only the three Danish police officers knew of it. The murderer must have felt threatened, and decided to give Irene a warning, and singled out an innocent victim with a connection to Irene.

Poor Isabell. What had the end of her life been like? Irene tortured herself with thoughts and images surrounding Isabell's murder. It was a sheer miracle that she managed to get home in one piece. During the drive she decided to tell the twins and Krister as much as she could. It would be in the newspapers very soon anyway.

Just after ten o'clock, Irene put her key into the lock of the door to her home. A heavenly smell of Jansson's Temptation hit her when she opened it. Sammie whirled toward her and welcomed her. The rest of her family was seated in the kitchen.

"Hi. It smells great," she said. Surprised, she noticed her hunger. She hadn't eaten since lunch. Then she saw the serious expression on the faces of Krister and the twins.

"We know what's happened," said Krister.

"Who has . . . ? How do you know?"

"Jonny Blom called and asked for you. You were going to fix a time to drive down to Copenhagen on Whitmonday. When I asked what you were going to do there, he said that you were going to assist in the investigation of the murder of Isabell Lind. Then I understood what you were doing in Vänersborg. You were speaking with Monika."

Irene couldn't keep her eyes from filling with tears; she had only the strength to nod. Krister took her in his arms. He held her close for a long time and Irene absorbed warmth and renewed energy. She freed herself in order to get a big piece of paper towel with which to dry her tears and blow her nose. Through the teary mist she saw her daughters' pale and resolute faces.

"I'm going to try and tell you exactly what's happened, but it's a long story," she said.

Chapter 9

YOU SHOULDN'T EAT JANSSON'S Temptation right before you go to bed, especially if you have problems that can affect your night's sleep. Irene lay awake and tried to digest her agonizing thoughts and that anchovies-in-cream-sauce dish until the early hours of the morning. When dawn broke, she fell into an uneasy slumber.

The alarm clock buzzed at six thirty on the dot. Irene felt as if she had spent the night in a clothes dryer. Her body was stiff, and she was reluctant to get up. There was only one sensible thing to do. She went down to the laundry room and put on her newly washed jogging suit, tying her jogging shoes on the way out.

An early-morning chill was still in the air, and the sky was covered by thin gray veil-like clouds, but they looked as though they would blow away during the day. She started at a pretty high speed in order to get her pulse rate up. As usual, she took the turn down toward Fiskebäck's small boat harbor and up along the back roads toward Långedrag. A short run of five kilometers would have to be enough. It was best not to be too late for the morning prayers since she was already in disfavor with the superintendent.

THE OTHERS were already seated when Irene steamed in. She mumbled something apologetically about the car not wanting to start. Since everyone knew Irene's almost-thirteen-year-old Saab, they didn't question her excuse.

"Now that everyone is here, we can start. Jonny is on vacation but he was briefed before he left. So it's just Tommy and Fredrik who haven't heard the big news."

Andersson paused for the sake of effect.

"Birgitta and Hannu are getting married tomorrow."

Fredrik and Tommy's faces clearly showed that it was news to them. Before they could gather their thoughts the superintendent continued,

"The Copenhageners have been in touch. A young Swedish prostitute has been found murdered, and apparently the murder bears the signature of the murder-mutilator, though she wasn't completely dismembered. In any case, Irene and Jonny are driving down to Copenhagen on Monday to get more information. Today, Hannu and Irene will continue to inquire into the names that have arisen during the investigation concerning Marcus Tosscander. We'll release his identity after the weekend."

Hannu asked permission to speak. "I've found Hans Pahliss and Anders Gunnarsson. They live in Alingsås."

"Try and get ahold of them. Fredrik and Birgitta, how is it going with the investigation into Robert Larsson?"

Fredrik still hadn't really recovered from the big news, but Birgitta gave an account of the results to date.

"He isn't trying to hide the money. Instead, he's trying to show it. That is to say, to launder the dirty money. We've had Wonder Bar under surveillance for three days. The number of customers has been noted and we have looked into what it costs to get into the club. If the entrance fees declared by Robert Larsson on his tax forms are correct, then an average of two hundred people visit the club every day. It can't possibly be that many. We make it an average of sixty-three. But we are going to keep an eye out for a few more days before we bring him in again."

"Speak with the prosecutor first," Andersson advised.

"We will."

"How is it going with Jack the Ripper?" Andersson asked and turned toward Tommy.

"Still no new information. Today I'm going to question his latest victim again. She was too upset when I spoke with her the first time. It doesn't feel right that we aren't getting any tips. There were long articles in both *GP* and the *Götesborgs Tidningen* the day before yesterday, but no one has called in. And soon it will be the weekend again."

"He only strikes on the weekends and downtown. Mostly around Vasagatan and its side streets," Andersson concluded.

"Does that provide any clues?" Irene asked.

Tommy nodded and shrugged his shoulders at the same time. This could be read as both a yes and a maybe.

Hannu and Irene went into Irene's office to continue planning.

"What do you think about my driving out to Pappa Tosscander's this morning while you contact Pahliss and Gunnarsson?" said Irene.

"Sounds good. Then we can speak with them this afternoon."

Irene called Emanuel Tosscander. He was still listed as "senior physician" in the phone book. According to Jonny he had been retired for a few years.

"Tosscander," a deep man's voice answered.

If Irene hadn't known about his previous profession, she would have guessed him to have been a high-ranking military officer.

"Good morning. My name is Irene Huss. I'm a police inspector—"

"I've already spoken with one policeman. Marcus is in Copenhagen. You'll have to look for him there."

The voice was ice-cold and dismissive.

"We have good reason to believe that Marcus has been the victim of a crime," Irene said calmly.

After a split second, the question came like a gunshot, "What kind of crime?"

"That's what I need to speak with you about. I'll be there in half an hour. Good-bye."

Before Tosscander had time to protest, Irene hung up the phone. She grabbed a cup of coffee on her way out for extra strength.

THE LARGE one-story brown brick house was located only a five-iron shot away from Hovås golf course. The whitebeam hedge around the house was several meters high, and only the flat roof of the house could be seen from the street. Irene turned in through the gap in the hedge and bumped onto the poorly maintained driveway. Both the house and the yard were characterized by slight decay.

The front door was opened before she had time to stretch her hand out and knock with the heavy bronze knocker shaped like a lion's head.

"Criminal Inspector Irene Huss." Irene held out her hand. Emanuel Tosscander responded with a short, firm handshake.

He was the same height as Irene. His body was slim and fit, his hair thick and silver-white. Marcus had inherited his beautiful eyes from his father. His face was deeply tanned and surprisingly wrinkle free. Emanuel Tosscander was a very handsome man.

"Senior phys—Emanuel Tosscander," he said. He stepped aside and halfheartedly gestured her inside.

The hall was gloomy, with a dark tile floor and moss green woven tapestry hangings. Irene followed Tosscander's straight back into an enormous living room. Large picture windows ran along the long side of the room. But no sunlight could squeeze through the heavy vegetation in the backyard. The entirety of the large room was filled with a dusky half-light. The furniture was big and heavy, made of dark wood and dark brown leather. There were large Oriental rugs in reddish brown tones on the floor. Not even the paintings on the walls could cheer up the room. They were sober landscapes and dim portraits. Not a single plant sat in the windows.

"Please sit down," Tosscander said mechanically. As for himself, he remained standing.

Irene sank down onto an uncomfortable rock-hard leather chair. "Thanks. I'd like it if you would sit down, too," said Irene.

At first he looked like he wanted to protest, but something in Irene's voice made him obey. He sat on the edge of the sofa and observed her coldly. But Irene could sense some concern behind his frosty demeanor.

It was just as well to inform him of what had happened to Marcus since it would be in the papers in a few days anyway. Irene got right to the point. "It was good of you to see me. I have something serious to tell you. First, I need an answer to a question. Did Marcus contact you during the first week of March?"

"No."

"Are you absolutely certain?"

"Yes."

"When was the last time you spoke with each other?"

"That's none of your business!"

"Yes, it is. We're investigating a crime."

"What kind of crime?"

"Murder."

Irene looked him straight in the eye. He was the first to glance away. He stared at his overgrown yard for a long time, then he turned toward her. "We haven't spoken with each other since the first week of December."

"Why not?"

"We . . . had a fight."

"Why?"

"That's really none of your business!"

"Again, I'll have to remind you that we are investigating a murder."

"Of whom?"

"My condolences, but it has to do with Marcus."

Slowly, all color disappeared from the handsome face. The even sunburn took on a sick yellowish tone. Right in front of Irene's eyes, Emanuel Tosscander aged ten years in as many seconds. He sank backward onto the sofa without taking his eyes off her. Finally, he was able to whisper, "It . . . can't . . . be true."

"Unfortunately, it is. Marcus had a very unusual tattoo made in Copenhagen. The body we found a few weeks ago outside Killevik had the same tattoo. There are also other things that add up."

"No! Not murdered and dismembered!"

Anguish could be heard in his voice and seen in his eyes. He slowly rose from the sofa. In an almost normal tone of voice, he asked, "Will Marcus's name be published in the press?"

"Yes. We have to do so in order to find possible witnesses."

"My name . . . ! What are people out here going to say? You must understand. I forbid you to publish his name in the newspapers!"

He got to his feet upset and pointed an accusing finger at Irene. She was getting angry. Sharply she said, "Sit."

The command word usually worked on Sammie and it also did on the surprised Tosscander.

"Marcus probably came home to Göteborg during the first week in March. That's when he met his killer. A killer who we have good reason to believe has murdered before. There is a significant risk that he will continue. That's why we must find him. You should also be anxious to catch your son's murderer."

Tosscander looked as though he had just been boxed on the ear.

"Why were you not getting along?" Irene repeated.

He didn't answer.

"My guess would be that he told you he was gay. Is that what happened?"

The jaundiced look of Tosscander's face gave way to a blush that spread up from his throat.

"That's not true! It was just a passing fixation. I don't know how many girlfriends he brought home over the years! He isn't gay!"

"How many girlfriends has he brought home over the years?"

"What business . . . I don't know."

"Try and count."

Tosscander glared at Irene but looked like he was thinking. Finally he said, "Four or five."

"Four or five girlfriends in thirty years. Can you give me their names?"

"No. Just one. The others I only met once or twice. Angelica Sandberg was a kid from the neighborhood with whom he was together for several years."

"When was that?"

"Well . . . it was probably about ten years ago. She's married now. Lives in the States."

"But her parents still live here?"

"Yes."

Irene wrote the name in her notebook. There were reasons for trying to get in touch with Angelica.

"He never brought any male friends here?"

Tosscander stiffened. Guardedly he said, "No. Not the last few years. When he was younger he did, of course . . . but not since he moved away from home."

"Was he always alone when he came to visit?"

"Yes."

"He never spoke with you about a male friend?"

"No."

"No name ever came up?"

"No."

Tosscander sat crumpled on the sofa as if he had given up the battle. It seemed as though the truth had begun to sink in.

"Mr. Tosscander, I need to ask a few routine questions. Is that all right?"

He nodded weakly.

"How old are you?"

"Sixty-nine."

Irene would never have guessed. He looked considerably younger.

"Where were you senior physician before you retired?"

"I was an ear, nose, and throat specialist at Sahlgren Hospital."

That kind of a specialist couldn't be all that familiar with autopsy methods, thought Irene.

"Does Marcus have any siblings or half siblings?"

"No."

"I understand that your wife died . . ."

"Ten years ago. Breast cancer."

Suddenly, he stood up and looked sharply at Irene. "Now I'm glad that she's dead so she doesn't have to experience this . . . disgrace!"

That's how he felt about his only son's death. It was a disgrace to him.

THE VISIT to Emanuel Tosscander depressed Irene. Since Hovås wasn't that far from Fiskebäck, she decided to drive home for lunch.

It was strange to come home in the middle of the day to an empty house. The mailbox was overflowing with advertisements. She almost threw out a card along with them, but just before she dropped the whole pile into the paper recycling bag she saw a glimpse of it inside a double-folded advertisement for Hemglass ice cream. Curious, she took a closer look at the colorful card. It was a picture of the familiar view of Copenhagen with the Little Mermaid in the foreground and glittering water behind. The message itself as well as Irene's name and address, was written with a black India ink pen. The street and postal code were perfectly correct.

The Little Mermaid is dead.

That's all it said. The card had been postmarked in Copenhagen two days earlier. Irene quickly dropped the card onto the table. Normal mail handling had probably resulted in a lot of fingerprints on the card but there could still be something useful left.

What did it mean? Was it a warning or a threat? Who had sent it? The answer had to be Isabell's killer. No one else would send that message.

But why? Several police officers were working on the case, both here and in Copenhagen. Why had the murderer chosen her?

She got an envelope and carefully placed the card inside.

A thought struck her. The message was in English. Maybe it was from Tom Tanaka, who was trying to contact her. The idea seemed rather far-fetched but she decided to pursue it anyway. Yet when she took a closer look at the handwriting, it didn't have any resemblance to Tom's elegant script in the message she had received at the Hotel Alex. The style on the postcard was heavy block letters. Still, she would leave the card with the technicians at the police station, together with the earlier message from Tom. She had saved it.

She took out her cell phone and found Tom's number. He answered almost immediately.

"Hi, Tom. This is Irene Huss."

"Hi. I suppose you are calling because of Isabell."

"Yes. But first I need to ask you a question. Did you send me a post-card?"

"Absolutely not. I never send postcards."

"That's what I thought, but I had to check. I've received a postcard from Copenhagen with—"

She had to stop herself for a moment and think about the word for mermaid in English, but in that moment she remembered that it was written on the postcard.

"A photo of the Little Mermaid. On the back it says, 'The Little Mermaid is dead.' Nothing more. I don't know how I should interpret the card."

Tom was quiet for a long time. She could hear his heavy breathing. Finally, he said, "It's a warning. The murderer knows exactly where you are. The murder of Isabell Lind is also a warning to you. I told you that when she disappeared."

"Do the police know that you called your contact at the Hotel Aurora and asked about Isabell?"

"No. He came here when her body was found and was completely hysterical. I managed to calm him down. We were lucky because a girl had called the hotel and asked about Isabell just after my call. The police only know that one of the girls at the escort service called because Isabell didn't come back after her job at the hotel. That's why the police think my contact's questioning the hotel staff resulted from the call by the girl at Scandinavian Models."

"I think it's important that the police in Copenhagen not know about you and Marcus. I haven't revealed your identity to my Swedish colleagues."

"Good."

"No one seems to have realized how . . . close you were, you and Marcus."

"No. We were very discreet. For different reasons. Marcus didn't want the policeman he was living with to know about our relationship."

"And you haven't told anyone about the two of you?"

"No. Just you."

"I'm coming down to Copenhagen on Monday night and have booked a room at Hotel Alex again. Unfortunately, I'm going to have a colleague with me. A male colleague. It means that I can't move around as freely."

"I understand. We'll be in touch."

"Yes. Good-bye."

"Be careful. Good-bye."

Irene had a vague feeling of concern after the phone call. Was Tom in danger too? She couldn't rule out the possibility.

POLICE TECHNICIAN Svante Malm took both the cards and promised to do a graphological comparison and look for fingerprints as soon as possible.

Hannu was sitting in his office waiting for her. Irene told him about the postcard. He reflected, then said, "Are you really going to go to Copenhagen?"

"You mean it could be dangerous?"

"Maybe."

"He knows my address, and he can easily get to me here! And as far as we know, the murderer could just as well be in Göteborg as Copenhagen." She took a deep breath and then said with conviction, "I have to catch him."

Hannu nodded. He knew Irene well enough to realize that this killer had good reason to feel hunted.

"What have you found on Pahliss and Gunnarsson?" she asked.

"Hans Pahliss is a doctor. Researcher. Virologist. He is in France right now at a conference. I reached Anders Gunnarsson. Dentist. He's willing to see us. He has a private practice by Vasaplatsen. On Fridays he finishes early. He could meet us around three o'clock."

"Perfect. Then we'll have time for coffee before we go."

* * *

RUSH-HOUR traffic was already heavy. The flex-time system meant that the bells of freedom starting ringing around lunchtime on Friday for lots of people.

Irene managed to find a free parking space on Storgatan. "This should be a good omen. I need one, especially when I consider how crazy this investigation has been," she sighed.

They found the entrance to Anders Gunnarsson's office without any problems. He shared the space with two colleagues. According to the shiny brass sign, they were Rut and Henry Raadmo, probably a married couple.

Irene called on the house phone. Almost instantly a scratchy male voice came over the speaker. "Who are you looking for?"

"Dentist Anders Gunnarsson. We have an appointment at three o'clock," said Hannu.

"Welcome. Second floor."

The entry lock buzzed and Hannu opened the heavy door. A broad, short flight of red marble steps led up to the stairway. Those who were brave could step into the rickety elevator, which dated back to the early years of the twentieth century. Since Irene and Hannu didn't want to risk getting stuck for the rest of the afternoon, they took the stairs.

Anders Gunnarsson had opened the door to his office and stood there, waiting to greet them. Irene recognized him from the wedding photographs as the tall blond one of the couple. His hair was a bit longer than it had been in the pictures. He stretched out his hand in greeting and smiled a bright white smile. His handshake was dry and firm. Then he showed them inside.

They entered a sober waiting room whose color scheme was light gray and old-fashioned rose. At once Irene suspected that Marcus Tosscander had helped decorate the room. When they came into the employee's lounge her suspicion was confirmed. There was a small kitchen area done in steel and black, with a floor of polished cherry-wood and a dining set in the same style as Tanaka's. Everything looked clean and fresh. The whole office appeared to be newly renovated.

"Please sit down and I'll put on some coffee. We're all alone in the office. Everyone else goes home around two o'clock on Fridays," said Gunnarsson.

Irene and Hannu sat in the creaking leather chairs. They still smelled new.

Gunnarsson was in the process of measuring the coffee when he stopped and looked at Hannu. "Why did you want to speak with me?" he asked.

"Marcus Tosscander," Hannu said shortly.

"Has something happened to him?"

Concern was evident in the dentist's voice. His blue eyes glided between Irene and Hannu. It was Irene who answered. "We have reason to suspect so."

A deep sigh escaped Gunnarsson. "Hans and I were speaking about him last week. We thought it was odd that he hadn't been in touch. We actually joked that he had decided to stay there in Thailand."

"Thailand? He was in Copenhagen. . . ."

"Of course. But he called me and said that he was just home for a quick visit in order to pack some summer clothes in a suitcase. He had suddenly been invited to go on a trip to Thailand. Apparently, one of his cameras was broken so he wondered if we could lend him one. But when he found out that it was at home in Alingsås he lost interest. He said that he wouldn't have time to come all the way to our place that evening. I advised him to buy a cheap one in the duty-free shop."

Irene felt her heart skip a beat. Finally, a bit of a scent out of all the false leads!

"When did he call you?"

Gunnarsson wrinkled his brow and thought about it. Finally he said decidedly, "It had to have been at the beginning of March. Right at the beginning. We spoke about the renovation here. It was almost complete."

"Did Marcus design the office?" Irene asked even though she already knew the answer.

"Yes. You have no idea how much it needed freshening up."

He stopped abruptly and looked sharply at Irene. "What has happened to Marcus?"

Evasively, Irene said, "We aren't entirely sure. After this talk with you we hope that additional pieces will fall into place."

Hannu broke into the conversation. "How did you know Marcus?"

"We have been friends for several years."

"How long?"

Gunnarsson thought for a moment before he answered. "Six years."

"Good friends?"

Gunnarsson smiled. "It started with a short relationship between the two of us. An intense week, but I realized that it wasn't possible to have a relationship with Marcus. He is very . . . flighty. I wanted something more stable and understood that Marcus wasn't the man for me. Shortly thereafter I met Hans and we are still together."

"But you kept in touch with Marcus," Hannu prompted.

"Of course! We get together often and we have many of the same friends. He is an amazingly kind and pleasant person. The best friend you could have—" Gunnarsson interrupted himself and seemed to be searching for words to explain what he meant. Uncertainly, he said, "Marcus is a warm-hearted person. He is charming and thoughtful. But when it comes to relationships, he is . . . artificial. He can't be faithful and quickly gets turned on by new guys. The longest relationship he's had was with Hassan, an Egyptian who was a guest researcher at the university here in Göteborg. I think it lasted for three months and that's an absolute record for Marcus."

"Was that a long time ago?"

"Four years. I remember because they were at our engagement party."

"Hans isn't bothered by the fact that you and Marcus were together?"

Anders Gunnarsson gave Hannu an appreciative look and smiled. "When you have entered into a partnership, as Hans and I have, naturally you have to discuss how you both feel about infidelity. Fidelity is important to Hans and to me. Hans has never been jealous of Marcus since our relationship ended before Hans and I got together."

Irene asked, "Who was Marcus's partner before he moved to Copenhagen?"

She got a shrug of the shoulders in response.

"No idea. We last met at the Glögg party that he held on the Eve of St. Lucia, before he moved. That was the last time we saw each other. I don't know if he was 'with' anyone."

"You didn't think any of the people present might have been his partner?"

"No. It could have been anyone or no one. When it comes to Marcus, nothing is obvious. And he has actually gotten into trouble before."

"What do you mean? How so?"

Gunnarson searched for the right words. "He is drawn to the . . . dangerous ones. And puts himself in danger. That Hassan was an example. A pretty nasty type who definitely leaned in the direction of sadism. Marcus came over to my place one time wearing a turtleneck sweater when it was twenty degrees* outside! He is always so fashion savvy that I asked why he was walking around in a turtleneck. In response, he pulled down the collar and showed deep marks from a rope on his throat. Somehow he . . . managed to joke about it."

"Is Hassan still in Sweden?"

"No. He's dead. He was killed by a lunatic at a gay club in San Francisco two years ago. Nine people died and Hassan happened to be one of them."

"I remember that. The killer was a prostitute. He had been subjected to things at the club that made him crazy for revenge," said Irene.

Gunnarsson arched his eyebrows and nodded. "That's right. That's the kind of club Hassan hung out at and that says everything about him."

"And about Marcus," Hannu added.

"He didn't frequent those types of clubs but he was drawn to that type of man. I think that describes it as exactly as possible."

In her mind, Irene saw the contours of a colossal sumo wrestler. Odd, maybe dangerous.

The dentist took a deep breath and stared at Irene. "Now you have to tell me what has happened to Marcus!"

Irene nodded. "Yes. But first I need to ask one last question. Do you have Marcus's address in Copenhagen?"

"No. He said that he would call when he had decided on where he was going to live."

"But he never called and gave you his new address?"

"No."

"It seems strange that you didn't wonder why he hadn't been in

---

* Twenty degrees Celsius is equivalent to sixty-eight degrees Fahrenheit.

touch. And why didn't you miss Marcus before now if he'd left for Thailand at the beginning of March? That's two and a half months ago."

"As I said, we started wondering a few weeks ago. But that's the way it is with Marcus. Long periods of time can go by without hearing anything from him. Especially when he is working intensely or has a new relationship going on. It's happened several times. He's disappeared with some new love and then appeared later as though nothing has happened."

"How long have these episodes lasted?"

"Anywhere from two days to two weeks."

"But never as long as over two months."

"No. But when he called at the beginning of March he said that he didn't know how long they would be gone."

"They? Who did he go with?"

"He didn't want to say. He just laughed when I asked and said I would never be able to guess."

"Never be able to guess. . . . That would mean that you know this person."

"Maybe. But I have no idea."

"Exactly what did Marcus say when he called at the beginning of March?"

"We started by talking about the renovation and about how it had progressed. I invited him for dinner the next night but he declined. He was going to go to Thailand with a friend, but he didn't say who the friend was. Then he asked about borrowing a camera. Then he said that he had to end the phone call and pack the things he needed for the trip."

"Did he say where they were traveling from?"

"No. But I assumed that it had to be Landvetter since he was here in Göteborg. But maybe he was only here because he had to pack his summer clothes."

"Could he have been traveling with a woman?"

"When he was younger he went about with girls . . . to keep up appearances for his parents. He told me about that. And personally I've seen how women are drawn to him. But he stopped that in the last few years. He doesn't need women as his alibi any longer."

"Did he have sex with women?"

Gunnarsson shook his head. "No. Never. He is gay through and through. Those are his own words."

Irene decided that it was time to tell Anders Gunnarsson the truth. She started by asking, "Did Marcus talk about a tattoo he had done in Copenhagen?"

"No."

The dentist shook his head but then stopped suddenly. "Actually . . . maybe. I asked how things were going for him in Copenhagen. Then he said he had something that would show what an indelible impression the city had left on him. Then he laughed mysteriously. Indelible could refer to a tattoo."

"We happen to know that Marcus had a unique tattoo done in Copenhagen . . ." Irene explained about the dragon tattoo and the murder-mutilation victim in Killevik. Anders Gunnarsson burst into tears. His sorrow seemed deep and real. Neither Irene nor Hannu knew how to comfort him, so they let him finish crying. His sobs began to diminish after a while. He got up and went to get a Kleenex and dried his eyes. With bent head and closed eyes he took deep breaths. When he had calmed himself, Irene said, "I understand that this must be a terrible shock for you."

Gunnarsson nodded. His eyes, shiny with tears, reflected sincere grief and pain.

"When is Hans getting back from France?"

"On Thursday, the twenty-seventh."

"Is he in Paris?"

"Yes."

"Could you be so kind as to inform him that he should come to the station on Friday? He can call and ask for an appointment with me or Hannu Rauhala."

They rose and thanked him for the coffee and the information. Gunnarsson followed them to the outer door. When he shook hands Irene felt his hand trembling faintly, which hadn't been the case when they had greeted each other. Impulsively, she took his hand in both of hers and said, "Will you be OK? Do you want us to call someone or drive you somewhere?"

Gunnarsson shook his head. "No, thank you. It's very kind . . . no, thank you."

Irene pulled a calling card from her pocket. "Call my home number if you come up with anything else that could be important. I'll be there all weekend."

Gunnarsson took the card and stuffed it into his shirt pocket without looking at it.

On their way back to the station, Hannu asked Irene, "Could it be a sex game that got out of control?"

"It's not impossible. But why dismember and clean him out? And take away certain muscles? It seems very . . . well planned."

"Well planned?"

"Yes. A suitable place must have been chosen in advance to enable the murderer to do all that he did to the body. So he must have decided to kill his victim beforehand."

When Hannu agreed, Irene felt an ice-cold chill. That was what was so terrible. Carmen Østergaard, Marcus Tosscander, and Isabell Lind had never had a chance. The murderer had already decided. Beforehand.

Chapter 10

FOR ONCE KRISTER DIDN'T have to work over the weekend. Irene's mother and her significant other, Sture, were invited for dinner on Whitsunday in order to give a full account of their wine trip to the Moselle Valley. Krister was looking forward to it with eager expectation because, naturally, he was hoping for some really exciting samples from the wine district.

Mamma Gerd radiantly handed over two bottles to her son-in-law. Irene saw an expression of disappointment pass over his face but he quickly regained his composure. He warmly thanked his mother-in-law and gave her a big hug. Then he turned the bottles so that Irene could read the labels: Ockfener Scharzberg. Even she knew the brand was available at the state liquor store. But little Mamma didn't know that. She rarely went there since she hardly drank any alcohol.

Sture wasn't very familiar with wines, either which Irene realized when he smiled and said, "Gerd and I made a find. We bought a whole case of these bottles in a grocery store for twenty-five D-marks. Amazingly cheap!"

"But didn't you drive around to different wineries? To do wine tastings and so on . . . ?"

"Of course, but those wines were so expensive," chirped Mamma Gerd.

Irene pretended not to notice her husband's low moan.

There were seven of them for dinner since Katarina had invited Micke to join them. He, too, was still feeling the effects of the accident so they had chosen to join the quiet family dinner at home instead of going to a big party with friends. Perhaps they just wanted to spend some time alone. Irene's watchful eye noted their warm looks and stolen touches. It really seemed to be serious. They had been together for almost two months, a new record for Katarina.

Jenny was going out later that night. Her band was playing at a newly opened club with her as the lead singer! Irene's daughter was in seventh heaven and seemed to be somewhere else. Out of pure distraction she almost put a piece of steak on her plate. At the last second she realized what she was about to do—meat!—and quickly put it back on the serving dish.

Krister had put together a wonderful menu for Pentecost. It was perhaps a bit too heavy for Whitsuntide, but Irene and Katarina had been allowed to request their favorite dishes. As an appetizer, they had crab Thermidor, crabmeat baked in a wonderfully spicy wine sauce, served in the shells.

Jenny ate pale celery sticks that she dipped in spicy tomato salsa.

Without revealing what he really thought, Krister served the wine his mother-in-law had brought, along with the first course.

The steak was sliced and covered in dark gravy. Cooked cauliflower, asparagus, lightly steamed sugar peas, peeled tomatoes, and Hasselback potatoes were the main course.

Krister had chosen Clos Malvern to go with the main course and, according to him, the wine had a heavy bouquet, a strong burned and smoky taste, and hints of both chocolate and sun-drenched berries. The hot sun and winds of South Africa had left their mark on this strong dark red wine.

"The wines are so full bodied and flavorful because they fertilize the wineries with elephant dung," Krister announced with the utmost seriousness.

His mother-in-law and Sture opened their eyes wide and said to each other, "Really! Just imagine!"

But Irene knew her husband well and shook her finger at him. He arched his eyebrows innocently and toasted his wife.

IRENE HAD taken the bus into the city. They were on a holiday schedule since it was Whitmonday. She hadn't thought about that when she and Jonny had made their appointment, and now she was almost twenty minutes late.

Jonny was standing outside the police station, huddled against the bitter wind. Based on the sour expression on his face, he had been standing and waiting for quite some time.

"Hi. Sorry, but the buses . . ."

"You knew that it was a holiday. Women and time!"

Sour was Mr. Blom's first name today, thought Irene. Obviously he was annoyed about having to come home from Stockholm a day earlier than planned and she was the one who was going to suffer because of it. Then again, though she had arrived late, at least she had apologized. If only she had been allowed to go to Copenhagen on her own.

"We should try and get there by eight at the latest, in time for a late dinner and a big *bier*," she said briskly.

"*Bier?*"

"Beer. A big Danish beer."

"Oh."

That was their entire conversation as they drove the length of Halland's coast. Since Irene was acquainted with Jonny's driving, she had insisted on getting behind the wheel of the bureau car. For the most part, Jonny sat dozing with his head hanging. He didn't wake up until they had driven onto HH-Ferries in Helsingborg. But he was first in line at the cafeteria. A large draft beer, and bread with a chunk of coarsely ground liver pâté with pickles, made him thaw out considerably. Irene went for the coffee and a plate of shrimp. She wasn't able to finish the slice of bread under it.

They were sitting in the car again after twenty minutes, and then it was time for Irene to drive across the clattering ramp with the same chilly feeling in her stomach as before.

Since she was familiar with the route, they made their way pretty quickly to the highway heading toward Copenhagen.

"Could you go through everything you know about Isabell Lind one more time? It would be good if you could refresh my recollection," said Jonny.

Irene went over everything she knew. But she didn't mention Tom Tanaka.

"I don't know much about the murder itself yet. We'll find out more tomorrow. But Metz said that the murder of Isabell bears the signature of our murderer even though she wasn't dismembered. That seems strange," said Irene.

Jonny nodded. Then he quickly changed the subject. "What is the hotel like?"

"It's really nice. I booked the rooms via the Internet. It's the same hotel I stayed in a few days ago. The breakfast is amazing."

"Are there some nice hangouts in the area?"

"It depends on what you mean by nice hangouts. The hotel is centrally located and everything is close by. It's just a matter of choosing."

Jonny nodded in response. Irene noticed that he started paying more attention to the areas they were passing through the closer to Copenhagen they came.

THEY EACH had a single room. To Irene's silent joy they were not located on the same floor. She took the second-floor room and Jonny, the room on the third. Thanks to this, she would have much more freedom to move around. She suspected that Jonny had similar thoughts, but for entirely different reasons.

They agreed to meet downstairs in fifteen minutes. Even though Irene wasn't particularly hungry after the pile of shrimp she'd had on the ferry, she realized that it was about time for dinner. If she ate too late, she would have a hard time sleeping.

The room was just as nice and fresh as the one she had had last time. She washed under her arms, put on a few strokes of deodorant, and touched up her makeup. She told her reflection that it wasn't for Jonny's sake but for her own.

In a cosmopolitan fashion Irene led Jonny over broad H. C. Andersen Boulevard. Restaurant Vesuvius looked warm and welcoming. The heat of the pub and the smell of cigarette smoke hit them when they stepped through the glass doors. They were shown to a little table by the window.

"Shit. The menu is in a different language," Jonny muttered.

"No. It's in Italian, Danish, and English," said Irene.

"Hell, that's exactly what I'm saying."

He ordered a calzone, "so you know what you're getting." Irene ordered *passera mira mare*, which turned out to be fried red snapper with mussels in a white wine sauce. Jonny needed two strong beers in order to wash down his pizza while Irene was content with one Hof. Tomorrow was another day.

When they got back to the hotel, the bar was overflowing. A big group of Swedes filled the room, making noise. There was a sign on the wall announcing that it was a "Jell-O shot evening." The guests were trying the gelatin drinks with a great deal of enjoyment and enthusiasm and, based on the rate of consumption, the Jell-O shot was definitely approved. A man sitting on a bar stool had fallen asleep with his head and arms on the bar. No one was paying any attention to him, and the noise gradually increased with the rate of consumption.

"That looks like fun," said Jonny.

Irene continued toward the reception desk. When she had gotten her room key from the smiling receptionist, she turned toward Jonny and said, "We're supposed to be at Vesterbro at eight o'clock. I'm planning on eating breakfast at seven-fifteen. Should I call your room before—"

She stopped when she saw Jonny's back disappear into the crowded bar.

In the room she took out her cell phone and dialed Tom Tanaka's number. He answered immediately.

"Tom."

"Hi. Irene here. I'm at my hotel now. The Hotel Alex."

"The same as last time," Tom noted.

"Yes. Has anything happened?"

"No. The newspapers haven't printed any details about Isabell's murder, just that she had been strangled and bound to the bed with handcuffs."

The handcuffs were news to Irene but she didn't admit it to Tom. Instead, she said, "Did Marcus tell you that he was going to go to Thailand with a . . . friend? Or did he just say that he was going home to Göteborg?"

Tom sounded harsh when he finally replied, "He didn't say anything about Thailand. Just that he was going home."

"Not a word about Thailand?"

"No. Who's said something about Thailand?"

"He called an old friend when he got home to Göteborg at the beginning of March. Marcus told him that he was on his way to Thailand with a friend."

"Apparently our dear Marcus had quite a few friends whom he didn't talk about."

Irene could hear deep bitterness in Tom's tone. "Unfortunately, yes," she replied.

Irene dreaded having to ask the next question but she was forced to. "Tom . . . this friend in Göteborg whom we spoke with implied that Marcus liked . . . *hard* sex."

She didn't know if her meaning was clear in English, but it was the only thing she could come up with. Tom seemed to understand. "I don't have the slightest intention of telling you about my sex life with Marcus. But of course . . . he was keen on some variations."

"Even . . . dangerous variations?"

"Not so that he would get seriously injured. Not like that. Maybe a little . . . spanking."

Irene didn't understand the word "spank," but based on the almost amused tone Tom used, she drew the conclusion that it had to do with a softer type of force. For fun.

"I'm sorry to have to ask these questions, but we need to try and find out what happened to Marcus."

"It's OK. I still want his murderer to be caught and punished. It's unfortunate that you don't have the death penalty in Scandinavia."

Irene trembled uncontrollably. Dear Tom still had a dark side. She hadn't realized it at the beginning of their acquaintance, but she was starting to understand that Tom had hidden depths he wasn't about to reveal to her. And why should he? Thanks to him, they had been able to determine the identity of the dismembered body in Killevik and that was the important thing.

A thought started growing in Irene's head. Maybe Tom could bring them closer to Marcus's killer. She asked, "Tom . . . since you know Copenhagen . . . do you know if there is a place for necrosadists?"

"Necrosad . . . !"

He was surprised by the question. But after thinking a bit he said, "There are several places for sadomasochists. But necrophiles! No. But . . ."

He stopped to think again. "There are videos that show necrophilia and some illegal films that show actual murders. But, of course, if someone wants them, they can get them."

"Did Marcus ever show any interest—"

"In necrophilia? Absolutely not! He was so alive and absolutely not interested in death!"

"Thanks for letting me ask these questions," she said.

"No problem."

They wished each other good night and hung up.

She sat for a long time thinking in the growing darkness of the room. Somewhere there had to be a connection between the three murder victims. A common variable. The police officer? The doctor? Or both?

Sex. All three of them were particularly sexually active. Carmen Østergaard had been in the business quite a while and Isabell was new to prostitution. But both of them had worked with sex professionally.

Anders Gunnarsson had said that Marcus was always ready for sex and that he was drawn to *dangerous types*. Did he do it for money? Hardly, especially as he made a very good living from his work. Money wasn't his problem. Did he buy sex? Not very likely either. With his looks he wouldn't have needed to pay.

No matter how she twisted and turned, she couldn't find a logical connection between the three victims. She gazed out through the mullioned windows. The lights of the big city were hard and artificial. The shadows between the sources of light were deep and black. Perfect for a killer.

IRENE FELT well rested after eight hours of deep sleep. She called Jonny's room at a quarter past seven, and after ten rings she heard the receiver picked up. Then, with a crash, it fell to the floor and she could hear Jonny's muffled "Damn it!" He finally managed to get the receiver to his ear.

"Jonny . . . Jonny Blom," a cracked voice bleated.

"Time for breakfast," Irene chirped.

"Breakfas . . . God damn—"

The receiver on the other end of the line was slammed down, and Irene felt both anger and dejection. Having to drag Jonny around Copenhagen was like having a ball and chain around her ankle. A hungover Jonny was a catastrophe. There were some good moments when he was sober, and he could even be useful. But if he felt half as bad as he had sounded on the phone, he was going to be worthless.

Irene went down and ate a delicious breakfast. She took her time. The sun outside was already shining brightly, and it looked like it was going to be a beautiful day.

Jonny never showed up in the breakfast room.

Back upstairs she changed into a short-sleeved light blue linen shirt. She kept the dark blue pants on but put on her black loafers. She took off her socks as a gesture to the summery feeling she had. She decided that the dark blue linen blazer would have to do as a coat. With her big canvas bag nonchalantly hanging over her shoulder, she looked more like a tourist on a shopping spree than a cop on the trail of a killer.

She called Jonny before she left the room, and after several rings he managed to answer the phone. Irene could only hear a guttural mumble, and then the receiver hit the cradle again.

With a sigh, Irene decided to let him sleep.

SHE WALKED down to the Vesterbro police station. It hadn't even been a week since she was here last, but it felt like an entire year had passed. Maybe it was the change in the weather that gave her this feeling. Last week she had been cold and had shivered, and now she was enjoying the warm wind's promise of summer.

Beate Bentsen, Peter Møller, and Jens Metz were already sitting in Bentsen's office. The air was thick with smoke. Irene hesitated on the threshold before she stepped into the room. Møller seemed to sense why. He opened the window. Whether the air outside was any cleaner was debatable but at least it diluted the nicotine concentration in the room.

Everyone greeted her warmly and welcomed her back, even if the reason for her return might have been more pleasant.

"Weren't there supposed to be two of you?" Beate Bentsen asked.

Irene had hoped to avoid that particular question but realized that was wishful thinking. "Yes . . . but my colleague wasn't feeling well this morning. I thought it would be best if he could sleep."

"Does he need a doctor?"

"No. It will pass on its own. Eventually."

"A hangover," Jens Metz whispered theatrically.

He winked meaningfully at Irene. She was ashamed of Jonny's behavior. Personally, he wouldn't have the good sense to be ashamed, she thought, and her irritation grew.

"We'll start without your colleague and you'll have to try and bring him up to speed when he gets here. Both Jens and Peter were present at the Hotel Aurora when Isabell Lind was found."

Beate Bentsen looked at the two inspectors over the rims of her French designer glasses.

Jens Metz leaned back in his chair and linked his sausage-like fingers over his belly. The backrest protested nervously but Metz didn't seem to hear it. Or maybe he was used to chairs whining under his weight.

"We got the call on Thursday afternoon, May 20, that a dead woman had been found at the Hotel Aurora by some painters. Peter and I got there shortly after four thirty. The medical examiner had already arrived and was inspecting the corpse. Here you can see the pictures of what we were faced with."

Metz bent forward, breathing heavily, and shook some photos out of a thick envelope.

Irene started with a picture of the room. It was taken from a high angle. The photographer must have been standing on a tall stool or a ladder.

Under the bare window, an overturned nightstand lay on the floor next to a lamp with a broken plastic shade. A bed could be seen in the rear next to the wall. Another bed had been placed in the center of the room. Isabell was lying on top of it.

Irene took out another photo. It was an enlargement of the bed with Isabell's body spread out on top.

Her hands were chained with handcuffs to the high wooden bed-posts. She was lying on her back, completely naked, with her legs spread apart. There was a deep incision from the top of her collar-bone all the way down to her pelvic bone. Mechanically, Irene noticed that the incision hadn't bled very much. There was, however, a good deal of blood under her, from her waist down to her separated legs.

Irene switched to the next photo, which was a close-up of the head and neck area. Strangulation marks from a noose were evident on her throat. Isabell's eyes were wide open, and her tongue hung out of her mouth, dark and swollen.

Irene was completely unprepared for her reaction. She was barely able to make it to her knees by the wastepaper basket before she threw up. The entirety of the delicious Danish breakfast came up.

When she was done, she got up on shaky legs and stammered, "Excuse me . . . I'll go and wash the basket . . . but this girl was a friend of my daughters' for many years . . . lived next door . . . and stayed over and ate with us. . . ."

"We understand. It's difficult when you know the victim," Bentsen said soothingly.

Irene quickly grabbed the basket and slipped down the corridor. She knew where the bathroom was.

She cleaned the basket and blessed the fact that it was made of plastic. Woven rattan would have been worse. She bathed her face with ice-cold water and washed her mouth clean. Then she saw her pale face in the mirror and mumbled half inaudibly to her reflection, "It's not just the fact that I knew you. It's my fault that you died. I led the murderer to you. Oh, Bell!"

Her throat felt thick with suppressed sobs, but there wasn't time for sorrow right now. For Bell's sake she was forced to try to be professional and objective. And what would the Danes think? One Swedish police officer is lying in bed at the hotel with a hangover, and the other pukes when she sees pictures from the murder scene.

Her Danish colleagues were sitting in the same places, waiting for her arrival, each with a fresh cigarette. The smoke made her feel ill again, but she braced herself.

"I'm sorry. It's OK now," Irene said and sat down.

She didn't pick up the close-up of Bell again, but turned to Jens Metz instead and asked, "What did the medical examiner say?"

"She had been dead more than twelve hours but less than twenty when she was found. He thought that fifteen to seventeen hours was a good guess. It matches the time she disappeared. She was strangled first. That's the cause of death."

"So she was dead when the trauma to her abdomen was inflicted?"

"Yes."

Thank God, thought Irene.

Metz picked up the enlargement of the photo of Isabell on the bed. He said, "The medical examiner thinks that she was chained with the handcuffs first. There are marks on the wrists that indicate she struggled to get free. Then she was strangled. As soon as she was dead, the murderer started striking her pubic bone with a heavy object. The bone was completely crushed, just like with Carmen Østergaard and your guy . . . what's his name."

"Marcus Tosscander," Irene added.

"Marcus. Both he and Carmen display exactly the same type of injuries. The object was also driven into her vagina and rectum. They were heavily damaged. Finally, he slit her open. According to Professor Blokk, he used the same incision that Østergaard and your guy had. Notice how careful he has been not to cut through the navel. The words are Blokk's, not mine." Metz made an ironic face.

"The object was not left in the room?" Irene asked.

"No. Blokk estimates that it was a sturdy, short clublike object."

"Could it be a large baton?"

Irene could hear that her voice sounded unsteady when she asked the question.

Metz looked surprised when he answered. "That's actually what Blokk guessed, but we really don't know."

A baton. The police officer, she thought. And she was sitting in a room with three officers who had known about her private search for Isabell.

Metz picked up the photo of Isabell on the bed. He studied the scene thoughtfully before he said, "The knife that was used was powerful, a hunting knife or an autopsy scalpel. According to Blokk, the murderer would have had a heck of a time with the breastbone even if he had had a proper knife. With the other two victims, the breastbone was sawed through with a circular saw, but here he must have decided not to worry about opening the chest."

"Why not? Wouldn't it have been easy to bring along a circular saw?" said Irene.

For the first time, Peter Møller responded. "Maybe he didn't have access to the saw this particular night. But it's probably because a circular saw makes a lot of noise. Even at the Hotel Aurora they would have reacted to the sound of a circular saw in the middle of the night."

It sounded like a plausible explanation. Metz nodded in agreement before he cleared his throat and continued. "We found out from the staff at the hotel that a woman had called and asked about Isabell. First she had asked for a guest who was called Simon Steiner but when the porter said that there wasn't a guest with that name, she got worried. That's when she asked about Isabell."

"Did any of the employees at the hotel see Isabell?"

"No, but we know why. The top floor was closed due to renovation. The room that Isabell was found in was one of the last ones to be fixed. The other rooms were still empty because they had just glued the carpets down and the smell was horrible. No one will be able to stay in those rooms for quite some time. We found marks on the emergency exit door that leads to the back lot behind the hotel. Someone picked that lock as well as the lock on the door of the hotel room. Our theory is that the murderer met Isabell outside the hotel and took her up to the top floor via the back stairs. He probably fixed the locks ahead of time."

It was quiet in the room while they contemplated the likelihood of this theory. Irene decided that it sounded very logical.

Metz took a puffing breath and continued, "We traced the phone call from the young woman to Scandinavian Models, an escort service."

Irene waited for the follow-up that never came. Now Metz should have talked about his visit to Scandinavian Models. He could have used the line that "It was a private investigation to help Irene," or whatever, but he didn't offer any explanation.

"The interrogations there have provided a good deal of information. The business is new and has only been up and running for a few months. All four of the girls have been there from the beginning. They share a large apartment in the same building in which the company is located."

"Did they move from the address that Isabell's mother had?" Irene jumped in.

"No. They've lived there the whole time."

So Bell had given Monika the wrong address in Copenhagen on purpose. Of course, it had seemed odd that the girls didn't have a phone in their apartment.

Irene remembered Bell's inclination to run away when she was younger, how she had wanted to disappear so that her mother would worry. Had Bell chosen to be unreachable? Maybe it made her feel grown-up, free, and independent. She had had to pay a high price for her so-called freedom.

"Who owns Scandinavian Models?" asked Irene.

"An American. Robin Hillman. A nasty guy. This is the third bordello he's started. He's worked 24/7 from the get-go. The girls are paid fairly well but they really have to work hard."

Metz winked and smiled knowingly after the last comment. Irene thought that he was disgusting. Why didn't he say anything about his visit to the bordello?

Peter Møller took over. "When he thinks he has made a big enough profit, he shuts down the business, goes bankrupt, or sells. Of course, there's no money left in the company. A colleague I spoke with says it's estimated that he must owe a minimum of twenty million kronor in unpaid taxes. It may be a much higher sum, but no one knows. He has the best tax lawyers in the country working for him."

"Have you spoken with Hillman?" Irene asked.

Møller shook his head. "No, he's in the States. Left on Friday morning, after we found Isabell. Someone probably tipped him off, and he felt things were getting too hot to handle."

"When is he coming back?"

"His wife didn't know."

"His wife?"

"Yes. Jytte Hillman. Danish. They have two small children and they live—very well off—in Charlottenlund."

"Where is that?"

"North of Copenhagen, along Strandvejen."

Irene remembered the fashionable neighborhood she had driven through on her way home the week before.

She looked at Møller's blond hair with its sun-bleached strands, his short-sleeved light gray shirt in thin silk, and well-pressed chinos in a slightly darker shade of gray. He looked healthy with his suntan. Suddenly, it struck her that she didn't know where he had gone to get his tan. Thailand? Also a question that had to be asked. But not right now; she would have to wait. Instead, she smiled and said casually, "Is the house located on the right side of the road?"

Møller raised his eyebrows and said ironically, "Of course. Own beach and dock. Hillman paid nine million kröner for the place. His occupation, as listed in the phone book, is businessman. Business seems to be going well."

Birgitta Moberg had said the sex industry brings in more money than the drug trade in the USA today. It's called an *industry*. Industries produce products for consumption. Women, men, children, animals . . . all are sucked into this industry, enslaved, converted to money, broken down, and spit out as worthless industrial refuse.

In order to stop her thoughts, Irene asked, "What have you found out by questioning the other girls at the bordello?"

"Isabell was requested via phone by a man who called himself Simon Steiner. He called around ten o'clock on Wednesday night. He asked specifically for Isabell and wanted her immediately. She was free at eleven. Petra, the one who took the phone call, said that Isabell hailed a taxi and left just before eleven. We've found the taxi driver and the time matches. He dropped her off at the Hotel Aurora at five minutes to eleven. The driver doesn't remember if there was a man waiting for her outside the hotel."

"Have you found anyone with the name Simon Steiner?"

"No."

Beate Bentsen suddenly cleared her throat and said, "The fact is, I knew someone named Simon Steiner. He lived here in Copenhagen but died four years ago. Lung cancer." She put out her half-smoked cigarette.

Metz suddenly looked interested and asked, "Who was he? Could he have a relative with the same name who's still alive?"

Bentsen shook her head. "No relatives with the same name, as far as I know. He was a retired real estate agent. Widowed."

"No children?"

"No."

Irene thought she heard a slight hesitation in Bentsen's voice but she wasn't completely certain. The superintendent's face didn't reveal anything. Since none of the other inspectors seemed willing to ask the question, Irene decided to do it. "How did you know Simon Steiner?"

"He was a good friend of my father's. They were childhood friends."

It was a simple explanation but Irene still felt uneasy. It seemed to be quite a coincidence that the superintendent had known a man with exactly the same name. Still, the explanation was credible. A dead man couldn't possibly be the murderer they were looking for, but someone could have easily used his name. But why *that* name?

Irene had to interrupt her train of thought when Metz said, "Now I want to hear everything you know about Isabell Lind."

Irene summed up everything she could remember about how Isabell had ended up in Copenhagen. She also told them about her own investigation at Scandinavian Models at about the same time Isabell's murder must have taken place. Jens Metz gave a start and gave her a sharp look. She calmly looked back into his small light blue eyes whose almost white lashes gave the impression that he didn't have any.

Surely now he will mention his visit she thought, but he didn't. Instead, he looked away quickly.

She did not talk about her visit to Tom Tanaka. She wouldn't breathe a word about his role in the investigation.

She finished by telling them about the postcard with its short message.

"The Little Mermaid is dead," Metz repeated thoughtfully.

"But in English," Irene clarified.

The three Danish colleagues looked grave. Møller was the one who said it. "To your home address. The murder of a girl you knew, here in Copenhagen. Murdered according to the rituals we recognize from two other murders. A warning can't get much clearer."

"But why me? Several police officers, both in Göteborg and in Copenhagen, are working on this investigation," said Irene.

She could hear the fear in her own voice. Metz looked at her expressionlessly before saying, "You must know things that make the killer feel threatened. Maybe you can't see how important these details are and that's why you haven't told us about them. But he thinks you're a threat."

A block of ice lodged itself in Irene's stomach. What Metz had just said could be interpreted as a threat. It sounded like a well-intended warning, but it could just as easily be—Irene warned herself not to overanalyze. There was a risk of becoming paranoid. Yet she had to tread cautiously and think about every word she uttered when she was with these three people.

Hurried steps were heard in the corridor, and the door to the office was thrown open with a bang. Jonny Blom stood on the threshold, swaying. With bloodshot eyes he looked at his colleagues, each in turn, before saying, "Excuse me. I overslept. They said this was where you were meeting."

Irene fervently wished that he would close his mouth. The stench of garlic and stale alcohol mixed with the cigarette smoke in the room.

"This is my colleague, Jonny Blom," she said stiffly.

Jonny politely shook hands when he was introduced to the Danish colleagues. Metz pounded him on the back and said, "Dear friend, you look like you need a big cup of coffee. What do you say about going to Adler's?"

Everyone got up. Metz kept a firm grip on Jonny's shoulders and led him through the corridor.

CAFÉ ADLER was located just around the corner from the police station. It had a strong turn-of-the-nineteenth-century feel to it, with dark heavy wood paneling and decorative Art Nouveau mirrors. The glass counter inside the entry door was loaded with delicious pastries. Irene decided to get a Danish with chocolate and her own pot of coffee. She felt a strong need for caffeine. One look at Jonny Blom almost made her ask the friendly woman behind the counter if it was possible to get the coffee intravenously. He looked like he needed it.

Jens Metz asked Jonny if he wanted a "little one." Jonny said that he craved a Danish schnapps even though it was only ten o'clock in the morning. When the dark schnapps came, Jens toasted with his coffee cup and Jonny with his shot glass, just like two old friends.

I wonder what the reaction would have been if I had been the one with the hangover and had arrived two hours late, thought Irene. She was quite certain that no one would have pounded her on the back and called her "dear friend" or offered her an eye-opener. The Danish colleagues would have thought that an intoxicated female police officer was an abomination, probably a drunk, and a bad cop.

Jonny stuffed himself with an éclair and a Danish pastry. His expression brightened after the schnapps, and he looked like he was enjoying himself in the smoky atmosphere. He smiled and raised his glass to Irene. "We should have these kinds of coffee breaks at home in Göteborg," he said.

Irene smiled in response but she could feel her entire face tighten.

She suddenly became aware that Beate Bentsen wasn't participating in the general conversation. The superintendent was sitting with her chin in one hand, staring blankly out the dirty café window. Her look was very far away. Irene decided to ask her the question that had been burning inside her.

"Did you tell anyone else I was looking for Isabell?"

Beate Bentsen gave a start and at first didn't seem to understand what she had said. Irene repeated the question. The superintendent lowered her gaze before she answered. "Just after you left, Emil came into the restaurant. I had mentioned that you and I were going to eat dinner there. I was going to invite him for dinner, but he only wanted to have a beer because he had already made dinner plans."

Emil had been chewing on a baguette when Irene had seen him around ten o'clock at night at Tom Tanaka's. He hadn't been eating in the little windowless employee lounge but right behind the store counter. Emil definitely hadn't gone on for dinner later, anywhere.

Beate cleared her throat with difficulty and quickly gave Irene a sideways glance before continuing. "He asked what we had spoken about and I told him that you had a murder-mutilation case in Göteborg that was very similar to Carmen's well-publicized murder. Then it struck me that Emil is out a lot and knows Copenhagen's nightlife. I asked him if he'd heard of Scandinavian Models but he hadn't."

"So you told him that I was looking for a girl who worked at Scandinavian Models and that her name was Isabell Lind?"

The superintendent nodded.

Irene's brain was humming. Emil, Emil.

Emil who knew about her contact with Tom Tanaka.

Emil was Beate Bentsen's son and had found out from her that Irene was looking for Isabell in Copenhagen.

"Maybe I should speak with Emil. He may have asked other people about Scandinavian Models and about Isabell. Can I have his address and telephone number?" Irene said nonchalantly.

For the first time during their conversation the superintendent looked directly at her. The look was clearly hostile, though her voice didn't show it. "Why do you want to speak with Emil? I can do that. I need to speak with him anyway. He hasn't been in touch for a week."

Irene nodded. She couldn't get any farther with Beate Bentsen. Her reluctance to let Irene talk to her son was very clear.

Irene became aware that Peter Møller was watching her. She turned her head and their eyes met. He smiled faintly, his gaze one of admiration. Irene understood that he had overheard the conversation between her and the superintendent. Did he think that she was a clever police officer, willing to ask the right questions? Or was it appreciation for her as a person and a woman? To her vexation, she felt herself blushing. Peter Møller turned his blue glaze toward Jens Metz, who was speaking to him and the remainder of the group.

"No, this won't do. Let's go and look at the crime scene."

He got up, puffing, and helped Jonny to his feet. They walked out the door, laughing, with Jonny pounding Jens on the back. Anyone seeing them would never guess that they had known each other for less than an hour.

THE SUPERINTENDENT didn't go with them to the Hotel Aurora. Peter Møller drove the car and Irene sat next to him in the front passenger's seat. They didn't exchange a single word during the two-minute car ride. Jonny and Metz, in the backseat, jabbered all the more.

The painters had been complaining. They wanted to get into the murder room because it was the last one to be renovated. According to them, they couldn't do anything else in the meantime, but the police hadn't budged. The disgruntled painters had started on the hallway. The police officers had to step over buckets and wend their way between ladders in order to get to the room at the end of the hall.

Aside from the body, which was no longer lying on the bed, everything was as it had been in the photographs. The bloody mattress was still there and the nightstand and the floor lamp were still lying, knocked over, by the window. The room was small and the bathroom was minimal. It seemed to have been a double closet that had been turned into a toilet and shower.

"The question is, do you pee in the shower or shower in the toilet?" Irene commented.

Møller smiled but the other two didn't hear her. They were talking by the bed.

Irene could hear Jonny ask a question but she couldn't make it out. She did, however, hear Metz's reply. "Not a single one. He probably used gloves the whole time. We haven't found the keys to the handcuffs or the object that was used to mutilate the abdomen or the knife used to cut her open."

"So no fingerprints or tools were left in the room," Jonny remarked. He wrinkled his brow and tried to look thoughtful and intelligent. Irene was fed up with him.

The rust-colored stain on the mattress made her shiver. A large pool had coagulated under the bed and a footprint could clearly be seen at its edge. One of the officers, or a technician, had probably stepped in it. All of this blood had poured out of Isabell's body. It wasn't surprising that she hadn't bled much from the incision. There wasn't much blood left in her and no blood pressure to pump out the last few drops.

Irene had a deep feeling of discomfort and she wanted to get out of the room as quickly as possible. She didn't think that the visit here had added anything to the investigation.

The whole time a name echoed in her head. Emil. How was she going to obtain his address? Maybe he was listed in the telephone book? Something told her that the telephone directory for Copenhagen had to be a hefty volume. It was just as well to wait until tomorrow and see if Bentsen had reached her son.

The next moment it struck her: Tom had to know Emil's address and telephone number. Her skin tingled when she realized that she couldn't call him right away. She would have to have patience and wait for a good opportunity.

THE OPPORTUNITY came when they were going to eat lunch. They went to the same restaurant as last time. Irene understood that it was Peter and Jens's regular hangout. When she had placed her order she excused herself and headed toward the ladies' room. She checked to make sure that there wasn't anyone in the other stall, then she dialed Tom's number.

"Tom speaking."

"Irene Huss calling."

"Hey, my favorite cop. Are you coming to visit me?"

"I would love to, but it's not possible. My colleague . . ."

"I understand. What did you want to talk about?"

"Beate Bentsen . . . Emil's mother . . . told him that I was looking for Scandinavian Models and Isabell Lind. I need to get in touch with him."

"Why?"

"To ask him if he told anyone else."

Tom's answer was a long silence. When he finally started speaking, a chilly undertone could be heard in his voice. "Our dear Emil certainly keeps on surprising us. Do you think he's the one who leaked it?"

"Leaked . . . but I never said that it was a secret that I was looking for Isabell. I never thought it would be dangerous for her."

"I haven't seen Emil for a week. Not since the night you were here."

"That's exactly one week ago. Does he usually stay away that long?"

After a long pause, Tom said, "It's happened. But usually he shows up every few days. Sometimes I've even asked him to come in when I've needed help in the store. Since he isn't employed, he comes and goes as he wants."

"Do you have his address and telephone number?"

"Yes, one second."

Irene heard the desk drawer pulled out. She guessed that he was sitting in his office and had just reached for his Rolodex.

"He lives on Gothersgade. Near the Botanical Gardens."

It sounded funny when Tom tried to pronounce Botanical Gardens in Danish. But Irene didn't laugh. He gave her the street address and telephone number. Summing up, Irene asked, "What do you know about Emil?"

"He studies law. That's what he says anyway. He lives in a big apartment that he inherited from his father. It's big enough that he can rent out a part of it. I suspect that he lives on the income from the rent. He's twenty-two years old. Doesn't draw a lot of attention to himself."

Irene was very close to asking Tom if he had had a "relationship" with Emil but decided not to. Such a question might destroy the relationship of trust they had built.

She dialed Emil's number as soon as she had finished the conversation with Tom. After ten rings she gave up. He wasn't home.

The food came at the same time as her arrival back at the table. The portions were lavish. Jonny had already accepted Danish food traditions with great enthusiasm. The young waitress set a schnapps glass filled to the brim in front of him. Jens Metz slapped her on the bottom and winked mischievously when she glared at him in irritation.

"Don't look so sour. A little clap on the rear is a compliment," he laughed.

The waitress quickly replied, "It depends on who's giving it!"

Irene could have applauded but managed to control herself. Jens looked cross, though he immediately cheered up after taking a big swig of beer.

They went back to the police station after lunch. Irene managed to reach Svend Blokk via telephone. The professor of pathology was absolutely convinced that the same murderer had been at it again. The abdominal incisions of both the dismembered victims matched Isabell's incision. The damage to the lower abdomen was also identical. Blokk was most intrigued by this last victim, since she still had all of her organs.

Irene was close to throwing up into the receiver. She had never reacted so strongly to a murder investigation before. Maybe when she was a rookie, and they had gotten a very rotten corpse to deal with . . . but no, not even then. In her emotional chaos after Isabell's murder, a much stronger feeling had begun to make itself known. It had been there for a while but now it surfaced and asked to be taken seriously: revenge.

She wanted vengeance. She wanted to avenge herself for having been used for the killer's purpose. She wanted to avenge herself for having been made responsible for Bell's death. She wanted to avenge the sorrow that Monika Lind's family was forced to go through. She wanted to avenge the terror Bell must have felt when she realized that she was going to die, and she wanted to avenge the desecration of Bell's dead body.

She would take revenge.

THE QUESTIONING of the three remaining girls from Scandinavian Models didn't add anything new to the investigation. They had closed the establishment for a few hours in order to be interrogated by the Swedish police. From what Irene understood, their establishment was open to customers fourteen hours a day, seven days a week. The girls worked in seven-hour shifts.

"Robin . . . Mr. Hillman . . . says that it's important now, in the beginning. The customers need to know that we're accessible. We're going to build a circle of regulars," Petra had said. Her tone of voice had been businesslike. She sounded as if she were describing the start-up of a health-food brand.

Irene wanted to yell at her and tell her to go home to Malmö on the next ferry. But she didn't say anything. The way Petra was sticking out first her chest and then her tight-pants-clad bottom in Peter Møller's face told her that it wasn't worth it.

THEY ATE dinner at Copenhagen Corner that evening. The three Danish officers had suggested the restaurant to their two Swedish colleagues and Irene knew right away that it was a good choice.

They were seated at a table on an enormous glassed-in veranda that faced the open Rådhuspladsen. The atmosphere was cozy, with lots of green plants, and the staff was pleasant.

Jens Metz and Jonny Blom ordered beer and a Danish schnapps straight away. Peter Møller and Irene satisfied themselves with one large beer apiece while Beate Bentsen ordered a glass of white wine.

Irene had tried calling Emil Bentsen several times during the afternoon without success. Jonny had had time to sleep for two hours at the hotel before Irene phoned his room and woke him up. Now he was sitting jovially exchanging toasts with Jens and looked as though he was really enjoying himself.

"When are you leaving tomorrow?" asked Jens.

"After lunch. We're just going to take copies of some of the interrogations and of the technical examinations. It's definitely your case, but it will be best for us to have information, too, since the murderer is still at large. No one knows what he'll do next," Irene replied.

A gloomy silence swept over the table but was quickly brushed aside by Jonny's comment. "He can do whatever he wants, as long as he stays in Copenhagen. Then we can come here every now and then."

Jonny and Jens drank to that. Their laughter resounded from the glass walls.

Irene noticed that Beate Bentsen seemed withdrawn. She was slowly rotating her wine glass between her fingers, staring down at the swirling liquid. Her thoughts seemed to be very far away. She looked tired, there were deep furrows in the corners of her mouth.

"Did you reach Emil?" Irene asked.

The superintendent gave a start and looked at Irene, confused. "What? Emil? No."

With the last word she bent over her glass again.

Irene felt strongly that something was wrong. But she couldn't stop now. "Do you think we can reach him tonight or tomorrow morning?" she asked.

Beate looked irritated. "I don't know. He lives his own life."

"I understand that. But for the sake of the investigation, it's important to clarify who knew that I was looking for Isabell. We need to know whom he told." Irene tried to sound calm and reasonable.

Beate looked at her sharply, then she nodded and looked away. "I can't get ahold of him." she admitted. "I was at his apartment today but he wasn't home." she sounded worried.

Irene thought quickly, then asked if he had left a note or a message for her at his apartment.

"I don't have a key," Beate Bentsen said.

Irene almost gave it away. The sentence was already rolling off her tongue—*but doesn't he have a tenant who can open it for you*—when she realized what she was about to reveal. She quickly swallowed the sentence and became mute out of sheer terror. She had come close to exposing Tom Tanaka! She could feel that she was starting to sweat.

Beate didn't seem to have noticed anything. Almost whispering, she continued, "He says that he doesn't want me to come and go in his life just as I please. That's why I don't have a key."

Irene could come up with several reasons why Emil wouldn't want a mother who was a police superintendent to suddenly show up at his home. She nodded, without saying anything.

Beate suddenly burst out, "It's so strange! He seems to have disappeared!"

The three men turned their heads simultaneously and looked at her. Jens peered good-naturedly from the depths of his fatty jowls and asked, "Who has disappeared?"

Bentsen took a deep breath and looked morosely. "Emil. I haven't heard from him in a week."

Clearly Beate was worried, and Irene had a feeling that she had good reason to be. Impulsively, she put her hand on the coarse linen-clad arm of her colleague and said, "When we're finished here, we'll take a taxi and go to Emil's apartment. I'll come along. If he's home, I can ask him my question directly. Then it'll be taken care of."

Beate shrugged at first. Then she nodded.

Chapter 11

THE DINNER HAD BEEN superb. Jens Metz had entertained them with stories about the work of the Copenhagen Police Department, and Jonny had countered with glimpses from the everyday lives of his Göteborg colleagues. They had laughed and passed a very enjoyable couple of hours.

Just before eleven o'clock, Beate Bentsen touched Irene's arm and said in a low voice, "Shall we go?"

Irene nodded. They got up and excused themselves. Peter Møller asked if he should escort them but they assured him that it wasn't necessary.

After the increasing warmth and cigarette smoke of the restaurant, the night air of Rådhuspladsen felt refreshing. They hailed a free cab and Irene remembered to let the superintendent give the directions. At Gothersgade they paid for the trip and asked the cabdriver to wait five minutes. If they hadn't come back before then, he could leave.

Emil lived in a beautiful old stone house dating from the beginning of the twentieth century. The house itself was of red-brown brick, richly embellished. Sculptured faces on the building's friezes gazed down at the two women through the half darkness.

They were lucky. A man was coming down the stairs and opened the door, giving Beate a friendly smile. He probably recognized her as Emil's mother, thought Irene.

Broad marble steps led to an airy stairwell. At the far end of the hall, light streamed in from a rectangular elevator window. The elevator was considerably younger than the remainder of the house. They were quickly carried up to the fourth floor; the car stopped with a gentle bounce.

The hallway had been recently renovated, revealing Art Nouveau designs along the walls and around the lead-framed stairway windows. It must be unbelievably beautiful when the sun shines through the multicolored glass windows, thought Irene. They were dark now since street light didn't reach to the top floor. The walls were newly glazed in pale yellow, and a talented painter had covered the heavy outer doors in an old-fashioned style using a dark chestnut brown color for a hand-drawn pattern.

Beate Bentsen walked with determined steps up to one of the two doors on the landing. It said EMIL BENTSEN on the blue ceramic plate, which contrasted with the elegance of the rest of the entrance. If one looked closer, it could be seen that the little pink border under Emil's name was made up of pigs. The first stood on all fours and the others stood behind, each with its forelegs resting on the back of the one in front. There were ten pigs in a row, copulating.

Beate didn't give the pigs a glance. She rang the doorbell forcefully. It echoed behind the massive door, which remained closed. Irene put her ear to the door. All was quiet; no movement could be heard. She got down on her knees and peered through the mail slot. On the floor she could glimpse newspapers, advertisements, and some envelopes.

"He hasn't been home for several days," she said.

Just when she was about to get up, Irene became aware of the smell coming through the open slot. It was so faint that she hadn't noticed it at first. But this smell, even if ever so faint, was well known to a murder investigator.

At first she didn't know what she was going to say to Beate. In order to buy some time, she asked, "Did you look through the mail slot when you were here earlier today?"

"Yes, I saw the pile of mail. That's what got me so worried."

Irene swallowed before she asked the next question. "You didn't notice anything unusual?"

"No. Why?"

Irene looked quickly at Beate. It was quite possible that the superintendent hadn't noticed the smell as she was a heavy smoker. Her sense of smell might be diminished, but not Irene's. A faint but unmistakable odor of corruption was coming through the mail slot.

Beate Bentsen managed to get the building's owner using Irene's cell phone. Judging by the tone of the conversation, they were old acquaintances. He hadn't gone to bed, and since the women didn't have a car, he promised to come and give them the keys personally.

The superintendent's face was pale green when she ended the conversation. With a gesture of exhaustion she handed the phone to Irene. "He lives very close by. It will only take him a few minutes by car."

Then the remote expression returned to her face. Irene decided not to bother her with chitchat. They stood in silence outside the door with its racy sign.

All of Irene's instincts were signaling with red warning lights: the smell wasn't coming from old, forgotten trash. Someone or something was rotting inside the apartment.

THE ELEVATOR swished quietly up to the top floor and the building's owner stepped out. To Irene's surprise he was as dark as ebony. He flashed a brilliant smile and introduced himself as Bill Faraday. He was tall and wiry. If Irene had been asked to guess his profession, she would have said he was a dancer. The last thing she would have guessed was that he was a real estate lessor.

Faraday pulled an enormous set of keys out of the pocket of his expensive-looking leather coat. He searched for a long time among the different keys before he fished out one with a joyful exclamation. The key slid easily off the ring and, with a click as it turned in the lock, the door opened.

Beate stepped in front of Faraday. Brusquely, she said, "Thanks, Bill. We'll go in ourselves. Can we keep the key?"

If he was surprised by this dismissal, he didn't show it. With another beaming smile, he turned on his heel and disappeared into the elevator. Bentsen waited until it had started descending before she opened the door completely and, with a wave of her hand, invited Irene in.

The smell was evident in the hall. Irene turned on the light and looked around. It was big and airy and the ceiling was very high. A soiled folk art rug in shades of wine red lay under the large pile of mail and newspapers. The only furnishings were a hat and coat stand and a large mirror with a gilded frame. A naked lightbulb hung from the ceiling.

At random, Irene chose the closest door on the left. It turned out to lead into a large dirty bathroom, which smelled stale. A sour-smelling terry-cloth towel had been thrown on the floor among empty toilet-paper rolls and shampoo bottles.

The next door led into a kitchen, which was equally messy. Encrusted dishes and smelly pizza boxes overflowed the filthy counter. But this wasn't the dominant smell in the apartment. Irene realized that Beate Bentsen was following right at her heels. Irene understood. The superintendent was afraid of the nauseating smell and of learning where it was coming from. She didn't dare find out on her own.

As if she had read Irene's thoughts, Bentsen took a step toward a closed door and said, "Emil's music room is in there. The door next to it leads to the living room and over there is the bedroom."

Irene went directly to the bedroom door. It wasn't completely closed.

The stench hit her as she opened the door wide.

Irene whirled around and tried to keep Beate away but she had glimpsed enough and rushed past Irene. Bentsen stopped by the bed as if frozen in place and stood stock-still without making a sound. Irene hurried to stand beside her.

Emil lay with his hands and feet bound. Rope this time, instead of handcuffs, Irene registered automatically. He was naked. The killer had left his mark on Emil's abdomen. Beate Bentsen began moaning; soon her moans had risen to a hysterical scream. "It's gone! He's taken . . . It's gone. . . . ."

Irene also saw that body parts were missing. The murderer had mutilated his victim.

I T WA S a long night. Irene didn't get back to the Hotel Alex until just before 4:00 a.m.

I'm never going to fall asleep, she thought. She didn't remember anything after that until she was awakened by the telephone at eight thirty. Half asleep, she fumbled the phone to her ear. She came awake after she heard Superintendent Andersson's booming voice. "Naturally, I called the police station to talk to you since you're supposed to be there working. But I didn't get you or Jonny so I had to try and understand a gruff-speaking Dane. At least I've understood that you found another dismembered victim! What the hell are you doing?"

Irene felt offended and tried to protest. "I'm not the one going around killing people!"

Andersson ignored her objection and continued. "And where are you and Jonny? You're lying in bed at the hotel sleeping!"

Irene was finally awake enough to get angry.

"I was there last night when the latest victim was found, and I didn't get to bed until five o'clock!" she hissed angrily. She added an hour while she was at it because it sounded better. Andersson wouldn't be able to refute this information. There was a short silence on the phone before the superintendent started speaking again. In a considerably calmer tone, he said, "You were there?"

"Yes."

"Who was the victim?"

"Superintendent Bentsen's son."

The silence that followed was very long, but she knew her boss and was preparing for another explosion. "What the hell are you saying? Bentsen's son! It can—"

She interrupted him. "This murder bears the signature of our killer. His victim was bound, split open, defiled and mutilated."

When the superintendent's voice could be heard again, it sounded serious and sensible. "Irene. He's working close to you. He's probably still in Copenhagen and he has struck again at someone connected to you."

"That's not entirely certain," said Irene. "The medical examiner reported that Emil Bentsen has probably been dead for a week. The murderer could already be back in Göteborg or wherever it is that he lives."

"So this victim was killed at the same time as that girl, Isabell?"

"Yes. The murders are connected. Jonny and I have to stay here another night."

"Why? Can't the Danes report to us as to what their investigation turns up?"

"I found a business card on Emil Bentsen's bulletin board in his bedroom. It was hanging pinned under another piece of paper and only one corner was sticking out. But I recognized the corner. It was Marcus Tosscander's business card. You know, the one that has Tosca's Design on it."

She could hear Andersson gasping for breath. Irene worried that he was going to have a heart attack but he sounded relatively normal and collected by the time he spoke again.

"OK. Look for more connections to Marcus today. But you're coming home tomorrow! This is getting expensive. We can't pay for two police officers to stay in Copenhagen. . . ."

He stopped himself and Irene realized that a thought had struck him.

"Was Jonny with you last night when you found Bentsen's son?"

"No."

"Where was he?"

Irene hesitated about telling the truth, which was *He was sitting and drinking with his Danish colleague Jens Metz*. She decided not to.

"No idea. I was with Beate Bentsen. She was worried because Emil hadn't been in touch for so long and I agreed to go with her to his apart—"

The superintendent interrupted her. "So Jonny wasn't there when you discovered the murder. What excuse does he have for not working?"

Irene chickened out again. "Don't know."

"I'll call his room and ask. And Irene . . . be careful."

"Of course. I'll call tonight."

A RED-FACED and hungover Jonny Blom entered the breakfast room when Irene had almost finished eating. He sank down in the chair across from her and sighed. "Andersson called. He was in a horrible mood. Why was he jabbering about my not being with you last night? What corpse was he ranting about?"

"Go and get some food and I'll tell you."

In a pedagogic tone, Irene explained what had happened during the night.

When he heard that they had found Emil's body and in what condition, Jonny sat up straight in his chair and seemed completely sober. The look he gave Irene was full of doubt.

"Is it true? Beate Bentsen's son?"

Irene nodded.

"That's the damnedest thing I've ever heard! How's she holding up?"

"She had to be taken to the hospital. Had a complete breakdown. It wasn't a pretty sight. The killer cut away his penis, one chest muscle, and one buttock."

Jonny looked at the remainder of his ham sandwich with distaste. He set it aside on his plate. "What a sick bastard!"

For once, the two of them were in agreement.

"I've booked us for one more night. We can keep the rooms we have and, Jonny . . ." She leaned forward over the table and said seriously, ". . . I would be very grateful if you could stay sober this last day. Andersson was right when he said that the murderer is working close to me. And you're close to me. For your own safety, you should—"

Jonny's face turned red, and he got up so quickly that he knocked over his half-full cup of coffee. "You're no damn chief or boss over me! You have no say in what I do!"

Furious, he stormed out of the breakfast room. Irene sighed loudly. It looked as though it was going to be yet another day of schnapps drinking.

JUST AS Irene had thought the night before, it really was beautiful when the sun shone in through the multicolored glass windows in the stairwell. But she couldn't enjoy the play of colors on the walls when she and her three male colleagues stepped out of the elevator and walked up to the door of Emil's apartment. Jonny looked at the blue ceramic sign in surprise and bent over in order to check out the pigs. He mumbled something but he didn't comment out loud.

He had ignored Irene on the car ride over to Emil's apartment. Her appeal for restraint with respect to alcohol had not gone over well.

When they inspected the crime scene during the night, Irene had realized that the other door on the landing belonged to the rental portion of Emil's apartment. It was made up of two large rooms with a communal kitchen, hall, and bathroom. Neither of the rooms seemed to be rented currently. A large door in the kitchen that was locked led to Emil's bedroom.

The rooms were almost identically furnished; each held a wide bed, a large fancy dresser with a mirror above it, and a leather recliner with a floor lamp next to it. On the floor were worn but beautiful folk art rugs. The closets were empty as well as the dressers. Everything was covered by a thick layer of dust, which indicated that no one had lived in the rooms for several weeks, maybe even months. The only thing that made the rooms different was the color scheme. One of them was decorated blue, the other green. Both the rooms had wonderful views of the Botanical Gardens.

The kitchen and the bathroom were dusty and dirty, but not as filthy as Emil's. There was actually a certain degree of impersonal order discernable.

Jens Metz turned around and breathed old booze in Irene's face. "We're going to let the technicians search for hair strands and so forth in both of the rental rooms. We have lots of hairs from the Hotel Aurora since the victim there was found in an old hotel room. We're going to search Emil's apartment thoroughly. It's going to take a hell of a long time but if we're lucky we'll find hair or something else that matches," he said.

Irene nodded. She couldn't speak since she was holding her breath. The question was who had the most repulsive mouth odor, Jonny or Jens.

They left the rental area and entered Emil's apartment. The smell of decaying flesh still hung in the air even though the body had been taken to the morgue. Irene opened the window in the kitchen. The technicians were in the process of collecting evidence in Emil's bedroom. A short, rather rotund young man looked up at the police officers through the door opening, and said, "This is going to take a while. There is more dust and shit than you can imagine. It doesn't look like the guy ever cleaned."

"Fingerprints?" Peter Møller asked.

"Tons."

"Anything of interest?"

"It looks like there are a lot of semen stains on the mattress and the bedclothes, but they appear to be older. We found a fresh semen stain under the bed. It's very small but I think it will be enough for a DNA test. It looks like someone wiped up something with a rag, here by the bed. It'll show up clearly when we light the area."

"Did you find the rag?"

"No. The murderer probably wasn't stupid enough to leave it behind."

"Where is the area that was wiped clean?"

"Here." The technician pointed at the floor just below the head of the bed.

Peter Møller nodded and turned to Irene. "Finally, we may have a bit of luck. The murderer slipped up and left some traces. If it's from him, that is. Emil could have left a sample before he was killed."

"You mean that if the semen belongs to the killer, he achieved climax through performing his rituals, and cleaned up afterward but missed a spot under the bed?"

"Yes."

The bright sunlight fell on the only picture in the room, a large framed black-and-white photo of a man in an incredibly exposed pose. He was half sitting against some large pillows. The focus was on his very erect penis. Even though his face and upper body were a bit fuzzy, Irene recognized him. She hadn't done so during the shock and chaos of the previous night. Now she saw that the model was Marcus Tosscander. What was even worse was that she recognized the type of photograph. Tom Tanaka had two of them hanging in his bedroom.

This realization hit her like a blow to the head. She needed to speak with Tom as soon as possible. He would probably be questioned since the police knew that Emil usually hung out in Tom's store. But they wouldn't find out anything from Tom. Emil's murder would just confirm his suspicions about the police in general and the Vesterbro station in particular.

The four crime inspectors backed out into the hall. They had to leave the bedroom to the technicians for the time being.

"Since there are four of us, I suggest that we each take a room to check. Jonny can take the bathroom; Peter, the kitchen; Irene can take the other room—the music room—and I'll take the living room," said Metz.

No one else came up with a better suggestion so each went to his or her assigned room.

Irene opened the door and stopped abruptly on the threshold to the room. She recognized this smell: marijuana smoke. She hadn't noticed it the previous night either. That evening's investigation had been cursory. There hadn't been time or personnel for a more careful investigation of the apartment.

She entered the music room and closed the door after her. The smell of pot mixed with the stale smell of a room that hadn't been cleaned or aired out. It was large and practically unfurnished. The morning sun shone in through the dirt-streaked and curtainless window. A withered brown plant in a little plastic bucket was placed in the middle of the window's marble ledge. Irene tore off a leaf. She crumbled the dry leaf in the palm of her hand and sniffed. It was a marijuana plant.

The floor was covered with a wall-to-wall carpet, which at some point in time had been light yellow. The dominating color at present was nicotine brown. The room had probably originally been used as a library. A built-in bookcase of dark wood ran along one of the walls. Emil had sloppily torn down some of the shelves in order to make room for two huge speakers and an impressive stereo setup. Along the sides of the speakers were overstuffed CD shelves. CDs and CD cases lay in random piles on the floor.

Irene assumed that Emil and his friends had laid on the floor to listen to music since there wasn't any furniture to sit on. They could have rested their eyes on the posters that decorated the walls. Irene took a closer look at them. They showed various rock groups with names like Warriors of Satan, Deathlovers, and Necrophilia. The band members were depicted in different stages of decay. Worms crawled out of holes in their skulls. Despite this, they were standing and jamming on their instruments and bellowing out their lyrics. The living dead.

The thought of the state Emil had been in when they found him—rotten and dead—made the pictures on the walls seem like mockery.

The majority of the CD covers resembled the posters.

Irene tried to imagine the fantasies that could lead a young man to like this type of picture and music. She jumped when the door behind her was yanked open.

"Why did you close the door?" Jonny asked.

"Come in and shut the door behind you," said Irene.

Uncertain, Jonny did as Irene had asked him.

"Sniff," she ordered.

He took some loud breaths.

"Pot," he determined.

"Yep. In the window is a marijuana plant but the smell is coming from the filthy rug. A hell of a lot has been smoked in here over the years."

Jonny looked at the pictures on the walls in bloodshot wonder.

"Shit," was his opinion.

"I agree. But it shows that he was drawn to necrophilia."

"Damn!"

"Again, I agree. But it's in these circles that we must look for our killer. Not just a necrophile but a necrophile who supplies his own corpses."

The wheels of logic had started turning in Jonny's fuzzy brain. With a clever smile, he said, "So it can't be Emil we're after."

"No. But he most likely knew his killer."

Jonny finally remembered why he had come to summon Irene. "Møller found something he wants to show us," he said.

They left the music room and almost ran right into Peter. He was standing in the hall, staring into a closet attached to the wall. Irene and Jonny stood beside him in order to see what he was looking at.

The large closet contained a worn leather jacket, a black trench coat, and two police uniforms.

"We shouldn't touch the clothes. There could be evidence on them," said Møller. His voice sounded strained. Irene guessed that he was thinking about the police officer who had shown up on the periphery of the murder of Carmen Østergaard. Her body become hot all over. Thoughts were going off like fireworks in her head.

Was it really possible? Could *Emil* be the police officer? Of course, his mother was a police officer. The photo on the wall and the business card proved that Marcus and Emil had known each other. Emil matched the description of the officer that the prostitute had given in connection with the investigation of Carmen's murder. Was this where Marcus had been living during his time in Copenhagen? Not unlikely. Where were his things? His car? Why hadn't Emil rented out the rooms again? Why had Emil himself been killed?

The answer to the last question must be that Emil somehow had become a threat to the murderer. Irene also saw another possibility: the killer had found sexual release during the murder. Perhaps desire had gotten the better of him and Emil was the only one around. The thought was nauseating, but Irene decided to bring up this hypothesis with Yvonne Stridner when she got the chance.

Jens Metz had rejoined the others in the hall. His heavy breathing could be heard in the silence. Finally, he said sincerely, "Now I feel damned sorry for the superintendent."

They should try and speak with Beate Bentsen as quickly as possible, thought Irene. Tentatively, she asked, "May I come with you to the hospital and speak with her?"

"Why?" Jonny asked sourly.

"Because Emil and Marcus knew each other. The model in the photo above Emil's bed is Marcus Tosscander. This is probably where Marcus was living. How much did Beate know about Emil's life? His sex life? There's a lot that I would like to ask her," said Irene.

Jonny looked irritated, but didn't say anything.

"You can come along. I'll call the hospital and see if we can speak with her. If it's possible, we'll go there right after we've eaten," said Peter Møller.

"I'll try and get Svend Blokk. He should be able to tell us if it's the same murderer. Actually, have you thought about the fact that the first two murders were different from the last two?" Metz pointed out.

"You mean because he hasn't cleaned out Isabell and Emil?" asked Jonny.

"Exactly. Plus the fact that the chest hasn't been opened. Maybe it's because he hasn't had access to a circular saw. That's probably also the reason he hasn't cut off the head and other extremities. Maybe we should be asking ourselves whether we could have a copycat murderer?" said Metz.

That was a possibility, but Irene's intuition said that it was the same killer. No copycat could have known the details of the mutilation and defilement of the first two victims since the media hadn't had access to all the facts. But she agreed that there were certain striking differences between the first two murders and the later ones. It was almost as though the last two were incomplete.

Irene became terrified by the word that popped into her head: incomplete. She would keep it in mind and come back to it when she had more information about the new murders.

Peter stuffed his hand into his coat pocket and pulled out a closed plastic bag. "I found this far back in the pantry. A bit of pot. Pretty strong."

"It matches the smell in the music room. The door has probably been closed since the murder. The posters and CDs show that Emil had an interest in necrophilia," Irene told him.

Møller and Metz went into the music room. They looked at the wall decorations in silence. Møller bent down and picked around among the CDs and covers. When they started walking toward the door again, Møller said to Irene, "It seems to mostly be death metal and black metal. He wouldn't have had to have been a necrophile to listen to that kind of music. There are a lot of youngsters who think it's cool. But I agree that he seemed to be obsessed with death."

He made a gesture at the poster hanging closest to the door. It depicted a guitarist, full length, standing and grinning at the observer, while worms crawled in and out of holes in his skull. Under the electric guitar his rotting intestines appeared to be hanging down to the floor. The words over the picture said: "There is no death!"

IT WAS a relief to come out onto the street again.

"It will be just as well if we eat lunch now," said Jens Metz.

Irene wasn't very hungry but realized that it would give her a chance to contact Tom Tanaka. There were certain advantages to having separate toilets for men and women.

They decided that after lunch Jonny should go back to the police station and make copies of the investigation reports about Isabell Lind. Naturally he groaned and mumbled, but deep down inside he must have been happy to be driven to the police station to sit in peace and quiet to deal with a stationary pile of paper. He obviously had a headache. But maybe he could get past it with an aspirin and some cups of coffee. A "little one" and some food would probably also do the trick.

Peter Møller called the hospital and asked if they could question Beate Bentsen that afternoon. After several discussions with the nurses, they mercifully were given a visiting time after three o'clock.

It was almost a quarter to twelve. If they hurried up and ate, Irene would have time for a visit to Tom Tanaka's before three. She became insistent that they eat an early lunch.

They walked to Gråbrødretorv and the small rustic pub Peder Oxe, known for its meat dishes and generous glasses of wine. All of them chose tender ox rolls in a divine cream sauce, black currant jelly, and a large helping of early spring greens. Everyone had beer. To Jonny's disappointment, he was the only one who wanted to have a schnapps. To save himself embarrassment he didn't order it, but his expression was that of a sad puppy who had been tricked.

Irene excused herself before coffee and slipped off to the ladies' room. She locked herself in the bathroom and took out her cell phone, then quickly brought up Tom's number on the cell phone display and made the call.

"Tom speaking."

"Irene Huss here. We need to meet immediately."

"Has something happened?"

"Yes, I need to speak with you."

"Are you able to, even with your colleague around?"

"Yes. If we can meet in half an hour."

"I can make it in an hour. OK?"

"No. There won't be enough time. It's important! Otherwise I wouldn't have called you!"

He must have heard the desperation in her voice.

"OK. I have company now. Come in half an hour. Call when you're outside the door and I'll come down and open it for you."

Irene pulled a comb through her short hairdo and ruffled it a bit. To her surprise, she had started liking her short hairdo. For the sake of appearances, she put on some more lipstick. She smiled at her own reflection for practice. It was important that she look casual while she was serving up a white lie to her colleagues.

She dropped down next to her steaming cup of coffee and said, "I think that I'm going to try and speak with the girls at Scandinavian Models again. I'd especially like to talk to Petra one more time. Now that the initial shock is over, she might remember more from the night Isabell disappeared."

"Do you think it will add anything? We have already questioned the girls several times," Peter objected.

"I know, but I want to make one last attempt."

Peter shrugged to show what he thought of the idea. To Irene's relief, the three men started talking about soccer. She sat quietly and pretended not to know anything about the group matches for the European Championship.

When she had finished her last cup of coffee, she smiled apologetically and said, "I think I'll head out. So long."

"I'll pick you up next to the entrance to Vor Frue Kirke at 2:45," said Peter.

"Fine."

Irene faintly recalled that this meeting place was in the immediate neighborhood. She realized that it was going to be difficult to get to Vesterbro and back in time. She would have to take a taxi.

Irene called Tom from the taxi. The driver turned in on Helgolandsgade and Irene paid. Without hurrying, she went through the entrance door. Even though it was broad daylight, she looked around the courtyard carefully. The run-in with the skinheads was still fresh in her mind.

Tom was already standing at the window. He opened the door, welcomed her, and shuffled up the stairs. Irene shivered when she heard his strained breathing. He sounded like a mountain climber without his oxygen at the top of Mount Everest. Tom was dressed in a silver-colored satin outfit for the day and he had wound small silver threads around his knots of hair.

With a chivalrous gesture he held open the door to his bedroom and invited Irene to step in. The room looked just the same. If Tom had been entertaining someone there, he had had enough time to put things in order again. When he started to walk toward the door that led to the corridor, Irene said, "Tom. Could we please stay here in the bedroom?"

Tom raised his eyebrows ironically. "In the bedroom?"

When he saw the serious look on Irene's face he hurried to add, "Sorry. Bad joke."

"It's OK. Why don't you sit on the bed?"

Without arguing, Tom lowered himself heavily onto the edge of the bed.

"Tom. Prepare yourself for horrible news. Emil Bentsen was found dead in his apartment last night. Murdered. Based on the evidence so far, he was killed a week ago. His body carries the signature of our killer. The signature of Marcus and Isabell's killer."

She watched for Tom's reaction. At first nothing happened; he sat immobile, like a massive gray stone. Slowly, a dull moaning sound rose toward the ceiling. Even though Irene had expected a reaction, she was still surprised. The hair on the back of her neck rose. Tom's plaint sounded wordlessly and terribly through the room, traveled desperately out into the hall, and died away in the far reaches of the apartment. He began rocking his large body back and forth. His moaning decreased in intensity until finally it ended. But he continued to rock his enormous body back and forth.

Irene was about to continue when he hissed, "That devil! You have to catch him!"

"I'm going to try but I need your help."

Tom nodded. Irene pointed at the framed photographs on the wall and said, "Why didn't you tell me that these are photos of Marcus?"

Tom looked sincerely surprised. "I didn't think about it actually. And he's only in one of the photographs. The other model is a friend of his."

Irene took a closer look at the two pictures and realized that he was right.

Marcus was sitting right at the edge of the water. The sun glistened on the droplets on his young sunburned body. He was smiling into the camera. The wind was playfully blowing the hair above his forehead. He was resting his hands on his knees, which were slightly bent and very wide apart. His condition was amazing. The photo had been taken from the water's edge, looking up, and the whole picture breathed sensual joy and acceptance of one's own sexuality. Irene had to admit to herself that it was one of the most exciting pictures of a naked person she had ever seen.

The other model was standing in profile, leaning against a rugged stone wall, which seemed to be part of a building. He appeared to be muscular and well built. The picture was taken against the sun so it was impossible to make out his face. Irene could see that his long hair was combed back and had been put in a thick ponytail. The photographer had managed to create the illusion that the sunbeams originated from the top of his erect penis.

Irene had to admit that the photographer was talented.

Suddenly, she had a strong feeling that she recognized the man. She stepped closer but her memory failed her. The direct light pulled his face into darkness, yet she definitely recognized the man. But where had she seen him?

"Do you know who the friend is?"

"No, he never said."

"You've never met him?"

"No."

"Did Marcus give you these photos?"

"Yes, right before he left. Framed and ready. I just needed to hang them up."

"Do you know who took them?"

"A photographer in Göteborg, but I don't know his name."

"Did you know that Emil also had this same kind of photo of Marcus over his bed? Not the same pose, but it is Marcus."

Tom gave a start. "No. I didn't even know that they were that well aquainted."

"But you knew that they knew each other?"

"Yes. The first time I saw Marcus, he came into the store with Emil. Marcus came up to me right away and started talking. Emil bought some things and didn't participate in our conversation. I never got the feeling that they were . . . together. They seemed more like friends. That's the only time I saw them together."

"Marcus never spoke about Emil?"

"No."

"And you never asked?"

"No."

"Did Emil ever speak about Marcus?"

"No. Never."

"You don't know very much about the personal lives of either Emil or Marcus? You never asked?"

For the first time, Irene felt a reserve on Tom's part. His tone of voice was icily neutral when he replied, "No."

"Why not?"

"If you don't ask any questions, then you don't have to answer any."

That was as close to the truth as you could get; Irene realized that she wasn't going to get any personal information out of Tom.

"But Marcus spoke of 'my police officer' and said that he lived with a police officer, right?"

"Yes."

"We found two police uniforms at Emil's place. And Emil had a rental unit that was part of his apartment. Do you think Emil could have been the policeman Marcus was staying with?"

Tom sighed. "Good God . . . Emil! It could have been Emil. I sold him a police uniform about a year ago."

"Do you remember when?"

"It was right in the beginning when I had just taken over the store. Almost two years ago. It was the first time we met."

"He only bought one? Not two?"

"One."

Irene said, after some hesitation, "Emil found out from his mother that I was looking for Isabell Lind. When I left Beate Bentsen at the restaurant, it was eight thirty. Emil came in just after that. He couldn't have known, then, until eight thirty. I saw him here with you around ten o'clock. At about the same time, a man named Simon Steiner called Scandinavian Models and requested Isabell Lind be sent to the Hotel Aurora, a stone's throw from your store. Who would Emil have had time to tell that I was looking for Isabell?"

A loaded silence ensued. Finally, Tom answered, "He must have called the killer from his cell phone. Can't you trace calls from cell phones as well?"

"I don't know if it's possible at this point. I don't even know if they found his cell phone. Do you have his number?"

Tom shook his head. "No."

A thought struck Irene. "Did Emil have your number?"

"No."

"Did Marcus?" A hint of a smile could be seen in one of the corners of Tom's mouth, when he answered. "Of course."

"And you gave it to me."

Tom raised his massive head and looked her straight in the eye. "I trust you," he said.

An unspoken question lingered above their heads: did she trust him?

Irene looked at the massive figure in front of her, seated on the edge of the bed. He had known both Marcus and Emil. As a police officer, this fact should cause her to be on her guard. He was a grotesque figure in the eyes of many people: frightening and at the same time inviting ridicule. But Irene had felt his sincere grief over Marcus's murder. She had also seen his lust for vengeance and realized that he was dangerous. He had meant what he'd said when he'd asked her to catch Marcus's killer.

"I trust you, too. Without you we wouldn't have identified Marcus as quickly, and you have always answered my . . . close questions truthfully."

Tom hid his smile when he heard Irene search for the English word for "intrusive"; it became instead "close questions." Irene understood English much better than she spoke it. He knew what she meant and he hadn't corrected her. He hadn't done that a single time during their sometimes stumbling conversations.

"I'm doing everything I can to help you," he said.

Irene looked at the clock and saw that it was high time she went on her way.

"Can you call me a cab?"

"Sure."

Tom reached for the telephone on the nightstand and pushed a speed-dial button. He instantly got an answer and ordered the car to the street behind the back lot.

He rose from the bed in a cumbersome fashion and went to the door that led to the stairwell. Before he opened it, he turned toward Irene and said, "We'll keep in touch, like before. But be on your guard. Keep a good lookout."

"The same goes for you."

Tom nodded. "I understand."

She called Scandinavian Models from the taxi. Petra didn't answer. Instead, a hoarse, sexy voice introduced herself in Danish as Heidi. Irene explained who she was and asked for Petra but was told that she was unavailable. Irene quickly decided to take a chance. In an official, neutral tone she said, "Petra told me what time Jens Metz arrived on Wednesday the nineteenth. But I happened to write it down sloppily and I can't see if it says eleven thirty or eleven forty."

Irene could hear Heidi flipping through the logbook. Her smoky, dark voice said, "Eleven thirty."

Irene was overjoyed. But her voice didn't reveal a thing when she thanked Heidi for her help.

Irene saw Peter Møller outside the entrance to the church before he saw her. He was standing on the top step next to the entrance, peering out at the people passing by. She knew that she was late and she quickened her steps. Peter caught sight of her and raised his hand to wave. Without haste, he sauntered down the steps toward her.

"Sorry, Peter. I went into a store and forgot the time."

She smiled apologetically and tried to look female and scatterbrained.

Peter nodded, but she felt him subject her to careful scrutiny. Without wasting unnecessary words, he piloted her over to the parked BMW. As usual, he held open the passenger-side door for her.

He slid smoothly into the heavy stream of traffic.

"Did you find out anything new?" he asked.

"I couldn't get Petra. She wasn't there. But I got confirmation for something I had been wondering about."

She explained that she had been outside Scandinavian Models at about the same time Isabell was murdered and that she had seen a man who looked strikingly like Jens Metz go into the bordello. After forty-five minutes he still hadn't come out. Heidi had admitted that it really had been Jens Metz.

"How should we deal with this information?" she asked.

Peter sat quietly for some time.

"Don't say anything to Jens. His visit to a bordello doesn't have anything to do with Isabell's murder."

"But don't you think it's an amazing coincidence?"

"Maybe not. Jens could have become curious about Scandinavian Models after you mentioned it. Maybe he went there to get a closer look. And then he thought about other things when he was there. . . ."

"You don't think it's the least bit suspicious?" Irene persisted.

Peter gave her an amused look before he said, "As I see it, he has a perfect alibi. You were standing outside keeping an eye on him."

He had a point there.

They turned onto a wide avenue with impressive beech trees lining both sides. The immense network of branches met in the middle and had braided themselves together like an enormous vaulted ceiling. The half-light of the avenue contrasted sharply with the sun-drenched surroundings.

An arrow pointed toward a parking lot. Peter turned in and stopped inside a white marked box.

Tall oaks shadowed the well-tended flower beds in the hospital garden. The hospital itself was a low yellow stucco building. Even though the building looked idyllic and romantically old-fashioned, the barred windows on the bottom floor dispelled this impression.

A discreet brass sign next to the entrance informed visitors that they had come to Queen Anne's Hospital.

"This is a psychiatric hospital," Peter informed her.

"I'd assumed that." Irene had to try not to sound sarcastic.

The heavy entrance door was open and led to a spacious hall with pillars in a Roman style supporting the white painted ceiling. It looked fresh and newly decorated.

"She's in Ward Three," said Peter.

The door on the left bore the number one, and that on the right, number two. Consequently, Beate Bentsen should be located one floor up.

There weren't any bars on the windows of the second floor, but the door to the ward was locked. They had to ring the bell and wait for a nurse.

One of the largest men Irene had ever seen—even compared with Tom Tanaka—filled the doorway when the door was finally opened. Under his curly blond beard and tangled head of hair, which seemed to be joined, a deep voice emerged. "Who are you looking for?"

Neither Peter nor Irene managed to reply. The giant was used to this reaction.

"I'm Erland. One hundred and sixty kilos, two meters ten. An old basketball player who has gained a few kilos."

Irene heard a hint of a titter in his bass voice. Peter had finally managed to get his act together and said, "Crime police. We've been given permission to visit Beate Bentsen."

The superintendent was half sitting in a raised hospital bed. Her hair lay, uncombed, over the pillow like a mass of copper red steel wool. Her eyes were closed when they came in, but when she heard them she turned her head and looked at them.

Beate Bentsen had aged several years in the past day. Her skin was gray, and her face, free of makeup, had a sunken look to it. If you didn't know better, you would have thought she was suffering from a fatal disease. But in reality her soul and her mind had received a deadly blow, thought Irene. No parent should have to see his or her child in the condition Emil had been in when they'd found him.

Beate's gaze cleared when she saw who it was. She raised herself up on one elbow with difficulty and nodded to them. "Good of you to come. I thought about calling you."

Her lips were cracked and dry and her hand shook when she reached for the water glass on the nightstand. She took a greedy gulp. She put the glass back, coughing.

"We should have brought flowers," Irene said apologetically.

The superintendent waved off the idea with her hand as she finished coughing.

"Not necessary. I'm going home tomorrow."

Was that really possible? She didn't look like she was in any condition to be released. As if she had read their thoughts, Beate continued, "I had an acute psychological crisis. But my doctor was here after lunch and he says that it's over. I'll have to continue with the medicine but I'm not sick anymore so I don't need to be in the hospital. But I'll be on sick leave for a while."

The long speech seemed to wear her out. She sank back onto the pillow.

Peter inhaled as if he was about to say something but Beate was ahead of him. "I thought about calling you because there is something important I haven't told you."

She looked Peter straight in the eye. "You will remember that I told you about the real estate agent Simon Steiner. He was my father's best friend and died of lung cancer four years ago. All of that is true but there is something else. He was Emil's father."

Last week someone who claimed to be Emil's dead father called and requested that Isabell go to the Hotel Aurora. The killer must have known who Emil's father was, thought Irene.

"Who knew that Simon Steiner was Emil's father?" she asked.

"No one. It says 'father unknown' on his birth certificate. I never even told my parents that it was Simon."

"Did Emil know who his father was?"

"Yes. He inherited the apartment and a good deal of money when Simon died."

Beate sighed before she continued. "I might as well start from the beginning. I had known Simon all of my life. He was a few years younger than my father but they had been friends since they were kids. My father met my mother and married her. Simon married my mother's sister Susanne a few years later. Susanne was diagnosed with MS the same year they were married. They didn't have any children. My aunt was very sick off and on."

Beate stopped in order to take a drink of water.

"There was a twenty-one-year age difference between Simon and me. I was twenty when our relationship started and twenty-two when Emil was born. I knew then that Simon would never leave Susanne. The poor thing was paralyzed and wheelchair bound—"

She stopped abruptly. Maybe she could hear the bitterness in her voice as she uttered the last sentence. In a more controlled tone, she continued, "He took good care of me and Emil. He was the one who bought me the apartment where I still live. It's worth a great deal today. He paid child support the whole time up until his death."

"How could he be ordered to pay child support if he never admitted to being the father?" Irene asked.

"He wasn't ordered to pay. It was done in a voluntary and generous spirit. But I wish he hadn't left his apartment and money to Emil."

"Did you know about it in advance?"

"No."

"His wife didn't inherit?"

"Susanne died three years before he did. She was tougher than anyone could have predicted."

"But you wish that Emil hadn't inherited?"

"Because that's when he found out who his father was. He was furious. He thought that I had deprived him of contact with his father. Using the argument that his father had never attempted to reveal his paternity even though they saw each other several times a year didn't affect Emil's opinion one bit. He believed that I was the one who had stood in the way. I couldn't keep him from moving into his own apartment. He was eighteen years old."

"So the relationship between the two of you wasn't the best?"

"No. Not for the first two years after his move. But recently we started spending more time together, even though he only let me into the apartment once. I didn't say anything but he knew what I thought . . . we mostly met at my place or in a pub. We were getting along better and better. I'm very grateful for that now . . . that it's over."

Beate's voice broke, and heavy tears rolled down her cheeks.

Would she have the strength to answer the questions that had to be asked? To Irene's relief, it was Peter who paved the way. "Were you aware of Emil's odd taste in music?"

Beate reached for a package of Kleenex. She fished one out and dried her eyes. "Of course I saw his so-called music room. . . . It was horrible. But we never discussed it. He would only have become angry."

"We found two police uniforms in his closet. Did you know about them?"

Now Beate hesitated. When she started speaking, her voice sounded very tired. "I didn't know that he had two. One is my old uniform. He asked to borrow it for a masquerade ball and I never got it back."

"How long ago was that?"

"About two years ago when he got in touch with me again after the move. That's probably why I never asked for it back. I didn't want to anger him and have him cut off contact again."

Irene decided to take the risk and ask the question burning inside her. "I got the impression that you and Bill Faraday know each other well. He came right away, on short notice. . . ."

"He's my lover."

The answer came so quickly that neither Irene nor Peter was ready with a follow-up question. To Irene's relief, Beate smiled faintly at them.

"You should see the looks on your faces. Mouths gaping open! I met Bill when Emil inherited the apartment. I was required to get in touch with him because he owns the building. Emil was so young when he moved in but there weren't any big problems. The building is a very old cooperative with old-fashioned and complicated rules. Bill owns and manages the property, but the tenants own their apartments. The tenants pay a management fee. It's that, plus the rent, that provides an income for Bill."

"Like a private tenant-owner's company," Irene said.

"Yes. Bill manages several properties."

Peter cleared his throat and announced that he wanted to ask a new question.

"You knew that Emil was . . . gay. Do you know any of his partners? Has he had a steady boyfriend recently?"

Beate shook her head. "No. He never confided in me. I've had the feeling that he has been very lonely. That's what the parent of a homo-sexual child is most afraid of, that they will be alone. If he had had a steady . . . friend and a secure relationship, he probably wouldn't have been so restless."

Maybe his preferences had been so particular that it hadn't been easy to find a like-minded individual.

"Did you know the people Emil rented rooms to?" Peter asked.

"No. He handled that himself. I have the feeling that he only rented the rooms out now and then. Of course it provided some extra income but he had the income from Simon's assets to live on. Thank God they are placed so that he can't . . . couldn't spend the money. The income was paid to him each month."

"I've heard that he was studying law," said Irene.

"It didn't go very well," Beate said shortly.

"Did you know that Emil often hung out in a gay sex shop in Vesterbro that is owned by one Tom Tanaka?" Irene continued.

Beate looked incredibly tired. She tried in vain to wet her lips.

"I know that he was often seen at different gay hangouts. But I don't know if he spent a lot of time in Tanaka's store."

It was clear that Beate didn't have the energy to talk anymore. Peter could see it as well.

"Take care of yourself, Chief. We can talk again when you are feeling a bit stronger."

"Thanks. I'll call if I come up with anything. My brain almost feels paralyzed right now," she whispered.

Irene felt deep sympathy for Beate. The image of Isabell's dead face floated past for one second. A strong pang of guilt hit her. In a sense, she was an accessory. The murderer was working close to her; involving her was his intention. Catching the murderer was something she owed his violated victims. Now it had become personal.

"SHE DIDN'T seem to know anything about his sex life," said Irene.

"Maybe it's just as well," said Peter.

They sat in the comfortable BMW and zoomed at an even speed toward downtown Copenhagen. Peter skillfully maneuvered the car into the parking spot in front of the Hotel Alex.

"Are you going to eat now?" he asked.

Irene saw that it was only five thirty. "In an hour. Then I'll go across the street; the food is good there," she said.

"I'll pick you up here."

"You shouldn't feel like you need to. . . ."

"I don't feel like fixing dinner tonight. I had already planned on going out to eat."

He stepped out of the car and quickly went around and opened the passenger-side door for her. Irene thought it was a bit embarrassing. She decided that it must be because she wasn't used to it.

A LONG hot shower followed by a short cold one raised her spirits. She relaxed, wrapped in a clean bath towel, a smaller towel wound around her wet hair. For a while she sat in the only recliner in the room with her fingers clasping the bottle she had just taken from the mini-bar. She slowly drank the cold Hof.

Her brain felt sluggish and overwhelmed by the events of the past few days. The murderer must have shown up at some point. Where? When? She couldn't locate him among all of her unsorted impressions. But she knew that he had been close by. He had been in Copenhagen a week ago, on her previous visit. Was he still here? Irene felt convinced that he wasn't. It was high time for her to return to Göteborg.

She longed intensely for Krister and the girls. She went to get her cell phone and called home.

Just before six thirty, Irene went downstairs to the lobby. They had put up the "Jell-O shot evening" sign in the bar again. She saw Jonny at a table in the bar together with two men and a woman. He lifted a small glass filled with pink Jell-O.

She didn't bother going into the bar. She was content. There would be no discussion about who was going to drive tomorrow. She exited through the revolving door and waved at Peter, who was walking toward her.

They went back to Restaurant Vesuvius. The head waiter was a gray-haired older man who showed them to a table for two in the smaller room with the movie-star photos on the walls. Two younger women sitting at a table by the window looked at Irene with undisguised jealousy and Irene became keenly aware of the fact that she was in the company of a very attractive man. When Peter stood near her in order to pull out her chair, she caught a whiff of his good aftershave. Light, masculine, and sensual. Could be Armani.

He pushed her chair in and when he leaned forward she could feel the warmth of his breath on her neck.

"It's been a busy day for you. Now you have to relax," he said. He smiled encouragingly at her when he seated himself across from her. "Do you want wine?"

She hesitated for half a second and then common sense took over.

"No, thanks. I have to drive tomorrow. Jonny is already in fine form in the bar. He's drinking Jell-O shots with a group of people. Something tells me it will be a quiet trip home."

Peter laughed. His eyes were as blue as the short-sleeved Sand shirt he was wearing. The top two buttons were open, revealing blond hair. A thin gold chain glimmered against his golden brown skin. He had hung his light-colored linen jacket on the back of his chair.

She still had on her dark blue linen pants, which at this point were wrinkled. She had managed to press them a bit with the iron in the hotel room, but they weren't pristine. Her linen jacket was still in good shape. She wore a new silver-gray satin top under the jacket. Her feet in blue suede sandals were bare.

"Beer then. What would you like to eat?"

"Something spicy that will make my spirits soar."

"How does *gamberoni sole mio* sound? Giant shrimp in a lobster sauce with cayenne pepper."

"That sounds perfect."

"Good. I'll have that as well. A drink before dinner?"

She hesitated. "OK, one. A dry martini, please."

The drinks came to the table very quickly. Peter and Irene raised their wide glasses in order to toast. Their eyes met and Irene felt her cheeks become hot. Damn the man for being so handsome!

A chill suddenly ran down her spine. Her brain became crystal clear. The police officer.

Mechanically, she took a sip of her drink as she thought feverishly. She put down her glass and said in as natural a tone of voice as she could muster, "You never had a chance to tell me where you got your tan." She smiled encouragingly but didn't get a response.

He looked into his glass. Finally he said, "I wasn't planning on telling you. I was in South Africa."

"How exciting! How long were you there?"

"Three weeks. A tour and safari."

"How wonderful, to get away in March when the weather is so bad. . . ."

"It wasn't in March. We . . . I left on April 1."

A month after Marcus's supposed trip to Thailand; Marcus had been dead for almost a month already. Peter's sunburn also seemed to match better with three weeks in April than with a few weeks the month before.

But there were tanning salons. You could maintain a tan. She had to confirm the date Peter had taken his vacation.

He seemed unwilling to talk about his trip. The conversation became strained. Irene decided to start a new topic: Copenhagen as a tourist city. Peter thawed out a bit but the intimate feeling was completely gone. Irene felt that something had come between them despite the wonderful food and drink.

What had happened on the trip to South Africa? Had he *really* been in South Africa?

They finished dinner at ten o'clock. He escorted her back to the hotel but didn't show any interest in following her inside.

Chapter 12

JONNY WAS ASLEEP BEFORE they left Copenhagen. He woke up when they rattled onto the ferry. Irritable, he tottered into the ferry's candy store and pulled a wrinkled shopping list from his coat pocket. Absentmindedly, he put bags of Drungelvrål, Dumlekola, and gummy bears into the shopping basket for his four kids. Irene noted that he didn't buy anything for his wife, unless the bottle of Black Velvet he purchased in the liquor store next to the hotel was for her.

Jonny cheered up after consuming a strong beer in the cafeteria. Irene had two cups of coffee. He fell asleep again as soon as they got into the car and didn't even wake up when they drove down the ramp.

The trip home along the coast of Halland went by quickly and uneventfully on the new highway. Jonny slept all the way to Kungsbacka. Jonny had to make a quick pit stop at Statoil. Irene filled up the car while she waited.

She dropped Jonny off outside his row house in Mölndal and continued home to Fiskebäck. It was almost two o'clock and she was hungry. She planned to unpack the car and get a bite to eat. Then she was going to drive to the station and speak with Andersson.

At three thirty she stepped into the superintendent's office. He looked up from a stack of papers lying on the table in front of him.

"Hi. Good that you came. Where's Jonny?" he asked.

Irene tried to look surprised. "He hasn't come in yet?"

She was reluctant to reveal her suspicions to her boss. Jonny had probably gone straight to bed and was fast asleep now.

"No. When did you get home?"

"At two thirty. I dropped him off at his home so that he wouldn't have to carry his things around with him and so that he could pick up his car. He hasn't arrived?"

"No."

"Maybe the car wouldn't start. . . ."

"Possibly. While we're on the subject of cars, that 'Mats' from Copenhagen called. He's so damned difficult to understand but I got that they've found Marcus Tosscander's car."

"Marcus's car! Where?"

"In a garage. He said that I should tell you it was in Emil's garage."

Emil's garage? Emil had a garage? Where?

" 'Mats' wants you to call him. He gave me some blasted number in Danish but I didn't understand it. Fours and threes . . . completely incomprehensible!"

Irene smiled.

"I'm thinking about asking for extra money for language assistance for these joint investigations."

Since she had the numbers for both Peter Møller's and Jens Metz's direct lines she said, "I'll call from my office. Then I'll report to you. Prepare yourself because it's going to take quite a while. Load up the coffeemaker."

She nodded in the direction of the old coffee pot, which was standing on top of Andersson's bookshelf. In recent years a coffee machine had been installed in the corridor but Andersson had kept his percolator. Irene knew that he always hid a package of coffee in the bottom drawer of his desk.

"YES. THIS is Inspector Metz."

"Hi. Irene Huss. Thanks again for your assistance."

"Thanks to you, too. It got real quiet here in Copenhagen after you left. Nothing is happening."

Metz laughed and Irene politely laughed, too, before she interrupted him. "You spoke with my boss and said that Marcus's car was found in Emil's garage."

"That's right. There's a garage under the building. Some of the tenants have parking spaces in the back lot but Emil had a spot in the garage. We did a routine check and found a Swedish-registered red Pontiac convertible. It turns out that it belongs to Marcus Tosscander."

"The photo above Emil's bed . . . the model is Marcus Tosscander," Irene said. "I wasn't sure when I saw it the first time, his face is so fuzzy. But I've seen other similar pictures of Marcus. The picture in the

bedroom and the calling card on Emil's bulletin board clearly point to
their having known each other. The car in Emil's parking spot confirms
it. I also think we can go ahead and assume that Emil was the one Marcus was staying with during his time in Copenhagen."

"Quite possibly."

"Both of them fell victim to the same killer. That must mean that
they knew him."

"That's what we think as well. But the question is, why didn't Emil
report Marcus missing? And why did he let that nice car stand there in
the garage?"

"Maybe he didn't have a driver's license?"

"Maybe. I'll check into that. But then why did he have a parking
space? And where is *his* car?"

"Have you heard anything from the medical examiner yet?"

"Yes. Emil had been dead a week, just as we thought. The exact time
of death is difficult to pinpoint but Blokk says that it was either late
Wednesday night or Thursday during the early morning. He was strangled with a noose. Probably a very thick rope, judging by the marks on
his neck. Isabell Lind had an identical strangulation mark.

"Have you found the rope?"

"No. There wasn't one at the Hotel Aurora or in Emil's apartment. We haven't found the instrument the murderer used on their
pelvises either. Blokk thinks it's some sort of a hard baton. In the preliminary report he actually says 'a baton of ordinary or large police
issue.' "

The police officer, again. Irene's skin crawled. It made her ask,
"Before I forget, when was Peter Møller in South Africa?"

"In April for three weeks. Why?" Jens Metz sounded very surprised.

"I apologize; it is not relevant. I asked about his vacation yesterday
and he seemed so unwilling to talk about South Africa, I felt embarrassed. It's not that strange to be interested in an unusual vacation des-
tination and want to ask about it, is it?"

Irene hoped that Jens would accept her half lie and leave it at that.

"It's not strange that he didn't want to talk about it," Metz said dryly.
He went on, "We've sent both of Emil's uniforms to the technicians.
Several dark stains could be seen on one of them that looked very sus-
picious."

"Blood?"

"Could be."

Irene came up with something. "It's odd that all of Marcus's belongings seem to have disappeared. As if someone wanted to remove all traces of him. Where are his clothes? After all, he went home to Göteborg at the beginning of March to pack his summer clothes for the trip to Thailand. Why aren't his winter clothes still in Emil's closets? And where are his work things? We know that he had brought them with him to Copenhagen because he did several jobs while he was there."

"We're in the process of searching the rest of Emil's building, the attic, and the basement. Maybe his things are hidden somewhere."

"Please call as soon as something interesting shows up."

"I'll do that. Take care."

Irene went into Andersson's office. The newly made coffee smelled wonderful. Hannu Rauhala was also there. Irene congratulated him on his change of status.

"So there was no honeymoon right after the wedding?"

"No."

Had it been anyone else, Irene probably would have asked when they were going to take one, but she knew that it wouldn't do any good with Hannu. If he didn't want to tell, he wouldn't. She would have to ask Birgitta when she got a chance.

"I've just spoken with Hans Pahliss. He's coming here tomorrow at around four o'clock," said Hannu.

Irene made a mental memo to be there for the questioning. It would be very interesting to hear what the virologist had to add.

They poured the freshly brewed coffee and Irene started on her long report.

Neither the superintendent nor Hannu interrupted her. Her presentation still took almost two hours. Andersson pressed the tips of his fingers together and hummed. Hannu fixed his gaze on a spot just past her left ear. Both showed signs of deep concentration.

Finally the superintendent said, "Since Emil and Marcus knew each other, we have to assume that they knew the murderer. The question is whether he's in Göteborg or Copenhagen."

"Both places," said Hannu.

"He has clearly murdered in both cities, but I'm asking where he lives," Andersson clarified.

"Both places," Hannu repeated.

Was he teasing the superintendent? Irene looked at Hannu in surprise, before the lightbulb went on.

"You mean that the murderer is actually a resident of both cities?" she said.

"At the least, he has strong connections to both of them."

"Marcus talked about his doctor in Göteborg. He indicated that he could be dangerous. At another point, he said that the police officer in Copenhagen could be almost as dangerous."

The superintendent interrupted her, irritated. "That's what your protected informant told you. What is this nonsense? Why can't we know his identity? The police uniform was found at Emil's, and you said yourself that a lot of evidence points to Emil masquerading as a police officer."

"But we don't know for sure. That's why I need to keep my informant's identity a secret. Especially after what happened to Isabell and Emil," Irene said obstinately.

Andersson snorted. "And what would happen if you told us here in Göteborg? Do you think one of your colleagues here—"

He was interrupted by a noise at the door. Jonny opened it and entered. He looked sober and smelled of soap but he couldn't do much about his bloodshot eyes.

"Hi. I've sorted through the photocopies I brought from Copenhagen from the investigation of Isabell Lind's murder. Jens Metz will send the final autopsy report when it's done."

Without difficulty he went up to Andersson's desk and put the pile of paper onto the stained desktop.

Andersson looked at Jonny bitterly. Then he sighed loudly and turned to Irene. "OK. I can understand your misgivings."

GETTING HOME was wonderful. Krister had made the rounds of the market and stocked up. He was off work the next day and wouldn't return until Saturday afternoon. When Irene stepped over the threshold he was busy seasoning pork chops with garlic and spices. Jenny was standing next to him, looking dissatisfied. She didn't comment on her father's choice of food. Instead, she continued to fill her greased pan with sliced tomatoes and squash. Katarina was chopping iceberg lettuce, which she put in a bowl together with corn and cucumbers.

Sammie, as usual, was the first to greet Irene and did so with unreserved joy. But her husband and children weren't far behind.

Katarina was depressed. The doctor had told her that she couldn't train for at least two months. No damage to her skeleton was visible on the X-rays but pain and limited mobility in her neck and back were still troublesome.

"There's a risk of chronic pain if I'm not careful," she said.

"What treatment did he recommend?" Irene asked, concerned.

"Acupuncture and physical therapy, which I'm already doing."

"She was referred to an orthopedist who specializes in whiplash injuries," Krister said.

"What if I can never compete again! As it is now, I don't even have the energy to train," said Katarina. She was on the verge of tears.

"You can devote yourself to walking the dog. Dogs are wonderful exercisers. And it looks like we'll soon have Sammie's son in the house," said Krister.

"What? No! I don't have the energy for two dogs," Irene groaned.

"*You* don't have the energy?! You're never at home," said Jenny.

This stung. Weakly Irene said, "Never home . . . it's not that often that I have to go to Copenhagen or anywhere else. It's just with this case—"

Jenny interrupted her, "You're never home anyway. It's always work, work, work. But the rest of us really want to have a little puppy. He's so adorable!"

"I haven't said that I would really like to have a puppy," Krister protested.

Both of his daughters looked at him meaningfully. Jenny said pointedly, "And who was it who was completely beside himself yesterday when we went to look at him? 'Oh, so cute and cuddly'!"

"You went to look at the puppy yesterday?" asked Irene.

"The lady called. She wants to get rid of him by the end of next week or the beginning of the week after. Then he'll be eight weeks old. None of us have found someone who is interested . . . so the girls and I went to look at him," Krister said apologetically.

"And of course he was adorable," Irene sighed.

"Adorable!" her family said in unison.

"SOMETIMES YOU fall into your own trap," said Tommy Persson.

He didn't try to hide his joy. They were sitting in the office they shared, taking an extra cup of coffee to get the Friday morning started. Irene had just given him the short version of what had happened in Copenhagen. And summed up with the fact that the Huss family would probably have to take one of the puppies.

"Everything at our house revolves around the puppy who's coming. Sara has bought food dishes and chewing toys and God knows what all," Tommy said, defeated.

"I hadn't thought about starting over with a puppy again. Vet visits, raising them, and training. Yuck! It's like having kids again." In order to change the subject, Irene asked, "How is it going with Jack the Ripper?"

"OK. I have a theory that I'm working on. Two of his victims talked about a certain smell he had. Now the last girl has come up with what it was."

Tommy stopped and paused dramatically before he slowly said, "Food."

"Food?"

"Yes. Kitchen odor. The smell seems to come from his clothes or maybe his hair. My theory is that Jack works in the kitchen of a restaurant. The pubs usually stop serving food around twelve. It takes at least one and a half and sometimes two hours to get the kitchen in order. You know that seeing as how you're married to someone in the business."

Irene nodded. Krister was rarely home before two when he worked evenings.

"All four times, Jack has made his move between one thirty and three in the morning. Always in Vasastan. I'm thinking about taking a look at the pubs in the area. Especially the kitchen staffs."

"You can eliminate Krister right away. He's too big and fat to match the description. And too old. Jack is around thirty if I remember correctly."

"Krister isn't the first person I would suspect in this case," Tommy said.

* * *

IRENE SPENT the rest of the day in front of her computer. The only interruption was lunch at the employee cafeteria of the nearby insurance office. The chicken casserole wasn't too bad, but Irene thought longingly about the lunches in Copenhagen. Jens and Peter were probably sitting at a nice pub with an ice-cold beer in front of them right now. Suddenly her light beer felt very thin.

The report she had to write about events in Copenhagen turned out to be a long one. She mentioned the photo of Marcus that hung above Emil's bed. It was too important to leave out. But she sneaked in the little lie she had served the superintendent and Hannu earlier that morning, namely that she had recognized Marcus from the pictures in the photo album that they had found in his apartment. Even if some of the pictures had been naked studies, they weren't in the same league as that framed photo. It occurred to her that it might be useful to try to locate the photographer. He must be well known. But who could provide information about a photographer who took these kinds of photos? Irene had to get copies of the photos from Copenhagen before she could attempt to find him.

She called Jens Metz. As luck would have it, he was in his office. He promised to arrange to send her a copy of the photo over Emil's bed.

"Do you need it in the original size?" he asked.

"Not necessarily. But not too small."

"OK. I'll take care of it."

Before they hung up, Irene thanked him again for the friendly treatment she and Jonny had received in Copenhagen, and Jens countered politely by inviting her down again.

After some hesitation Irene took out her cell phone and called Tom Tanaka. It rang several times before he answered. When she heard his hoarse voice she realized that she had awakened him.

"Tom speaking."

"Hi. Irene Huss. Sorry to wake you."

Tom mumbled something unintelligible in response. Irene decided to keep the phone call short.

"It's important. Can you arrange to let me have copies of the photos you have on your bedroom wall?" she asked.

It was quiet for some time. Irene assumed that Tom was trying to wake up and understand what she had said. Finally she heard his gruff voice. "I have a Polaroid camera. Is it good enough if I use that?"

"I don't know. Maybe. We can always make an enlargement."

Personally, she wasn't among the most chipper of morning people so she understood his irritation about being awakened. But it was actually one thirty in the afternoon. As if he had realized how grumpy he sounded, he hurried to add, "I know a guy who can make real copies of the photos. But it will take a bit longer. Then you can have them enlarged."

"That would be really nice of you. Could I suggest that you take the Polaroid pictures with your camera and send them today and then send the others when they are ready?"

"I'll take care of it."

Irene decided to get in one more question. "You haven't come up with the name of the photographer or the name of the other model?"

"No. Marcus never mentioned them. He had the pictures with him when he came here for the last time. They were ready to hang. Without asking me, he took down the two paintings I had on the wall and put up his instead. He said that they should hang there while he was gone so that I wouldn't forget him."

To her surprise, she suddenly heard a man's voice say something in the background. She also heard Tom say, "Soon." Who was with him? A vague feeling of concern overcame her. It could be heard in her voice when she said, "You're being careful, right?"

"Absolutely. You, too."

After he'd hung up, she was unable to free herself from her feeling of concern.

She spent the time until four o'clock finishing the report, then turned off the computer with a feeling of liberation. Her body felt stiff. Her neck and shoulders popped when she stretched. She would have to take a really long run tonight to chase the stiffness from her body. Not to mention the high living in Copenhagen, which had settled around her stomach. Her jeans had felt tight this morning. But her period would be coming in two days, so that might also be the reason. In any case, she needed some serious workouts over the weekend.

On the way to Hannu's office she picked up two cups of coffee. When she pushed open his door with her foot, she could see that there was a man sitting at the desk, but it was Hans Pahliss, not Hannu. Irene recognized him from the pictures in Marcus's photo album. He looked up from the pile of papers he had been reading.

A sharp brown gaze focused on her over the edge of lowered reading glasses. His dark hair was a little too long and hung untidily across his forehead. It looked as though he had run his hand through it several times. His face was pale, with sharp lines, and showed heavy blue-black beard stubble. His body seemed to be thin. Irene got the impression that Pahliss was several years older and significantly shorter than his partner, Anders Gunnarsson.

Irene smiled and said, "Inspector Irene Huss. I brought some coffee. Would you like milk or sugar?"

"Milk, please."

"Then I'll go and get one with milk. Hannu can take this one."

She placed both steaming cups on the desk and went out again. She caught sight of Hannu at the far end of the corridor. He had just reached his office when she returned with Hans Pahliss's coffee.

The virologist was packing his papers into a large briefcase. His thin hands, with their long, sensitive fingers, nervously closed all the locks and set the combination numbers. If she hadn't known his profession she would have guessed he was a pianist. He folded up his frameless reading glasses and put them in the chest pocket of his suit jacket, clasped his hands in front of him on the desk, and looked challengingly at Irene.

"Well," said Hans Pahliss.

There was no question in his voice. It was a command to start the conversation.

"Anders Gunnarsson has probably talked to you about what has happened," Irene started.

Hans Pahliss nodded.

"How well did you know Marcus?"

"We were good friends."

"Did you speak with Marcus when he called at the beginning of March?"

"No."

"Why not?"

"I wasn't home."

"Did Anders tell you that he had called?"

"Yes."

"What did Anders say?"

"What did he say? That Marcus had called. That he was in a hurry because he was going to pack for a trip to Thailand."

"Did Marcus say who he was going to travel with?"

"No. We speculated a bit about it."

"Did you come up with who it could be?"

"No. It could have been anyone."

"Were you aware that Anders and Marcus had been together?"

"Yes."

"How did that affect your feelings toward Marcus?"

"It didn't affect me at all."

"Not at all?"

"No."

Pahliss hadn't touched his coffee mug. He maintained eye contact with Irene. A quick thought about the unfairness of nature flickered through Irene's brain. Long eyelashes like that should not belong to a man. The next thought that struck her was how different Anders Gunnarsson and Hans Pahliss were. The dentist had been open and talkative while the virologist seemed to be his exact opposite.

Hannu had been sitting quietly during Irene's preliminary questions but now he leaned forward suddenly and said, "Have you been to Copenhagen?"

Pahliss looked both surprised and irritated when he answered. "Of course."

"As a tourist or for a longer period of time?"

"I was a guest researcher for two months at the state hospital."

Irene realized that she had been holding her breath. Hannu continued without showing that he noticed. "When was that?"

"February and March 1997."

"Where did you live?"

"What does it matter? What does this have to do with Marcus—"

He stopped, struck by a thought.

"Of course. I understand. Naturally, Marcus also stayed with Emil," he said shortly.

Irene's pulse rate increased so much that her ears hummed. Did she have a predisposition to high blood pressure, like the superintendent?

Her voice was almost shaky when she asked, "Did you live with Emil Bentsen when you were in Copenhagen?"

"Yes. I got his address from an acquaintance here in Göteborg. His rooms were centrally located, cheap and good. I gave the address to Marcus when he asked me about places to live in Copenhagen."

"You gave him Emil's address?"

"Yes."

"But then you knew where Marcus was living in Copenhagen."

For the first time something that could be interpreted as a smile crossed Pahliss's face.

"We didn't know. Marcus went around and asked everyone he knew about places to stay in Copenhagen. He was loaded down with addresses when he left. He was going to stay at a hotel the first few days and then let us know when he had decided on a permanent address."

Hans Pahliss suddenly seemed to discover his mug on the desk and took a large gulp of the lukewarm coffee.

"But he never did?"

"No."

They finally had an explanation for how Marcus had ended up at Emil's. Irene's thoughts were interrupted when Hannu asked, "Who gave you Emil's address?"

For the first time, Pahliss looked uncertain. But when he realized that the police officers had noticed his hesitancy, he said with assurance, "Actually one of my exes. Before you ask: yes, Anders knows him and we hang out as friends."

His tone of voice sharpened.

"Who?" Hannu repeated.

"Pontus Zander."

"How did he know Emil Bentsen?"

"No idea."

"How can we reach Pontus Zander?"

"The emergency room at Sahlgren Hospital. He's a nurse. Otherwise he lives on Kungshöjd."

Pahliss gave them Zander's address and telephone number.

Irene quickly asked the next question. "You were in Copenhagen in February and March of 1997. Did you return there at the end of May that year?"

Pahliss shook his head with emphasis. "No. I didn't return until just before Christmas 1997."

"Did you live with Emil Bentsen then?"

"No. It was just for four days. Anders was with me. We stayed at a hotel."

"Did you keep in touch with Emil after you had moved?"

Pahliss looked uncertain again. "No. I sent a Christmas card that year but there was nothing else."

"Did you spend time with Emil while you were living there?"

Now Pahliss became irritated. "I didn't live with him. I rented an apartment from him. We hardly saw each other. During the two months I stayed there I was rarely home before ten. Then I stumbled into bed and slept. Research is not a nine-to-five job."

"What did you think about Emil?"

"Nothing. As I said, we didn't spend any time together."

He stopped and looked sharply at Hannu. "Why are you asking about Emil Bentsen?"

Irene was the one who revealed Emil's murder. Hans Pahliss didn't interrupt her. When she was finished, he sat in silence. Finally he whispered, "What is happening? First Marcus and now Emil . . ."

Irene tried to choose her words. "There have been two other murders that bear the signature of this murderer. But those victims were women. It is the dismemberment and . . . a few other things that indicate it's the same killer. Our medical examiners say that the killer's method points to a strong familiarity with autopsy procedures," she said.

Irene paused dramatically in order to see Pahliss's reaction. There was none. She continued, "We think that both Marcus and Emil knew the killer. There is a possibility that you and Anders also know him. You happen to be a doctor and may also know others who could—"

"No! None of the doctors I know could do such a thing! Doctors don't do that sort of thing!"

"You aren't aware of any rumors about a colleague who has particular tendencies?" Irene asked calmly.

Pahliss was still upset. His temper was hidden beneath a calm surface but his voice was filled with rage when he answered.

"No! Absolutely not!"

He squeezed his interlaced hands so tightly that the knuckles turned white.

Hannu said in an expressionless voice, "We're searching for a terrifying killer. He's going to kill again. And he's probably in your vicinity."

The effect on Hans Pahliss was like that of a bucket of ice-cold water. First he sat frozen, then he slowly loosened up. He crumpled up in his chair and put his hands over his face. Neither Irene nor Hannu said anything. After some time he took his hands away and looked at both officers. He was teary eyed. He said, "It's possible that he is close to me. I just don't know who he is. Marcus was drawn to men with, as you say, particular tendencies. He had other men as well. I guess you could say that they were more normal. But it never lasted. He was driven by his search for the . . . exotic. If he stayed with someone a longer time it was always one of these special types."

"Did you notice any signs that might point to Marcus's being drawn to necrophilia?"

Pahliss gave a start. His terror wasn't for show. "No! Never."

"Would you like to tell us more precisely what preferences he had?"

"Odd men. A lot of sadomasochism. But he never discussed his sexual adventures with me and Anders. We knew him only as a very good friend."

Anders Gunnarsson had known him as more than a friend. But according to Gunnarsson that relationship had ended after only one week. That's what Gunnarsson had said. Irene decided to speak with the dentist one more time.

"Do you know if Marcus was ever together with a doctor?" she asked.

The virologist thought for a moment. Then he shook his head. "Not that I know of."

As he spoke he stiffened and gazed up at a point above Irene's head. In a strained voice, he added, "Last summer . . . we were picnicking at Marstrand. We were a group of about ten people drinking wine and eating good food. I remember that Marcus got pretty drunk and started talking about a new guy he had just met. 'He's great. He's my new personal physician,' or something along those lines. Then he started laughing as if he had said something very funny."

"He never mentioned that guy again?"

"No."

Assurance was growing inside Irene. The doctor existed. And he was here in Göteborg.

HANS PAHLISS had gone and the feeling of the coming weekend began to descend over the offices on their floor. People had started going home; soon only the people on call would be left. A few hours of relative calm would engulf the station and then the weekend would start. Sirens would start blaring after darkness covered the city. It never got completely dark at the end of May, and the evening was warm. Teenagers who felt the end of the term drawing near would go out partying and let out a whole year's worth of frustration. The adults, feeling "continental," would congregate at the city's restaurants and bars with outdoor seating. Together with the usual weekend quota of robberies and assaults, it pointed to a difficult night for the Göteborg police.

"How did it occur to you to ask Pahliss if he had been in Copenhagen?" Irene asked, curious.

Hannu shrugged his shoulders. "Just a whim. I thought about his conference in Paris. If he had been to Paris, then he could also have been to Copenhagen," he said.

"We should try and talk with this Pontus Zander as soon as possible," Irene thought out loud.

Hannu nodded. "I'll look for him."

Irene couldn't keep from saying teasingly, "You're not in a hurry to get home to the wife?"

Hannu's bottomless gaze passed quickly over her face before he answered, "She's staking out the strip club until ten tonight."

In an attempt to brush her silly comment aside, Irene said, "How is it going? Will they be able to get Robert Larsson for laundering money through the club?"

"Maybe."

When would she learn that you couldn't get Hannu to make any personal comments? This man made Greta Garbo look like an exhibitionist.

To change the topic, she asked, "Are you on call this weekend?"

"No."

"I am. If you get Pontus Zander, arrange a good time and place with him. Put a note on my desk and I'll take care of the questioning."

"I will if I can't meet him tonight. If I can, I'll take it myself," said Hannu.

"OK. Have a good weekend."

"You, too."

Chapter 13

THE NOTE WAS LYING in the middle of the desk. It was the first thing Irene saw when she stepped across the threshold of her office on Saturday morning. She put the coffee mug down on the desk with a yawn and read:

Pontus Zander is coming at 11:00. He worked the late shift last night. Didn't have a chance to ask him anything on the phone. P.Z. seems to be our link between Marcus and Emil.

Hannu

It was an unusually wordy message for Hannu. Irene hoped that he was right. Zander could be the breakthrough they had been waiting for, the explanation as to how the clues from Göteborg and Copenhagen came together.

IRENE WAS deeply engrossed in routine duties that had been piling up when the intercom beeped and reception announced that a Pontus Zander wanted to see her. She turned off the computer and took out her authorization card.

She immediately knew who Pontus was when she stepped out of the elevator and looked through the glass wall toward the reception area. He was tall and blond, and looked a lot like Anders Gunnarsson. Apparently Pahliss was attracted to a certain type. The difference was that Pontus had longer hair, pulled together in a neat ponytail at the back of his neck.

Pontus stood talking with two uniformed police officers. They were laughing and seemed to know each other, which wasn't all that surprising since Pontus worked in an emergency room. Irene cleared her throat lightly before saying, "Pontus Zander?"

He stopped in the middle of his conversation and smiled at Irene. "Yes, and you must be Irene Hysén?"

"Huss."

They approached each other. His handshake was warm and firm. The two patrolmen said good-bye and went out through the main entrance door.

Irene made a stop at the coffee machine when they got to the fourth floor. With a steaming mug in each hand, she led Pontus into her office. She placed one mug on the desk next to her chair and the other in front of the visitor's chair.

"Please sit down," she said and gestured toward the chair.

Pontus Zander sat. The sun shone on his blond hair and a ray was reflected in his steely blue eyes, which were framed by thick dark eyelashes.

"I don't know if my colleague had time to tell you what we wanted to ask you about," Irene started.

She intentionally allowed her question to hang in the air. Pontus answered immediately, "No, I was very stressed when he called. We got a guy with hemorrhaging varicosities in his throat at the same time as five people injured in a minivan accident. Plus the usual bunch of emergencies that had been sitting and waiting for several hours. It was tough last night. God!"

He rolled his eyes and sighed. Irene was not absolutely certain as to what bleeding varicose-something was but she decided not to pursue the matter.

"As you know, we're investigating the murder of Marcus Tosscander. Did you know him?" she asked instead.

"Not very well. We met at a party that Anders and Hans had. And at their wedding, of course. But otherwise I actually haven't spent any time with Marcus."

"You two never dated?"

Pontus looked genuinely surprised. "No, as I said, we didn't know . . ."

"Marcus wasn't always diligent about getting to know his partners . . . beforehand. Are you absolutely sure that you were never together?"

Now Pontus had a mischievous look on his face. He smiled when he answered, "To be honest, I actually tried flirting with him at the wedding but he wasn't interested. He only had eyes for a big dark-skinned American named Leon. A real motorcycle-and-leather queen."

"Does Leon live in Göteborg?"

"No, Los Angeles. He's a doctor. A virologist, just like Hans. That's how they met and became good friends. Leon's research concerns various HIV viruses, and Hans works with the herpes virus."

"Do you know if Hans and Leon have been more than friends?"

"I actually don't think they've ever been together. They aren't each other's type."

"But Marcus and Leon were?"

Pontus pursed his lips and thought before he replied. "Leon was Marcus's type. That much I can say."

"But you weren't."

"No." Pontus sighed lightly.

It was about time to discuss Copenhagen. In a neutral tone of voice, Irene said, "Exactly when did you live in Copenhagen?"

He looked surprised. "How do you . . . Almost three years ago."

"When exactly?"

"In October '96."

"What did you do there?"

"We have an exchange program within the union. You trade jobs and living quarters with a colleague in another Nordic country. Loads of fun!"

"How long were you in Copenhagen?"

"One month. But what does this have to do with Marcus—"

"How did you end up at Emil Bentsen's?"

Now Pontus looked confused. "What does that matter? Isn't it Marc—"

"I'll get back to that. Could you please answer my question?"

"OK. The colleague who I was going to trade with was named Lise. Lise called two weeks before I was going to leave for Copenhagen and she was completely distraught! There had been a fire in her building and it wasn't possible to stay in her apartment because of smoke and water damage. But she promised to arrange a place where I could live and she did. I know that she put an ad in the paper and got some replies. She decided on Emil Bentsen's apartment and that's where I stayed the whole time."

"I understood from Hans Pahliss that you recommended that others rent from Emil when they needed a place to stay in Copenhagen."

"Yes. The location and the rent are excellent."

"What did you think of Emil?"

"He's a little . . . strange. I didn't see much of him. I was out on the town when I wasn't working. But he was weird."

"Weird? What do you mean?"

Pontus sat for a moment searching for words. Finally he said, "He played strange heavy metal at the highest volume. Completely incomprehensible music. It seemed to me that he was sneaking around. A few times I had the feeling that someone had been in my room while I was out, and sometimes I heard someone moving on the other side of the door in the kitchen. It led into Emil's apartment. And one time I clearly saw and heard the door pulled shut when I came out into the kitchen early in the morning. God! He was scaring me half to death!"

"Was anyone else living there aside from you?"

"No, but I was only paying for one room."

"Were you ever inside Emil's apartment?"

"No. I kept my distance from him. I don't really know what it was, but I didn't like him."

"Yet you recommended his place to others?"

"Of course. It's impossible to find a cheaper place at such a good location. And you don't have to hang out with Emil if you don't want to. He didn't make any attempts at getting to know me, except for that strange sneaking around."

"Who else have you recommended Emil to?"

"Hans Pahliss and a guy at work named Sven. Emil asked me to put up a notice in a good place about his room for rent. He gave me some flyers with little strips at the bottom that you can tear off. Emil's name and address were on the strips. I put one up at work and the other in the union offices. And I put one up at a club. Are you familiar with the Sodom and Gomorrah Club?"

Irene was very well acquainted with Göteborg's largest gay club. If Pontus had put up the flyer there three years ago, it would be hopeless trying to track down everyone who might have taken a strip.

"Could you please tell me why you're asking about Emil and Copenhagen?" Pontus requested.

Irene described the connection between Marcus's murder and Emil Bentsen's. Pontus was visibly shocked when she spoke of Emil's murder.

There had only been a little article about it in the Swedish papers, with no mention of a name.

Pontus sat quietly for a long time after Irene had finished her account. Finally he said, "It feels horrible that two people I know have been murdered by the same person, and because I recommended Emil to Hans and, in turn, he recommended him to Marcus . . . I know it sounds silly but I feel responsible."

Irene admitted they shared that feeling. Her guilt after Isabell's death would not go away.

She leaned back in her chair and looked at Pontus's beautiful face, which reflected anguish. Up to now he had seemed very sincere. Yet he could be a skillful liar who was concealing the truth. Had he been closer to Marcus than he was willing to admit? With these thoughts in the back of her mind, she asked, "Since you work in the health-care field, do you happen to know if Marcus was in a relationship with a doctor during the summer and fall of last year?"

Pontus shook his head. "As I said, we didn't know each other that well. I haven't seen Marcus except for the few times I've already told you about."

"Have you heard any gossip about a doctor who has somewhat odd preferences?"

"Odd?"

For the first time Pontus looked suspicious. Carefully, Irene said, "The kind that Marcus was drawn to. Sadomasochism. Maybe even necrophilia?"

"Necro . . . absolutely not!"

He was very upset. Soothingly, Irene said, "I'm asking because of the way in which Marcus was dismembered. Our medical examiner believes that Marcus's murderer is a sadistic necrophile. The way in which he was dismembered points to someone who is familiar with autopsy procedures. Marcus is said to have referred to a doctor he knew, who could be dangerous. And Hans Pahliss heard Marcus talk about his 'personal physician.' "

A faint hint of red suffused Pontus's cheeks. His distress could be heard in his unsteady voice. "Just because you're gay, people think you're perverse! I don't know of any gay person who does the things you're talking about!"

"You knew Marcus."

Pontus took some deep breaths in order to calm himself. "I've just told you that I barely knew Marcus. I guess there was a reason he wasn't interested in me and was attracted to Leon instead."

He took one more deep breath before continuing, "Of course there are guys and girls who like different things, but I don't know of anyone who is even remotely in the vicinity of necrophilia. I've never heard of anyone either. Obviously, I know that there are necrophiles but sadistic necrophilia . . . it sounds terrible! I don't actually think I know what it means, but thinking of the horrific thing that happened to Marcus . . ."

He left the sentence unfinished and shook his head again.

"So you haven't heard any rumors about a doctor who likes what I just mentioned?"

"No. Of course there are gays on the medical staff, and one or two maybe . . . but I've never heard anything like that. Which I would. We actually have an organization for gays in the health-care field of which I've been a member for several years and know almost everyone in it. If there was such a rumor, then I would have heard it."

Irene was about to ask if lesbians were allowed to join but upon consideration, decided that they probably had their own group. If not, then it was probably the same in the homosexual world as it was everywhere else, where men were the norm and women the exception. The question was interesting but there was hardly a reason to ask Pontus about it, thought Irene.

But an idea was forming in her head.

"How often do you have meetings of this organization?"

"The first Monday of every month."

Irene leaned forward and looked at her desk calendar. "The next meeting will be this Monday," she said.

"Exactly."

Irene looked up from the calendar and made eye contact with him. "I'd like you to discuss what you heard from me today with the people at this meeting. Tell them that Marcus may have been in a relationship with a man who's a doctor. Mention that you became very upset when I started asking about someone with sadomasochist interests who leans toward necrophilia. Tell them how angry you became and that you gave me an earful about people's prejudices," she said.

Pontus looked completely uncomprehending. Finally, he stammered, "But . . . but . . . oh God . . . why?"

"To get a discussion started. When people start talking, you should keep your ears cocked and try and remember what is said. Maybe someone has had a run-in with a doctor who turned out to be dangerous. It may be worth a try."

Irene was aware that she was appealing to him, but if it could get them closer to the doctor's identity, it would be a real break. Everything depended on whether or not Pontus would go along with the suggestion.

His forehead wrinkled as he stared through the heavy glass windowpane in Irene's office. He nervously straightened the already smooth hair on the top of his head with the palm of his hand, then took his hand away, turned from the view over the gloomy dark brown brick building of the Insurance Office, and said, "OK. I'm willing to give it a try for Marcus and Emil's sake."

"That's very kind of you," said Irene. "I'm going to give you some phone numbers where you can reach me."

"DO YOU think we should release more details to the press about Marcus's murder?" asked Irene.

Superintendent Andersson muttered, "The vultures have gotten enough information."

Andersson had stopped by around lunchtime, not because he was on duty over the weekend but because Irene suspected he didn't have anything better to do. Maybe he felt lonelier than his staff thought. He looked more unkempt than usual today, in worn brown pants and a washed-out, wrinkled shirt. At some point it had probably been forest green but over time it had taken on a faded, military green hue.

Irene continued, patiently coaxing, "I'm thinking about the fact that Marcus was in Göteborg for one or two days at the beginning of March. We know that because he called Anders Gunnarsson. And the neighbor lady saw that he had been home and watered his plants while she was in the hospital. We've asked the other neighbors but none of them recalls having seen him. I'm wondering if he might have been spotted somewhere else in the city. Maybe at a club or something."

Andersson considered this suggestion. Finally he said, "Didn't he tell that dentist that he didn't have time to drive out to Alingsås to get the camera he wanted to borrow?"

"Yes."

"Then I think he was in a hurry."

"You mean you think he came home to Göteborg, packed some clothes for the trip to Thailand, and left again right away? Maybe he didn't even stay overnight in the apartment?"

"Exactly. There weren't any sheets on the bed. But we've checked departures to Thailand from Sweden, Norway, and Denmark during the first week of March. Marcus Tosscander wasn't on any of the passenger lists. He should have been if he was booked on a flight."

After the last sentence, Irene had goose bumps all over her body.

"That means Marcus was tricked. The murderer never intended to take him to Thailand. He had decided to kill Marcus from the very beginning," she concluded.

Andersson nodded grimly.

"It seems that way."

Irene forced herself to continue, "Then the big question is, where was he murdered? And then where was he dismembered? It doesn't necessarily have to be the same place."

"No. The technicians have checked the bathtub and the drain in his apartment, but there were no traces of human tissue or blood."

"Do you know what the analysis of the trash bags and the tape have shown?"

"It's the most common type of black trash bag on the market. It can be purchased at every hardware store and every gas station and so on. The tape is regular masking tape that you use when you paint. It can also be purchased anywhere. The only interesting thing the technicians found was traces of rice powder on the tape and inside the bags."

Irene nodded. "That's what we suspected all along. The murderer must have worn latex medical gloves. How commonly is rice powder used, compared to regular talcum powder, on medical examination gloves these days?"

"No idea. We'll have to ask the technicians. But the murderer has actually left a clue behind or, rather, two."

At first Irene was genuinely surprised. This murderer seemed more like a malicious being than a human who might leave a trail. Of course he was in fact a tangible person, and, as such, it was possible to trace him through the evidence he had left behind. Even if the leads in this case were very few. But at some decisive moment he would expose himself. Irene had been waiting for it to happen. Perhaps he was, reluctantly, beginning to reveal himself now. Anticipation caused her pulse to quicken as she leaned over the desk and looked at the superintendent.

"What kind of evidence?"

Andersson smiled contentedly when he saw her restrained excitement.

"Hairs. Two of them. They were in the sack, under the lower part of the body. And they don't belong to Marcus Tosscander because they're too light. Svante has sent one of them to his colleagues in Copenhagen. It will be a direct hit if they've found hairs from the same person at one of their crime scenes."

"Have they found rice powder at the crime scenes in Copenhagen or in connection with Carmen Østergaard?" Irene asked.

"I don't know. You'll have to ask Svante. He's in touch with Copenhagen."

IRENE FOUND police technician Svante Malm in the Forensics break room. He was sitting, his eyes closed and his back leaning up against the wall. At first Irene thought that he was asleep, but when she hesitantly approached, he opened his eyes slightly. A happy smile crossed his long freckled face. He quickly ran his fingers through his carrot red hair in a futile attempt to make himself presentable. Wisps of hair stood up on the top of his head. He looked like he had just awakened.

"Now you caught me red-handed," he said.

"Sorry if I woke you."

"Not at all. I was meditating."

He smiled again and got up to get some coffee from the pot on the hot plate. Irene had just had three cups of coffee after lunch, so, just to be different, she declined his offer. When he had seated himself at the table with his aromatic-smelling mug, Irene asked how much data he had on the murders in Copenhagen. She had copied the information with respect to Carmen Østergaard herself, but she hadn't had a chance to read it over.

"As far as the murder of Carmen is concerned, it has been determined that the murderer was wearing rubber gloves there as well. They found talcum powder on both the body parts and in the sacks."

"Talc? Not rice powder?"

"No, regular talc. Because of allergies they've recently begun to use rice powder, instead of talc, on examination gloves."

"Did the sacks reveal anything?"

"The body parts of each corpse were found in the same type of black trash bag. The only difference is the way they were sealed. Marcus's sacks were taped with masking tape. Carmen's were tied together with nylon string. According to my Danish colleagues, strong string of the household kind was used. Unfortunately, that type of string is very common and is used throughout both Sweden and Denmark."

"But Andersson said that you had found two hairs in one of Marcus's sacks."

"Yes. I sent one of them to Copenhagen, but haven't heard anything yet."

"It'll probably take a while. Isabell Lind was murdered in an old hotel room. Naturally there were a lot of hairs."

"Yikes. Then we'll have to bet on the other crime scene where that guy was found."

"It was also very dirty."

"Were you there?"

"Yes. I was there when he was found."

An image of Emil's desecrated corpse suddenly flashed before Irene's eyes. The scene was crystal clear. She started talking about the murders of Isabell and Emil in order to dispel the agonizing picture.

Svante Malm absorbed her information. Finally, he said, "Strange. The murders of Carmen and Marcus are almost identical. Just like the murders of Isabell and Emil. The medical examiner is still convinced that we're dealing with the same murderer. What kept the killer from completion? From cleaning out the bodies of the victims and dismembering them?"

Malm had put his finger on exactly the question that was gnawing at Irene. Why hadn't he finished the dismemberment? Incomplete. Irene remembered that word had come to mind earlier.

"One theory is that for some reason he didn't have access to the circular saw he had during the last two murders. Another reason could be lack of time," she said.

"Maybe so. A third factor could be the lack of a suitable place to carry out the dismemberment. Remember, it's a messy procedure. To avoid being caught, he'd have to have the ability to clean up afterward."

Malm fell silent as he thought.

"The internal organs and heads of the mutilated victims were never found. What did he do with them? And with certain muscles that were removed."

Irene replied, "Yvonne Stridner thinks that he's a cannibal. That he's eaten the muscles. Apparently, this occurs with necrosadism. Have you run across anything like it before?"

Malm shook his head heavily. "No. The closest is probably a woman who was suffering from postpartum depression. She put her newborn baby in the oven and baked it. But she didn't *eat* it. Damn! That was one of the worst things I've seen."

Irene was happy that she had already finished her lunch, even though it was trying to come up again. Normally, after so many years in the field, she was hardened, but this was so disgusting that she had no defense against it. Cannibalism. The most forbidden and repulsive act.

She quickly changed the subject. "I actually came here to ask you about something completely different. Is it possible to make decent enlargements of Polaroid photos?"

"You should ask one of the photo guys about that. But I don't think there are any problems if the initial picture is sharp."

She would have to depend on Tom's skill as a photographer. Thinking of skill as a photographer reminded her that she should start looking for the person who had taken the pictures of Marcus and his friend.

IRENE FLIPPED randomly through the Yellow Pages. Lots of different photographers and studios were listed. Who could have taken the pictures of Marcus and his friend? She put the phone book aside with a sigh and decided to wait until later to make inquiries, until after photos from Tom had arrived. If she was lucky, they would be on her desk with the morning mail on Monday.

It was five o'clock and time to go home. Since Krister had the night off, she was looking forward to a nice dinner, just the two of them, for a change.

Katarina was going out with Micke, and Jenny had a gig at the student union with her band. Polo. Strange name for a pop group. But it was going well for them. That evening's gig would be the biggest yet. Jenny had been feverish with excitement all week and could speak of nothing but the approaching performance. Krister had cautiously wondered if parents were allowed to come and listen, but at this hint Jenny had thrown a fit. It was the most embarrassing thing she had ever heard! Her old parents were going to stand there and bring the average age in the place up several notches! How awkward could it get!

It would have to be a cozy night at home for the old fogies. They could always entertain themselves by petting the dog.

Irene smiled at her thoughts. The truth was that she wanted to do nothing more on Saturday night than eat a good dinner. But afterward she was definitely planning on petting something other than the dog.

Chapter 14

MONDAY MORNING STARTED NORMALLY but things began running amok a little ways into morning prayers. The door opened and an inspector stuck his head in and said, "There's a Dane on the phone. And he insists on speaking with Huss."

Irene excused herself. She was escorted by her colleague to her office. He told her, "I said that you were conducting a case review and wondered if he could call back later. He told me to go to hell!"

"That sounds like a Danish colleague I know," Irene said. She smiled.

She closed the door. The call had been transferred so she picked up the receiver.

"Hey, Jens," she said.

"Hey, yourself. Hope you have plenty of time."

"Plenty of time?" she asked, surprised.

"You have a hell of a lot of explaining to do!" Metz roared into the receiver.

Irene hadn't noticed his anger until now. He was royally pissed off for some reason. Why? She had the uncomfortable feeling that the anger was directed at her.

"A lot of things have happened here in Copenhagen. Despite the fact that you've gone home! But you have left traces. Everywhere!"

Irene heard him pause in order to lower his voice a notch or two before he continued, "I'm sitting here with Tom Tanaka's cell phone in front of me. There are about twenty numbers programmed into it. One of them has been traced to a cell phone belonging to Marcus Tosscander. Another is your cell phone number. How do you explain that?"

Irene's pulse began to race from fear.

"What's happened to Tom?" Her voice rose to a falsetto but she didn't care. Not Tom! Not Tom! she said desperately to herself.

"He's lying unconscious at the hospital. He was attacked and severely wounded, stabbed last night."

"But he never leaves his apartment!" Irene burst out.

"The attack occurred in his apartment," Metz said dryly.

How was that possible? Irene remembered his code locks and heavy doors. Had he let the perpetrator in himself? She became aware that Jens was speaking again and she straightened up in order to listen.

"Peter is on his way to you. He has two videotapes with him, which we found in Emil's apartment. They're very . . . interesting. For both you and us. And I can tell you that we've identified the owner of the hair you found in one of the sacks with Marcus's body parts."

He paused for dramatic effect and Irene realized that she was holding her breath.

"The hair comes from Emil Bentsen."

"Emil?" Irene repeated, amazed.

Her brain went on strike. Then the wheels began to turn and she managed to say, "But Emil himself was murdered!"

"You'll have to look at the tapes. Then you'll understand. The stains on one of the police uniforms were human blood. We're matching them against that of Carmen Østergaard and Marcus Tosscander. The results will be ready tomorrow morning at the earliest. Peter should be in Göteborg between eleven and twelve. Order a good lunch. It will be a long one."

After a curt good-bye, Irene put down the receiver. Her thoughts were spinning chaotically. What was she going to do? Her attempt at keeping Tom outside the investigation had failed. He was alive but seriously hurt. And this was plainly her fault.

She made up her mind. She rose and went into the room where her colleagues were still meeting.

When she opened the door, they turned their questioning faces toward her.

"Some dramatic things have happened in Copenhagen, which make it necessary for me to add to my report," she said decisively.

SUPERINTENDENT ANDERSSON had flown through the roof. Irene was used to it but this fit had lasted longer than usual. When he was done scolding, it was clear Irene had landed in the soup.

The reactions from her other colleagues were largely condemnatory. Tommy was the only one who smiled supportively.

When his irritation had abated, the superintendent decided that Hannu and Jonny should be present during Irene's meeting with Peter Møller.

"So that we can be sure our Danish colleague walks out of here alive," Andersson concluded, with a dark look in Irene's direction.

She restrained herself from answering. Possibly, she hadn't dealt with things in the best way when she consciously withheld facts. Despite this, she still felt convinced that she would have done the same thing if she had the chance to do it all over again. Her attempt to protect Tom had failed, but she had really tried.

The fact that Jonny was in a terribly whiny mood didn't help things. His bloodshot eyes and minty-smelling breath gave rise to the suspicion that he was hungover. Had he continued to drink after returning home from Copenhagen? After morning prayers, he whined several times about how unsociable Irene had been in Copenhagen. Finally, her irritation overcame her. She pulled him into her office and closed the door in Hannu's face. Aggressively, she shoved her face toward his and said in a low voice vibrating with restrained fury, "It's possible that I've dealt poorly with this case and I've been thoroughly reprimanded by the boss for my mistakes. But in any case, I've tried to do my job as best I can. That's more than I can say for you! You were loaded from your first step onto Danish soil until we went home! Is that what you call being sociable?"

Jonny was still in shock from being dragged into a room without warning. He couldn't come up with anything to say in self-defense. But Irene could see dark anger rising in his bloodshot eyes. After a period of silence, the anger was transformed into gushing hatred. Without a word, he turned and tore the door open, almost stomping on Hannu, who still stood outside. Hannu thoughtfully looked at Jonny's back disappearing down the hallway. Then he turned his gaze on Irene.

"He needed to hear that," he said.

Her anger left Irene as quickly as it had come. She felt emptied of any strength, both mental and physical. She sank into her chair, exhausted. Hannu came in and closed the door behind him.

"Have you known about Jonny's drinking problem for long?" she asked.

"I've had my suspicions for about a year."

"I hadn't really thought about it until the trip to Copenhagen. What made you suspicious?"

"He's often sick on Mondays or comes in late. Smells of old booze sometimes. On Fridays he disappears early in order to make it to the state liquor store before it closes. He uses a lot of breath spray and cough drops. And he's always drunk at parties."

When Irene thought back, everything Hannu cited added up.

"He needs help. What do we do?" she asked.

Hannu shrugged. Irene realized that he was right. What do you do when a colleague has a drinking problem if he refuses to acknowledge it? Jonny would go crazy if they tried to get him help. Talking to the boss wouldn't do any good. Andersson hated employee problems. What a "fuss," he would say, and mumble, and pretend they didn't exist.

With a sigh, Irene decided to leave Jonny's problems hanging. She had enough of her own to deal with. Peter Møller was expected to show up in two hours.

PETER ANNOUNCED his arrival at the front desk at eleven thirty on the dot. With an unpleasant, tingly feeling in her stomach, Irene took the elevator down to accompany him to their unit. Their meeting was stiff and cold, just as she had expected. The intimacy of the restaurant visit had vanished completely. Had it ever been there or had she just imagined it? Irene was unsure where she stood with him as she breathed in his wonderful scent. His expression was neutral and he displayed no special feelings. Dressed in a thin light gray blazer, dark blue pants, and a chalk white shirt without a tie, he looked like a bank director on his day off. Definitely not like a police officer.

He held a briefcase in cognac-colored leather in his right hand. Expensive. Probably his own, thought Irene.

He greeted Hannu as he entered the office. Jonny hadn't arrived yet. Irene asked them to be seated. Peter, with the briefcase in his lap, started by saying, "We need a VCR."

"Not a problem. We have one in the break room," said Irene.

Peter shook his head. "Not the break room. Someplace where only we can see."

"I can take care of that," said Hannu. He disappeared into the corridor.

When he had closed the door, Irene said, "Tell me what's happened to Tom."

Her distressed tone of voice didn't escape Peter's attention. He observed her closely before he said, "If only I could understand how the two of you ever hooked up."

A faint smile could be detected in the corner of his mouth. Irene felt a bit more at ease.

Peter took off his cotton blazer and hung it over the back of his chair. "Tanaka closes the shop at eleven o'clock on Saturday evenings. His employee, Ole Hansen, also worked on Saturday. Hansen was in the employee's lounge just before ten thirty. As you know, it's located between the shop and Tanaka's apartment."

He stopped when Hannu returned with Jonny in tow. Jonny greeted Peter warmly but avoided looking at Irene. As far as he was concerned, she was empty air. If Peter noticed the tension, he pretended not to. He picked up where he had left off.

"Hansen heard a noise inside Tanaka's apartment."

"A shot?" Jonny asked.

"No. A crash, from a broken window. Hansen hurried after Tanaka, who went into his apartment. Hansen, standing in the doorway to the kitchen, saw Tanaka disappear in the direction of his bedroom. Almost immediately, he heard a terrible commotion. He describes it as a roar, and the sound of people fighting."

The roar had probably come from Tom. A sumo wrestler summons up power and instills fear in his opponent with the help of loud screams, thought Irene.

"Hansen dialed the emergency number on his cell phone as he was running toward the bedroom. When he got there, he saw Tanaka lying on the floor in a rapidly growing pool of blood. The room was covered with it. A large blood vessel in his throat had been cut and his blood was pumping out."

Irene's stomach knotted when she pictured the scene in her head.

"Hansen saw a man dressed in black, wearing a hooded sweatshirt, disappear through the window. Hansen didn't see his face, only his back. But he got the impression that the man was large. Not fat, but tall, with a large build."

"Did he take anything?" Irene asked.

"Yes. A picture. Apparently a framed photograph. According to Hansen, there had been two on the wall. Now only one of them is left."

"What's the subject of the picture that's still hanging there?"

"A naked man sitting in the water."

The culprit had taken the backlit picture of the man standing in profile, leaning against a stone wall—the one that had sparked in Irene a faint feeling of recognition. He had left the picture of Marcus. She jumped out of her chair and said, "The mail!"

Without paying attention to her colleagues' curious looks, she ran to get it. She heard Jonny say, "She's been knocked totally off-kilter. This investigation has taken its toll. Women can't see their limitations."

To her joy, she heard Peter reply, "I don't see her that way. Strong-willed, but definitely not off balance."

With shaky fingers she started sorting her mail. There! She recognized the stiff exclusive envelope that was just like the one she had gotten Tom's message in at the Hotel Alex. Triumphantly, she went back to her office bearing the white envelope and impatiently cut it open.

Two photographs floated down onto the desktop. Without a word, Irene pushed the pictures in front of Peter and Hannu's surprised eyes. Jonny's curiosity got the better of him and he drew closer in order to get a glimpse.

"How did you get these?" Peter asked, amazed.

Irene leaned back in her chair and said, "I'll start from the beginning. But first I want to know if Tom is going to make it."

Peter smiled widely for the first time since his arrival. "Of course. He's had several blood transfusions and he'll recover."

The smile faded a bit when he continued, "The problem is that he lost so much blood that his brain may have been affected. But the doctors don't know yet."

At least Tom wasn't going to die from his injuries. Irene would have to take comfort from that.

It didn't take very long to explain her dealings with Tom to Peter. Since Hannu and Jonny had just heard it all, they studied both of the photographs. As Irene was finishing, Hannu looked up from the picture he held in front of him.

"I recognize this guy. But I can't recall who he is."

He turned the photo around. It was the backlit picture. Irene nodded.

"That's exactly what I thought. Do you recognize him, too?" she asked Jonny.

He shook his head without looking at her. Peter took the picture and looked at it for a long time.

"No. I can't say that I recognize him," he said finally.

Irene took the picture back and stared intently at it, as if to force the man to turn toward the light. She had to put the photo down finally.

"It's getting close to movie time," Jonny said, and grinned.

They rose and went into an empty interrogation room where there was a TV with a VCR.

"We usually use this room for children we believe have been subjected to abuse," Irene explained.

Peter nodded and put one of the films into the VCR.

The first thing they saw was a naked body lying on a long table. The table was covered with strong, see-through plastic. Scaffolding and miscellaneous junk could be seen under and behind the table. In the background, a sturdy tackle hung from a chain fixed to the ceiling. It appeared to be a large industrial building. Above the table, a bare lightbulb emitted a harsh light.

There was absolutely no doubt that the person on the table was dead. The camera zoomed in on a long incision that ran along the front of the corpse's abdomen. It was obvious that the internal organs had been removed. At first it was difficult to decide if the body was male or female, since both chest muscles and the genitals had been cut away. But based on the curves of the hips and the thighs, Irene concluded that the body was that of a woman.

Peter hit the pause button and spoke. "We found these two films in a hidden compartment in Emil's bookcase. These are copies that you can keep. There is no soundtrack on either of the films. This is Carmen Østergaard's body. Neither the actual murder nor the rituals performed with the body afterward are shown. As you can see, the pelvic area is severely damaged. What follows now is the dismemberment itself. That's Emil's thing."

Peter started the tape again. Emil Bentsen walked into the frame with a large circular saw in his right hand. He was dressed in a police uniform. When he stared at the camera from under the police cap, he looked absurd, almost comical, if it hadn't been for his expression. His thin face was completely distorted, and his eyes stared wildly. He grinned and motioned toward the camera.

The camera zoomed in on the body again, this time on the head. Irene had time to see Carmen's wide-open eyes and swollen tongue, sticking out of her mouth, indicating she had been strangled. Then Emil stepped in front of the camera and the screen became completely dark.

The next scene showed Emil as he sawed off Carmen's head. He had positioned himself on the far side of her body, so he wouldn't be in the way of the camera. As the head rolled to the side and fell to the floor, he raised the circular saw in the air in a show of victory. He bent and picked up the head, took a tight grip on the hair, and showed off his trophy proudly. The circular saw, with its red-colored blade, was still spinning. Emil turned it off, placed it on the plastic-covered table, and stepped close to the lens, Carmen's head dangling from his outstretched hand. Irene saw his lips moving. He seemed to be talking the whole time. His chin and goatee were covered with drool.

"Stop!" Hannu screamed.

The scene ended and the next one started. Emil stood leaning over the body again, in the process of starting the saw. Peter Møller stopped the video.

"Back up," Hannu instructed.

Without commenting, Peter did so.

"Stop," Hannu said again.

Again they saw Emil move toward them with the sawed-off head held out in front of him.

"Play it slowly," said Hannu.

They watched the replay of the horrible scene in slow motion.

"Stop!"

Peter paused the picture instantly.

"Look in the lower left-hand corner," Hannu said and pointed at an indistinct light curvature. "Can you back up a little?"

Peter did as he was asked. Slowly, the size of the little curvature grew and became longer. It was still barely discernible down in the corner of the picture. Then it disappeared.

Peter rewound the tape and played the sequence again.

"It's definitely the tip of a finger. The person who's filming this scene doesn't want the head near him," said Hannu.

"You're absolutely right. We've played it with magnification. It's the index finger of a left hand. The entire nail is visible," said Peter.

Peter started the tape again.

Now they watched Emil saw off Carmen's arms and legs. When he was done, he grabbed both of the severed arms and shook them above his head in a second show of victory. His entire face was transfigured with joy.

That's where the video ended.

"Altogether, it's thirteen minutes," Peter informed them.

"Does the next film show the dismemberment of Marcus Tosscander?" Irene asked.

"Yes. And they're strikingly similar," Peter answered.

The other video began with the same panning over the body, which was in exactly the same condition as Carmen's had been before Emil's appearance. Marcus was lying on a sturdy piece of particleboard that could be glimpsed under the clear plastic, resting on two trestles. Bare cement walls could be seen in the background. But this room was much smaller than the one in the first film. Irene guessed it to be a basement or a garage.

Emil was dressed in a police uniform this time as well, and he held the circular saw in his hand from the start. Now he was used to the camera and didn't obstruct the cameraman's view when he sawed off the head. Without changing his position vis-à-vis the camera, he held up the head and roared with laughter. Then he cut off the arms and legs. In conclusion he took one of Marcus's legs and lifted it straight above his head. That was the final picture.

"Ten minutes," Peter said dryly.

"Damn, this stuff is sick!" Jonny exclaimed.

Irene felt ill. At the same time she realized the importance of the videos.

"Have you been able to locate where the dismemberments took place?" she asked tensely.

"With respect to the first murder, we have a theory that the dismemberment may have taken place in an old, abandoned shipyard building. There are several of those out by Frihamnen, a few kilometers from Hellerup. That's where the sacks were found. We have people going through all of the abandoned shipyard buildings with a fine-tooth comb. If we don't get anything there, we'll go through industrial sites. It's a huge job, but we're going to do it."

"How about the location where Marcus was dismembered?"

"Harder. It appears to be a basement. It's probably located in Göteborg, since he was found here."

Irene nodded and said, "I think that's a correct assumption. There was no reason to transport Marcus's dismembered body to Göteborg. The risk of getting caught at customs would always exist."

"We know that he was alive when he came to Göteborg at the beginning of March," Jonny pointed out.

"Yes. He called Anders Gunnarsson. And according to a neighbor lady he had been in his apartment because the plants were watered and his summer clothes were gone," Irene agreed.

Hannu had been sitting motionless during the entirety of the last film, but now he turned to Peter and said, "That means that Emil and his accomplice also came along to Göteborg."

"I think the accomplice was already in place. He was waiting for Emil and Marcus here," Irene said.

Jonny was still noticeably pale but now he cleared his throat and asked, "Why didn't Marcus drive his car when he came home to pack?"

"A very good question. But that's the obvious answer to why we haven't gotten any positive leads when we asked the different ferry lines about the car. His red American vehicle would be very conspicuous," said Irene.

"That's why," Hannu said.

The other three turned their questioning looks toward him.

"Because it was conspicuous," Hannu said.

Irene thought hard but didn't understand Hannu's meaning.

"They were going to leave from Landvetter," Hannu continued.

Jonny's paleness was replaced by a flush of annoyance. "How do you know that?" he hissed angrily.

"They were going on a long trip to Thailand. It wasn't a good idea to leave the car parked for an even longer time on the street. Marcus didn't have a garage. Emil did, so they parked Marcus's car in Emil's garage, and took Emil's car to Göteborg. Or maybe his accomplice's."

Peter nodded and said, "We'll go through all of the facts again. But this time we'll look for Emil's car. I think you are right."

"Were all three of them planning on going to Thailand? Or at least is that what Marcus believed?" Irene said thoughtfully.

"It's very possible," said Hannu.

"Did you notice that there weren't any internal organs or muscles left in the bodies in the films?" Peter wondered. He continued without waiting for an answer, "Our theory is that they were placed in different containers. In the film where Carmen is dismembered you can see the rim of a large plastic bucket. It's standing right next to the table she's lying on. Our thinking is that the head and the internal organs were placed in that bucket and covered with cement. The bucket was then sunk out in the ocean. The sacks floated, as you know."

His Swedish colleagues pondered this theory.

"You think the same thing happened with Marcus's head and organs?" Hannu said finally.

"Yes."

"And the buttocks and muscles were eaten by those sick bastards?" Jonny exclaimed.

Peter answered neutrally, "Probably."

He ejected the tape and put it back in its case before he went on, "Blokk watched both videos last night. He said that Carmen had probably been dead for at least eight hours before Emil started dismembering her. Rigor mortis is already fully developed."

"And Marcus?" asked Irene.

"He was probably dead a shorter period of time. Blokk guessed five hours. As you saw, the leg bent a bit at the knee when Emil picked it up. The jaws and the arms were completely stiff. Blokk said that he was going to analyze the films frame by frame. Then he can see if there is livor mortis and so on."

Irene realized that it was way past lunchtime but she assumed that the other three didn't feel particularly hungry either.

"These two videos explain why Isabell and Emil weren't dismembered. Sawing off the head and the extremities was Emil's job. He wasn't there when Isabell was murdered. Certainly, he was there when *he* was murdered, but not as a mutilator," Peter said dryly.

"He was indirectly involved in Isabell's murder. He was the one who tipped off the murderer that I was looking for her, and he must have given him the name of Simon Steiner," said Irene.

"Emil may have told the murderer his father's name earlier. But the murderer and Emil must have been in contact directly after Emil spoke with Beate, after your restaurant meeting," said Peter.

"He couldn't have known before then that I was looking for Isabell," Irene agreed.

"Why would he kill an insignificant little whore you were looking for?" Jonny asked.

Before Irene had a chance to answer, Hannu said, "A practical joke."

It sounded ridiculous, but the more Irene thought about it, the less far-fetched it seemed. Was Bell's murder a warning from a twisted brain? Or a joke?

"Emil's accomplice has suddenly become very active. There were two years between the murders of Carmen and Marcus. Then he murders Isabell and Emil within an interval of just a few hours. And a week and half later, Tom is stabbed!" she exclaimed.

"We don't know if Emil's partner stabbed Tanaka. It could have been a regular burglar. But as he took the photo in the bedroom, we have to assume that the break-in is connected to everything else," Peter observed.

"And we can probably assume that it was Emil whom Marcus meant when he spoke about his police officer. The question is, who's the doctor?" said Irene.

She told them about Pontus Zander's promise to keep his ears cocked at the next day's meeting for gays in the health-care field.

"Gays in the health-care system! I'll be damned if they're going to look at my ass!" Jonny snorted.

They decided to eat before watching the tapes one more time. Peter wanted a solid lunch because he was planning on driving home directly afterward.

"You're not going to stay here in Göteborg for one night?" Irene asked.

"No. We're short-staffed. Jens has had to take over as superintendent for Beate. She'll be on sick leave a few more weeks."

He wouldn't let himself be persuaded. Finally, Irene gave up. She wanted him to leave with a good impression of Göteborg's pub life so she decided that they would eat at Glady's Corner. She lifted the phone receiver to reserve a table. If you're married to the master chef, it should be possible to arrange things on short notice.

THEY WERE given a table but had to wait until two o'clock. Jonny excused himself by saying that he had work piled up, but Irene had the suspicion that it was mostly out of fear that he would have to pay for himself. Glady's was one of Göteborg's best pubs, with a star in *Guide Michelin*, but not the cheapest one.

Irene quickly realized that the three police officers weren't really dressed for the establishment. Peter might be able to pass as business casual. But since it was after the lunch rush and the dinner guests hadn't started streaming in yet, there shouldn't be a problem. The headwaiter was among the snootiest Irene had ever come across; they had never gotten on well. Not that they had that much to do with each other, but sometimes she couldn't avoid needing to speak with her husband. If the headwaiter happened to be the one who answered the phone, an icy chill soon floated over the wires. Irene suspected that she wasn't chic enough to be the wife of the golden pub's master chef, in his estimation.

Now he met them at the door. He wore a black suit and a white shirt, and bowed stiffly to them. Of course, he pretended not to recognize Irene. Surrounded by the scent of his exclusive perfumed aftershave, he showed them to a table by the far wall in one of the more concealed alcoves. With her biggest smile, Irene said, "No thanks. We would like to sit at one of the empty window tables."

He opened his mouth to respond but when their eyes met he closed it again with a snap. Without a word, he led them toward one of the window tables. In order not to admit complete defeat, he seated them at a table by the side of the window rather than in the middle. Irene decided to let it go.

The business lunch consisted of grilled cod cooked in a wok, with white wine sauce. All three chose the same dish, not least because of the price. For an additional one hundred and thirty SEK, they could have gotten an appetizer and dessert as well, but none of them was that hungry. The images from the video were all too fresh in their minds.

While they were waiting for food, they each ordered a large beer. Fresh-baked bread appeared. Its smell was seductive, and it was still warm enough for the butter to melt when it was spread.

So far, the day had been overwhelming. It was important to process all the new information. Peter and Hannu avoided talking about what they had seen and gone through during the last few hours. And Irene started to relax. The tension in her neck and shoulders began to ease, due to a combination of the beer and Glady's comfortable atmosphere. The restaurant, located in an old potato shop on the bottom floor of one of the larger stone buildings on Avenyn, was spacious but the architect had preserved small storage rooms and narrow passages, which added intimacy to the restaurant. The bare brick walls had been washed, and lighting points and candles placed in the holes in damaged stones. The chairs, in a late-eighteenth-century Gustavian style, were painted in sober light gray and covered in a blue-and-white-striped cotton fabric. White linen tablecloths and napkins completed the fresh look. Airy striped cotton curtains framed the only window, where the police officers were sitting. Irene could watch the passersby through the gauzy fabric without being seen herself. An ideal lookout spot, she thought. She realized a second later how much her work had affected her psychologically. She had to make an effort to concentrate on the conversation and the good food.

THEY WATCHED the videos with Peter one more time. Jonny joined the group before they started.

It was easier this time, since they knew what was coming. When the last painful image had faded from the screen, Irene said, "Why didn't Emil include the entire dismemberment process? It's easy to copy a videotape so that both Emil and his accomplice could have had one."

They pondered the question for a while. Finally, Hannu said, "He didn't want the other part. That's not what turned him on."

Peter nodded.

"Blokk said something similar. He said that the dismemberments with the saw reduced Emil's anxiety and gave him pleasure."

"The other one probably wanted the other pictures of the abuse of the body. Opening the abdomen and removing the internal organs and all that. Incidentally, I wonder if the murder itself is on tape?" Irene asked.

"It's very possible. But not certain. The primary thing wasn't to kill a person but what they did later with the body," Peter answered.

It sounded very much like what Yvonne Stridner had said at the beginning of the investigation.

"So the other guy is supposed to be the doctor, if I've understood this correctly?" Jonny jumped in.

"Yes. We think so since Marcus spoke . . ." Irene started.

"What if he's just as fake as the policeman?" Jonny said triumphantly.

"Fake?"

"Emil wasn't a police officer. Just dressed up like one. What if the doctor isn't really a doctor, but is just pretending. Goes around in a white coat and stethoscope and all that."

Irene stared at Jonny, amazed. It was the most intelligent thing he had come up with during the entire investigation. And he could very well be right. Irene nodded and said, "That's very possible. I've been thinking about the picture that was stolen at Tom's. The man in the photo, maybe he's the doctor. I've been trying to come up with a way of getting in touch with the photographer who took the pictures. He should know who the man in the backlit picture is."

"Have you asked Tanaka?" Peter wondered.

"Yes. Tom doesn't know who he is. It's a high-quality picture—"

She was interrupted by Jonny's loud snort but continued, "—and there shouldn't be that many photographers who could have taken it. The question is where to start looking."

"Among the photographers," Hannu answered.

Sometimes he really could be irritating. Irene told herself to be patient and waited for further exposition.

"He's a freelance photographer," said Hannu.

Jonny raised his eyebrows in surprise and started to say, "How do you—" but stopped himself.

At least he had learned something, thought Irene.

A freelance photographer? Probably. A photographer of this class probably worked on his own. But he might have a studio with employees. Irene realized that it was going to take time to find the photographer but they would find him.

PETER MØLLER left just before five o'clock. He planned on reaching his home by ten if all went smoothly. Hannu, Jonny, and Irene went to Superintendent Andersson's office in order to bring him up to speed on the surprising developments in the case.

Andersson declined to watch the videos. He fully trusted their judgment of the tapes' authenticity, he said.

They agreed that they would start the search for the photographer the next day.

Chapter 15

THE GIRL IN THE lab was a godsend. By nine o'clock she had made five sets of copies of Tom Tanaka's Polaroid pictures, as well as a good enlargement of both pictures. Irene had gone around among her colleagues with the picture of the man with the ponytail, and asked if anyone had seen him before. No one recognized him. Only she and Hannu seemed to have a feeling of familiarity. Or was it just their imagination?

Irene focused on the picture and tried to be objective. Yes, there was certainly something familiar about the high cheekbones and the contour of the ear, the chest and the arms. She stared at the picture until her eyes started burning.

She gave up. His identity was somewhere in the back of her mind, she was certain of it. She would eventually come up with it. She hoped it wouldn't take too long. They were working under a time constraint; the risk that the murderer would kill again was constantly increasing. It was obvious that the man in the backlit picture had known Marcus Tosscander. It was possible that he knew quite a bit about both Emil and Marcus. It was even conceivable that he was involved in the murders. It was very important to find this man.

Hannu was going to try to reach Anders Gunnarsson, and Birgitta was going to try Hans Pahliss. Irene took it upon herself to get in touch with Pontus Zander since she needed to speak with him anyway. There was a good chance that one of them would recognize the man in the photo. Maybe he moved in the same circles they did.

Irene realized pretty quickly that it wasn't possible to divide up photographers based on their areas of specialty. So they divided those listed in the Yellow Pages in four, with the same number of names in each. They would have to go through each list methodically, one by one. It was just a matter of getting started.

Irene started writing in the photographers' addresses on the map, in order to work out a systematic route. If she didn't get any leads quickly, it would take up most of the day and a good portion of the next one. But it would be worth it if they could put a name to the man in the backlit picture.

IT WAS three thirty and Irene had begun to feel a bit dejected. None of the men or women she had met during the day as she wandered between photography studios had been able to give her any tip as to who the photographer could be. However, several people had recognized Marcus. Apparently, he had done a lot of modeling before the design company got off the ground.

Now she was both sweaty and thirsty. The early summer heat had been pleasant at lunchtime but it had become oppressive during the afternoon. It was the first real summer day of the year, and one that had been longed for, but as far as Irene was concerned, it could definitely have held off a while longer. The car was boiling hot and her clothes were sticking to her body. Her deodorant sure wasn't lasting twenty-four hours, like the commercial had promised, a fact of which she had become awkwardly aware during the last couple of hours. She longed intensely for a cool shower.

Without any expectations whatsoever she slowly trudged up the worn steps to E. Bolin's Commercial Photography Company, Incorporated, on Kastellgatan. "Corporation" always sounded fancy, but the facade of this office was not impressive. The outer door was insignificant and its paint had peeled off in big patches. The bell didn't work, so Irene had to knock hard.

The man who opened it was a surprise. Her first thought was that he must be a photo model. He was a bit taller than average, slim, and looked like he was in good shape. His eyes were amber brown and matched his short hair perfectly. The bangs were longer and stood straight up in straggling pieces. The look was so nonchalant and sporty that it must have taken him at least half an hour to arrange it. After more scrutiny, she realized that he was older than he had seemed at first glance, over thirty rather than under.

He smiled charmingly and said, "Hi. What can I help you with?"

"Hi. Irene Huss, from the police." She had her ID ready and pulled it out of her pocket.

The man raised his eyebrows slightly but didn't move from the doorway.

"Really?" he said.

"I'm looking for the photographer Erik Bolin," Irene said.

"At your service," said the man at the door.

He made a slight bow and took a step into the hall so that she could get past. Irene entered his studio.

If the exterior wasn't impressive, the interior certainly was. It was obvious that the entire premises had recently been renovated.

The walls in the hall were painted light gray, and the floor was a warm cherrywood. The studio itself, a large illuminated room, was located straight ahead. Those walls were white but the floor was the same as in the hall. The door to the right stood open and led into a rather large and airy kitchen. Black, steel, and cherrywood flooring.

"When did Marcus Tosscander design this interior?" she asked.

Now Bolin arched his eyebrows. "Did you know about it or could you tell?" he asked.

"I could tell."

"Bravo. He has, or had, his own style. Absolutely luscious. I love it."

"When did he design it?"

"A little more than a year ago. The renovation itself was done last summer. Would you like some coffee?"

"Yes, please."

They went into the ultramodern kitchen. Irene sat on a kitchen chair, which certainly wasn't any ordinary kitchen chair. The welded-steel frame and the skillfully woven chair seat of sturdy hemp told her that it was "designed." Erik Bolin turned on an espresso machine. He was busy for a long time with all of the utensils required to press out an itty-bitty cup of coffee from the sputtering and puffing machine. Irene preferred huge buckets of Swedish coffee but for lack of anything better, this would have to do. Caffeine was caffeine.

Apparently the machine could make two cups at a time, because Bolin set down two minicups on the kitchen table's slate top. He placed a small plate with rice cakes between them. Was the man dieting? He didn't look like he needed to. Or maybe that's why he looked like he did?

Her thoughts were interrupted by Bolin's question. "Is this about Marcus?"

"In a way. Did you know each other well?"

He smiled sorrowfully. "Yes. We were very good friends."

"How long had you known each other?"

Bolin thought a bit. "Four years."

"Were you together?"

"Together . . . it happened in the beginning . . . but we've just been friends the last two years."

"Did you take any pictures of Marcus?"

His dark amber eyes began to glow.

"Tons! He loved being in front of the camera, and the camera loved him. It's like that with some people."

Irene pulled out the envelope with the two Polaroid pictures.

"Did you take these?"

He picked up the pictures and cast a fleeting look at them. "Of course."

Irene was close to yelling, "Bingo!" but she managed to stop herself. She apologized to Erik Bolin and excused herself for a little while. Then she called her colleagues on their cell phones and told them that she had found the photographer.

"Do you know who the other man is?" she asked when the phone calls had been taken care of.

"Nothing more than that Marcus called him Basta."

"Basta? What is that a nickname for?"

"No idea."

"When were the pictures taken?"

"Last summer, at the beginning of August."

"Almost a year ago. Where did you take them?"

"In Løkken."

Løkken was in Denmark, on the west coast of Jylland, quite a ways from Copenhagen. But it was in Denmark! Irene had to force herself to concentrate on the follow-up questions.

"How was it that you happened to choose Denmark specifically? And Løkken? It's a ways to drive."

"Because of the amazing sand dunes. I took lots of wonderful pictures!"

"There aren't any sand dunes in these two photos," Irene pointed out.

"No. Marcus chose the pictures he wanted to have. He wasn't at all interested in the sand," Bolin answered knowingly.

"I've seen another picture of Marcus. Where he's leaning back against some large pillows. He's a little fuzzy but his—"

"Oh, that old picture. We took that one here in the studio. It was one of the first naked studies I did of Marcus. Personally, I didn't like it but Marcus loved it. I enlarged it and gave it to him as a Christmas present. I took it at the beginning of our friendship."

"What were the photographs used for?"

"What do you mean?"

"Were they going to be printed in magazines or did you make posters or . . ."

"Come," said Bolin.

He got up quickly and went out into the hall and then led her farther into the large studio. He gestured toward the walls.

Framed black-and-white pictures hung all around them. Some were of naked people, both men and women, but most of them were portraits. All proved Irene's first thought correct: a very skillful artist had taken them.

"I take a lot of commercial photos since I work with advertising. It feels like a great privilege to work as an artist sometimes. I've had some exhibits that have gotten good reviews. The pictures from Løkken were displayed at my last exhibit half a year ago. I called it *Affirmations*. It was shown at the Pic Ture gallery."

Irene felt completely uncultured.

"Come," Erik Bolin said again.

He went over to a door that was built into the white wall. When he opened it, Irene caught a glimpse of frames lined up in the closetlike space. He started flipping systematically. Occasionally, he stopped with a soft triumphant shout and pulled out a picture, which he leaned against the wall. When he had finished rummaging and selected six of them, he seemed satisfied.

"These, plus five more, which are hanging on the wall behind you, were part of the exhibit," he said.

Irene heard the pride in his voice, and in her estimation it was justified.

All of the pictures were very sensual. The picture of Marcus was somewhat different from the one Tom had on his wall. Here he sat leaning forward more, with his arms freely resting on his knees. His left hand loosely held his right wrist, and his right hand obscured most of his genitals. He was smiling a confident, sexy smile and looked right into the camera with eyes glittering mischievously. The wind was tousling his damp hair, and the sun glittered in the sea spray on his body. A perfect body, thought Irene. The body of a Greek god. Which Emil and his partner had turned into a torso.

One of the pictures represented a young woman sitting on a chair with two small children. The smallest child appeared to be almost a newborn and slumbered, leaning against her chest. The older child stood with his head leaning against her knee and looked directly into the camera. At the most, he was two years old. All three were naked. The woman was a stunning beauty with Asian features. Her long black hair billowed around her and the children. Without doubt she could sit on her hair. The whole picture breathed love and warmth.

"My family," Erik said with pride in his voice.

Irene's chin dropped. She had thought that Bolin was gay. But now, if the woman and the children were his family—! She asked, "Is that really your wife and children?"

"Yes."

"Does she know about . . . you and Marcus?"

Erik Bolin suddenly looked serious.

"She knew that I was bisexual when we got married. With Marcus it was a short-lived passion. Though he and I kept in touch afterward."

Irene would have loved to have continued to dig into their relationship but she suspected that his answers wouldn't be completely truthful. Instead, she concentrated on the picture of the backlit man. It was the same photo that had hung on Tom's wall.

"Did you take several pictures of this man?" Irene asked.

"Yes. But there wasn't much time. This was the best picture. It's the kind of picture you dream about being able to time just right. With the sun rays spreading out from his glans. Wonderfully sexy! I named it *Penis Power* but the gallery didn't think it could be called that, so it was changed to *Manpower*."

"Tell me about the meeting with Basta."

Bolin seemed to be searching his memory before he spoke. "Marcus's cell phone rang. He answered and seemed really happy when he understood that Basta wanted to get together. Marcus explained where we were. It was easy to find us because there was an old lighthouse right next to where we were hanging out. After about an hour, I saw a jeep approaching on the beach. It turned out to be Basta."

"Weren't there a lot of curious people standing around and watching what you were shooting? Marcus was naked after all."

"We were working a bit toward the north where there aren't all that many people. And it was quite late in the afternoon. I started taking the first pictures of Marcus around five o'clock."

"And Basta came later?"

"Yes, around seven. I finished the last roll of Marcus, and when that was done he suggested that I should photograph Basta. He was a good-looking guy so I agreed. It was actually Basta himself who came up with the idea of leaning with his back against the stone wall at the base of the lighthouse tower with his dick in the air. It turned out really well."

"How long did Basta stay?"

"Max, two hours. He watched when I shot Marcus and then I took the pictures of him. Then he left."

"Did it seem like they had a relationship?"

At first Bolin looked uncertain, but then he shrugged. His voice sounded rough when he said, "Before Basta left they had a go behind the lighthouse."

Again Irene felt a strong desire to press him about his relationship with Marcus, but she stopped herself. That wasn't what was most important right then. What was urgent was trying to figure out Basta's identity.

"Marcus never called him anything but Basta?"

"No."

"Describe Basta."

"The same age as Marcus and me. Tall. Over six feet. In good shape. Probably lifts weights. Shoulder-length hair, relatively blond. Yellowish blond, you would probably call it. He had it pulled back in a ponytail."

"Did he speak Swedish or Danish?"

"Swedish."

"Dialect?"

"I don't remember exactly, but I think he was from Göteborg. Yet he didn't have the typical thick dialect. I would have remembered if that had been the case."

"Were his license plates Swedish or Danish?"

"No idea. He parked the jeep on the beach, maybe a hundred meters away."

"Eye color?"

"Blue. I think."

"Could I borrow this one from you?" Irene said and held up *Manpower*.

"Sure."

"Do you still have the other pictures you took of him?"

There was a chance that Basta's face might be clearer on one of the other pictures.

"Yeah . . . somewhere. But I only took one roll of him."

"How many pictures are there on one roll?"

"Twelve."

"Can you try and find the pictures for me?"

"Certainly. But a major client is coming here in a while. I'll have to look after he's left."

"If you find them, maybe you can leave them in reception at the police station. Put them in an envelope and write my name on it."

Irene held out her card. Erik Bolin took it and put it in the pocket of his jeans.

"A WHOLE day wasted! Couldn't you have found him earlier?" Jonny grunted.

Was he serious? Irene gave him a sharp look and determined that he was. It was late and her blood sugar was low and she was tired. Her anger rose and she snapped, "Be happy I found him. Otherwise you would have had to trot around town tomorrow, too!"

"About tomorrow. How are we going to organize it?" Birgitta interrupted in order to break up the quarrel.

Strange, she was usually the one who became most upset at Jonny and his comments. Maybe things were different now that she had become Mrs. Rauhala. But of course she was thinking about keeping her last name and continuing to be called Moberg. Nothing could be seen yet of her pregnancy, even though she had purchased new pants in a slightly looser style than the jeans she usually wore.

"Are you going to get the other pictures of that Bastu guy? What did the photographer say?" Andersson asked.

"*Basta.* Yes. Bolin is going to leave them at reception tomorrow."

"Then we'll have to hit the street looking for Basta. Strange name," the superintendent muttered.

"Has anyone managed to access Marcus's computer yet?" Birgitta wondered.

"No. We haven't found anyone who is good enough with computers," said Andersson.

"I can give it a try," Birgitta offered.

Irene made a note to herself that she should try to reach Pontus Zander. Maybe the feeler put out at the meeting for gays in the health-care field had yielded some profit.

IRENE MADE one last attempt just after eleven o'clock, right before she was going to go to bed. Pontus answered at his home number.

"Did you get any information?" Irene asked straight out.

"No. But, God, what a discussion we had!" he exclaimed.

"Start from the beginning."

"OK. I pretended to be upset after being questioned by you. 'As if there were gays in the health-care field who devoted themselves to necrosadism,' I said in a loud voice. There really was a hot discussion, just as you'd hoped. You should have heard it! But no one said anything about necrophilia or other horrid things. Everyone agreed that this was a result of the police's general homophobia. Ha ha!"

Irene didn't feel that she was particularly homophobic and didn't really understand what was so funny. She giggled politely into the receiver so that he would continue.

"We usually wrap things up around ten o'clock. No one had any interesting gossip. At least none that I could hear. But now the hook is baited and lowered. It's not too late to get a bite. Goodness! This is really exciting!"

Exciting wasn't the word Irene would have used when she thought of the murderer and his victims. She thanked Pontus for his help and asked him to be in touch if he heard anything interesting.

She set down the receiver and she crawled into bed. An irritating thought was gnawing at her that made it impossible for her to sleep.

It was something she had overlooked. Something she should have thought of during the day. But she couldn't come up with what it was.

It was nearly twelve thirty when she fell asleep out of sheer exhaustion.

"IS THERE anything for me?" Irene asked.

She leaned forward toward the window in reception and was so prepared for a positive answer, she already had her hand stretched out to take the envelope.

"Let's see . . . Huss . . . Irene Huss. . . . No. There's nothing here."

The friendly brunette behind the glass windowpane smiled apologetically. Irene was incredulous.

"Are you sure? A photographer by the name of Bolin was supposed to leave an envelope for me here during the morning."

"Sorry."

Irene was crestfallen, but had to pad away empty-handed. Maybe Bolin hadn't found the roll of film? She decided to call the photographer and find out what had happened. She would have time; five minutes remained before morning prayers.

While she was dialing, her eyes rested on the framed photo of the man in the backlit picture. She knew she should recognize him. If only he had shown a little more of his face, and if only the picture hadn't been taken in direct sunlight, then . . . She sighed and gave up. The picture, which stood against the wall, had already been the source of many witty comments from people who had been in the room.

Irene let the phone ring ten times before she hung up. Seven thirty was probably too early for the advertising business. She would have to wait until after morning prayers.

SUPERINTENDENT ANDERSSON held a short morning review. The bright sun flooded the room. A premonition of the approaching end of the school term hung in the air. The superintendent didn't seem to notice the beautiful weather outside the window. He was deeply engrossed in some papers lying in front of him on the table. He looked up from them and searched for someone with his eyes, peering from behind lowered reading glasses. He stopped at Irene.

"The technicians send greetings. The investigation of the postcard from Copenhagen hasn't provided anything more than an interesting thumbprint on the stamp. The other fingerprints on the card probably came from you and the mailman. But they'll keep the card in case we find other fingerprints or other written messages that we want to compare. Our colleagues in Copenhagen are going through Tosscander's car. They'll be in touch when they have something interesting to say."

"Did they say anything about how Tom Tanaka is doing?" Irene asked.

"No," the superintendent said shortly.

Tom was apparently still a sensitive topic for Andersson. Irene decided to try and call Copenhagen to inquire as to Tom's condition.

"Today Birgitta is going to attempt to get into Tosscander's computer. Irene is in touch with the photographer Bolin and is trying to get pictures of that guy with . . . well, you know . . . in the air. Jonny is going through the last of Marcus Tosscander's videos—"

The superintendent was interrupted by Jonny's irritated mumble.

"What is it?" Andersson said, irritated.

"Those films are damn difficult! A lot of queers jumping each other! Damn!"

"I realize that you don't think they're terribly amusing to watch. But you have to. We can't miss a single film. Think about the movies we found in Copenhagen!"

"Yes, but all of Tosscander's movies are commercial videos. Not home movies," Jonny tried to protest.

"Watch them! All of them!" Andersson ended the discussion.

Jonny continued to mumble discontentedly, though in a somewhat lower tone.

"Hannu will have to help Irene look for that Basta guy. And Tommy has informed me that there are some developments in the search for Jack the Ripper," Andersson continued.

Irene sent a questioning look at Tommy, who responded with a thumbs-up. It would be great if they could catch that idiot. He hadn't been out on the prowl the previous weekend. Maybe the young women in Vasastan had become more careful. Or maybe something else was keeping him off the streets.

"Fredrik is at Financial Crimes. Apparently there's a good chance of pulling in Robert Larsson for economic fraud. Since we don't have witnesses anymore we'll never get him for murdering Laban," Andersson informed them before they rose from morning prayers.

THE FIRST thing Irene did when she returned to her office was to dial Erik Bolin's number. There was still no answer. She remembered that he had a family. He might still be at home. After a brief search in the phone book she found Erik, photographer, and Sara Bolin, dental technician, at an address very close to where she lived.

Irene only heard one ring before the phone was answered.

"Sara Bolin," a strained woman's voice said in a proper Göteborg dialect.

"Good morning. My name is Irene Huss. I'm looking for Erik Bolin."

"Who are you?"

Irene was surprised by the question but answered, "I'm an Inspector with the Crime Police and I've been in touch with Erik about a case and . . ."

"For goodness' sake! Don't be so long-winded! Have you found him?"

Irene was dumbstruck and couldn't come up with anything more intelligent than "Who?"

"Erik, of course! I called early this morning!"

"Wait a second. Has Erik Bolin disappeared?"

It became quiet for a moment before Sara Bolin's shaking voice could be heard again. "Yes. Didn't you know?"

"No. I'm looking for him with respect to a case . . . a person he knew."

Now Sara's voice became guarded. "I understand. Marcus."

"Exactly. Did you know him?"

"No. I've never met him. He was . . . Erik's."

There was a pause.

"Did I understand you correctly? You have reported Erik missing?" she asked carefully.

"Yes. When I woke up this morning, his bed was empty. He didn't come home last night."

"Is he gone overnight occasionally?"

"Yes. But he always calls. And he always calls if he's going to be late. He often is, at his job."

"Didn't you miss him last night?"

"Yes. But he called earlier yesterday afternoon and said that he would be late. So I wasn't all that worried when it was nine o'clock and he hadn't come home. I was mostly irritated. I called the studio but he wasn't there. So I went to bed. I was very tired and must have fallen asleep as soon as my head hit the pillow."

Irene agreed it was worrisome that Erik Bolin was missing. "Do you have a key to the studio?"

"No. Erik has the only key."

Irene was about to ask why they didn't have an extra key at home, but realized that was a question she should ask Erik and not his wife.

She made up her mind. "I'll go to the studio and see if I can get inside."

"Thanks."

She almost collided with Hannu on the way out.

"Come on. Erik Bolin has disappeared," she said quickly.

Without asking any questions, Hannu went to get his jacket.

DURING THE car ride to Kastellgatan, Irene briefly went over what she knew about Erik's disappearance, which wasn't all that much.

"He quite simply never came home last night," she concluded.

"So, according to the wife, he's often late but always calls home," Hannu ascertained.

"Exactly."

"So he has time to meet boyfriends."

"You mean in the evenings? Before he goes home to his family?"

"Yes."

Hannu was right. The previous day, Irene had had a strong feeling that she should have dug deeper into Erik Bolin's relationship with Marcus and Basta. Now she regretted her omission.

"Could it be a triangle drama?" she asked.

Hannu asked, "How so?"

"If Marcus loved Basta and Erik loved Marcus and Basta loved Erik . . ."

She stopped and thought the sequence through to see if she had said it correctly. She had. Resolutely, she continued, ". . . then maybe Basta murdered Marcus. In order to get Erik."

Hannu said, "Hardly. Remember Carmen Østergaard. And Isabell and Emil. It doesn't fit."

Irene had to admit that he was right. But there was something in the thought that she didn't want to let go. Would Erik and Marcus have continued their relationship on a friendship basis for several years?

The pictures of Marcus were taken through the eyes of a man in love. And would the man in love let his lover go to have sex with another man behind an old lighthouse? Not on your life. Even if, according to Anders Gunnarsson, homosexuals could sometimes have a more relaxed view of unfaithfulness, they still weren't immune to jealousy.

Something in Erik Bolin's story didn't add up. She had sensed it yesterday but hadn't really realized it until now. Now she was more concerned and unconsciously increased her speed, despite the heavy traffic.

"Fifty," Hannu pointed out.

A glance at the speedometer showed sixty-five. Embarrassed, she eased off the gas pedal.

THE OUTER door of the studio was just as it had been the day before. Irene knocked hard and long without any response. Hannu opened the metal lid of the mail slot and peered into the hall. He stood for a long time and looked without saying anything. When he turned toward Irene, he looked very serious.

"We have to call a locksmith," he said.

Irene pulled out her cell phone and did as he had said. The locksmith would come within half an hour. She ended the conversation and leaned forward in order to see what Hannu had seen.

Inside the door were a lot of newspapers and mail. Glass shards and a piece of a broken silver-coated wooden frame could be seen at the periphery of her field of vision. Several large rust brown stains were visible on the light pinkish-colored floor.

"There's been a violent struggle in there. It looks like dried bloodstains on the floor. There weren't any pieces of glass or a broken frame on the floor when I left yesterday around four thirty," said Irene.

Hannu nodded, expressionlessly, an unfailing sign that he was worried.

While they were waiting for the locksmith, they read the names of the other tenants in the building. The house had five stories, with two apartments on every floor. They decided to wait to question the neighbors until they had more information about what had happened in the studio.

The locksmith arrived and opened the door. He disappeared as quickly as he had shown up.

The light in the hall was on. Both Irene and Hannu stopped in the doorway in order to get an overview of the situation. One of Bolin's framed gallery photos was lying on the floor, completely broken into pieces. The glass was crushed, the frame was broken into small bits, and the picture itself had been cut into strips. They were wide enough that Irene could make out the shape of an infant's head against a woman's chest in one of them. It was the photo of Erik Bolin's family.

From a door on the left, which had been closed when Irene had been there the day before, a trail of rust red stains led to the outer door.

Hannu saw it first. He gave a start and Irene followed his eyes to a point above her right shoulder. She screamed. The floor rocked.

Erik Bolin's head lay on top of a hat rack, gazing at them with half-closed eyes.

"Stand still," said Hannu.

He pulled his cell phone out of his pocket and called for backup.

"WELL, WELL. Now Irene is home again and they're starting to drop like flies here in Göteborg," said Jonny.

He laughed loudly in order to show that it was a joke but none of the others were smiling. Andersson gave him a dark look that effectively silenced any more such comments. The superintendent turned to Irene and said, "Could you sum up your actions yesterday and today?"

Irene gave an account of her visit to Bolin's studio. She went to get *Manpower* from her office since Fredrik Stridh and Birgitta Moberg hadn't seen it. Then she told them about her conversation with Sara

Bolin that morning. She briefly mentioned the visit she and Hannu had made to Björnekulla in order to inform the widow of her husband's death.

"She had a complete breakdown. A pastor and relatives are there with her now. We'll have to wait to ask any new questions for a couple of days."

Irene tried to gather strength for what was coming. She was still under the effects of the scene that had met them when they went into the studio.

THEY HAD carefully stepped up to the closed door. Hannu had opened it with his toe cap. There was a spacious bathroom inside. A naked, headless body lay in the huge bathtub. From her position in the doorway, Irene saw that the body looked like Emil's, except for the fact that the head was missing. Hannu took a few steps inside the room, watching where he put his feet. There was a lot of blood on the floor.

"Cut open. Trauma to the pelvic area. Genitalia and chest muscles are cut away," he ascertained.

"Can you see if the buttocks are missing?" she said.

"No. There's a lot of blood and . . ."

He stopped and shook his head before retreating.

"We can't do much before the technicians have done their stuff," he said.

Irene was grateful to have avoided seeing the mutilated body. It was an accusation against her, personally. She should have known that Erik was in danger. He had taken the picture of Basta, and that picture had almost cost Tom Tanaka his life. *Manpower* was the connection between Tom and Erik Bolin.

Everything was as it had been in the studio, except that the place where the destroyed photo had been hanging was empty. A blank. The police patrol arrived and the technicians came soon after.

Hannu stood in front of the salt-sprayed study of Marcus for a long time before he turned to Irene and said, "You're right. Erik was in love with Marcus."

They heard a commotion at the outer door. Irene and Hannu turned and saw Professor Yvonne Stridner in person sail into the hall. This was highly unusual.

"Where's the body?" she said in a high voice to no one in particular.

She expected that one of the servants would answer. Police technician Svante Malm gestured silently toward the bathroom door and then returned to the blood trail under the hat rack. Stridner was in such a hurry that she missed the head on the shelf, but no one stopped her in order to draw her attention to it.

After barely a minute, the professor asked in a loud voice, "Have you found the head?"

Without taking his eyes from what he was doing, Svante Malm pointed up at the ordinary wire hat rack with its macabre decoration. Even Stridner became speechless at the sight.

"STRIDNER SAYS that she thinks Bolin has also been strangled but she wasn't sure. She'll be in touch when she has taken a closer look at the body," Irene concluded.

No one interrupted her while she was talking, but now the superintendent sighed. "To cut off the head! What a sick thing to come up with!"

"A new element," said Hannu.

"It was Emil's job to cut off the head and limbs. We've seen that in the videos. And the murderer didn't bother to do so in Emil's and Isabell's murders." Irene said.

"Then why is he starting with this now?" Andersson asked.

Irene remembered what Yvonne Stridner had said that time when Irene visited her at Pathology. Stumbling, she attempted to explain. "His inner images have changed. He sees things inside that he needs to act out. According to Stridner, it's an incredibly strong urge. Clearly, he has added this thing with the head to his inner image."

Andersson nodded and tried to look like he was following this explanation.

Jonny asked permission to speak. "About this thing with the pictures, one of Marcus's videos is different from the others. It's more like one Emil would have liked. Lots of blood and slaughter. Interestingly enough, it's of women, not a lot of queers. Damned sick, anyway."

"What's it called?" Hannu asked.

"Don't remember," Jonny answered.

"Go get it," said Andersson.

Reluctantly, Jonny sauntered off to his office. He came back with a video in hand. Hannu reached out for it.

"It doesn't say anything on it," he determined.

"It's a copy of a feature-length film. The title is at the beginning," Jonny informed them.

Hannu disappeared into a room with video equipment. While they were waiting, Birgitta informed them that she had found Marcus's password.

"He had saved it in Netscape Bookmarks. Guess what it is?"

She paused for effect and looked around at the curious faces in the room. She slowly turned her notebook, which she had in her lap. In black ink it said: 69 Hotnights.

"Hot nights? That's ridiculous!" Irene exclaimed.

"I've found a customer and address list, different jobs, and so on. I'll print out the things that seem interesting," Birgitta continued.

"Have you found any names we recognize yet?" asked Irene.

"Not yet. But I've barely had time to look at them."

Hannu came in with the videotape in hand. He had put the cassette back in the cover.

"It's *The New York Ripper*," he said.

Everyone looked puzzled, and finally he realized that he would have to explain himself.

"It's illegal. It shows real murders."

"A snuff movie?" Fredrik asked.

"Yes."

"But aren't those just tall tales? I was under the impression that it was never proved that there were actual murders in the films," said Birgitta.

"I know the names of three of them that show actual killings. One of them is *The New York Ripper*," Hannu said firmly.

Irene turned toward Jonny.

"Was this the only movie with this kind of content?" she asked.

Jonny nodded sullenly.

"Was there any element of sadistic sex in the other films?"

"Yes. Sick types with leather whips and several guys on top of one guy and that sort of thing. Disgusting!"

"They're not very different from heterosexual porn films," Irene said dryly.

"Of course, you're very familiar with those," Jonny sneered.

"Yes. As everyone is well aware, I've spent a good deal of time in Vesterbro. You don't need to see the films. It's enough just looking in the display windows," she countered coldly.

Jonny snorted but didn't continue the dispute.

"I'll leave this with the technicians," Hannu said and disappeared again with the video cover in a careful hold.

"Maybe I should try and call Copenhagen? It would be interesting to know if *The New York Ripper* is among Emil's videos," said Irene.

The superintendent nodded.

"Do that. And inform them about this latest murder."

He turned toward Fredrik Stridh.

"Take some guys and start knocking on doors as soon as possible. This bastard has had incredible luck but it has to run out at some point. And this time the trail is fresh and we can go after him quickly."

Irene nodded. "And he has actually left evidence behind. He must have been panicked when he destroyed the photo of Bolin's family. Why? Well, the picture he wanted wasn't in the studio. Because it's standing here."

She pointed at *Manpower*, which was leaning against the wall just inside the door.

"Do you think that picture is so important that he's willing to kill for it?" Andersson objected skeptically.

"Yes. Think about what happened to Tom Tanaka. There are probably only two enlargements of *Manpower*. Marcus had one of them. He deposited it, along with the picture of himself, at Tom Tanaka's before he left for his supposed vacation. For some reason he let the other picture of himself leaning against the pillows hang in Emil's apartment. Either Emil got it from Marcus or he took it after Marcus was dead. But Basta found out where *Manpower* was, probably through Emil. And he knew that Erik Bolin had the other enlargement along with some small pictures and negatives. But there wasn't as much of a hurry with Bolin. Basta probably didn't think that we would find out who had taken the pictures."

"According to the preliminary report from Stridner, Bolin has been dead for more than twelve hours. That means the murderer must have arrived pretty early in the evening. Someone may have seen him," said Birgitta.

Irene wasn't so sure about that. Kastellgatan was relatively quiet and calm, without many shops. But there was always a possibility.

PETER MØLLER answered the telephone despite the fact that it was after six o'clock. Irene couldn't hear any guardedness in his voice; instead, it sounded as though he thought it was nice that she was calling. She started by asking if *The New York Ripper* was among Emil's films. Peter promised to find out. When she had relayed the day's discovery of the latest murder he became very serious.

"He's following you," he said.

That wasn't what Irene wanted to hear. The short hairs rose up on her neck and she shivered, despite the summer heat. Peter wasn't the first one to point this out. And she had thought about it herself many times lately. The murderer was close by.

"How's Tom?" she asked in order to change the subject.

"He's conscious but very tired. The doctor said that he had to be sewn up with over a hundred stitches. Your friend Tom is beautifully embroidered."

Irene's heart ached in sympathy. Poor Tom, who was so appearance conscious. She remembered the silver threads he had twisted around his hair knots and his blue nail polish.

"Could you please say hello to him from me? Actually, can you buy a bouquet of flowers from me? I'll send money."

"Buy flowers! If I could understand what you and that . . . OK. I'll do it."

It was quiet for a moment and Irene was just about to end the phone call when Peter said, "Jens told me that you had asked him about my trip to South Africa. That you thought I became cross and strange when you asked about it."

"Yes . . . it had to do with the fact that Marcus had talked about a police officer who worked in Vesterbro, and then he was tricked into going to Göteborg with the promise of a trip to Thailand . . . and you were tan," she tried to explain.

She quietly blessed the fact that the Göteborg police didn't have videophones. A blush spread across her cheeks. Peter's answer strengthened her wish that videophones might never become standard.

"The trip to South Africa was an attempt at patching up my marriage. But it didn't work. The trip was a catastrophe from beginning to end."

He paused and then added, "It's too bad that you brought up that trip. I became . . . upset. Otherwise it could have been a very pleasant evening . . . and night, for both of us."

Irene was surprised. At the same time she became aware of the tingling warmth spreading between her thighs. Peter was beautiful. His eyes were so blue and his body so muscular and agile. He smelled good and he moved in a sexy way. Her breathing quickened. God! Two police officers almost having phone sex, while talking about a bestial murderer!

She couldn't help but laugh. Half joking, she said, "Maybe I should drive down to Copenhagen and visit my good friend Tom?"

"Do that. I promise to take good care of you."

Before they hung up they agreed to call each other again soon.

Irene was forced to sit in the room for a while, until the pressure in her pelvis ebbed.

"IT SEEMS as though the first part of the address list is customers but at the end there are several pages with names and addresses of different guys. I found Anders Gunnarsson and Hans Pahliss listed there. They were listed together. Erik Bolin is also there and a lot of other names that I don't recognize since I haven't been involved in this investigation," said Birgitta.

She set down a bundle of papers on Irene's desk.

"Thanks. I'll take them home and read them tonight. Krister is working and the girls aren't home either. It'll be a perfect time to sit and work," said Irene.

But she suspected that her concentration would be disturbed by fantasies of what might have happened that night in Copenhagen.

Chapter 16

SVANTE MALM KNOCKED ON the doorjamb before he stepped through the open door. Irene looked up from the pile of printouts from Marcus's computer. She set down her coffee mug in order to avoid getting stains on the papers. It was the fourth mug of the morning and she was actually starting to wake up.

"Thought I would drop by and bring you up to speed. I missed morning prayers. You need to know about some developments."

Svante sat in Irene's visitor's chair. He declined the offer of coffee. Irene pulled out pen and paper and got ready to take notes.

"My colleague in Copenhagen and I have been exchanging information the last couple of weeks. They have better resources than we do and they can get results a lot faster. Now we think we have enough evidence from the murderer that we can run a DNA profile. And we've also found fingerprints."

"Fantastic! But what kind of evidence? And where were the fingerprints? He used gloves, it seemed."

"For the most part. But he made a mistake here and there."

Svante put his right hand up in the air and started counting the mistakes, at the same time he let his fingers point toward the ceiling, one after another.

"One: the semen stain found in Copenhagen under that murdered guy's bed. Two: saliva from the stamp on the postcard you received. We also got an extra bonus there. Three: there's a clear thumbprint in the middle of the stamp! You often push with your thumb when you attach a stamp. For some reason he wasn't wearing gloves then. There's always the risk that it could belong to the mailman but we've just found a new trump card. . . . ."

He paused for effect. Irene discovered that she had scooted forward in her seat and was leaning over the desk, as if she were hard of hearing.

"The videocassette that Hannu brought us yesterday. We could eliminate Jonny's and Hannu's fingerprints right away. We found Marcus's and Emil's prints on the cover. But there were only two prints on the video itself, Emil's and that of an unknown. We've secured the unknown thumbprint. And it matches perfectly with the thumb on the stamp!"

Irene stared at Svante and exclaimed, "I'll be damned! He's been smart, and had incredible luck, but he hasn't realized how dangerous a series of small mistakes are, when put together!"

"He has become too arrogant and self-confident. A bit sloppy. If you catch him, we'll definitely be able to nail him. Even if he denies it." Svante sounded very pleased.

"You haven't gotten anything in on Erik Bolin yet?"

"No. Several samples will come from the autopsy today. Stridner's assistant called. That young girl, what's her name? Britt! Britt Nilsson called from Pathology and said that they had found a skin scraping under Bolin's nails. Apparently the body also has injuries that are indicative of a serious struggle."

Something clicked, but when Irene couldn't grasp it, she tossed it off as her imagination, and asked instead, "So Erik Bolin fought with his killer?"

"The evidence points to it. But you'll get a preliminary report today."

"Probably."

"The bloodstains on the police uniform in Copenhagen are from Marcus Tosscander but those on the baton turned out to be significantly older. They came from a prostitute who was killed two years ago."

"Carmen Østergaard! You mean that her blood was still on the baton after two years?"

"Apparently. There were traces of blood in the hole for the leather strap and on the leather itself. Most of the blood had been wiped or rinsed off, but there was still enough for a positive test. According to our colleagues in Copenhagen, it can't have been used after the murder."

"Wasn't there a baton with the other uniform?"

"No."

"And no signs of bloodstains on that uniform?"

"No."

"Were the bloodstains on the real uniform or on the one Emil bought in the gay shop?"

"On the one he bought in the shop."

So Emil hadn't dared to use his mother's uniform during the dismemberment itself, maybe out of fear that she might sometime ask to have it back. A thought struck Irene.

"Wasn't there any of Carmen's blood on the uniform?"

"No. Though it had never been washed."

Irene thought. "On the video, Emil was wearing a uniform when he dismembered Carmen. That must mean that he had still another uniform at that time," she said.

"Very possible."

Svante was already on his way into the corridor when Irene heard his farewell. "Good-bye. We'll be in touch when we know more about Bolin."

Irene brooded for a long time about the mystery of the absence of Carmen's blood from the uniform worn during her dismemberment. That *must* mean Emil had had a third uniform. Where was it now? Maybe he had burned it afterward if it was very bloody? And bought a new one for the dismembering of Marcus?

Irene trembled. That meant that Marcus's murder had been planned long in advance. Which must mean that Carmen's murder had also been planned. Were the strange assaults on the two prostitutes in Copenhagen shortly before Carmen was murdered the first clumsy attempts at trying to secure a mutilation victim? Third time was the charm, in that case.

The description the police had of "the policeman" matched Emil, and the description of "the doctor" matched Basta. And what was it that had clicked when Svante Malm started talking about Stridner? Something that Stridner had said? Something that her assistant had said? Irene had only met Britt Nilsson a few times and that had been a while ago. No, it was useless. To her irritation, she was forced to give up. But something had definitely registered.

She went through every name on the lists from Marcus's computer. Even names that only popped up in connection with job requests were noted. All of them would be checked. It would be a huge job but Irene felt convinced that Basta was hiding behind one of those names.

He *could* be a link between the victims and the murderer. But another certainty had grown ever stronger inside her: *he* was the murderer they were looking for.

"I THINK we have him!"

Tommy stormed into the office they shared. He seemed elated. Normally, Tommy was calmness personified.

"I've come directly from the prosecutor. We're going to get him immediately. He's at work right now."

"Who?" Irene asked, confused.

Tommy stared at her. Then he exploded, "Jack the Ripper, of course!"

"*The New York Ripper* and Jack the Ripper. . . . It's a bit much now," Irene said, trying to make a joke of her blunder.

Tommy gave her a sharp look before he continued. "I went through the employee lists of all the bars in Vasastan and its surroundings. I checked all males between the ages of twenty and forty. What a job! But it paid off. Yesterday I found Rickard 'Zorro' Karlsson. Thirty-two years old and works as a dishwasher at a pizzeria on Molinsgatan."

Irene formed a silent whistle with her mouth. A dishwasher at a pizzeria, just a stone's throw away from the pub where her husband worked as master chef.

"He got the nickname Zorro from his fellow inmates in prison. He raped a waitress who was working at the same bar that he was. After the rape, he carved two deep Z marks on her thighs with a meat knife. Afterward he couldn't explain why. He was convicted of aggravated sexual assault and he got seven years."

"Dare I guess that this was max four years ago?" Irene said ironically.

"Almost right. Four and a half. The crime happened in Gävle. After his time in prison he moved to Göteborg. His brother works as a cook at another restaurant here in the city but Rickard didn't get a job there as a dishwasher. He works at the pizzeria instead."

"When did he start?"

"In February."

"And at the end of March, Jack the Ripper started to wreak havoc," Irene determined.

"Yup. And now I've checked his time sheets against the times of the rapes. All of them have occurred when Zorro was working a late-night shift!"

"And the prosecutor has given the OK to pull him in right away?"

"Yup. Fredrik is tagging along. See you!"

His good-bye echoed from the corridor. Strange how everyone seemed to be in a hurry to leave her office today.

Personally, she was stuck with all of the names on Marcus's computer lists. Her intuition hadn't given her the verdict when she went through them but she felt certain the murderer's name was there.

Two names connected with Marcus weren't on the lists: Pontus Zander and Tom Tanaka. Irene knew of them so she noticed they were missing. That meant there were probably other people close to Marcus who were not listed in the computer. The absence of Pontus's name wasn't as remarkable as the fact that Tom's name was missing. According to Pontus, he and Marcus had never been well acquainted. But Tom and Marcus had been.

Irene sighed. It felt hopeless but she had to start the phone calls. Just as she reached out for the phone it rang. She grabbed the receiver.

At first it was quiet on the line but she could hear quick, nervous breathing.

"This is Angelica Hendersen," said a thin female voice.

The name didn't mean anything to Irene. Cautious, but in a friendly tone of voice, she said, "OK. And what can I help you with?"

"Marcus . . . I knew Marcus Tosscander. Have you caught the killer?"

"No. Not yet."

"It's so terrifying. I can't understand it . . . Marcus!"

To Irene's dismay, the woman started sobbing. There was no point in trying to comfort her. Irene patiently held the phone and waited for the crying fit to ease. It took a long time but the woman finally calmed down. Sniffling, she said, "Forgive me. But this is a shock for me."

Irene heard her blow her nose. Her voice sounded steadier when she started speaking again. "I live in Los Angeles. I came home yesterday to visit my parents. They told me what had happened to Marcus. It's . . . horrendous! They didn't want to tell me anything before I came home because they knew how sad I would be."

"How did you know Marcus?"

"We grew up together."

"In Hovås?"

"Yes. I was named Sandberg at that time."

The lightbulb came on. This was the girlfriend Marcus's father had desperately tried to drag out as proof of his son's heterosexuality. Irene had actually thought about contacting her, but since no more women's names had come up in connection with Marcus, she had forgotten about Angelica.

"I visited Emanuel Tosscander today but he didn't want to talk to me about the murder. He said that I should contact an Inspector Huss at the police station if I wanted to know anything. Please, tell me what you know," Angelica Hendersen pleaded.

"Yes, I will, if I can ask you a few questions afterward."

"That's fine."

"Even if the questions might be a little sensitive?"

"Yes. I promise to answer them," Angelica replied in a firm voice.

Irene told her about the investigation from the very beginning but without going into great detail. She outlined the connections between the murders of Carmen Østergaard, Marcus, Isabell Lind, Emil Bentsen, and Erik Bolin.

Angelica didn't interrupt her account. Her response, when it finally came, took Irene aback.

"Despite everything, I'm not completely surprised about what happened to Marcus. The connection to violence and to the other victims, that also adds up."

Irene collected herself after her initial reaction. "Why aren't you surprised?" she asked.

"He needed excitement and danger. Together with sex. If you understand."

Several people had said the same thing in similar words. Irene understood but still said, "Explain a bit more. Or why not tell me about your relationship with Marcus from the beginning?"

"Maybe that would be best. We've known each other all our lives. He was a year older than I. Our parents were neighbors and spent a lot of time together. We were best friends, played with each other all the time, and were always together, too. When we were teenagers, there was a bit more . . . making out between us. In hindsight, I've realized that I was always the one who took the initiative. But I didn't have any experience with other boys, and I thought that Marcus and I were very much in love with each other. Because I really loved him. During my entire childhood and youth there wasn't anyone else. He went along with cuddling and making out, but never sex. I was naive and romantic and thought that it would sort itself out on our wedding night. That he was saving himself for that."

Angelica stopped herself.

"You never sensed that Marcus was gay?" Irene asked.

"No. Never. As I said, I was very naive and I'd had a protected childhood. That's why the realization was so traumatic."

She blew her nose discreetly before continuing. "The summer I turned eighteen, Marcus asked if I wanted to go with him to Crete. I was overjoyed. Somewhere inside me, hope started growing. The Greek sun and warmth would get Marcus's hormones to wake up, and we would finally have sex. Because I really felt I was mature enough for it. We landed at the airport in Chania late in the afternoon, so by the time we had checked in and gotten things sorted out with the hotel room, it was time for dinner. The hotel we were staying at was located in Platania. It was right by the beach and couldn't have been more romantic. I still remember that night. We were sitting at a beachside tavern watching the sun disappear into the Mediterranean. The food was fantastic and we had shared a bottle of wine. We had also had some whiskey in the hotel room. I wasn't used to it and became a bit tipsy. Marcus suddenly got up from the table, mumbling an apology. I thought that he was just going to go to the bathroom. But he never came back. I sat and waited for him for more than an hour. When the staff started looking at me strangely, I paid and went up to the hotel room. He didn't show up during the night."

"Didn't you report him missing to the hotel staff? Or the police?" Irene asked.

"That came later. I fell into an uneasy sleep in the early morning hours and slept until nine o'clock. When I woke up, a very clear memory came back to me. Just as Marcus had gotten up and hurried away, a man dressed in military clothes did the same, and I got the impression that they had nodded at each other faintly. As if they knew each other. But it was impossible. Marcus had never been to

Crete before. I managed to convince myself that I was mistaken and that I had to do something. But I didn't know what. Maybe something bad had happened to Marcus. I went out on the streets and wandered around aimlessly a while without knowing what I was going to do next. Then I saw the jeep."

Angelica took a deep breath. "A military jeep came driving at a high speed down the main street of Platania. It was forced to slow down because of a car that was turning just a few meters away from me. A military man was sitting in front, driving. Marcus was in the backseat with the man I had seen at the restaurant the night before. He was still wearing a uniform. The jeep disappeared from my line of sight. I totally panicked. I rushed into the telegraph office, which was located a few hundred meters farther down the same street, and requested a phone call home to my parents. When Pappa answered, I started screaming that Marcus had been arrested by the military and was probably being taken away to some Greek prison. Because my father is a man with good international contacts, he promised to find out what had happened to Marcus right away. He called the consulate in Athens, which in turn contacted Heraklion in Crete. Pappa had told me to be in the hotel room two hours later. He called me like he had promised but he hadn't gotten any information yet. I remember that he told me to go and eat and swim and he would be in touch around four o'clock. I didn't have the energy to eat or sunbathe. I sat glued to the phone instead. Pappa called at four o'clock and I could tell by the sound of his voice that it was hard for him to tell me what had happened. In the end, I understood what he was saying. Marcus had been found. He was with a high-ranking military officer at the military base in Maleme. They weren't on the base but in the personal home of the officer, and Marcus was there of his own free will. I still remember Pappa's sympathetic voice when he asked if I wanted to come home right away or stay the whole week as planned. You aren't going to believe me, but I chose to stay the whole week. I hadn't really accepted what Pappa told me. I thought that I had to be there when Marcus came back. Surely everything would turn out to be a misunderstanding. Not even then did I realize Marcus was gay. Not even then . . . I didn't want to see the truth."

She stopped herself again.

"When did you realize that Marcus was gay?" Irene asked.

"When he showed up after three days. Just as bright and cheerful as usual. I was at the point of collapse. Actually, I was just as pale as I had been when I arrived in Crete. It wasn't fun to lie by yourself on the beach, and I didn't have enough peace of mind to do it. But Marcus was tan over his whole body. He certainly didn't have any tan lines from a bathing suit! When I asked what the marks around his wrists and neck were, he only laughed and hugged me. But the marks were terrible; his skin was chafed and covered with sores. Even I could see that he had been tied up. He was sweet with me and was in his usual cuddly mood during the afternoon. In the evening he got dressed up and invited me out to dinner. After dinner we went to a disco. Not fifteen minutes had passed before he disappeared again. But this time I understood what had happened. He had met a man again."

"When did he come back?"

"Late the next morning, but by then I had had enough. There were two sweet Norwegian guys living in the same corridor as we were and I basically moved in with them."

At the last sentence she laughed. Apparently not all her memories from the trip to Crete were unpleasant.

"Did you speak with Marcus afterward about what had happened?"

"No. That's what was so weird. When we went back home on the plane we didn't say a word about his disappearing. Anyone who saw us must have believed we were a young couple in love traveling home from a very nice vacation. And we never talked about it later either. But our relationship changed. The making out and the cuddling ended, but, strangely enough, we continued to be the best of friends. We've continued to stay in touch through the years. I write to him a few times a year and he calls me. In recent years it has mostly been e-mails back and forth."

"Haven't you wondered why he hasn't been in touch during the last few months?"

"Yes. At Easter. He always sends a greeting or gets in touch. But he didn't this year. I was a bit upset but that's the way it was with Marcus. I could go a long time without hearing from him, but when he did get in touch it was always as though no time had passed since the last time."

"When was the last time you had contact with Marcus?"

Angelica thought a moment before replying. "He sent an e-mail on Stan's fortieth birthday. Stan is my husband. His birthday was February 3. I had reminded Marcus when we spoke on the phone New Year's Eve. I never thought that he would remember, but he did."

Irene was struck by a thought. She looked down at the pile of lists lying in front of her on the desk and asked, "Do you know if Marcus had access to a computer when he was in Copenhagen?"

"Of course! He couldn't work without his computer. Before he moved to Copenhagen he bought a laptop. I don't remember what brand it was but he was completely satisfied with it."

Obviously, that was why Tom Tanaka wasn't on any of the address lists. All of the new names and design projects after the move were on the new computer. It had disappeared without a trace, like all of Marcus's other belongings in Copenhagen.

Irene gave Angelica her direct number and got Angelica's parents' telephone number. She would be staying in Sweden two weeks.

Dark rain clouds towered over the city, warning of a serious afternoon rainstorm. Irene pondered, not paying attention to the weather.

Marcus's clothes, computer, cell phone, pens and papers, toiletry items—everything was gone. Except for the car and the three framed photographs Erik Bolin had taken.

One victim had taken pictures of another victim. One of the pictures had hung over the bed—and, moreover, the murder scene—of a third victim. Who demonstrably had participated in mutilating the victim in the picture! It was all connected in some sick and curious way.

The pictures. Because Bolin had been murdered and Tanaka seriously wounded in the murderer's hunt for *Manpower*, one could reasonably assume that the picture was important. Because the man in the photograph was the murderer? Irene couldn't come up with any other reason.

The car. Why hadn't they gotten rid of Marcus's conspicuous car? And what kind of car did Emil have?

Irene decided to ask Peter Møller. Her heartbeat sped up when she dialed his number.

To her disappointment, Jens Metz answered. He sounded less irate than he had the last time they'd spoken. Irene presented her questions. Jens answered, "The investigation of Tosscander's car hasn't revealed anything. It appears to have been standing untouched in the garage since the owner disappeared."

"What kind of car did Emil have?"

"The make? A Range Rover."

A Range Rover. A jeep. Erik Bolin had said Basta had arrived in a jeep the time his picture was taken. Had Basta borrowed Emil's jeep?

"Where is it now?"

"It was parked out in the yard. We've taken it in for a forensic examination. The investigation into the attack on your friend Tanaka has come to a halt. A witness saw a tall dark-clothed man jump into a white parked car that was standing just outside the entrance to the backyard. He had the hood of his sweatshirt pulled up. Before he started the car, he threw a large picture into the backseat. According to the witness, he was alone. He wasn't sure about the make of the car. Probably an old Jetta or something similar. But we've gotten some interesting tips from Emil's neighbors. According to them, a tall man with a ponytail has occasionally lived at Emil's. And, according to a neighbor lady who lives under Emil, he's Swedish. She's heard them talk with each other. The other neighbor has only run into the guy a few times in the elevator."

"Have they been able to give a more detailed description?"

"Tall, muscular, about twenty-five years old, shoulder-length dark blond hair in a ponytail. The man who had been with him in the elevator said that he thought the man was an artist because he had paint on his hands and a large sketch pad under his arm."

Artist? Then if this was the killer, all Marcus's references to "my personal physician" were meaningless. No matter how much he would have liked to, Marcus couldn't possibly have transformed an artist into a personal physician.

Jens Metz asked about the new murder in Göteborg. Irene told him the little she knew. When they hung up they agreed to allocate every resource to stopping the murder-crazed beast. There couldn't be any more killings.

"Right now it's quiet here because he's wreaking havoc in Göteborg. But something tells me that he'll be here again soon," Jens concluded ominously.

When they had hung up, Irene thought about his last sentence. Why Göteborg and Copenhagen? Was it possible to figure out some sort of connection between these two cities and one of the names on the list? That name might only be on Marcus's missing computer, but all they could do was check the names they had and hope for a little luck.

Birgitta Moberg stood in the doorway like a God-sent angel and said, "Hi! Did you find any names that seem familiar? No? Then I can help to make some calls. We'll divide the pile."

"You're a pal! Just let me know if you need a favor in return."

"Well . . . you can babysit in a few years."

HER DAUGHTERS were in the kitchen, well under way with dinner, when Irene came home. Krister was working late and wouldn't be home until past midnight.

Jenny was pouring steaming vegetable broth over thin-sliced vegetables. Irene could make out tomatoes, carrots, squash, and onion. A faint smell of garlic whirled up into the air, betokening the perfect amount of seasoning in the casserole.

Katarina was spicing large ground-beef patties with generous dashes of black, white, and green pepper. When they had turned a delicious golden brown color in the frying pan, they would simmer in some cream and a little bit of soy sauce. Those who had iron stomachs could add even more pepper at their discretion. Irene usually added a bit extra.

Jenny opened the oven door and scooted the pan with the potato wedges over in order to make room for her vegetable casserole. Irene knew what was expected of her. She got out the ingredients for the salad. It was boring to make salad but it was the family's collective opinion that that was what she was best at when it came to the cooking arts.

"We aren't going to be in Borås until eleven. Mattias and Tobbe are leaving earlier to set up the stuff so that everything will be ready when we get there," said Jenny.

"Are you going to Borås?" asked Irene.

Jenny sighed loudly and rolled her eyes.

"You're more scatterbrained than Grandma! If someone tells you something, like, in the beginning of the week, you've forgotten it by the end."

Irene faintly started remembering a short conversation with Jenny a few days earlier. Then she had talked about the band having gotten a gig in Borås. But was it really so soon as this weekend?

"We've been allowed to jump in at the last minute for the Wawa boys. They're huge. This is an awesome opportunity. We're getting paid really well."

The blush on her cheeks wasn't because she had a fever. Her eyes were lit up from excitement and happiness. This was what Jenny had dreamed about for the last couple of years. Irene felt affection mixed with sorrow rise within her. Sorrow over the fact that time went by so quickly. Soon the girls would be all grown up. She quickly landed in reality again with Jenny's next comment; she was far from being able to accept her daughter as an adult.

"And everything is sorted out with the hotel. It's going to be so cool!"

"The hotel? Are you going to stay at a hotel?"

"Naturally. We won't be done until after one o'clock. And by the time we've packed all of our things, half the night will have gone. We were able to take over the Wawa boys' room reservation."

Irene stared at her daughter. She would soon be turning seventeen but she was far from being of age. And now she was going to stay at a hotel in Borås with a strange group of guys. Irene didn't have any idea what they were like. With an effort, she tried to conceal the anxiety in her voice as she asked, "Will you get your own room?"

Jenny shrugged and said, "Don't know. Think so."

Contradictory thoughts were darting here and there in Irene's brain, but before she had time to reach a decision, Katarina said, "Polo is in the process of becoming superpopular. You have to understand, Mamma. Jenny might be the next Nina in the Cardigans!"

Jenny blushed with delight at her sister's praise. Irene hadn't seen her this happy for a long time.

Now she realized: she had to let Jenny go to Borås.

Katarina continued enthusiastically, "Micke and I are driving there to listen to them. Then we're going home to Micke's to sleep there. It's nearby."

Irene could have informed Katarina that the distance from Micke's parents' house in Önnered to her own was barely a kilometer as the crow flies and only slightly longer if one used the asphalt roads. But she didn't have the energy for that discussion. She had the feeling that she had lost something. And she knew what it was. Her daughters' childhoods would never come back.

Mostly in order to have something to say, she asked, "Is Micke well now? And how does your neck feel?"

"Both of us are feeling much better. I'm allowed to start training lightly after midsummer. Real training and stuff. Not this stupid physical therapy I'm doing now. Just watch how I'm going to catch up! That Ida Bäck better not think she can keep her gold medal in the National Championships next year!"

Irene felt very proud of her daughters now. Each of them, in her own way, was a goal-oriented fighter.

Heavenly smells started emanating from the oven. Katarina was browning the beef patties. Irene felt hungry. She quickly set the table and put out a pitcher of ice water.

A calm whimper at knee height reminded her that it was high time for Sammie's dinner. Two mugs of dry food mixed with the leftovers from yesterday's beef sausage was a culinary treat, according to him. Irene stared at the dry brown pebbles, which looked suspiciously like rabbit droppings. Even though she loathed preparing food, she would never be tempted to eat dry dog food. Not even if it had been soaked in hot water.

THE POLICE movie was over just after midnight. Irene turned off the TV, stretched, and yawned. Goodness, how confused and messy it seemed to be at police stations in the USA. Large open office spaces where the desks stood close together, and every attempt at creating a close relationship was doomed to fail. Collared whores, drug dealers, and murderers walked past each other between the desks. In the middle of it all, cops stood and quarreled and fussed about their work problems. And everyone went around indoors armed. It would seem to be too easy for a suspect to pull a gun out of a holster amidst the general confusion.

Was it really like this? If that was the case, Irene felt sincerely sorry for her colleagues on the other side of the Atlantic.

She cleared away her coffee cup. Just as she had expected, Sammie came padding after her into the kitchen. It was high time for the last rounds of the night.

The rain had slowed to a drizzle. The air was fresh but still mild. Steam rising from the warm earth smelled good. The early summer foliage was at its most beautiful and everything breathed hope in the face of the oncoming summer. Judging from appearances, a student party was being held at a nearby house. Two skinny birches decorated with balloons stood on either side of the front door as a sign. A young man in a white shirt and dark pants stumbled through the open door. Heaving sounds could be heard by Irene and Sammie. The young man clung to the nearest birch for support and both he and the propped-up birch fell straight into the pool of vomit.

The future is ours, Irene thought.

Sammie became uneasy and whimpered when he saw the boy struggling with the birch tree. It didn't get any better when, with loud curses, the boy swayed upright, grabbed the birch, and threw it down the steps. Sammie started barking heatedly. Of all strange behaviors, this took the cake! Personally, he loved trees and never fought them! He used them for their proper purpose. He demonstrated by lifting his leg toward a lilac bush.

Irene had to drag her furiously barking dog away by his leash. A lap around the soccer field would have to do. A wet dog wasn't the nicest thing to have in bed and Irene knew that he would jump up as soon as she had fallen asleep. They should have dealt with that when he was a puppy, but it had been so charming when the chubby little dog, struggling, crawled into their bed.

Irene suddenly felt as though she was being watched. They were on the far side of the soccer field that bordered on woods. She looked around but couldn't see anyone. The feeling wouldn't go away.

Sammie didn't notice anything out of the ordinary; he sniffed the ground as usual. The energetic wagging of his tail revealed that an unusually attractive female dog had passed by a little while ago.

Irene's nervousness increased. Going home, the dog hesitated; someone was standing behind the trees, watching her. Sweat broke out over her entire body under the tight nylon rain jacket. Fear made her yell at Sammie, "Come on, you stupid dog!"

He was so perplexed that he followed without protest. She hadn't been imagining things. When they began walking briskly, she heard a twig break. Someone had stepped on a dry branch. The young birches stood tightly together. It was impossible to see anything in the deep darkness between the trees. In a flash, she made up her mind. In a fake, hearty voice, she said to Sammie, "Now we're going to run home to master!"

Bewildered by his mistress's quick mood swing, he hesitantly started trotting, but pretty soon he got into the swing of things. He increased his speed and ran with the leash taut as a cable behind him.

While she ran, Irene fumbled with her house key. She held it, ready, in a tight grip inside her jacket pocket. As luck would have it, she had switched on the outside lighting when she went out. Even though her hand was shaking, she managed to get the key in the lock. She quickly pulled the dog inside, shut the door behind her, and locked it.

Without taking off her shoes she went straight through the house, checked that the patio door was locked, and switched on the outdoor lights facing the yard. Then she switched off all the lamps on the ground floor and checked the windows just in case, even though she knew that they were closed. Quietly, she crouched beneath a window, so that she couldn't be seen from the outside. She peered out but didn't see a single living creature. Only the light rain and the wind, setting the trees' leaves in motion.

A thought struck her: the second floor. What if the girls had left a window ajar? With a pounding heart, she ran up the stairs. But she had worried for no reason; all of the windows were closed, including the ceiling window in the combined hall and TV room.

From Jenny's room she could look out over the backyard, which was lit. None of the neighbors had their outdoor lights on. The yard was small and well illuminated by lighting from the patio and the street-lights on the other side of the sidewalk.

Her pulse reverted to a normal rhythm. Had there really been a person watching her from the stand of trees? She had definitely heard a twig break, but a deer or some other animal might have caused it.

Irene had always depended on her intuition and it had never let her down. She wasn't afraid of the dark, but maybe a figment of her imagination had scared her this time. All of the talk about the murderer being close to her had naturally affected her. Isabell's murder and the postcard that had come directly afterward had been directed at her, personally. The murderer must have thought that Irene was getting close to the truth of Marcus's death far too quickly. He had killed Isabell as a warning, but maybe also to send up a smoke screen to complicate the investigation of the murders of Carmen Østergaard and Marcus Tosscander.

But why had he needed to kill Emil Bentsen? They were partners—principals and accessories in both crimes. Yet Basta had carried out the murder of Isabell on his own. Had Emil become frightened when Basta told him about the murder? They must have met soon afterward.

Emil's mother had asked him if he knew Isabell or had heard of Scandinavian Models. Isabell was lured to the Hotel Aurora only an hour later. By whom? Not by Emil, who was in Tom's store. Irene had seen him there with her own eyes. Bell was murdered by the person Emil had spoken with just after his conversation with Beate Bentsen. That person must have been Basta.

Maybe the picture over Emil's bed had reminded Basta about the pictures Erik Bolin had taken the previous summer. *Manpower* was proof of the connection between Marcus and Basta. It had taken him some time to get Tom's copy of the photo, but in the end he had succeeded. If Tom hadn't happened to go into the bedroom he wouldn't have been injured. The primary thing hadn't been to kill Tom, but to get the picture.

But it had been his intention to kill Emil Bentsen and Erik Bolin. There were elements of mutilation and rituals. Wouldn't it have been enough to break into Bolin's and steal the pictures? Why had it been necessary to murder him?

The answer turned Irene's blood to ice: because he liked killing. He wouldn't hesitate to do it again. Just the opposite: it was an instinct, an obsession. And he wouldn't have any objections to the next victim being a certain female criminal Inspector. That would be killing two birds with one stone.

This thought made her pulse race again though there hadn't been a single movement outside. Irene looked at the clock. Almost thirty minutes had passed since she'd locked herself in the house. Krister would soon be home. And almost at once, she heard Krister's familiar steps coming up the cement walk to the front door.

Suddenly, she understood Basta's strategy. She jumped up from the bed and rushed toward the stairs. The front door opened below and the light from the sconce outside spread into the dark hallway in an ever-growing fan shape. Krister stood out as a massive shadowy figure in the door opening. He stretched his hand to turn on the hall lamp.

With a primal scream Irene threw herself down the stairs. Krister jerked, which saved him from receiving a heavy baton blow on the head. It caught him on the side of his throat instead. He fell with a deep grunt.

Irene threw herself with all her weight against the strong black-clad man who had sneaked up behind Krister. With her head lowered, right shoulder first, she lunged at his chest. He was off balance from the blow he'd aimed at Krister and he tumbled backward out the door and fell into a half-sitting position. As he fell, he dropped the baton, which hit the pavement with a thud.

Irene stopped her movement forward by grabbing the door frame. The man quickly got to his feet, and his right hand darted under his jacket. Irene saw a knife blade glitter under the light. She did the only thing possible given the situation: she slammed the door shut. Then, with shaking fingers, she turned the lock.

Chapter 17

"HE HAD THE HOOD of his sweatshirt pulled down tightly. I didn't see much of his face but I'm absolutely sure that I recognize him," said Irene.

Andersson looked at her thoughtfully. Finally he nodded and said, "I've sat and looked at that damn porn picture several times and I don't know if I'm imagining it, but I also think that there's something familiar about him."

"Me, too," Hannu agreed.

The others at Monday morning prayers shook their heads regretfully.

The attack at Irene's home had happened late Friday night. Colleagues and technicians had searched through her house and its surroundings for evidence over the weekend. Rain had fallen during the night, which made the search difficult. The only positive find was the impression of a Nike athletic shoe, size eleven, in a flower bed on the short side of the toolshed that separated the Husses' house from their neighbor's. Basta must have hidden behind the shed, waiting for Krister to come home.

Krister had become dizzy after the blow but he hadn't passed out. A police car drove him to Sahlgren Hospital to be checked. They confirmed that he had suffered trauma, with heavy bleeding and swelling. He would have to take a few days off work and go easy for a while.

Krister accepted his diagnosis with a grumble. Irene heard him say that to be attacked from behind by a crazy murderer was nothing compared to the experience of opening the door of one's own cozy home and being met by a howling demon coming at him! He had never been so close to a heart attack in his life.

Irene was truly grateful that they had come away from their meeting with Basta as well as they had. By now she had seen far too many who hadn't had the same luck.

"The baton he had with him wasn't a normal policeman's baton. It was dark brown or black. And it wasn't made out of rubber. It sounded like he'd dropped a baseball bat when it fell against the concrete slabs of the walkway. And it seemed longer than our batons," Irene said at morning prayers.

"Probably hickory or mahogany. The police in the USA and some Asian and African police corps use them," said Hannu.

"Was the baton found in Emil's closet a regular rubber baton?" Andersson asked.

"Yes," said Irene.

"And there was blood on it from that tart," the superintendent mentioned.

"Yes. Carmen Østergaard's blood. That murder was committed two years ago. The conclusion has to be that the weapon used during the recent murders was this wooden baton," said Irene.

And her husband had been knocked down with that baton. Fear chilled Irene. She hadn't had any objections when the superintendent placed an officer at their house during the weekend and wouldn't oppose keeping the guard there until Basta had been caught. As if he had read her thoughts, Andersson locked his gaze on Irene and said, "We'll continue to post a guy at your house. It's clear that that idiot is out to get you. And you aren't going out on any investigations on your own! No personal projects for a while! He's biding his time, waiting for the right opportunity."

Irene was uneasy, not because the superintendent was talking about her private investigation in Copenhagen, but because she realized how right he was. Basta had been very clear about his intentions. He wasn't afraid of attacking her family. Their daughters had carefully been instructed not to open the door for strangers, not to go out alone in the evenings or at night, and to take other necessary safety precautions.

"What a horrible job you have!" Jenny had sighed. For the first time in her life, Irene almost agreed with her.

"Are we getting closer to identifying this man?" Andersson asked.

Birgitta asked permission to speak.

"I've called everyone on the lists from Marcus's computer. I've been able to cross off most of them right away. They've been business contacts. But there are several interesting people in his phone book.

I haven't been able to get a few of them. I think many of the ones I've already spoken with have had interesting reactions. Some have said, 'Am I in his phone book? We've only seen each other once,' and others, 'Am I still in his phone book? We haven't seen each other for years.' I think this means that Marcus was very careful about keeping track of his partners and even one-night stands. That's why I think it's highly likely that Basta is on the list."

Irene had avoided the boring lists of names on purpose but realized now that there was every reason to get to work on them. Birgitta was right. Basta was probably in there somewhere. Give the thing you fear a name and gain control over it, thought Irene. Loudly she said, "What can the nickname Basta stand for?"

"Basta. Bastu. Bastuklubb!" Jonny grinned. "Steamy! Like a bathhouse."

"Maybe he's strict. Basta could refer to that," Birgitta suggested.

"There could be something there. Marcus was evidently a masochist. Basta could mean a strict enforcer," Irene agreed.

Hannu spoke up. "I've been thinking about the location where they dismembered Marcus. On the video you can see a window high up on the wall. Twice you can see blinking lights that are moving. It's dark outside. The lights can clearly be seen. I've contacted a friend who is an air traffic controller and have shown it to him. He says that the first light you can see is that of a helicopter taking off and the other is an airplane that's landing.

"That's a clue. But which airfield can it be? Landvetter?" Andersson wondered.

"No. The plane is small. It must be Säve. That's the only one with enough traffic for there to be two light aircraft in ten minutes. I'm thinking about checking to see if there are any interesting locations nearby," said Hannu.

Irene thought this seemed soundly reasoned. They had to start looking for the location and this was a start. Everyone else had been completely focused on the macabre scene that had played on the television screen. As usual, Hannu had been thinking for himself.

"And we'll return to our lists," Irene pointed out and nodded at Birgitta.

"It's probably safest that way. To have you here in the station," the superintendent muttered.

IRENE PUT a red mark next to the names of people she couldn't contact and those she thought would be interesting to meet face to face. She had gone through over twenty names and put a red mark next to five of them. If Basta wasn't among these five, then she would have to go back to the list and go through more names. It was boring and time consuming. There wasn't much police action, drama, or glamour in this kind of thing. But that was how you solved a crime: you didn't set aside any project until it had been thoroughly checked and judged to be exhausted.

Just as she was stretching her hand out to make the twenty-fifth call, her phone rang.

"Inspector Irene Huss," she answered.

"My name is Hen . . . Henning Oppdal," said a soft man's voice.

Irene couldn't decide if the man was stammering because of a speech impediment or just because he was nervous. She sensed a faint Norwegian accent. The name didn't mean anything to her.

"What can I help you with?" she asked in a friendly manner.

"I know Pontus. He said that I should . . . should call you."

Pontus? Irene needed to think before she recalled him.

"Ohh, you know Pontus Zander. Do you also work in the health field?"

"Yes. I'm an X-ray technician."

This was followed by silence. Each was waiting for the other to continue.

"Why did Pontus think you should contact me?" Irene finally asked in order to move the conversation along.

"I told him about something. A terrible thing I experienced over the winter. Pontus had apparently spoken with you about the mur . . . murder of Marcus Tosscander. And you had talked about some sick things. Like nec . . . necrophilia and stuff like that."

"That's right. We know that Marcus's murderer is involved with things like that. Did you know Marcus?"

"No, I've never met him."

"But you've experienced something that may have a connection to necrophilia. Have I understood you correctly?"

"Yes. At the end of January I met a guy at a bar at the Central Station. We met and, well, we were attracted to each other. After a while he thought we should leave to . . . together. We walked along Stampgatan. I thought we were going to go home to his place, but it wasn't like that."

"Sorry for interrupting, but what did he look like? Did he say his name?"

"He was tall and in good shape. Shoulder-length hair pulled back in a ponytail. I don't know his real name. He just said that his name was B . . . Basta."

Irene felt her pulse rate increase but didn't say anything. Henning continued. "At the cemetery that is right next to Sta . . . Stampgatan, he said, 'We'll go in here. I have a really cozy place here.' I thought it sounded strange and it was below freezing that night. But I went along anyway. It was dark and terrifying! But he walked straight to a large mausoleum with an iron door. Then he took out a key and unlocked it. I was scared to death. I turned and rushed toward the ga . . . gates. As luck would have it, he had left them open."

"Did he run after you?"

"I don't know. I'm a long-distance runner. I run several mi . . . miles a week. He wouldn't have had a chance if he had tried to catch me."

You should thank your lucky stars for that. You've probably never been that close to death before, thought Irene. She said aloud, "Where was the mausoleum located? In the cemetery itself, I mean."

"Straight ahead. Maybe a hundred meters from the entrance."

There was every reason to investigate the mausoleum. Stampen's old burial ground was known for lavish graves and mausoleums. At the last moment, Irene remembered that she wasn't allowed to go out alone. It would be best to ask a colleague to accompany her.

"Is it possible for you to come to the police station? I have a photo I would really like you to take a look at," she said.

"I cou . . . could probably do that. I'm off work tomorrow."

"Can you come around nine o'clock?"

"That would be fine."

Irene thanked him for calling and put down the receiver.

Wow! Basta had been cruising on his own in January, without Emil. Or hadn't he planned to kill Henning? Was the cemetery just a morbid place to have sex that attracted Basta? Thank God they'd never know, since Henning got away. But maybe she could find evidence there, maybe someone hadn't been so lucky?

Irene decided to check out the grave right after lunch.

BIRGITTA AND Irene had eaten a good lunch at the Central Station's restaurant. The bustle of people outside contrasted with the turn-of-the-century atmosphere of the restaurant. The dark wood paneling on the walls made for a calm atmosphere even if the restaurant was completely full. The daily special, pasta marinara, was definitely approved. While they were eating, Irene described Henning's phone call.

Birgitta listened without interrupting. When Irene was finished she said, "We need to take a look at the mausoleum, if we can find the right one. We'll probably have to check out several of them."

Irene nodded. "What do we do?" she asked. "How should we proceed?"

Birgitta took out her cell phone and said, "We'll call Hannu. He'll know."

She speed-dialed a number. "Hi, sweetie. Where are you?"

It sounded strange to Irene to hear Birgitta call Hannu "sweetie." But maybe one gets used to it, she thought.

Birgitta said, with a look at Irene, "Of course. But first you have to help us with something. We need to look in some mausoleums at Stampen's old cemetery. No, not dig up. These are the kind of graves that have doors and walls. Like little houses. Irene got a tip today that has to do with Basta. Do you know who to talk to when you need to have those doors unlocked?"

She listened and nodded before she said, "OK. Call if it works out." Birgitta handed the phone to Irene.

"Hi, Irene. I asked Birgitta to see if you can come along when I question Sara Bolin. But there won't be enough time today. Can you come with me tomorrow morning?"

"No. I'm going to meet the witness who provided the tip about the graveyard. But after eleven will be OK," said Irene.

"Then I'll get in touch with Sara and make an appointment after eleven."

Irene ended the call and gave the cell phone back to Birgitta, who put it in her bag again.

"Hannu knows someone who works in Cemetery Administration. He's going to call there first. He'll let us know as soon as he learns anything," said Birgitta.

If there was anyone Irene knew who could open graves, it was Hannu; she was absolutely certain of that. That's why it didn't come as a surprise when Hannu phoned twenty minutes later and informed them that an administrator would meet them at the cemetery gates at three o'clock.

IT WAS still overcast but a mild breeze swept through the city and dried up the streets. Birgitta and Irene walked to the old cemetery.

"Henning Oppdal and Basta went exactly this way on a late January night. The X-ray technician thought that he was going to get a good fuck but instead Basta lured him into the cemetery and unlocked an old mausoleum. No wonder the guy was badly scared," said Irene.

"Lucky for him," Birgitta replied.

And it probably was. On a warm afternoon in June, the parklike old cemetery looked tranquil and inviting. Ideal for a contemplative walk. It was the last place one would think of as the site of macabre necrophilic rituals.

A corpulent older man stood outside the gates. He was wearing a worn brown tweed suit and sweating heavily even though it wasn't particularly warm. He wiped his forehead and face with a large blue-checkered cotton handkerchief.

The female police officers walked up to him and showed their IDs as they introduced themselves. When he greeted them, he held out a surprisingly soft little hand that was completely soaked with perspiration.

"Gösta Olsson from Cemetery Administration. This isn't really according to regulation but my boss didn't think it was necessary to consider this a grave opening, because then we would need a judge's permission. We're only going to take a look and see what the miserable Satanists have been up to. Amazing that they've gotten a key! It must be a copy since we hold all of the keys to the old graves. Many of the families have died out but the graves are protected as historical monuments. They're unique because . . ."

The round man talked uninterrupted and gesticulated widely until they reached the larger grave sites that were clustered almost in the center of the cemetery. There were two mausoleums on one side of the gravel path and three across from them. They towered, like a Manhattan of the dead, over the other graves in the cemetery.

These mausoleums were impressive. They were somewhat larger than small cabins. Two were covered with white marble, one with black slate, and two with red granite. Their doors were either heavy iron or copper plated.

"Do you know which of the graves they had a key to?" Gösta Olsson asked.

"Unfortunately not. Our witness was scared and doesn't remember," Irene answered apologetically.

Apparently, Hannu had represented the case as one of suspected Satanism. Irene saw no reason to enlighten the administrator.

Olsson sighed heavily and passed the handkerchief over his face once more.

"It's best if we go through all five. If you knew how much misery these Satan worshippers have caused! They turn over gravestones and cover them with wax and stearine. One time they even tried to dig up an old grave! It held the remains of a bishop who died at the end of the 1800s. But people who were living in the house on the other side of the street saw that there was some devilry going on so they called the police."

Here he was forced to catch his breath, so Irene took the opportunity to suggest, "Maybe we should start with the closest one?"

She pointed at the copper door of one of the marble crypts.

"Certainly, certainly," the administrator said nervously.

He had to play with the lock for some time before it slowly gave way. The door was reluctant to open and complained loudly. It hasn't been opened for many years, thought Irene.

It smelled like a damp, musty cellar. Irene switched on her powerful flashlight and let it swing over the coffins, which were piled on top of each other along the walls. She counted nineteen of them. It was so full they couldn't have jammed in one more. The dust on the floor seemed to be untouched. She shook her head and turned toward the administrator. "No. No one has been here for years."

"Suspected as much, because this family died out in the forties. But we've had two funerals in the last few years at the one next door. Very

tragic. It was a father and son, but I think that the son's wife was pregnant so there's a survivor. But somehow the wife was involved in the
father's murder. . . ."

Irene didn't hear the rest of Olsson's litany. She looked as if spell-
bound at the verdigris-encrusted copper plate on which two newly
engraved names shone clearly: Richard von Knecht and Henrik von
Knecht, who had died in November and December 1996, respec-
tively.

That had been one of the most complicated cases Violent Crimes
had ever been faced with. In the end they had solved it, but at the cost
of many lives. The murders had had their origin in betrayal, hate, jealousy, and greed.

The motive for the murders they were investigating now was alien
to the emotions of normal people.

Irene shivered despite the relative warmth of the day.

Gösta Olsson inserted the key and unlocked the door, which slid
open on well-oiled hinges. A moss-covered marble angel, almost the
size of an adult, kept vigil beside the iron-clad door. Irene looked into
the cold stone eyes and wished that the sculpture could speak. It had
probably witnessed a thing or two.

The administrator stepped to the side and let Irene enter the mausoleum first. She walked down the slippery steps, switched on her
flashlight, and let the beam play around the room. Before she stepped
down, she carefully shone the light across the floor. Footprints could
be seen on the dust-covered stone floor.

"Fresh footprints. They could, of course, be from the funerals of two
and half years ago, but I think they're too distinct for that," said Irene.

Ten wood and metal coffins stood in rows along the walls. The two
closest to the door were shinier than the others, and Irene could read the
names on the metal plates. Richard von Knecht was in the lower one;
his son, Henrik, was on top. Irene inspected Henrik von Knecht's coffin. She saw a groove in the metal. It was very recent and shone like a
fresh scar right below the lid. When she looked closer she discovered several similar cuts. It wasn't difficult to figure out how they'd been made.
The lid was heavy and whoever had opened it needed to prop it up.

What should they tell the interested administrator? After a while
she made up her mind, and walked back out into the sunlight.

"There are clear signs of Satanic activities in there. Entering might destroy evidence. Police technicians will arrive as soon as possible. Can we keep the key?" she asked.

Gösta Olsson became confused. He anxiously wiped his already shining head with his handkerchief. Hesitantly, he said, "Well . . . I don't know if I'm allowed to, but as you are police officers and want to investigate this problem we've had with Satan worshippers . . . I guess there can't be anything wrong with lending you the key, even though according to regulations we're not allowed . . ."

As calmly and professionally as possible Irene said, "We will borrow the key to let in the technicians. You can speak with your boss in the meantime. If he wants the key returned right away then call me on my cell phone. We'll go straight to your office with the key. If there are any problems, the police will take full responsibility."

Irene handed her card to Olsson, and patted him on his shoulder, then pointed him in the direction of the cemetery gates. Reluctantly, the administrator started moving.

When he had disappeared through the gates Irene turned to Birgitta and said, "This is the one. Someone has been here, digging around in Henrik von Knecht's coffin. We have to lift the lid and see what's happened."

Birgitta made a face without saying anything. She had seen worse things than a corpse that had been dead for two and a half years.

They went into the mausoleum together. Irene set the lit flashlight on top of the next coffin lid.

"Look at the grooves. They're recent," she pointed out.

Birgitta took a closer look and nodded. They positioned themselves on the long side of the coffin. Each took a firm hold of one edge of the lid.

"One, two, threeee," Irene counted.

They pulled with all their strength and managed to shift the lid.

The shrouded corpse of Henrik von Knecht lay inside. But that wasn't what made Irene and Birgitta recoil. There was also a head in a state of advanced decay next to the corpse.

"SO WE'VE found Marcus Tosscander's head. But there weren't any arms or legs in the crypt or whatever it's called," said Superintendent Andersson.

"Mausoleum," corrected Irene.

Andersson pretended not to hear her. He continued, "Under no circumstances is this allowed to get out to the press. If it does, Basta will know we're hot on his trail."

"Are we going to watch the graveyard?" Fredrik Stridh wondered.

"I've already posted a guard," Andersson replied.

The technicians had been working all evening to secure the scene. Svante Malm had shown up at morning prayers. Now it was his turn to speak. "Professor Stridner has promised to be in touch as soon as the identification of the head has been made with the help of dental records and X-rays. A medical odontologist will be present during the morning. But based on what remained, Irene and Birgitta have established that it is Marcus Tosscander's head."

The image of the decaying head quickly fluttered through Irene's mind. Marcus's beautiful features had vanished forever. A vague thought about the mortality of all beauty was forming in her head, but she had to let it go in order to concentrate on what Svante was saying.

"There's no evidence to support the theory that a murder was committed inside the burial chamber. However, we've found footprints. When we sorted out the ones Irene and Birgitta made when they went in, two sets remained. A pair of heavy boots, size eleven, and a pair of athletic shoes, also size eleven. Right now we're in the process of matching the prints to the one we secured over the weekend from the flower bed outside Irene's house. We've also sent copies to Copenhagen in case they have footprints from any of their crime scenes."

Where had there been a footprint? Irene strained to recall: there had been a print on the outer edge of the big pool of blood at the hotel room where Isabell was found. At the time, Irene had thought that it had been made by one of the police officers who had clumsily stepped in the blood. But what if she'd been wrong, what if it turned out to have been made by an athletic shoe, size eleven! That would be the first evidence incriminating Basta for the murder of Isabell.

"We've also found some long blond strands of hair, but they're very light and don't really match with the description of Basta," said Svante.

A thought struck Irene. "That could be hair from the older Mrs. von Knecht. She's very blonde."

"Very possible. They were found in the coffin, where the head lay."

Svante knelt and rummaged in his dark blue bag. Then he waved a paper in front of them.

"A fax from Copenhagen. They think that they've found the location where the first dismemberment took place. Apparently, the interior matches that on the video. It's a small shipyard north of Copenhagen that has been abandoned a few years, and will be torn down this summer. Our colleagues in Denmark have requested the fingerprints. It'll be interesting to see if the ones we believe belong to Basta are found at the Danish crime scenes," he said.

Irene had her misgivings but, on the other hand, Basta had made some mistakes. Each one of them had been small but, put together, the accumulation of evidence made a serious case against him. Now it was just a matter of determining his identity and catching him.

Irene glanced at the clock. It was almost 9:00 a.m. Henning Oppdal should arrive any minute. She excused herself.

HE DIDN'T look anything like the man she had pictured. The owner of the soft voice turned out to be a rather large man, in good shape, definitely not corpulent. He was of average height and about twenty-five years old. His thick black hair stood straight up on his head. A friendly blue gaze was aimed at Irene through thick glasses enclosed by round, steel frames.

Irene had turned *Manpower* toward the wall. She didn't want the picture to distract the witness.

"It was good of you to come, Henning. I have a picture I would like you to see a little later. But first, I'd like to ask some follow-up questions. Is that OK?"

"Of course," said Henning.

"Have you ever seen Basta at a meeting of Gays in the Health-Care Services?"

"No. Never," he answered firmly.

"Had you seen him earlier, before you met at the Central Station in January?"

"No."

"You've never seen him at a gay club or anywhere else?"

"No."

"Do you often go to gay clubs and other gay hangouts?"

"Yes. When I go out it's oft . . . often to those kinds of places."

"And you've never seen Basta at any of them?" she repeated.

"No."

"Do you have any idea who he is or where he can be found?"

Henning shook his head vigorously. "No. And I don't intend to look ei . . . either."

"You haven't heard anyone else talk about an event similar to the one you experienced?"

"No. But it's unlikely that anyone would talk about something like that. I haven't mentioned what happened to anyone except you and Pontus. And that was only because Pontus started talking about his conversation with you. About necro . . . necrophilia and stuff like that. Then I wanted to speak about it."

Irene nodded. She walked over to the picture, turned it around, and stepped to one side.

"Do you recognize this man?" she asked.

Henning stared at *Manpower*.

"It's not possible to see the face but it very well co . . . could be Basta," he said finally.

He smiled mischievously, adding, "Where can I buy this poster?"

"It can't be bought. It's an exhibition photo."

"Is Basta a photo model?" Henning asked, interested.

Irene decided not to reveal the photographer's identity. The papers had feasted on the murder of Erik Bolin. No one outside the police station was aware of the picture of Basta. Basta couldn't know that the police had already connected the attack on Tom to the murder of the photographer. He also didn't know where *Manpower* was right now, if Erik Bolin hadn't had time to tell him before he was killed.

"We don't know anything about Basta. Actually, we're not even sure that it's Basta in the picture. Right now it's just a suspicion. One among all of the leads we're looking into. I would be very grateful if you didn't speak with your friends about this picture. It may be very important but it could be a false lead," said Irene.

Henning managed to tear his eyes away from *Manpower* and looked at Irene. She started thinking about a friendly blue-eyed owl when he blinked at her from behind his thick lenses.

"OK. I won't say anything. But what a pi . . . picture!"

Irene understood his reaction but her own attitude was ambivalent. The dark silhouette in the sunlight felt more and more threatening and full of malice.

IRENE WAS on her fifth mug of coffee of the morning and she had almost finished writing the report on the questioning of Henning Oppdal when Hannu stuck his head in and asked if she was ready to tag along to the interview of Sara Bolin. She quickly hurried to finish and logged out.

Hannu drove as Irene leaned back against the headrest, trying to relax.

"Did the witness ask if we'd found anything in the mausoleum?" Hannu asked.

"No. He became completely absorbed by *Manpower*."

Hannu laughed. "I can understand that. Did he recognize Basta?"

"He said that it could very well be Basta. Hard to say for certain since the face is in shadow."

Hannu said, "Exactly. Then why is Basta so anxious to get this picture? We haven't found any of the other pictures Bolin took of him. Basta probably found them."

"There is a connection between himself and Marcus through the pictures Bolin took. But I don't think he functions like the rest of us. Could *Manpower* have become an obsession?"

"Maybe. But I put more stock in your first theory. He's cold. Ice-cold."

Irene felt that cold surround her.

SARA BOLIN must have been standing just inside the door waiting for them. Irene barely had time to take her finger off the doorbell when the door flew open. The woman in the photograph that Erik Bolin had proudly shown Irene less than a week ago opened the door. She was completely dressed in black and was even more beautiful in person. Her thick brownish black hair billowed like a shiny waterfall down her back and framed a finely chiseled face. Her eyes were large and slightly almond shaped; the nose, small and straight. Her mouth was generous with full, sensual lips. Her petite body didn't bear the slightest evidence of two pregnancies. Irene noticed that the woman in the door opening barely reached her chest.

Irene and Hannu introduced themselves and Sara Bolin let them into the pink-painted shoeboxlike row house. She held her arms tightly wrapped around herself, as if she were freezing. She looked very thin and frail in a black long-sleeved cotton shirt and black pants.

"Kristian is sleeping and Johannes is with the neighbor's kids, playing. He's only three and doesn't understand what's happened. Sometimes he asks about Pappa but he's used to his father working a lot and often being away."

Sara's voice broke and tears glimmered in her dark eyes. She turned her face away and said, "Please, come in."

She gestured toward a pair of open glass doors. The police officers entered the small living room and sat on a comfortable leather couch. The couch was light brown and the rug under the glass coffee table was light beige. Everything was free of stains and dust. Irene had a feeling that the little boys weren't allowed in this room.

"Maybe I should put on some coffee?" said Sara Bolin.

Before Irene had time to say yes, Hannu replied, "No, thank you. We won't be here very long."

Sara didn't insist but sank down onto a couch across from Irene and Hannu. She clasped her hands tightly in her lap. Irene could see her knuckles turning white.

"Have you caught him?" she whispered, almost inaudibly.

Calmly, Hannu asked, "Who?"

She gave a start and gave Hannu a look of disapproval.

"The one that did . . . that . . . to Erik."

"No. We're following several leads. Personally, do you have any suspicions of someone?" Irene asked.

Sara aimed her beautiful eyes at Irene and shook her head sadly.

"No. I don't understand who would want to . . . Why?"

"Erik was never threatened, never said that he felt threatened?"

"No. Never! He was the nicest person in the world. Liked by everyone," Sara said firmly.

Irene looked at her and nodded thoughtfully. "Right. Erik said that you were aware of his bisexuality when you got married. Is that true?"

The slender body collapsed. After a while, Sara sat up and said defiantly, "Yes. I knew about it. But I was the one he loved. No woman could want a better man than Erik. Why are you asking me this?"

"There are signs that point to sexual activity before the murder," said Irene.

It was repulsive having to inform the widow about this particularly sensitive point, but the fact was that Professor Stridner had identified semen on Erik Bolin's body. The strange thing was that it was in his hair. She hadn't found any in the rectum or anywhere else. The analysis wasn't complete so she couldn't say who the seminal fluid had come from.

If it turned out to have been from someone other than Erik Bolin, the technicians would send the DNA analysis to Copenhagen to match against the semen stain found under Emil's bed.

Sara's voice was tense as she replied. "We loved each other tremendously from the first time we met. There was a lot of passion in the beginning; we felt we were right for each other. He told me about his bisexuality before we moved in together. I can't say that he deceived me. He was completely open. But I didn't have a choice since I loved him so much. Either I had to accept his orientation or I would have had to leave him. The latter never felt like an option."

"Then you were prepared to share him with a man?" Irene wondered.

Sara started twisting a strand of her hair. It took a while before she answered, "No. Not to share him with anyone else. But I thought that his love for me was so strong that he had gotten over . . . that."

She fell silent and started absentmindedly making a knot in the strand of hair. To get her to continue, Irene said, "From what I understand he hadn't gotten over it."

Sara gave a start as if Irene had stuck her with a needle. With resignation she said, "No. When I was pregnant with Johannes I understood that he had been seeing someone else. It turned out to be Marcus Tosscander. We had a terrible fight. Then Erik said that he felt like half a person sometimes. He was missing something when he was together with me. It was . . . terrible."

"How did you react?"

"I left him. I moved out. But I couldn't function without Erik. Before Johannes was born I moved back. Erik made a solemn vow to try and resist his . . . other desire. I know that it didn't always work. But his relationships never hurt us. He was an amazingly good father and husband."

"Did you notice anything recently that could point to Erik's having had a new man?"

"No. Sometimes—"

She stopped herself and bit her lip. With a defiant gesture she threw her hair back, lifted her chin, and looked Irene straight in the eye.

"Sometimes he would work late. And he often worked far from home. I couldn't check what he was doing every second. I had to trust him."

Irene thought about the old saying *You see what you want to see.* She decided to change tacks and put her hand in her jacket pocket. Her fingertips touched the envelope holding the photos of Tom Tanaka's two pictures. She placed the pictures on top of the coffee table. Sara Bolin leaned forward and inspected both photographs. When she examined the picture of Marcus more closely, she recoiled. She realized that they had noticed her reaction and she said in a shaky voice, "The picture of Marcus didn't look like that. The one that Erik had at the exhibition."

"What do you mean? Is it the wrong picture?" Hannu asked innocently.

"No, not the wrong picture . . . but it didn't look like . . . this!"

With a shaking index finger, Sara pointed at Marcus's magnificent erection. In the exhibition picture, Marcus's hanging hand had nonchalantly concealed his sex. But Irene understood Sara's distress. The picture on the table radiated lust and desire: Marcus seen through his lover's eye.

Sara stared as though entranced at the picture, and finally she whispered, "He swore that it was over. He swore!"

Irene saw how close she was to bursting into tears. In order to distract her, Irene threw the picture of *Manpower* on top of the photo of Marcus.

"Do you recognize this man?" she asked.

For a second, Sara Bolin looked confused. Hesitantly, she picked up the picture of Basta and examined it. Then she lowered it and looked at Irene again.

"Of course I recognize the picture itself. It was part of the exhibition and it looked like this. But I have no idea who the man is."

"Erik never said anything about this man or mentioned his name?"

"No."

Irene saw that several nice pictures were hanging on the walls. A thought struck her. She pointed at the photos on the table and said, "I see you are displaying many of Erik's photographs on the walls. Is it possible that the enlargement of one of these two photos is hanging somewhere in the house?"

Sara's voice was harsh when she replied, "No. I decide what is going to hang on the walls!"

She was interrupted by a child's cry. She rose and said apologetically, "Kristian is awake. He's crying for me to come and change his diaper. It's always so wet when he's been sleeping and . . ."

The last part of the sentence faded away as she entered the hall. Irene turned to Hannu and said teasingly, "The parents of small children have such interesting conversational topics."

Hannu raised his eyebrows a fraction of a millimeter and said, "Really."

She was close to saying, "Just wait and see when it's your turn," but she stopped herself. Hannu would never sit and discuss his child's diaper status with anyone.

They got up at the same time and started toward the glass doors. Sara Bolin came out of a door a little farther down the corridor. In her arms she was carrying a baby, still warm with sleep, who had thrown his chubby arms around her neck and burrowed his dark head under her chin.

"Thanks for letting us stop by," said Irene.

Sara Bolin tried to smile bravely. "Naturally, I'm interested in seeing my husband's murder solved. Of course, I'll help any way I can."

The little one in her arms became conscious of the strangers in the house. He turned and looked at Irene. Her throat tightened when she looked into Erik Bolin's amber eyes.

HANNU CALLED Birgitta on the cell phone and they decided on a time to meet outside the station house. Fifteen minutes later, he and Irene picked her up in an unmarked police car. During the ride, Irene and Hannu had decided to eat lunch at the Göteborg City Museum. Birgitta had enthusiastically talked about the restaurant on the ground floor several times, but Irene had never been there despite repeated urgings. Now it would actually happen.

After circling for several minutes they managed to find a parking spot on Packhuskajen. It was a ways to walk but that was a bonus in the gorgeous weather.

Hannu held the door open for the ladies and invited them to step into the eighteenth century. Irene's eyes had a hard time adjusting to the half darkness under the restaurant's stone arches. The staff's clothes—rough homespun skirts and stiff white aprons—were reminiscent of bygone centuries.

"It wouldn't surprise me if today's lunch is cold herring with dill and chives and mashed rutabaga," Irene whispered to Birgitta.

They managed to get an empty table and ordered from the menu, which offered three lunch alternatives. Irene took a Creole brochette with potato wedges, and a light beer. Both Hannu and Birgitta chose the haddock in a white wine sauce with scalloped potatoes. Typical of newlyweds to choose the same thing, thought Irene.

The food was very good and Irene realized how hungry she was. Even if it wasn't the cheapest lunch special she had ever had, it was worth the money.

During the meal they sat and chatted about everything but the current investigation. The big news that neither Irene nor anyone else in Violent Crimes had heard—was that Birgitta and Hannu were in the process of renovating an older house in Västra Bodarna. An explanation of the location established that the house was a few kilometers southwest of Alingsås and not in Dalsland, which Irene had originally thought.

"We'll be moving at the beginning of August," Birgitta chirped.

It wasn't possible to overlook her happiness; it haloed her.

Had Irene felt that way when she and Krister moved into their row house twelve years earlier? Maybe something approaching it but not quite as strong. The twins had just turned four and were particularly active. Irene thought it was wonderful not to be squeezed into two rooms and a kitchen on Smörslottsgatan. Out in Fiskebäck they could let the girls run free on the lawn and in the playgrounds but, of course, under some parental supervision. The young Huss girls had been very adventurous and often ran off on their own adventures.

"And the property is three thousand square meters," Birgitta bubbled enthusiastically.

Irene raised her eyebrows and turned to Hannu.

"Riding lawn mower?" she asked.

He smiled faintly and shrugged. That could mean anything from "probably" to "who cares?"

During coffee Birgitta changed the subject and said, "Svante Malm and some technician from Copenhagen inform each other of all their findings and clues. It's saving double work. And Svante is sending some samples for testing directly to Copenhagen. The noose is tightening around Basta."

"I wish it would. And that we could identify him at some point," sighed Irene.

"He's killed too many times and left too many clues. We'll get him," said Hannu.

WHEN IRENE opened the door to her home at nearly six o'clock, she couldn't detect the slightest smell of food. Yet the whole family appeared to be at home, gathered in the kitchen. Laughter could be heard and something that sounded suspiciously like baby talk. Irene stood in the doorway but no one took any notice of her. Not even Sammie. Everyone's attention was concentrated on the fuzzy little bundle who was chasing Sammie and trying to nip his leg hairs and dignified whiskers. The result of his romance with the poodle champion had arrived.

Pappa Sammie was very upset. A dignified middle-aged man shouldn't have to put up with this sort of thing. He wasn't fond of youngsters either! Hyper-irritated over his obtrusive son's bad habits, he growled and laid the puppy out flat on the floor. The fur ball immediately turned up his almost hairless round stomach.

"Oooooh, he's sooooo cuuuuute!" Katarina crooned.

"How long has he been here?" Irene asked.

Now the family discovered that she had arrived.

"The old bag brought him over as soon as Jenny and I came home from school. She must have been standing outside, lying in wait," said Katarina.

"But she actually gave us a leash." Jenny tried to smooth things over.

"And he has all the vaccinations he needs," Krister added. He energetically waved a veterinary certificate to back up his statement.

"Uh-huh. And you think it's going to work with Sammie. He's used to being everyone's darling and the center of attention. I think he's too old to get used to living with a puppy," Irene sighed.

Krister brushed off her protests with the paper he was holding in his hand and said, "Oh! Now you're being pessimistic, kiddo. He'll get used to it. It'll be fun for him not to have to be alone when we aren't home."

"What do you think we should name him?" asked Katarina.

Irene looked at the little creature and then said acidly, "What about Tinkler? And do you see what he's doing under the kitchen table right now?"

Chapter 18

THE MORNING AFTER THE first night, it was clear to the Huss family that it was going to take a while for Tinkler to become house-trained and acclimated to his new environment. Sammie had openly shown his distaste toward the ill-mannered rascal. Tinkler adored his father even if it was doubtful that the dogs had a clear idea of the relationship. The result was that Sammie had desperately tried to crawl under the beds and hide in the recliner while Tinkler thought that it was a very funny game and stubbornly followed him. When Sammie became really annoyed and barked at Tinkler, the little one had been scared out of his wits and become sad. He had sat whining and crying in the darkness, abandoned. No one in the Huss family had slept many hours that night.

"Summer vacation starts tomorrow. Then we can keep an eye on him," said Jenny.

"Weren't you going to work at Domus over the summer?" Irene asked, tired.

"I don't start until Monday."

Irene turned to Katarina. "When does swim school start?"

"The fifteenth. And it's arranged—I'll be able to work both sessions," Katarina answered.

"How long will that be?"

"Six weeks."

"That means that we have supervision for Tinkler until the fifteenth of June. Pappa and I have our vacations three and half weeks later. What do we do with him between June 15 and July 8?" Irene wondered challengingly.

"Dog sitter—," Katarina started.

"That won't work at all! She can't take care of a little puppy. We have to be grateful she has the energy to look after Sammie. And she's on vacation after midsummer and won't start again until August 1."

The little problem in question came bounding in, wanting attention.

Katarina picked him up and burrowed her nose into his soft coat. Tinkler struggled wildly, wanting to taste some of her liver pâté sandwich. One of his eagerly jabbing back legs kicked over a full tea mug and spilled the contents over the entire table.

"My graduation clothes!" Katarina cried.

She jumped up and brusquely set the puppy on the floor. Maybe he was hurt or just very scared, but he began to cry pitifully. Katarina had tears in her eyes as she looked at her white trousers and white sleeveless top. Large tea stains decorated both pieces.

"Stupid dog!" she screamed.

The tumult woke Krister, who came down to the kitchen, heavy with sleep. When the situation was clarified, he oiled the insubordinate waves by offering monetary compensation for overtime, to be in effect the rest of the day. The twins were mollified.

"HOW'S IT going with the puppy?" asked Irene.

She looked at Tommy through the steam from her coffee mug.

"Just fine. She's actually very cute. Agneta has been home with her since we got her on Sunday. But now the kids are out of school, so they'll have to take care of her," he said.

"What's her name?"

"Nelly."

Irene finished the last of the coffee in her mug.

Strange, she hadn't noticed the slightest stimulating effect from the coffee. Maybe it had been mixed up with decaf?

"We searched Zorro Karlsson's house yesterday. And now we have him! He kept trophies. Three pairs of underwear and a shoe were in a box in his closet. The items have been identified by the victims."

Tommy sounded very pleased and he had every reason to be. He had wagered on a faint lead, the smell of food. But it had led to the perpetrator.

Irene got a bitter taste in her mouth when she thought about the things Basta had taken as trophies. Where did he store . . . Irene didn't have the energy to complete that line of thought.

Svante Malm looked in through the doorway and said, "Howdy. I'm going to provide a briefing at morning prayers. Isn't it about time for that now?"

His happy, smiling, freckled horse-like face and the red, gray-streaked hair standing on end made Irene think of healthy carrot juice. Get your eight hours of sleep and get into shape with carrot juice, she thought in her sour morning mood. She regretted it the next moment because she knew how Svante had slaved during the investigations of the murders, putting in lots of overtime. Basta might be tied to the various crime scenes by means of the tedious work of technicians.

"STRANGELY ENOUGH, the seminal fluid in Erik Bolin's hair appears to have been rubbed in. One theory is that when the murderer cut off the head and carried it out to the hat rack he forgot that he had semen on his hands. He probably carried the head by the hair and under the chin because we've also found quite a bit there. And the semen is not Bolin's. We ran a DNA profile and sent it to Copenhagen. It's an exact match with the semen found at one of their crime scenes. Under the bed of the guy whose name was . . ."

Svante looked down at his papers. To save time, Irene filled in, "Emil Bentsen."

"Exactly. Thanks. And incidentally, Irene, the shoe print in your flower bed matches the print in the blood at the hotel room where Isabell Lind was found. It's identical. In addition, in all likelihood the prints match the ones we found in the mausoleum at Stampen. That's a little less certain because the prints were in dust. No fingerprint matches were found. We can conclude that Basta hasn't been in trouble with the law."

Svante stopped and looked at Irene.

"Have you identified the guy?" he asked.

"No. We know what he looks like and that he's called Basta. He's been located in both Göteborg and Copenhagen. And he could be a doctor or an artist according to our witness statements," said Irene.

"Why don't you put out a warrant for his arrest?" wondered Malm.

"It's hard to decide. On the one hand we want to identify him as quickly as possible. And on the other hand we don't want him to know how close we are to him. We hope he thinks he's smarter than we are and that his overconfidence will be his downfall. But I don't know . . . maybe we need to put out an APB on him in both Denmark and Sweden at the same time and very soon. The difficulty is knowing when the right time is. If we do it too soon, he may go into hiding and if we do it too late, he may have time to commit a new murder," said Irene.

Svante nodded to show that he understood the dilemma. He looked down at his papers and continued, "We've enlarged the index finger-tip that can be seen in the video of the dismemberment of Marcus Tosscander. It's the index finger of a left hand and the nail is severely deformed. Here you go. There are five enlargements."

He pulled out the photographs from a brown envelope and passed them around the table. The superintendent, Irene, Hannu, and Jonny each took one. The tip of the finger wasn't round; it was flat and looked as if it had been chopped off. The nail covered just the nail bed, and its surface seemed to be dented. While the officers were examin-ing the enlargements, Svante continued, "On the floor of the burial crypt we've found some stains that could very well be seminal fluid. But unfortunately they've started decaying and are too dried out to be use-ful. But we found more stains on the shroud inside the coffin where Tosscander's head was lying, which are in better condition. We're working on them right now."

What if the semen turned out to have come from the same man who had left semen behind on the floor at Emil's and in Bolin's hair?

"What the hell is the sick bastard actually up to?" Superintendent Andersson exclaimed.

You don't want to know, Irene nearly said, but she managed to stop herself in time.

IRENE SAT staring listlessly at *Manpower*. She felt intensifying anger and hate directed at the black silhouette in the picture. At the same time she considered what might turn a person into a necrophile.

With a bang, the door hit the wall. Professor Stridner rushed in on clicking heels, dressed in a thin, light green dress of some shiny material, enveloped in the strong scent of Joy. Despite the fact that she was neither slender nor tall, she wore the dress with a superb con-fidence. Irene became uncomfortably aware of her own worn jeans and short-sleeved denim shirt. At least my sandals are new, she comforted herself.

Stridner came to a dead stop in front of Irene's desk.

"Where is everyone? Are you the only one who's on duty?" she asked.

"The superintendent went to a meeting and the others—," Irene began.

"I came here myself since I was in the neighborhood. I'm flying to New York but before that I want to hand over the preliminary autopsy report on Erik Bolin. The medical odontologists have also confirmed that the head in the burial chamber belonged to Marcus Tosscander."

While she was talking, she pulled out some papers from her elegant leather briefcase.

"Erik Bolin's," she said curtly, and threw them on the desk in front of Irene.

Without looking at them, Irene asked, "Is the mutilation the same type as with the previous victims?"

"Yes. The chest muscles, one buttock, and the penis. None of Bolin's internal organs were removed; however, the head was. It was cut off with an extremely sturdy, sharp knife. I would guess a knife similar to our autopsy knives."

"Why do necrophiles do this sort of thing?" Irene asked.

Stridner's forehead wrinkled. "The question is not phrased correctly. Necrophiles don't do this sort of thing. Necrophiles literally love dead people, but they don't kill them. Necrophiles who devote themselves to necrosadism are, thankfully, an exceedingly small fraction. As I've already told you, the type of murderer we're chasing right now is very rare. But sometimes they pop up and we become overwhelmed in the presence of what we regard as an inhumane atrocity. But actually a necrosadist isn't any more gruesome than any other kind of murderer. The result is the same: a murdered person, a life that has been snuffed out forever. What terrifies us is the abuse of the dead body after the murder. We see it as something sick."

While she was delivering her little lecture, Stridner clip-clopped around the room on her high-heeled pumps. She stopped in front of *Manpower*. Even after she had finished speaking, she remained, examining the picture.

"For a split second I had the feeling that I recognized this man. But I don't know. No one I know poses for porn pictures," she said finally.

Irene walked over to Stridner. "Interesting. Both Hannu Rauhala and I also think we recognize the man. None of the others are sure."

The professor leaned forward so that she could study the photo more closely. Suddenly, she straightened up and exclaimed, "Now I know! He works with us."

Irene realized that she had been holding her breath. She exhaled and asked, "Does he work in Pathology?"

"Yes. But he doesn't have a permanent position because he's a student."

A medical student? It was quite common for medical students to find extra work as autopsy technicians.

Her voice shook when Irene asked, "What's his name and what does he study?"

Stridner continued her examination of *Manpower*.

"I don't remember his name. But he's an art student. He was the one who made the copy of Marcus Tosscander's tattoo."

Basta had spent several hours sitting next to the mutilated upper body of his victim, making an exact copy of the dragon tattoo. The thought was nauseating.

"Erik Bolin took the picture. The man in the picture is called Basta, and he's probably Bolin and Marcus Tosscander's murderer. In addition, he's been linked to three murders in Copenhagen," said Irene.

Stridner did not move. "I have a hard time believing that anyone at Pathology would be capable of this. But we'll go up right away and try and find out his name. If for no other reason than so he can be exonerated and dismissed from the investigation," she said finally.

YVONNE STRIDNER rushed into the employee lounge with Irene in tow, like a skiff in her wake. There were only two people sitting there. The man had very dark skin and hair. Irene guessed that he was Indian. She recognized the woman as Britt Nilsson, a young, newly hired pathologist. It wasn't her name that had struck a cord when Svante Malm spoke about her, but the fact that he had referred to her as *Stridner's assistant*. The link to Stridner and Pathology had made Irene react.

Another person worked with Stridner, but not as her assistant; rather, just as an attendant. He was called Basta, and Irene had seen him in Pathology. Now she remembered the last time she had seen Basta. It was when she had asked for Stridner and he had pointed at the autopsy room, where the professor was in the process of performing a postmortem examination on pieces of Marcus. When he stretched out his arm and pointed at the autopsy room she recalled his well-trained arm muscles playing under his gleaming brown skin.

Basta had been helpful. He'd made a very skillful copy of Marcus's tattoo. Had he thought they would never be able to trace the origin of the tattoo? Or had he seen no way to say no when Stridner gave him the assignment? These were just some of the questions Irene wanted to ask when they caught him.

Stridner described Basta to the two employees in the lounge. Before she was finished, the dark man nodded. "I know his name . . . *hmmm* . . . could be Sebastian. But he's also called Basta, *hmmm* . . . called Basta. Not his last name."

He threw up his light-colored palms with an apologetic smile.

Britt Nilsson looked uncertain. "An attendant works here sometimes who matches the description. But I don't know his name," she said.

Stridner turned on her heel and said, "I have the employee records in my office. We have his first name to work with."

Irene could feel a draft when the professor swished past.

YVONNE STRIDNER pounced on her yellow-spined cloth binders. She studied "Employees 1998–1999." Her index finger wandered down the list. She stopped at a name and cried out, "Here! Sebastian Martinsson. Born March 7, 1970. Lives on Gamla Björlandavägen. His telephone number is also here."

Yvonne Stridner handed the binder to Irene so that she would also be able to read the entry. Irene wrote down the information on her notepad and thanked Stridner for her help.

She waved it off. "Don't mention it. Just make sure you catch him as quickly as possible. He isn't going to stop killing. Sooner or later he'll do it again. He's simply biding his time," she said.

She looked at her elegant watch. Something told Irene that the Rolex hadn't been purchased on some shady backstreet in Bangkok. Because it was sitting on Yvonne's wrist, it was one hundred percent certain that the glittering diamonds around the face were real.

"Now I have to get going! The plane to New York won't wait, even for me!"

IRENE CONTACTED Hannu and Birgitta on their cell phones. Jonny didn't answer his. A mechanical voice asked her to leave a message since the subscriber wasn't available, which meant that he had turned off his phone. Typical, but maybe it was just as well. Hannu, Birgitta, and she would be able to undertake the search and any possible arrest. She and Hannu had been in agreement that the prosecutor should be brought in immediately. Since Hannu was in Säve, looking for the location of the dismemberment, it would be fastest if Birgitta, who was in the station, spoke with the prosecutor.

They agreed to meet in Superintendent Andersson's office at three o'clock. He needed to have all the information before they proceeded.

Irene decided to check whether Basta happened to be in the Department of Pathology right that moment. His time sheet hadn't been filled out after June 4. Was he going to be off work for the rest of the summer? Irene checked the list. Basta had worked from March 4 to 12. He had been in Göteborg right after they believed Marcus had been dismembered. He had also been at work on May 31 through June 4. He had been in Göteborg when Erik Bolin was killed, as well. There were relatively large gaps in Basta's work schedule, anywhere from two to three weeks. Had he been in Copenhagen? She checked the dates of the murders of Isabell Lind and Emil Bentsen. An empty hole gaped then, as well as during the time Tom Tanaka was attacked.

Irene went into the empty corridor. She didn't see a living soul to ask about Basta. She walked down the stairs with heavy steps. Hesitantly, she stopped outside the door to the autopsy room. Sharp howling from a bone saw could be heard from within. She straightened up and opened the door.

Two autopsies were in progress. Britt Nilsson was at one of the tables, in the middle of picking out the organs from the chest. A belching sound from gases being pressed out of the windpipe could be heard as she picked up the heart and lung package.

Autopsies could seem disgusting, but no one was more aware than Irene of how important they could be. Only a dead body could tell the truth about what had really happened. The mute testimony of the corpse had to be taken down by keen and skilled medical examiners.

They had to interpret what the body was really saying in order to be able to make reparations and do justice to the dead.

A young autopsy technician was in the process of sawing open the skull bone of a dead man at the other table. Irene concentrated intently on the technician. He looked up when he became aware of her presence, turned off the saw, and stared at her.

"Who are you?" he asked in a rude tone.

"Inspector Irene Huss. I'm looking for Sebastian Martinsson."

"Now I recognize you. Sebastian is on vacation all summer. He's studying abroad. What do you want with him?"

He sounded friendlier after having recognized her and made no attempt to conceal his curiosity. Irene pretended not to notice.

"Thanks a lot. I'll call him at home and see if he's still in town."

She gave him a friendly smile and left the room at an even pace. Even if she was in a hurry she didn't want it to be too noticeable.

"I RAN into Superintendent Andersson in the corridor and we went together to the prosecutor. Inez Collin is handling this case," Birgitta began.

Andersson snorted but Irene was pleased. Inez Collin was sharp and always knew what she was doing.

"That's why Superintendent Andersson is already informed. We've saved a lot of time," Birgitta continued.

Hannu, Birgitta, Superintendent Andersson, and Irene were seated in Andersson's office. Steaming coffee mugs were placed in front of them as well as a bag of mazarin buns.

"Collin is working on a search warrant," Andersson added.

"Good. Then it's just a matter of driving out to Björlanda and picking him up," said Birgitta.

"If he's still in town. The guy in Pathology said something about Basta being off all summer to study abroad," Irene said.

"Abroad? He's sure as hell not supposed to leave Sweden when we're finally close to bringing him in!" the superintendent exclaimed, displeased.

"Hopefully not. But the risk is there. I suggest that we take a locksmith with us to save some time."

"I'll take care of that," said Hannu.

"I'm going with you," Andersson muttered.

Irene sensed that his nerves wouldn't allow him to remain at the station to await their return, with or without Basta.

THE GRAY three-story concrete house dated from the earliest "million houses project," a program to provide affordable shelter for the poor. In an attempt at softening its gloomy facade, all the balconies had been painted a bright red during the eighties. Over the years, exhaust fumes from the heavily trafficked Björlandavägen had toned down the color to a brownish red. Colorful graffiti on the walls did a better job of livening up the environment, but since it was of varying artistic quality, the impression was mixed.

The lock on the door to the building was broken so it was just a matter of stepping inside the dirty stairwell. The walls inside were also covered in graffiti, even though it was mostly edifying invectives in the form of different sexual slurs and only a few pictures.

The name plate on the second floor read S. MARTINSSON. The four police officers positioned themselves outside the door and Irene rang the bell. She felt her heart rate increase. She was finally about to see Basta, eye to eye.

After five rings, she realized that he wasn't home. Or, if he was, he wasn't planning on answering the doorbell. Irene opened the lid of the mail slot and peered in. She could see an advertisement on the floor and the corner of a yellow rag rug. The apartment seemed quiet and empty. Irene could hear Hannu's voice behind her saying, "OK. You can come now."

When she turned around, she saw him turn off his cell phone and put it in the inside pocket of his jacket. In five minutes the locksmith arrived. He was a big cheerful Finn who spoke a singsong Finnish-Swedish as he opened the door. If he noticed the superintendent stomping with impatience, he didn't comment.

When the lock clicked, he opened the door wide and threw out his hand in an inviting gesture. "There you go!"

Andersson stepped over the threshold first. Before they took a closer look at the apartment, they split up in order to check and make sure that Basta hadn't hidden himself somewhere. The little studio apartment was quickly searched. The hallway was small and cramped.

There were two closets. One of them contained wire storage bins and the other held cleaning implements. The bins were as good as empty aside from a pair of ski gloves, two thick shirts, and a long light blue scarf knitted with thick yarn. A pair of well-polished light brown boots in size eleven stood on the floor.

There was an old vacuum cleaner, a green plastic carpet beater, and an ironing board in the cleaning closet.

The door on the opposite wall led into a small bathroom. It was so small that the toilet was placed as close as possible to the bathtub. The washbasin was squeezed under the window on the short wall. The walls were painted a shade of pale green like linden tree blossoms. The floor was covered in gray tiles, several of which were cracked. Irene opened the medicine chest and determined that it was empty except for a hairbrush and a squeezed-out tube of toothpaste. The entire space was meticulously clean and fresh.

On the hall floor there was a small sun-yellow rag rug. The hall lamp was broken but light flooded in from the open door as well as through a high picture window. Irene normally wasn't very sensitive to how people cleaned their homes, but even she had to admit that she had rarely seen such well-polished windows. White curtains woven in a pattern of flying seagulls hung on either side of the window. When Irene looked closer, she discovered that the curtains had been carefully starched.

Just to the left of the main door was a kitchen alcove a few square meters in size. A minimal stove, a fridge and freezer, and a few beige-colored kitchen cabinets shared the limited space. The small sink shone like a commercial for some miraculous cleanser.

The bedroom appeared to be sizable because it held almost no furniture. The walls were sponge-painted in a pale apricot color. In the middle of the floor was an old but faultlessly clean hooked rug in green and yellow. A bed with a simple green-and-white striped cotton bedspread stood along one of the shorter walls. By the window, there was a small pine kitchen table and two odd kitchen chairs. A cheap shelf unit from IKEA covered the entirety of the opposite wall. A small TV with a VCR stood on the middle shelf. There were no books but there were lots of videos and sketch pads in different sizes, organized in neat rows. On the bottom shelf were some stretchers for canvases.

"Wow, this guy really cleans and keeps things tidy!" Birgitta said, impressed.

Two pictures hung over the bed, the only wall decorations in the room. When Irene saw them she was speechless. She could only grab Birgitta's arm and point.

"You're pinching!" Birgitta cried.

When she looked in the direction indicated by Irene's index finger, she grew quiet.

The paintings were two portraits, one of a man, the other of a woman. Their heads seemed to be floating freely in the air, since the necks were not attached to any upper body.

"Carmen Østergaard and Marcus Tosscander," Irene said with an unsteady voice.

Andersson stepped up to the paintings and examined them attentively.

"Are you sure? I mean about the woman. I recognize Tosscander, of course," he said.

"I'm absolutely sure. It's Carmen."

Carmen's portrait background was violet-purple. Her wavy brown hair framed a pale gray face. Her wide-open eyes were weary and blank.

The background of Marcus's portrait was golden ochre, beautiful against his dark hair. The warm color contrasted with the greenish gray pallor of his skin. His eyes were also wide open and dull.

"Oh my God! He's painted their decapitated heads," Irene exclaimed.

Andersson took a step back in order to get another angle on the pictures.

"You think so?" he said.

"I'm sure. Don't you see?"

"It actually looks that way," the superintendent agreed.

Hannu stood by the bookshelf and flipped through the sketch pads.

"Come here and look," he said.

The other three went over to him. Without a word, he held out a large pad and showed them the sketches on the first page. They were of Carmen's head. Basta had drawn it from different angles. On some of them you could see the cut on the underside of the throat. There was no doubt about the fact that the head had been chopped off.

"Turn," Hannu ordered.

Irene turned the page and they saw the sketch for the painting that was hanging on the wall.

The following five pages held sketches of internal organs. Irene could make out a heart and intestines in varying thicknesses. She had probably understood subconsciously what was coming, but when it suddenly popped up she still was very upset. First there was a detailed sketch of a severed female breast, then an interior study of a female vagina.

Irene started to feel ill. Her hands shook as she turned the pages.

The sketches of Marcus also started with a study of the head from different angles. On the next page the sketch for the painting appeared. But when Irene turned another page, she got a severe shock. There weren't any still lifes of internal organs here. That would have been better. On the following pages there were portraits of Marcus in the exact same position and from the exact same angle. Yet each picture was different, since they represented the advancing decay of Marcus's head.

"Damn, what a sick bastard!" Andersson exclaimed.

"That's why he saved the head in the crypt," said Birgitta.

Hannu came out from the kitchen alcove and said, "The fridge and the freezer are empty. Cleaned out. He's not planning on coming home over the summer."

He jingled a small key ring and added, "I found these. I'm going up to the attic."

The next moment the front door closed behind him and they could hear him mounting the stairs.

"If Basta is abroad then it seems natural to guess he's in Copenhagen," said Irene.

"That's not really abroad," Birgitta objected.

"No, but he has some base there."

"Why didn't he tell his friend at work that he was going to Copenhagen?"

"Maybe he doesn't want anyone to know that he spends time there," said Irene.

"Do you think that over a period of several years he's gone to Copenhagen periodically without his friends at work knowing about it?"

"It's not impossible if he doesn't spend time with them outside work. He's only an hourly employee at Pathology."

"How long has he been working there?"

"Off and on for the last five years, according to Stridner."

They were interrupted by Andersson's voice. "Come and see this!"

He was looking into one of the two closets opposite the foot of the bed. Irene and Birgitta joined him. A sturdy leather jacket with a fur collar, a black suit, and a white shirt with a black tie hung in one closet. On the floor was a pair of smart black-laced shoes. In the other closet, a white doctor's coat hung, along with a short-sleeved green smock and a pair of green cotton pants with loose cuffs at the bottom. On the floor there was a pair of green wooden clogs with "Op 1" written in black India ink on the side of the wooden sole. There was a package of operating masks and a package of examination gloves next to the shoes.

"I don't believe it! 'My personal physician'!" Irene exclaimed.

"What nonsense are you babbling about?" Andersson hissed, irritated.

"Marcus mentioned something about a man to his friends almost a year ago. He called him 'my personal physician.' And here we have a doctor's outfit! Just like Emil was called 'my policeman' by Marcus, even though he was also only dressing up."

The front door opened and Hannu returned. He was carrying a Domus bag in each hand. He had hung a black shoulder bag in shiny leather diagonally across his chest. Without a word, he walked over to them and set down the bags.

Irene saw that they were filled with clothes. She could see a pair of white jeans and a pair of red swim trunks.

"Why did he bring his clothes up to the attic?" Andersson asked.

Hannu put the shoulder bag down on the floor and stuck his hand inside.

"These aren't his. They're Marcus's clothes. There's more up there," he said.

He took out a new EU passport with red covers and opened it. Marcus Tosscander's beautiful smile beamed out at the three officers.

"There's money here as well," Hannu continued.

He hauled out a long, thin, blue plastic pouch. A thick stack of bills lay inside.

"Thai *bats*," Hannu announced.

Irene got a lump in her throat. Up to the last minute, Marcus thought that he was going to Thailand.

Suddenly, Andersson clapped his hands together and said with determination, "Now we're going to catch him! We must try and locate relatives. Some relative should damn well know where he is! Check if he has forwarded his mail . . . and all of that, which you are really good at, Hannu."

Hannu nodded. If there was a relative, that person would be traced. And if Sebastian had left an address, Hannu would find that as well. But what would they do if he had managed to sweep away every clue as to his whereabouts? It would be a good idea to contact the police in Copenhagen, but that would have to wait until tomorrow. It was after five o'clock.

IT WAS almost eight o'clock when they met that night in the conference room to eat their ordered-in pizzas. Superintendent Andersson, Tommy, Irene, Birgitta, and Jonny sat around the table. Irene wondered how Andersson had reached Jonny. The last one to enter the room was Hannu.

The superintendent started with a recapitulation of the afternoon's events. In conclusion, he turned toward Jonny and said, "Since you're already initiated into the video film world, your assignment is to go through Sebastian Martinsson's film collection."

Despite Jonny's loud protests, he was assigned to this job. Then Andersson turned to Hannu and asked, "Have you found anything?"

Hannu nodded and looked down at his papers.

"Sebastian Martinsson was born in Trollhättan twenty-nine years ago. His father was a teacher. The parents divorced shortly after the son was born. His father died of cancer when Sebastian was thirteen. The mother still lives in Trollhättan. She's apparently an artist."

"Have you gotten in touch with her?" Andersson asked.

"No. No one answers at that telephone number."

Andersson looked displeased but cheered up after a little while.

"We'll have to contact our colleagues in Trollhättan so that they can go and get her. Or at least find out where she is."

Trollhättan was located barely twenty kilometers from Vänersborg. Irene felt a pang when she thought about Vänersborg, and Monika Lind. She decided to call and see how Monika was doing. Maybe Irene could hint that they were hot on the murderer's trail. It would, perhaps, be some comfort.

MONIKA LIND sounded a bit surprised at first when she heard Irene's voice on the telephone. She was pleased when she understood that Irene was worried about how the family was doing.

"It feels like I'm living in a black hole. Thank God, the semester is over now, but maybe it isn't good to have time to think. I blame myself for what happened to Bell. Why did I let her go to Copenhagen? But I could hardly stop her. I never understood that she . . . How could I be so naive!" she said.

"How's it going with the rest of the family?" Irene asked.

"Janne has taken it with composure. I think too much composure, at times. But he has been an amazing support for me and Elin. She's young enough that she doesn't mourn her big sister very deeply. But she has started asking for a dog. Janne would also really like to have one. Maybe it would distract us from the thoughts . . . what do you think? You've always had a dog. Is Elin too little?"

"Not if you and Janne realize that all the responsibility for the dog is yours. But a dog would certainly distract them, and the family would have a common interest. A little puppy demands a lot of care and it needs to be looked after and go to obedience school and . . ."

Irene stopped herself and thought. Then she said, "The fact is that Sammie has become a father. We have one of his puppies at our home. He's almost ten weeks old and terribly cute. But we've realized that having a puppy right now isn't going to work. Sammie is too old and doesn't accept having a competitor. The dog sitter is almost seventy and we don't know how much longer she'll have the energy to keep going. As a whole, our family is hardly at home. We're working and going to school and have a lot of extracurricular activities, you know how it is. He's a mixed breed of black poodle and an Irish soft-coated wheaten terrier. If you want, you can have him. He's very cute and sweet."

Monika considered before she said, "Yes, it would work out well with respect to the fact that I'm off work all summer. How much would he cost?"

"Elin can have him as a gift. You'll be doing us a big favor, just knowing that he'll be getting a good home."

"But it's far too much! What's his name?"

Irene was close to telling the truth, but she managed to stop herself. "Tinkler" didn't inspire much confidence. That's why she just said, "We haven't been able to decide yet. For the most part, we just say Little Guy."

"I'll talk it over with Janne. We'll be in touch tomorrow."

Irene thought that Monika Lind's voice sounded happier when she hung up. She hoped that the Lind family would take Tinkler.

Now the worst part remained—convincing her own family of the truth behind her actions.

Chapter 19

IT WAS AS HARD to convince the family as Irene had expected. After long discussions back and forth, the other three had to admit that it was difficult to merge their time schedules with young Tinkler's needs. The deciding factor was Sammie's obvious dislike of the whole situation. He was used to peace and quiet, long walks, and eating his food in peace. His son had sabotaged this comfortable existence. Sammie roamed around with his tail hanging, looking unhappy.

"It's possible that I may go to Trollhättan tomorrow. If the Linds want him, I'll take Tinkler with me and drive by Vänersborg," Irene said decisively.

Her family nodded gloomily. Jenny had tears in her eyes when she pulled the tousled charmer into her lap. Tinkler was ecstatic that she wanted to cuddle with him, and his little pink tongue went in and out during his energetic attempt to lick her face.

Sammie lay under Irene's chair and sighed deeply.

MONIKA LIND called just before Irene was about to drive to the station.

"We would love to take Little Guy!" she said, sounding really happy.

It took a few seconds before Irene's tired brain remembered that it was the way she herself had described the puppy the day before. She pulled herself together quickly and mentioned her possible trip to Trollhättan during the day. If it didn't happen, the Lind family would drive down and pick up the puppy the next day.

"SEBASTIAN MARTINSSON'S mother has been found. Her name is Sabine Martinsson and she was born in 1950. She's being released from the hospital today where she has been treated for acute delirium. Apparently she's a serious alcoholic," Birgitta started.

Andersson nodded and interrupted her. "I've spoken with our colleagues in Trollhättan. We'd better drive up there and talk with her ourselves. Hannu and Irene can leave now. Here's the address."

He handed the note to Hannu. Irene felt satisfied. Now Tinkler would ride in a car for the first time in his life and he would meet his new family.

The superintendent continued, "Svante Malm didn't have time to come himself this morning but he called me just a little while ago. Apparently, they can do some DNA test on the hair strands that were found in the hairbrush in the bathroom cabinet at Martinsson's apartment. He said that there were hair follicles left on some of them. They're going to compare them with the DNA profile from the semen stains that have been found at the crime scenes. He also asked me to tell you, Irene, that after a quick look at the handwriting on the postcard you received, he thinks there is a lot in common with Martinsson's handwriting. He's written quite a bit in his sketchbooks."

"Did he say anything about having found Marcus's laptop computer?" Birgitta asked.

"No. There're just clothes and sun lotion and stuff that people take with them when they're going on vacation. Strangely enough, they haven't found a suitcase," said Andersson.

Birgitta looked disappointed. Marcus's laptop would have filled in several blanks.

"Irene, before you leave, I want you to call Copenhagen and inform our colleagues there. You're the only one who understands Danish. Tell them everything we know about Martinsson and that we think he's going to some art school in Copenhagen," said Andersson.

The last was a possibility that Irene had introduced during the previous evening's pizza dinner. Her hypothesis was that Sebastian worked in Göteborg and studied painting in Copenhagen. When Andersson doubtfully asked why Sebastian hadn't moved to Copenhagen and gotten an extra job there, instead of doing all this commuting, Hannu had dryly replied, "He has his dream job here in Göteborg."

JENS METZ answered the telephone at the police station in Vesterbro. Irene gave an account of the information they had on Sebastian Martinsson. When she was finished, Metz was impressed.

"That's not bad. So he's connected to all the murders. Have you been able to check his videos? It wouldn't surprise me if you happened to find scenes where he has the lead role." Jens chuckled.

Irene felt nausea rising from her stomach when she thought about those scenes.

In conclusion, she asked about Beate Bentsen. Jens replied, "She has received extended sick leave. She took Emil's murder hard. And the fact that *he* was one of the mutilation murderers has cracked her completely. She'll probably be on leave all summer."

Irene felt a deep sympathy for the Danish superintendent. The thought that she was the mother of a necrophilic murderer was incomprehensible. How could Emil have turned out like that? Irene thought about the posters, videos, and CDs they'd found in Emil's apartment. She had a feeling that the films, which Emil consumed in large quantities, were very significant. The pictures that he built his fantasies around had taken up more and more of his life.

Jens and Irene agreed to be in touch if even the slightest lead showed up during the day.

"I already have your cell phone number," Jens said. He laughed nastily.

When they had hung up, Irene thought about his final words. He had taken her number from the address book in Tom's gold-covered Nokia. She actually hadn't dared ask Jens what Tom's condition was. It was still far too sensitive a topic.

The next phone call was to home, to Katarina. Irene asked her drowsy daughter to pack Tinkler's few earthly possessions in a sack: the bag with puppy chow, the two stainless-steel food bowls, the leash, and the chewy bone. He was scared to death of the duck that peeped so they could forget about that toy. However, it would be good if Katarina could find a book about raising a dog. Since the Linds weren't used to puppies it might be of use. And since Tinkler was Sammie's son, Irene knew that they would need it.

When the phone calls were taken care of she called for Hannu. Together they went out to an unmarked police car, a discreet dark blue Saab 900.

TINKLER WAS rested and energetic. It was clear he thought it was very exciting to ride in the car. Even before they started, he was standing in Irene's lap with his paws against the window, trying to see out. When he caught sight of Katarina, who was standing with Sammie on a leash and waving to them from the row of garages, he barked teasingly at the old man who hadn't gotten to come along. He was his father's son in every way, except for the fact that his coat was darker.

After barely half an hour, all of the new impressions became too much for the puppy and he curled up, exhausted, in Irene's lap and fell asleep instantly.

The handing over of Tinkler to the ecstatic Elin was accomplished without any major problems. And Irene managed to keep her from putting the puppy to bed in her doll carriage.

"Call if there are any problems" were Irene's farewell words.

When they were out of sight of the family, she took a deep breath and sighed. "That's that," she said.

"Puppies are hard work," Hannu commented.

"Just like small children," Irene quickly replied.

A faint smile could be seen in the corners of Hannu's lips.

THE AREa where Sabine Martinsson lived was a little way outside the city center of Trollhättan. They had a hard time finding the address, but after circling for a while they ended up in the right place.

The house had been built in the fifties but hardly anything had been done to it since. The whole area appeared to be in a state of decline. The windows in the main entrance were shattered and had been replaced by Masonite nailed up in a sloppy manner. Someone had painted a black swastika on the board. Irene pushed open the heavy front door and stepped into the graffiti-covered and urine-smelling stairwell. Both she and Hannu came to a stop as the door shut behind them.

A party was going on. It could be heard from the entrance. Irene looked at her watch, which showed a quarter to twelve. Some people were drinking their lunch. Directed by the laughter and loud voices, Irene and Hannu ended up on the second floor. A cracked ceramic sign hanging on the door read WELCOME TO SABINE AND SEBASTIAN'S. Under the sign someone had etched the word "cunt" with a sharp object.

The doorbell was broken. Hannu knocked loudly. The noise level on the other side of the door was too high for anyone to hear the knocks. When no one came, Hannu resolutely pushed down on the handle and stepped inside.

A man was lying across the dirty floor in the hall. Since he was snoring loudly, they knew he was alive and stepped over him without ceremony.

The party was in the kitchen. The air was thick with cigarette smoke. But the smell of smoke couldn't conceal the stink of garbage and unwashed human bodies. A woman and two men sat around a crowded kitchen table. A boom box in the window, turned up to the highest volume, belted out Elvis's seductive question "Are You Lonesome Tonight?" There was a big mess of unwashed glasses, a broken loaf of bread, an empty sausage skin, and a large carton containing cookie crumbs as well as empty chip bags on the table. A five-liter plastic jug was the centerpiece of the table. If it had been full from the beginning, then four people had consumed almost two liters of home-brewed liquor. Nothing in their behavior contradicted this assumption.

"Do you think we can get a sensible word out of her?" Irene asked.

"If we've driven all this way, at least we have to try."

That same instant, one of the men discovered the unwanted visitors. He was thickset and heavy. Course, light hair stuck out wildly in all directions around his head. His light blue irises swam around slowly in his bloodshot eyes. He clumsily tried to rise but fell back heavily into a kitchen chair. He started shouting, "Who the hell! What the hell . . . !"

Despite the monosyllabic words, they could discern a thick Finnish accent. Hannu quickly said something in Finnish. With a bang, the Finn shut his jaws, and by the stiff expression on his face Irene understood that he wasn't going to open them again for a long time. She took pains to use a soothing tone of voice when she said, "We're from the Göteborg police. We're looking for Sabine Martinsson."

The woman turned her narrow head and looked at Irene for the first time. Her thin henna-colored hair was pulled together into a slovenly ponytail on the top of her head. Her face seemed to have been marked by a life of extreme abuse, with deep lines around her eyes and mouth. But from her cheekbones and her large green eyes one could see traces of earlier beauty. Sebastian had inherited those cheekbones. Irene had been able to make them out in the backlit photo and had recognized them without being able to remember who they belonged to.

Sabine Martinsson slowly got up, using the tabletop as support. Sebastian had also inherited his height from his mother; she was almost as tall as Irene. She wasn't slender anymore; rather, she seemed hollowed out and undernourished. Only her stomach appeared to be round and full. Sabine Martinsson looked very sick. Her yellow T-shirt hung loosely over her bony shoulders. Under the thin fabric, the large nipples of her flat, hanging breasts were outlined. The torn black tights she wore should have been taut, but they hung limply around her skinny legs.

"Göteborg's . . . pig," she slurred.

She was missing a top front tooth as well as several on the bottom.

"We would like to speak with you. It's about Sebastian."

When Irene mentioned her son's name, it was as if a light flickered behind Sabine's deadened eyes. She straightened and said surprisingly clearly, "Has something happened to Sebbe?"

Irene took a step closer to the swaying figure and gently put her hand on Sabine's skinny arm. No muscles, just bone could be felt under the skin.

"We don't know. He's disappeared from his job. Do you know where he is?"

Now the older man came to life. He had been sitting and staring at the officers with narrowed eyes while his toothless jaws ground together. He started yelling, "Don't tell the damn pigs anything! Those damn p—"

Clumsily, he tried to get up but was quickly pulled down into his chair again by the Finn.

"It's cool. We're just trying to find her missing son," Irene said with a smile.

The man became confused. Maybe he was trying to figure out whether the police officers were there as friends or enemies.

"Sebbe? Sebbe . . . missing?" Sabine asked.

She spoke in a strained voice now as if it took an immense amount of energy to utter each word.

"Yes. He hasn't been at work for a while and he isn't in his apartment. Do you know where he might be?"

Sabine shook off Irene's hand and started walking unsteadily toward the kitchen door. She steadied herself against the door frame and took a few deep wheezing breaths before she started coughing. After a while, she set her course for the bathroom on the other side of the hall. She stumbled over the snoring man and fell headfirst, but luckily landed somewhat softly on his body. He coughed and continued snoring in another key.

"Did you hurt yourself?" Irene asked. She had rushed to Sabine's rescue as the woman toppled over. Now Irene helped her to her feet, noting how light the tall woman was. Sabine mumbled something and released herself from Irene's grip. Staggering, she took the last few steps into the bathroom and pulled the door shut with a bang. A short while later, the sound of gagging came through the thin door.

"Is she forcing herself to throw up?" Irene whispered to Hannu.

"Think so. She wants to clear her head."

When Sabine opened the door again they could smell the sour odor of vomit. She jerked her head without looking at the officers, and said, "Come. The living room."

She walked unsteadily ahead of them. The only furniture in the room was a dirty couch that, at the beginning of time, had been light blue and a broken rattan recliner. An empty easel stood in one corner. A small but brand-new color TV was enthroned in the middle of the floor. But the furniture was not what one paid attention to when entering the room.

Not one square centimeter of the wallpaper was visible. Sabine's paintings lined the walls. They were large and painted in roughly the same color scheme. The dominating tones were light purple, pink, and white. Here and there a light blue tone remained in a few of the pictures. Not a single warm tone was visible.

The paintings were portraits, but they were grotesque faces from terrible nightmares. Twisted, malignant demons stared down from the walls. For a while, Irene thought that a fat, Buddha-like man with a wide smile was the only figure who looked sympathetic. But then she saw that the Buddha's eyes were completely black and empty. Sabine had captured a cold, scornful person with her brushes. The icy colors strengthened the uncomfortable feelings the pictures inspired. Irene would never want to have any of them on her walls, even though they were skillfully painted.

Sabine sank down onto the sofa with a thud. Her chest heaved and she wheezed and coughed so that Irene became concerned. Did Sabine have pneumonia? But she had just been released from the hospital. As if she had read Irene's thoughts, Sabine puffed out, "Smo . . . smoker's cough. Shouldn't smoke."

Irene sat on the creaking, protesting wicker chair. She sent up a silent prayer that it wouldn't collapse. Hannu preferred to stand.

"What do you want with Sebbe?" Sabine wheezed.

Irene leaned forward intimately and said, "Sebastian's fellow workers are wondering where he's gone. He hasn't been at work for several days. Do you know where he is?"

Sabine shook her head. "No . . . he has nice friends . . . at work at the office."

"Office?" Irene repeated, surprised.

"Nice office. The best one in Göt . . . heborg. Cyhrén's." She grew quiet and stared listlessly at a purple-colored spirit from the abyss with a gaping mouth frozen in an eternal anguished scream.

"What do you mean when you say that he works at an office?" Irene asked again.

Sabine gave her an irritated look. "It's a funeral home. A good job. Needs money . . . expensive studies in Copenhagen."

Irene quickly jumped at the opportunity. "How long has he studied in Copenhagen?" she asked.

Sabine wrinkled her thin forehead. After a while her look brightened and she informed them triumphantly, "Several years!"

"What's he studying in Copenhagen?" Irene took pains to maintain a soft tone of voice.

Sabine straightened up on the filthy sofa and jerked her thin neck. "Painting. Art. I'm an art . . . hist, of course."

With the last word she threw herself forward and vomited a spot of yellow bile on the floor. Hannu pulled out a package of Kleenex from his pocket. He placed several on top of each other and wiped up the stain, then disappeared into the hall. Irene heard the toilet flush.

The thin woman on the sofa sat with her hands pressed tightly over her stomach. Beads of sweat glistened on her forehead.

Irene became really worried. "Do you need to go back to the hospital? We can drive you."

Sabine said, terrified, "No! There's no point! They'll just send me home. My liver and pancreas are gone. My fault . . . they say."

Irene could see how much it cost Sabine to answer their questions. Desperately, the woman struggled against the haze of alcohol and pain. She must care about her son.

"When was the last time you saw Basta?" Irene asked.

At first she couldn't understand what had gone wrong but when she saw Sabine's eyes glowing with hate she realized that she had blundered. "Don't say Basta!" Sabine hissed with rage. "How can you know . . . ? Not Basta! Sebbe! Sebbe!"

Hannu slid through the doorway. He gave Irene a wondering look but she could only shake her head in response. Carefully, she asked, "Do you not like it when people call him Basta?"

"No! No!" she said firmly.

"I'm sorry but that's the nickname he has given to other people. And his friends at work call him Basta. Sebastian himself can't have anything against it," Irene continued.

Sabine looked at Irene mistrustfully.

"Does he call himself . . . that?"

"Yes. Basta."

"His . . . shit heap of a father always called him . . . that," Sabine whispered.

So Sebastian Martinsson had used the nickname his father had given him when he was alive. But he had died when Sebastian was thirteen. The psychologists could probably figure out what this meant when they examined him. Too bad that he hadn't called himself Sebbe; then it would have been much easier to guess his full name.

Irene tried again. "When was the last time you spoke with Sebastian?"

Sabine leaned back, her hands still pressed hard against her stomach.

"I don't know. Maybe at Christmas," she mumbled.

Apparently mother and son were not in close contact, Irene concluded. She remembered something she had to ask. "Had Sebastian injured the tip of his left index finger?"

Sabine tried to focus her suspicious look on Irene. "Why . . . are you asking?"

"One of his friends at work said something about an injured fingertip.

It may be good to mention it if we need to conduct a search for him," Irene said innocently.

Sabine nodded and sighed. "He crushed it . . . in the main school door when he was living here . . . with me."

Her chest heaved after the long sentence as she fought for breath.

"Do you know where he lives in Copenhagen?" Irene asked.

"No. He's moved . . . different places."

She closed her eyes. Irene worried that she would fall asleep. Quickly, Irene asked, "Do you know the name of the school he's attending?"

Sabine opened her eyelids slightly. With difficulty she straightened up. Hesitantly, she said, "Not a school . . . Kreuger . . . Academy or something."

Kreuger? Wasn't he a Swede, the match king? Maybe he had founded an art school in Copenhagen? She would have to call her colleagues there as soon as possible.

For the first time Hannu broke into the questioning. He asked, "Sabine, is there a place out near Säve that Sebastian might have access to?"

"Säve? My little house . . . inherited from my parents. Can't live there. Burned down. . . ."

"Do you still own the house?"

Sabine nodded in response. She sat with her head hanging. Now and then a low groan escaped her.

Since Sabine had just been released from the hospital there really wasn't any sense in trying to have her admitted again. No one wanted to touch Sabine with a ten-foot pole. No one, except for her cavaliers in the kitchen.

When Irene got up to leave, Sabine's clawlike hand shot up and gripped the lower part of Irene's jacket hard.

"Find him . . . please," she wheezed.

Irene reassured her with the greatest sincerity, while at the same time freeing the jacket fabric from her grasp. "We'll do everything we can."

They stepped over the man in the hall, who was still snoring peacefully.

"WHAT WAS she talking about when she said that he works at a funeral home? Basta works in Pathology!" said Irene

She was holding on to the steering wheel as they zoomed toward Göteborg again, just above the speed limit. Hannu sat for a while before he answered. "The suit."

The man could be insanely irritating but Irene knew that he was often right and his conclusions correct. The irritating part was that he was the only one who understood what he meant but he thought it should be crystal clear to everyone. He went through several ideas mentally and then stated the last one, often monosyllabically. Everyone around him gaped and looked like an idiot. Right now only Irene was around him, but she was no exception.

"What damn suit?"

She hadn't meant to hiss, but it turned out that way. As usual, Hannu was unaffected.

"The suit in the closet," he said.

A sober black suit had hung in Basta's closet, with a white shirt and a black tie. A pair of black-laced shoes stood on the floor. Altogether, the prevalent clothing for employees at a funeral home when they were going to assist in burials.

"You're right. I had forgotten. The doctor's outfit was more interesting to me. Police uniforms and operating clothing . . . God! They're playing dress up."

"Both Emil and Basta knew what they were doing. It was never a game. They were planning and preparing for the murders of Carmen and Marcus," Hannu said.

Irene reminded herself of the scenes from the videotapes they had found at Emil's. Emil and Basta had procured a video camera and a circular saw before they killed Carmen.

"I'll find out where Sabine's house is located," Hannu said.

He took out his cell phone and called a number in his address book. Irene could hear someone answer and the start of a conversation in Finnish. The only part she recognized was something about "entry into the land register," but she wasn't sure if she had heard correctly.

Hannu turned off the cell phone and said shortly, "He'll call."

If Irene hadn't known Hannu she definitely would have asked "Who?" But now she knew him, so she didn't ask. She didn't doubt for a second that his cell phone would ring soon and they would get the address of Sabine's house in Säve.

"Have you ever heard of the Kreuger Academy?" she asked instead.

"No."

"I'll have to phone Copenhagen when we get to the station."

IRENE WOULD have liked to have taken a shower after their visit to Sabine Martinsson. The smell of dirt, human degradation, poverty, and destitution had an uncomfortable ability to stick to you. But it wasn't the first time she had wandered around in that environment and it would hardly be the last time, either. Like a wet dog, she shook off the worst of it and decided to start working.

Before she had had time to dial the number for Vesterbro her cell phone rang.

"Irene Huss."

"Tom speaking."

Joy made Irene's heart skip a beat.

"Tom! So nice of you to call! That means you've come home. How are you feeling?"

"That's right, I've come home. All things considered, I feel good. I've felt better. I should probably be thankful that I'm alive. But I'm not calling to complain. I wanted to thank you for the flowers. Your friend Peter Møller brought them to me. Beautiful orchids, which are actually my favorite flowers. Thanks."

A thought struck Irene: what if Basta was in Copenhagen and decided to take care of an unfinished job? Tom was the only one of his victims who had survived. Should she warn him? Hesitantly, she said, "Tom. We've gotten a lead. We probably know who the murderer is. Did Emil or Marcus ever mention the name Basta?"

The silence became loaded. Finally, Tom said shortly, "No."

"Do you know of any art school called the Kreuger Academy?"

"Not Kreu . . . no."

Irene heard him stop himself. When he didn't continue, she asked, "Did Emil or Marcus ever talk about someone they knew who was studying art?"

"Yes. For a while Emil rented to a guy who was studying art. I think his name was Sebastian. Is he the one called Basta?"

"Yes."

Again a fraught silence ensued.

"Is this Basta the murderer?" Tom asked finally.

"A lot of evidence points to him. He could be in Copenhagen right now. You must be on your guard. We don't know how he thinks. Maybe you're a failure he has to fix. You survived."

"Such a klutz. But he wasn't after me; he was after the picture on the wall. Why did he want it?"

"He's the one in the picture."

"Aha."

Afterward, Irene felt a deep and sincere thankfulness that Tom had made it through alive.

After two mugs of coffee, she called her colleagues at Vesterbro. Jens Metz answered, just as Irene had expected.

"Hi, Jens. Irene Huss. We spoke with Sebastian Martinsson's mother about an hour ago. We have good reason to believe that he is in Copenhagen now. She maintains that he's studying art at the Kreuger Academy."

"The Kreuger Academy? I've never heard of it but we'll find out about it pretty quickly. Anything else?"

"We're going to go out to an old house that is owned by Martinsson's mother. My colleague thinks that that's where Marcus Tosscander was dismembered."

"Now we're as good as certain that the old, abandoned shipyard is where Carmen was dismembered. We're in the process of comparing the video film and most of it matches. Did you get an address where Sebastian could be found?"

"No. The mother is an alcoholic and was completely drunk when we questioned her. She didn't have any idea about where he lives in Copenhagen."

"We'll have to start looking for that academy. But there won't be anyone there now. It's almost four o'clock on a Friday afternoon in June. The art school is probably closed for the summer."

"Quite possible. Have a good weekend. Keep in touch."

HANNU WAS leaning over a map when Irene entered his office. He put his index finger on a dot on the map and said, "Here."

Irene leaned forward and saw that he was scrutinizing a detailed map of northern and western Hising Island. His index finger was located just by the coast.

"We'll have to drive by Björlanda shooting range. Then it will be a matter of following a lot of small forest roads. We'll take the map with us," Irene determined.

Hannu nodded and put it inside his jacket.

IT WAS sunny and clear but the wind blew cold from the sea, if it still was the sea, since they were also close to the mouth of the river. Irene thought that the water had a browner tone, but it may have been her imagination.

For the last part of the trip, they had bumped along a barely visible gravel road. The only two houses along the road looked like old allotment garden sheds. They looked shabby and run-down. Sabine Martinsson's house, or what remained of it, was located farthest out toward the water, just fifty meters from the cliffs. Apparently it had once been a small summer cottage but now there wasn't much left of it. A half-collapsed brick column pointing accusingly up at the sky.

"It burned twenty years ago. No insurance," said Hannu.

They parked in front of the ruins and stepped out of the car.

"There," said Hannu.

He pointed at a decaying garage a bit farther back of the ruins. It was quite small but solidly built out of cement, with a roof made of corrugated steel. Rust had turned the roof a dull brown color. A little bird flew in and out of it through a hole in the roof.

The wooden entry looked dry to the point of cracking but it had a sturdy new lock. Hannu went back to the car and got a crowbar. He shoved it into the opening by the lock and broke it. With a dry crunch, the lock fell to the ground. The hinges whined stubbornly when he threw open the half doors.

Straight ahead there was a window situated relatively high up on the wall. Old junk was piled up beneath it. By the door Irene saw two trestles stacked up. A large piece of fiberboard leaned against the wall across from them.

Hannu was as motionless as Irene. He peered in without entering the garage. Then he pointed at the window.

"Look."

The June sky was still bathed in daylight, but through the dirty glass Irene could see the blinking lights of a plane, which was descending for a landing.

Chapter 20

MONIKA LIND CALLED ONCE over the weekend and asked why the puppy didn't want to lie in its brand-new basket in the evenings. He had wandered around and cried. Not until they had pulled him up onto the bed had he fallen asleep, completely exhausted. Irene recognized all of it. She calmed Monika by saying that Sammie had never used his basket either; they had sold it after a year. Monika thanked her for her reassurance and told Irene that they had named the puppy Frasse.

ON SUNDAY afternoon, Irene devoted some time to looking through the yellow pages. Under the heading Funeral Homes, she found Cyhrén's Funeral Home. Had Sebastian really been a member of the staff of the funeral home? Or had he just been an hourly employee, working sporadically? She decided to contact the funeral home the first thing Monday morning.

Later that same night Jonny Blom called. It had never happened before, despite the fact that they had been working together in Violent Crimes for twelve years. Katarina took the call and when she yelled: "Mamma! It's Jonny!" At first Irene hadn't known who was calling.

"This is Irene Huss," she said, waiting.

"Howdy. It's Jonny. I've found the films. The damn psycho is slicing and dicing his corpses to his heart's content. And he's dressed like a doctor. One who is op . . . rating."

He slurred the last word, but Irene had already sensed that he was drunk. Very drunk. She could understand that it might be an advantage to have a certain degree of blood alcohol concentration to make it through the films. But it also meant that his judgment was affected. There was a risk that he might damage one of the films. Cautiously, Irene asked, "Where are you watching the films?"

He immediately exploded. "What the hell! Do you think I'm

sitting at home showing them to my wife and kids? Obviously, I'm
at the station!"

"Good. Do you want me to come down?" asked Irene.

"For lack of anyone better. Hannu isn't home. I just called."

"OK. Are you in interrogation room number four?" The best video
equipment was in that room.

"Yes."

"Have a cup of coffee while you wait. I'll be down in twenty minutes."

"Coffee and coffee. You and your coffee!" he snarled.

"I'll be there soon. Good-bye."

Irene rushed out to the car. She blessed the fact that they had eaten
dinner several hours ago. She had a strong feeling that she wasn't going
to be hungry after the scenes she was about to see.

INTERROGATION ROOM number four was empty. Two unmarked
videos lay on the table next to a half-eaten cinnamon roll. In the light
from the ceiling fixture Irene could make out several wet rings on the
table, from bottles and glasses. She looked in the wastepaper basket,
but it was empty. Jonny had cleaned up before she had arrived.

She heard steps in the corridor and the door was yanked open.
Jonny had wet-combed his hair and he reeked of aftershave. The
effect was a bit comical, since he plainly hadn't shaved in two days.

"I'm going to the john. You can watch the films yourself. I've seen
enough."

Before Irene had time to reply, he shut the door. She could hear his
steps disappearing down the corridor.

Irene felt ill at ease as she looked at the black plastic tapes. They
felt threatening. She knew what they contained. A thought struck
her: were these the original cassettes or had Jonny made copies?
After a quick search of the room she assumed that these were the
originals. Because the equipment was at hand she decided to make
copies of the tapes herself. It was important not to cover them with
even more fingerprints, so she put on a pair of cotton gloves. When
the copying was finished she put the originals in plastic bags to send
to Forensics.

The films were just as horrid as she had expected. Worse, they were painfully long, each of them more than an hour. On the film showing the gutting of Carmen Østergaard, Sebastian wasn't wearing a mask or anything on his head, though he had worn a thick green mask and an operating cap during the dismemberment of Marcus. Otherwise he was dressed the same in both of the films—in a white buttoned-up doctor's coat, a green smock, and green operating pants.

Irene thought about Sebastian's clothing. On the doctor's outfit that they had found in his closet there wasn't the slightest trace of blood. In fact, it was just the opposite: the clothes had appeared to be newly washed. Based on that fact one could conclude that after his dissections Sebastian had deposited the soiled clothes with dirty laundry at work. The fact that there was a fresh set hanging in his closet could mean just one thing: he was preparing to cut up a new victim. A shortage of time combined with distance from a good dismemberment location had kept Sebastian from cleaning out Isabell Lind, Emil Bentsen, and Erik Bolin in the same way he had mutilated Marcus Tosscander and Carmen Østergaard.

With great care Sebastian had sliced open these two bodies and cut out the organs and the intestines. It was nauseating to see how carefully he examined every part he cut loose. But the worst were the close-ups when Emil zoomed in on his face.

His eyes, wide open, glittered feverishly. He rarely blinked when he was standing bent over a body. His lips were tightly pressed together while he concentrated on his work. A few times his tense face broke into one of the most charming smiles Irene had ever seen. He was immensely attractive when he smiled.

Irene took note of the fact that he threw the internal organs into a large plastic bucket, which stood on the floor to the side of the table they were using. It wasn't the same bucket each time; one of them was yellow and the other, red.

He placed the genitals and the muscles in clear plastic bags. With a shiver, Irene determined they were freezer storage bags. The thought of what he had done with the body parts was so horrible that she resolutely pushed it away.

WHEN THE last film was over, Irene gathered up the originals and the copies and went into her office. Without any great hopes she called down to Forensics, but to her surprise and happiness a voice answered, "Forensics, Åhlén."

"Hi. Irene Huss. Can I come down to you with two videos to go over for fingerprints?"

"Sure."

"It has to do with the mutilation-murders."

"OK. It'll be given priority."

"Thanks."

She rushed down to Forensics with the videos. Apologetically, she said that there were probably lots of fingerprints from Jonny Blom. "We weren't really sure what it was that we had found," she said vaguely.

"OK," Åhlén answered uninterestedly.

When she returned to her office she sat for a long time and looked out at the summer twilight. Her window faced east so she couldn't see the sunset itself but she could watch the sun paint the clouds a violet-red against the dark sapphire blue sky. As time passed, the light on the clouds weakened and they took on a softer violet tinge.

Irene caught very little of the magnificent display of colors. She was sunk deep in thought.

SUPERINTENDENT ANDERSSON started morning prayers by saying that the videos had been found. Andersson praised Jonny, who had diligently devoted the entire weekend to going through Sebastian's film collection. Jonny himself looked unusually pale and reserved. Irene knew that it wasn't because he was overworked.

"We've sent out an All Points Bulletin via Interpol. We don't know where Sebastian Martinsson is. Hannu has located his car in the vehicle register. A Volkswagen Jetta, 1989 model. The license-plate number is included in the APB. Hannu checked on Saturday and Martinsson's parking spot was empty. It's very likely that he's taken the car with him. A lot of things point to Copenhagen, but we don't know if that bastard is starting to sense that we're hot on his trail. He could have kept going and may be farther south in Europe."

A Jetta. The witnesses who had seen the assailant after the attack on Tom Tanaka had said that he had thrown the picture into a car, which was probably a Jetta, and driven away.

Right after the morning meeting Irene went to her office and called up Cyhrén's Funeral Home. A soft female voice answered almost immediately, "Cyhrén's Funeral Home."

"Good morning. My name is Detective Inspector Irene Huss. I'm looking for one Sebastian Martinsson and have been given the information that he works for you sometimes."

"One moment and you can speak with Mr. Danielsson," the woman replied.

After a few cracks and beeps as the call was transferred, an energetic voice could be heard. "Bo Danielsson, Director. What can I do for you?"

A quick thought flew through Irene's head: wasn't a funeral director supposed to sound sober and compassionate and not like a sports commentator on TV? But maybe it made the mourners and the shocked relatives get their acts together and quickly decide on their wishes for the funeral. She introduced herself and told him why she was calling.

"Sebastian Martinsson? Of course I recognize the name. One second!"

He put the receiver down on what might have been a desktop and Irene could hear him pull out some drawers. His powerful voice was soon heard. "Of course! Here he is! He has helped sometimes to carry the coffins. Strong guy!"

"Does he help out often?" Irene asked.

"No. Just sometimes when we need extra help."

"When did he start working for you?"

"Let's see . . . '94. He worked more often then than in the last two years, because he's started studying in Copenhagen. Before that, he studied here in Göteborg and then, of course, it was easier for him to help out at the last minute."

Irene could hear the surprise in her own voice when she asked, "Did he say that he was studying in Göteborg?"

"Yes. To be a doctor. Now he's doing his specialization training in Copenhagen. I always write down this kind of personal information about extra employees. So that you know what kind of a person you're dealing with."

Someone studying medicine inspires trust. So much trust that he probably got to take care of the keys to very special burial chambers. Is that why he said that he was studying medicine? Or was it his secret dream? It was interesting and certainly something that the headshrinkers were going to delve deeper into during the psychiatric examination. Irene decided not to comment on Sebastian's studies.

"May I ask a completely different question?"

"Sure! Of course!"

"Does Cyhrén's take care of the keys to the mausoleums at Stampen's old cemetery?"

"No. Cemetery Administration has those. We contact them when it becomes necessary to open one of the graves."

"Did you take care of the last two funerals for the von Knecht family?"

"Yes. Why are you asking about that?"

"Unfortunately, I'm not at liberty to say right now."

"Of course! I understand!"

Naturally, he didn't understand anything but nothing made people more willing to talk than the idea that they had the trust of the police.

"So the keys are only lent out when a new family member is going to be placed in the grave?"

"Exactly!"

"Does that mean that one of the pallbearers is trusted to take care of the key?"

For the first time during their conversation he sounded hesitant when he answered. "Yes. That probably happens."

"Can you look in your papers and see if Sebastian Martinsson was a pallbearer at the funerals of Richard von Knecht and Henrik von Knecht in November and December of 1996."

"Of course!"

The receiver bounced down onto the desk again. This time it wasn't enough that Danielsson pulled out the drawers in his desk. Irene heard him stomp about and after a little while she heard the sound of heavy boxes being pulled out. Vigorous steps moved toward the telephone and she had the funeral director's keen voice in her ear again.

"He's noted as a pallbearer at both funerals. They were buried in metal-fitted oak caskets that are very heavy. You have need of a strong man!"

Irene thought about how she was going to formulate her next question, but realized that it could only be asked straight out.

"Is there any way that Sebastian Martinsson could have had the key to the mausoleum in his possession?"

There was a decided pause. "The possibility is there. But only for a short period of time. We always ask for the key back from the one who's in charge of it. And we always check to make sure that the key is returned. It's a matter of the customer's trust!" Danielsson emphasized.

"How long could he have had the key?"

"At the most one day! We need to have it back the next day to give to Cemetery Administration. We're a big office with many employees and many projects. It gets very busy here sometimes. Usually, my right-hand man or I take care of the opening of old graves. They are rarely used. But if it has been a crazy day with many funerals, one of the pallbearers may be trusted to take care of the opening and locking of the crypt."

A day was more than enough time to get a copy of the key made.

"Thank you so much for taking the time to answer my questions," Irene concluded.

"No problem. Don't hesitate to contact us again if there's anything else," Danielsson said.

IRENE DEVOTED several hours to writing a report of Friday's questioning of Sabine Martinsson and the discovery of the possible dismemberment location out in Säve. At the end she also described her conversation with the funeral director while it was still fresh in her mind. Nowadays, police investigators had to waste time sitting at a keyboard for hours in order to produce a report. Formerly, civilian office workers had done that job. And the officers had been able to devote themselves to investigating crime.

Office work always put her in a bad mood. Now that mood improved slightly when Hannu stuck his head in and informed her that the technicians had found traces of human tissue in the old garage drain in Säve. The samples were being sent to Copenhagen and would be matched against Marcus Tosscander's DNA profile. The risk was that the material had decayed so much over time that no DNA could be extracted.

"It's amazing that the Danes can do DNA tests and other analyses in just a few days. While in Sweden the same tests take several weeks!" Irene exclaimed.

"The forwarding address for Martinsson's mail is a post office box in Copenhagen. Have you heard anything from our colleagues there?" Hannu asked.

"No. They were going to locate the Kreuger Academy today and try and track down Sebastian's address."

"It's supposedly difficult to find housing in Copenhagen."

"For sure. That's probably why he rented from Emil Bentsen in the beginning. My theory is that he couldn't put up with Emil's messiness. It was almost as dirty in his apartment as it was at Sabine Martinsson's."

"I've spoken with Social Services in Trollhättan. Sabine has been an alcoholic since Sebastian was little."

Since Social Services maintained absolute secrecy of its records, even in a police investigation, if no prosecution had started—and they only released information if the prosecution was of a very severe crime in which the penalty was more than two years in prison— Hannu must have had a contact inside the Trollhättan agency. Irene wasn't a bit surprised. "It couldn't have been fun growing up in a home with an alcoholic mother. Maybe his obsessive cleanliness is a reaction against the mother's slovenly habits. I'm thinking of his obsessively clean apartment."

Hannu nodded.

They went to get Birgitta and trooped across the street. The insurance office building's restaurant was serving pan-fried breaded fish with cucumber mayonnaise and potatoes, which was usually very good.

"A witness has appeared who says that he saw a tall, well-built man enter Bolin's Commercial Photography Company at around six o'clock on the evening that Erik Bolin was murdered. The witness is an older man who lives a few blocks farther down. He was out with his dog when he saw the man open the door. He noticed the ponytail in particular. Apparently he really dislikes ponytails on men," said Birgitta.

"Does he remember how the man was dressed?" asked Irene.

They spoke quietly, since not everyone in the lunchroom was a police officer.

"Black jacket, black jeans, and a small shoulder bag. I asked specifically about the size of the bag. We agreed that it was about nine by fourteen, or somewhat larger," said Birgitta.

"Big enough to hold a good-sized knife and some sliced-off muscle tissue. Too small for a head," Hannu said dryly.

"You think that's why he left the head on the hat rack," Irene clarified.

"Yes."

Irene tried to suppress the image of Bolin's dull eyes behind half-closed lids.

"Did the witness see a car that the black-clad man might have gotten out of?" Irene continued.

"No. I tried several times to refresh his recollection but he doesn't remember a car. Just a man walking into the building at the time in question. His description matches that of Sebastian Martinsson," said Birgitta.

"He probably arrived by car and left a few hours later without anyone noticing," said Irene.

"We've connected him to all of the murders. Now it's just Basta himself who's missing," Birgitta concluded.

"Sometimes I think that he's hidden himself here in the city and is laughing at us. And sometimes I think he has no idea that we are so close to him and he's walking around carefree on the streets of Copenhagen or somewhere else," Irene sighed.

"Just as long as we get him before he commits another murder," said Birgitta.

JENS METZ had been trying to reach her while she was out to lunch. Irene felt hopeful when she caught sight of the message to phone him. Had they found Sebastian? She quickly dialed Jens's direct number.

"Inspector Metz."

"Irene Huss here. You called me."

"Yes. We've gotten hold of Martinsson's address. Unfortunately, we haven't gotten hold of Martinsson himself, but we've put his apartment under surveillance."

"Great! Do you know if he's in Copenhagen?"

"Probably. The art school is called Krøyer Academy, not Kreuger Academy. It had closed but we managed to reach the director's secretary. She found his address in her records. She also said that the school is about to reopen and he is listed as an instructor for a summer course that starts today and lasts for three weeks."

"Then you can pick him up at the school?"

"That's what is really strange. He didn't show up for the beginning of the class. All the instructors were supposed to meet their students at the first morning lesson. But Martinsson never came. The secretary was very irritated but also confused. According to her, Martinsson had been so happy when he got the job. And then to screw up on the first day!"

"Then maybe he's left town. Maybe he suspected something and cleared out."

"The risk is there. We've sent inspectors to his address. His apartment is located here, on Istedgade. I have a hunch that he's here in the neighborhood. If he is, we'll get him."

"Have you been inside his apartment?"

"Not yet. It's better if he walks into the trap without suspecting anything. But if he hasn't shown by the evening, we'll go in."

"That sounds good. I hope you get him."

"If he's here, we will. I'll be in touch tomorrow."

"Thanks."

Irene felt her pulse pounding in her temples. Finally they were closing in on Sebastian!

Chapter 21

IRENE DIDN'T SLEEP WELL that night. In a dream, she ran after a fleeing shadow, through dark alleys and deserted streets. She kept growing closer, certain she would catch the black silhouette. But when she rounded the corner of a house she ran into a soft, formless mass. Out of the corner of her eye she saw a sturdy knife blade glimmer and realized that she was going to die. Her arms were leaden and she didn't have the strength to raise them to protect herself. The knife flew right in front of her face and, suddenly, in a lightning-quick arc, it dove down toward her heart.

Krister woke her and asked why she was screaming. When the question was repeated for the third time, she gave up and went down to the kitchen. A mug of milk warmed in the microwave and a piece of hard bread with cheese put her in a better mood. The clock read 4:10 a.m. when she crawled back under the covers, but it was impossible for her to fall asleep again.

"IRENE! COPENHAGEN on the line for you!" Tommy yelled.

Irene was on her way out to fill her coffee mug but she ran back to her chair. Expectantly, she pulled the receiver toward her.

"This is Irene. Have you found him?"

"Yes. But I need to ask a few questions first."

Jens Metz sounded very official and proper. Irene realized immediately that something wasn't right. *Oh no! Not Tom! Not Tom!* echoed inside her. Like an answer to her thoughts, Metz asked, "Have you had any contact with Tom Tanaka recently?"

Something in his tone of voice and the way he asked the question made Irene sense danger. She knew she must be careful about what she said.

"Tom called me a few days ago and thanked me for the flowers I had sent by Peter Møller," she said.

Irene was well aware of how easy it was to trace a cell phone call.

Metz's voice revealed real surprise when he exclaimed, "Did Peter take flowers to that . . . ?" He stopped himself before he had finished his sentence but Irene already knew how he felt about Tom.

"Yes. I asked him to," she said.

"Did he only thank you for the flowers?"

Why was Metz asking this? Now she was on full alert. With feigned ease, she answered, "Yes. Apparently he loves orchids. He also said that he had just come home and wasn't fully recovered."

Irene sensed Jens's silent misgivings flood toward her through the receiver. Finally, he asked, "You never mentioned Sebastian Martinsson's name to Tom, or that he was in Copenhagen?"

"No."

Irene's heart was beating fast. Tommy seemed not to notice anything as he was deeply engrossed in a text on his computer screen.

"Are you absolutely sure? You never said *anything* about Sebastian Martinsson?"

With a struggle, Irene controlled her voice as she answered, "No. I never spoke with Tom about Sebastian Martinsson."

She knew that if they ever pressured Tom on this point he wouldn't give a truthful answer. She was good at lying but he was a master at keeping quiet.

"We've found Sebastian Martinsson. Dead," Metz told her.

"Dead?" Irene repeated, surprised.

"Yes. We entered his apartment at around nine o'clock last night. He was lying on his bed dead, wearing a muzzle, his hands and feet bound. His stomach was cut open and his intestines were lying on top of his chest. According to the pathologist, Martinsson had been lying there, looking at his own intestines, for several minutes before he died."

Irene's head was spinning. She felt ready to faint. Her mouth was bone dry and she only managed to croak, "Oh my God!"

"It was one of the worst things I've ever seen," Metz said.

In an exaggerated, pedagogic tone of voice he continued, "But now you're going to hear something really strange. The pathologist has pinpointed the time of death as sometime early Sunday morning, between two and four. A witness who staggered home around three o'clock on

Sunday morning from a drinking party stopped and peed in the doorway next to Martinsson's. Suddenly, a black Mercedes stopped outside the door where Martinsson was living. A huge and amazingly fat Chinese man got out of the car, according to the witness, who wasn't completely sober. But he describes the Chinese man's strange haircut as small, hard buns on his head. And he maintains that the Chinese man had horrible scars on his face!"

Metz fell silent. For lack of a better comment Irene repeated, "Oh my God!" She couldn't come up with anything else.

"That's what we said. But Tanaka has six witnesses who swear that he held a party for them in his apartment. None of them left before five o'clock. We can't get them to budge. Every one of them is standing by this story. It'll be difficult to prove that it was him. Tanaka himself maintains that the witness might have been in his shop and seen his scarred face. Then, later, in his intoxicated condition, he imagined he had seen Tanaka again outside Martinsson's door but in reality it was another large man."

"Martinsson lived just a few hundred meters from Tanaka," Metz added. He paused dramatically. "The question then is how could Tanaka know Sebastian Martinsson's identity and address?"

Tom had a network of friends and contacts. Irene had mentioned the name Basta and said that he was studying at an art school called Kreuger Academy. 'Not Kreu . . . no,' Tom had answered, before he stopped himself. So he knew of the Krøyer Academy. And Tom most likely was acquainted with someone who could find out if someone at the academy was named Sebastian, but was called Basta, and where this Basta lived. Tom had made it very clear to her that Sebastian deserved the death penalty.

Trying to sound convincing, Irene said, "I haven't given Tom any information about Martinsson nor did I tell him we suspected the killer was in Copenhagen. Tanaka is a man with many contacts."

"We know. Also within the police," Metz replied in a poisonous tone of voice.

Thank God Tommy had left the room on an errand. She was alone in the office. In her hand she held her bright yellow Nokia. She slowly flipped through her address book. When she came to Tom's name and number, she started erasing them.

She would never call Tom Tanaka again.

It would be several years before she went back to Copenhagen.